MEMORIES OF ASH

BOOK TWO OF THE SUNBOLT CHRONICLES

INTISAR KHANANI

PURPLE MONKEY PRESS

Titles in the Sunbolt Chronicles
Sunbolt
Memories of Ash

Memories of Ash
Copyright © 2016 by Intisar Khanani
Published by Purple Monkey Press
All rights reserved.

Cover and Interior Graphics by Jenny Zemanek

www.seedlingsonline.com

ISBN: 0985665858
ISBN-13: 978-0985665852

MEMORIES
OF ASH

AUTHOR'S NOTE

A portion of the proceeds from the sale of *The Sunbolt Chronicles* will be donated to the United Nations Children's Fund. UNICEF fights for the survival and development of the world's most vulnerable children. Find out more at http://www.unicefusa.org

THE TIES THAT BIND

CRACK.

I glance up, holding tight to the thread of my spell as the mountains throw a thunderous echo back to us. My skin tingles with the brush of magic, as if unseen creatures skitter up my arms, over my back. Across the valley, forest birds take to the air, calling out as they wheel over the lake. I catch the pale white flutter of snow pigeons, the midnight silhouette of ravens, and high up the snow-dusted peaks, the great dark wingspans of a pair of griffon vultures.

Seated cross-legged beside me on the banks of the lake, Brigit Stormwind murmurs, "That was the first ward."

I nod. It has been some time since a traveler came our way, but the sound of our farthest ward triggering is not easily forgotten. Without knowing who approaches our valley, finishing my casting would be reckless. I could easily leave a trace behind that a mage might notice…But I promised myself that this time I would finish.

Before me the water lies smooth, no ripple disturbing its crystalline surface. Upon that polished expanse gleams the spell-cast image of my mother. Dressed in a pale pink kimono embroidered in shades of rose, she kneels before a tea tray, hands on her lap and face raised toward me. I have her eyes, though my skin has the desert tint of my father's people. Her lips, neither too full nor too thin, grace her face in harmony with the gentle roundness of her cheeks, while my own features remain hollowed by the fire that once consumed me from the inside out. By her very stillness I know she has detected some trace of my spell, the ties of blood and kinship that I have used to seek her out through the shields that surround her.

"Let it go, Hitomi," Stormwind says gently.

I release the tenuous thread of my casting with unexpected relief. I have attempted this spell half a dozen times now, but not once have I taken it to completion. I could have done it today had I not paused to observe her. The bitterness on my tongue has the singular taste of cowardice to it.

My mother's image breaks apart, replaced by the faint reflection of trees overhead. I watch the water's movement over the multi-hued stones covering the lake bottom. In the early morning light, they're every color of the earth: the burnished yellow of evening sunlight, a dreamlike lavender, grays dark as storm clouds and light as hope, reds both as bright as blood and as dark as death. The colors of life lie beneath the water, calling to me as if I might reach out and recover the memories I lost in ash nearly a year ago.

"These things take time," Stormwind says into the quiet.

"I started the spell with enough time to speak with her. I should have gone through with it."

"You did not know anyone was coming." She glances down to the water, her eyes more gray than blue in the tree-thrown shadows. "And when you seek truth, you must be ready for it."

"You don't think I am."

"You must be ready to understand, and accept, whatever you find."

I make no answer. I don't know what to say, how I would accept it if my mother truly intended to abandon me all those years ago.

Stormwind rises, readjusting her cloak against an autumn chill I don't feel. On the far shore the deep green of the pines and cedars are interrupted here and there by the fiery orange and red mantles still worn by the other trees. When I first came here, Stormwind admitted she had studied together with my father, which should mean many more years of health and strength for her. But she lost a part of her youth to a breather. Her silver-white hair, the deep creases around her eyes and mouth, the way the cold touches her, all these bespeak an age she should not yet feel.

"Let's see what we can of our visitor," she says. With a sweep of her hand, the surface of the lake stills. The water before us now reflects the forested path near the great deodar cedar that stands as our farthest ward.

"Closer," she murmurs, beckoning the image. The path reels out as if we were looking over our shoulders while riding at speed toward the valley. The cedar recedes, then disappears behind a curve.

"There," she says as a dark shadow obstructs the image. She raises her fingers and the image slows. But the shadow at its center persists, murky and unclear. For a long moment, Stormwind remains still. The shadow moves along the trail, growing larger in our view, but no clearer. Then she releases the image, her hand falling to her side. The waters of the lake ripple, lapping at the banks once more.

"They've used a shield," Stormwind says. "Without breaking the shield, we can't know who comes, or how large their party."

"We know there's a mage involved."

"That we do," she agrees. "Which means we know we need to hide you. Come." She starts along the path toward the cottage.

I follow after her. "Are you sure it's safe to meet them? I mean, why would they shield themselves?"

"Two reasons," she says, her voice sliding into the detached tone she uses when teaching. "To protect against attack and to keep from being traced."

"We found them easily enough."

"Because we looked at the path, not them. Had we known who they were and attempted to trace them, we would have had a hard time finding them without a focus for our trace."

Like a hair, or a well-worn bit of cloth.

But I don't like the idea of an unknown mage coming to Stormwind's valley. She rarely has visitors. When she does, they are locals seeking cures. Never mages. "Are you sure you want to wait here for them?"

Stormwind smiles, shaking her head as if my question is sweet, endearing, and very naive. "I'm not running. First, a mage would easily trace us using any one of a number of items from the cottage. Second, if they are coming for me, I would not lead them to you. And third, I am a high mage in my own right. I have done no wrong and can easily defend myself. The only thing I need to hide is you."

"You're sending me away." It isn't a question, but a flat-voiced statement.

"No. There isn't enough time for that."

I glance up at the high ridge that divides our valley from the next. The only passable path to our cottage cuts through it. On horseback, moving at a brisk walk, a traveler might easily cover the distance from the deodar cedar to the ridge in an hour and a half. It would take us half that time to get to the path ourselves on foot. But our tracks would be fresh, and anyhow, Stormwind isn't running...and I'm not leaving without her.

"Take the books up to the loft and pack them back into the trunk," Stormwind says as we reach the cottage. The single open room serves as kitchen and workroom and sitting room and bedroom, while the small loft above provides a cozy space for my own pallet.

I make a round of the room, gathering the books I've been studying under Stormwind's tutelage along with the charms I'm working on. Stormwind checks the charms we keep about the house, her fingers passing over them, gauging if they are hers or mine: the stone beside the hearth, used to keep the bread from burning; the glowstones in a pile over the mantle, for when we need light without the heat or flicker of flames; the seeker charm by the door, to help find wandering goats.

I climb the ladder to stow what I've collected in one of the trunks against the back wall of the loft. Stormwind joins me as I finish tucking the books in, adding the bag of charms I made to the trunk.

She shuts the lid, places her hand on top. "We'll ward it and bind it."

She really is worried. I kneel beside her worldlessly. She presses my palm against the trunk's lid and quickly traces a series of sigils on the wood with her other hand. They glimmer and send out tendrils of magic that trace the shape of my palm, flare around her fingertips, and then fade. With the trunk bound so, only Stormwind or I will be able to open it.

She rises and takes a quick inventory of the little room. There's a small collection of bags and boxes lining the wall beside the trunks. To my right lies my pallet with its nest of blankets. A small wooden statuette of a crow stands on a brick-sized stone beside my bed, its head bent, beak pressing a key to its breast. She focuses on it for a moment, then looks away.

"That's all, right?" I say, keeping my tone casual. I have no cause to hide the crow. Only she knows that it was carved by a breather, not a human. Right now the sight of Val's parting gift is oddly comforting.

She nods, moving back toward the ladder. "Everything else should be fine." She pauses with her feet on the first rung. "Hitomi? You remember that you're to act as my servant?"

"I remember." We've discussed this a few times, and I've played the part of serving girl during the few visits from locals we've had. It provides a simple explanation for all the rest of my belongings. "I am Hikaru, girl of all work, loyal unto death."

Stormwind chuckles. "Don't overdo it. Since we don't know what this is about, I want you to stay outside as much as possible today."

I hesitate. I could offer to collect deadwood from the forest—we need to stockpile more for the winter—but I want to stay close to the cottage just in case.

"I'll keep working on the roof," I say. It's perfect, really. We've spent the last two afternoons on the roof together, Stormwind teaching me what I need to know. I can easily work on my own. Best of all, I can keep an eye on our visitors. And I'll be near enough to help Stormwind if she should need me.

"It will keep me close but out of sight," I press when she doesn't answer.

"Very well."

Her easy agreement worries me further. As a mage, she could easily call for a far-off servant to return. Without charms to anchor it, magic may not reliably deliver messages across mountain ranges, but a summons sent across a valley would hardly go astray. Only if she fears she won't have the time or the leeway to do so would she need me nearby.

The last ward triggers as I tack down a new shingle, the hammer missing the nail as my skin prickles, an electric tingling raising the hairs at the back of my neck. This ward is silent, subtle, bound just to Stormwind and me, small enough that a visitor shouldn't notice it. I rub a hand over my neck, my eyes traveling up the path to the high pass.

Soon our unknown visitors will enter the valley, their progress masked by the forest. It will take a little while yet for them to reach the cottage. I pound down the waiting nail and then check the next few shingles for cracks. They're mostly in good condition, whole and still firmly attached. This past winter brought deep snows, but with just a few summer storms to cause damage, the roof has held up well since Val repaired it.

Perched on a roof, dreading the arrival of a mage, is probably not the best time to reminisce about a breather, but I have so few comforting memories. When Val brought me here, he was the only friend I had, the only memory aside from the fire that took my previous life. I didn't fear him as most would, didn't fear his ability to control those who meet his gaze, to take the life of those around him with a single inhalation. I assumed that, no matter his words, he would not use these talents against me.

As I peel off a broken shingle and check the wood underneath, I recall Val's hands at work, his voice warning me not to trust him, the faintest of butterfly touches on my wrist as he explained how, truly, I should fear him. Now, with distance and time between us, I wonder whether I was more foolish to be hurt by his words or to keep pushing my company upon him. He knows himself better than I ever will. If he believed himself a danger to me, shouldn't I have trusted that? Or was he merely trying to escape the thorns we had stumbled into, mage and breather becoming allies in a world where no such thing could exist?

Even now, nearly a year since his departure, I find that I trust him, trust the kindness with which he treated me, trust the wisdom and care he showed in nursing me back to health and delivering me here, to this valley, to study with Stormwind. As she said all that time ago: *A breather does not help a Promise become a mage.* And yet he had. It was dangerous ground.

I sigh, running my fingers over the weathered wood before me. There are no answers here, and Val is long gone, hidden away in the Amara Mountains with the breather prince he serves. According to my geography lessons, he is months away by horseback. I doubt I shall ever meet him again.

I look up at the faint thud of hooves against the packed dirt of the path. A man wearing a flowing desert robe, the warm brown of rich earth, rides at a quick trot down the path from the pass, followed be a second, riderless horse on a long lead.

I squint against the sunlight, studying the rider. He's tall and slim, his tan complexion strikingly similar to my own, though his features are sharp, hawklike. His robe falls open in front in the tradition of many desert folk. Beneath it, he wears a long-sleeved tunic and loose cream-colored trousers tucked into riding boots. A faint line of geometric embroidery circles the collar and outlines the two buttons on the front, markedly different from the attire of the local men and women I have seen this last year.

Strapped over his tunic, he wears a belt with a curved sword and a dagger as well as a small crossbow. Here in the mountains, there is no need for either blade. The crossbow might be useful against a larger predator, but even those are few and far between. He is not just any mage, then, but one trained as a warrior.

I continue to check the shingles, keeping one eye on him. Stormwind steps into sight, calling a greeting as she walks to meet him. He dismounts with alacrity, the faint reverberations of his voice—deep and not unfriendly—barely audible. They clasp hands, and then Stormwind gestures to the cottage. As she turns, I see the smile that tugs at her lips.

Friends, then. But who is he? And why would he bring a second horse?

I watch them converse as they lead the horses around back. Stormwind seems as unruffled as always. The mage's gait is long and easy, but when a bird takes flight from the long grasses growing near the trees, his head whips toward it. I can't tell if he is especially on guard, or if warrior mages never really let their guard down.

They close the horses in the goat pen, empty for the moment while our goats are out grazing. Stormwind untacks the chestnut while the mage tends to his own horse. They pile the tack outside the fence and head for the cottage door.

I perch sideways on the roof, digging out a bit of black rot and trying not to look as clumsy as I feel. This way, I can track them from the corner of my eye.

They continue to chat as they walk, and while I cannot make out the words, I can hear the rhythm and tone of their voices: familiar, pleasant, as if they are catching up with an old but dear acquaintance. The sound of it eases some of my fears.

As they're about to pass from sight, the mage glances my way, eyes hard and measuring. I remain still, neither moving to break his gaze nor allowing my expression to shift until he steps into the cottage.

Once the door latches behind them, I ease back on my heels, letting out a breath I hadn't realized I'd been holding. Of course he would assess me. He's a warrior mage, used to evaluating situations before he walks into them. And as a half-trained Promise—albeit better skilled than I was a year ago—

I am still unsworn to the High Council and would easily meet his definition of a rogue.

Perhaps I should have suggested Stormwind send me off to collect deadwood after all.

No.

I glare at the empty spot before me, then slap a new shingle in place and hammer it down with unaccustomed force. I'm not going to let fear drive me. And, like Stormwind, I'm not going to run.

AN UNEXPECTED SUMMONS

There's something powerful about being high up on a roof, a great shimmering expanse of lake off to the side, forested mountains rising to frame the wide blue swath of sky. With each swing of the hammer, each nail driven home to hold a shingle in place, I feel my blood thrum through my veins. Despite the lake breeze that cools me, my tunic sticks to my back, the taste of salt on my lips. Even as my arms tire, each swing of the hammer weighing heavier, I don't want to stop. It's a temporary magic, if you can call it magic at all.

The cottage remains quiet as the sun continues to creep toward noon. I descend from the roof once to refill my flask from the bucket Stormwind left. I can detect the faint murmur of voices, but with the door closed, I cannot catch the words themselves, nor can I hear any better crouched beneath the shuttered windows. It isn't until just past noon, my rooftop magic grown threadbare and the muscles of my arms aching, that Stormwind comes outside.

"Hikaru!" She steps around the corner carrying a bowl of stew.

I clamber down, hammer in hand. Stormwind tips her head toward the cottage, her brow furrowed and her pale eyes steely. "How goes the roof?"

"Not too bad." I ladle water from the bucket to rinse my hands. Is the mage listening, or is she simply warning me to exercise caution? "What about your visitor?"

"He is High Mage Harith Stonefall."

I raise my brows in question.

"He's one of the High Council's best rogue hunters."

"You're a *rogue*?" I can't keep the disbelief from my voice. It seems about as likely as her spontaneously breaking into song and dancing across the surface of the lake.

"The Council sent him because they expected I would be hard to find. They do not wish to waste their time looking."

I stand still, water dripping from my fingertips. To my knowledge, Stormwind has had nothing to do with the Council since I arrived here. "What does the High Council want from you?"

"Stonefall brought a summons. I must go back with him at once." The words are as abrupt and sharp as the crack of lake ice in the night. I experience a plummeting moment of nausea. Then I take the bowl from her and sit down cross-legged with it. A summons could mean anything. It's what she hasn't said, the things her expression won't let slip, that worry me.

"What do they want?" I repeat softly.

She stares down at the dirt by our feet. "I've been charged."

"With?"

She raises her gaze to me. The hollowness of her eyes has a familiarity that reaches back into the ashes of my past. It is a look that has no place in this quiet valley. "Treason."

The word hits me low in the gut. *Treason.* The same charges levied against the Degaths a lifetime ago in Karolene. "Tell me," I demand, all pretenses of eating forgotten.

She counts the accusations on her fingers. "Conspiracy to overthrow the High Council, conspiracy to assassinate First Mage Talon, perjury under oath, failure to renew my oaths of allegiance, and developing alliances with creatures inimical to the High Council."

"Creatures—" I stumble, wondering if someone somehow learned of Val. Then her other words catch up with me. *"Assassinate?"*

She looks suddenly old, weary. "Yes. The charges were brought forward by Arch Mage Blackflame. It seems he has won a great deal of support on the High Council."

Blackflame? "But you've had nothing to do with him this past year. What does he know about you?"

"My past."

I wait, but she doesn't elaborate. I've known since I arrived that Stormwind has some history with Blackflame, but I never learned what. She offered me shelter, and it seemed unnecessary to pry into a past she put behind her. Whatever it is, it has come back for her now.

"They're all false," I say into the smothering quiet. "The accusations."

"They are either false or greatly exaggerated."

She glances to the side, her gaze following the wall of the cottage. Nothing we've said should stand out to Stonefall as strange, other than perhaps Stormwind treating me more like a friend than a servant. And there are still things I need to know, especially if I don't manage to speak with her alone again.

"Blackflame's not on the Council, is he?" I ask, even though Stormwind would have told me of any changes.

"No, he's still one of the eleven assigned to serve the Kingdoms."

"Karolene?"

"Yes."

I nod. The High Council is composed of eleven arch mages, all elected to govern the use of magic in the Eleven Kingdoms. In addition to them there are eleven more arch mages, each appointed by the Council to serve a Kingdom, assuring the regulation of magic there and seeing to the welfare of the people. Without a seat on the Council, Blackflame's power should still be somewhat limited.

"Do you have any allies on the Council?"

Stormwind squats beside me, pitching her voice low. "Yes. Talon, for one. She serves as first mage on the Council now. As a high mage, Stonefall has no vote on Council proceedings, but he'll support me as well."

As far as I can tell, without a vote on the Council, Stonefall is irrelevant. Talon's position as first mage means she presides over Council proceedings and casts a vote only when the other ten arch mages reach a deadlock. Which might be very helpful in Stormwind's case.

"Will Talon help you, even though one of the charges involves her?" If Talon believes there's even a grain of truth in the charge of assassination, there's no reason for her to side with Stormwind. It's a brilliant ploy by Blackflame, cutting off Stormwind's most powerful support with such direct an allegation.

"Yes. She sent Stonefall with a private message for me. I'll meet with her on my arrival to plan my defense."

That's something, then. "How long will the trial run?"

"A week or two, I expect."

"Will you be free to come and go till then?"

"No. I'll be held in custody." Stormwind smiles grimly. "Stonefall won't say as much, but he cannot allow me to choose any option but to go with him."

"But..." I pause, remembering the greeting I had

witnessed, the very fact that he has let her out of his sight. "You're friends?"

"Yes."

"And he's still taking you to be tried on false charges?"

"He's a man of honor. He will not break his allegiance when no wrong has yet been done." She sighs. "But you're right. If Blackflame's reach is strong enough, he may prevail regardless of whether his allegations hold any truth."

There's the crux of it. The one thing I wish I knew. "How does he know you?"

Stormwind stiffens. It's the slightest of changes, her expression going from serious to set, her chin tilting up a degree or two, but I see it. "We…have a history." She glances toward the cottage. "Come in and help me pack when you're done."

"I'm done." I stand up so fast I nearly slop the stew out of its bowl.

Stormwind glances at the bowl, nods. "Then come."

I follow her through the back door, the room dark to my eyes. I set the bowl of stew on the counter and wait for my sight to adjust.

Stonefall leans against the table. He is a tall man, taller even than I assumed when I saw him seated on his horse. The fall of his robes around him bespeaks a desert elegance, austere yet beautiful. He must be in his late thirties, his beard and mustache carefully trimmed and showing no sign of silver or white. Dark hair curls at his temples.

"Master Stonefall," Stormwind says, her voice neutral. "Allow me to introduce my servant, Hikaru."

I incline my head.

"Peace be upon you." Stonefall's voice is deep, resonating.

"And upon you, peace." I meet his hawk-eyed gaze as a rabbit might, wide-eyed and still. He had not greeted me in the trade language of Karolene, which Stormwind used to introduce us, but in his own language. And I answered him in the same, a language I have not spoken a word of this past year: the language my father once spoke.

Stormwind clears her throat. "Let's get started. Come help me with the herbs, Hikaru."

I join her at the herb cabinet with its store of powders and prepared salves, medicinals for everything from severe burns to upset stomachs to insect bites.

"What shall I take?"

She's still teaching me, even here, in front of a mage.

Because however many times I may have set off on a journey before, I remember nothing of it now. "Herbs for illness," I hazard, aware of Stonefall's silent attention to our words.

"There'll be an infirmary there."

My lips twitch. "Salves for wounds and burns, then, in case anything goes wrong on the journey."

"Which ones?"

I rattle off a list. She agrees and leaves me to gather them together while she sorts through the charms she intends to take. I select the smallest of the empty jars from the back of the cabinet and quickly portion out the most vital ointments, not bothering with labels. Stormwind can easily differentiate them by scent. After hours of being required to sniff and sort both salves and herbs, I've developed a moderate proficiency in the skill myself.

"Done?" Stormwind asks as I close the cabinet door. She sets down her collection of charms beside the jars: a firestarter, a seeker to help locate objects, a couple of glowstones. Nothing for protection.

I nod, trying not to show my worry before Stonefall. I wish he would leave, go for a walk or check on his horses or something. I hate the steadiness of his gaze, the way he watches me utterly unfazed, even when I glance toward him. He shouldn't be so interested in me. He should have no reason to study Stormwind's help so carefully. And with his continuous attention, I can't even murmur a question unobserved.

Stormwind flicks a glance at Stonefall, a quick birdlike assessment. "I'd like to make a set of ward stones to take with me. Would you fetch a handful of stones from the lake?"

I try not to let my relief show; at least she's planning to take something useful with her. "Of course, mistress."

"About this big," she says, holding up her fingers to show me: no bigger than a walnut without its shell. Not that I needed to see. This is for Stonefall, so he doesn't suspect that I know more of magic than a servant ought to.

"Yes, mistress."

I hurry down to the edge of the water and select a dozen brightly colored small stones. I make a pouch of the bottom of my tunic to carry the stones back to the cottage and walk quickly up the path. But at the sound of voices through the open door, I slow, unsure if I should interrupt. It takes me a moment to realize they are discussing me.

"—a child of the desert," Stonefall says, his tone cold.

"Neither would I," Stormwind replies evenly. "She was brought to me still weak from an illness that broke her health and took her memory. You surprised her, earlier, greeting her in a language she didn't realize she knew."

"She remembered Tradespeak before her own tongue?" Stonefall says, calling the language of Karolene by its most widely used name. His voice has regained its rich timbre, bringing with it a sense of warmth. Was he actually upset at the idea of Stormwind keeping me as a servant?

"She is clearly not only of the desert. Perhaps Tradespeak is her mother tongue."

"Perhaps. How long has she been with you?"

"Almost a year now. And no, she has not recovered much of her memory as yet, though I guide her through meditations and do what I can to help her."

"You could bring her with you. The healer-mages at Mekteb-i Sihir might be able to help her," Stonefall suggests. I recognize the name—it's the school for sorcery where the Council has taken up residence for the year.

"No," Stormwind says, a little too abruptly. "I will take no one with me. She is not ready for such a journey and"—a tight pause—"I would not want Blackflame to take note of her."

"Because he would. Because of you."

"Yes."

"You're sure she'll be safe here? And your cottage with her?"

"I have no concerns for the house. As for her safety, this is the safest place I can grant her."

"Perhaps she should return to the desert, seek out her family."

I stand rooted to the ground, staring at the shadowed doorway. My family? What family would I have in the desert, with my father dead?

"I will mention it to her."

I look at the stones I carry. Stormwind is waiting for them, will soon begin to wonder where I am. I make myself take a step, then another, the gravel crunching beneath my boots.

Inside, Stonefall still sits at the table. Stormwind stands at the counter with her daypack. She has already packed the herbs and charms we had set out and a change of clothes. She takes the stones from me without a word, pouring them into a pouch and sliding them into the pack. "Let's go up to the loft. I'll need some additional clothes."

I follow her, aware of Stonefall turning his head to watch

us climb. There, Stormwind deftly retrieves a pair of mirrors from the first trunk. The frames are forged of the same metal, framing glass ovals formed from the same source and enchanted by the mage whose hand made them. The mirrors allow their users to communicate with each other, no matter the distance between them. Stormwind taught me to use them early this spring. We spent a week or two with them before she packed them away.

"I'll contact you," she promises me, handing me one. She slips the other into her pack. "Keep it near."

I glance toward the open trapdoor, but Stormwind seems unworried. No doubt Stonefall would expect her to leave some form of communication with me.

"What of the wards?" I ask. There are layered enchantments over the valley, spells that she created to keep herself safe from prying eyes before I ever came here.

A flicker of Stormwind's familiar dry humor lights her eyes. "I set them. I don't think I'll have a problem reaching you through them."

I hide the mirror behind my pallet. She planned amazingly well. Had she foreseen such a summons even then? Or was it merely the pragmatic approach of a woman who had seen the world and left it?

There is no way to ask her now, with Stonefall listening intently from the room below. Stormwind selects two of her finer dresses and adds them to her pack, then digs deeper and draws out a ceremonial silk robe. It is indigo embroidered heavily in silver with a scattering of pearls, far more elegant than the daily-wear robes stored at the top of the trunk. She shakes it out, pulls it on, and looks at me. The silver thread accents her bone-white hair, the deep bluish-purple silk offsetting her pale skin, flowing down to lap at the floorboards between us.

"You look...like a mage," I say. The robe transforms her from the reclusive woman with whom I have spent these past months to one who commands both power and respect in the world.

"I should hope so," she says dryly.

I hear Stonefall chuckle below us, and keep the rest of my thoughts to myself.

Within half an hour, Stormwind has nearly completed her preparations. In the main room, I gather provisions for their journey: three small loaves of bread, a block of goat cheese wrapped in cloth, dried fruits and nuts, and a packet of dried meat we had put by for winter.

"I'll ready the horses," Stonefall says. With a slight nod toward us, he rises and departs. I carry the food to the vacated table and add it to Stormwind's pack as she watches. When I look up, there is regret and sorrow and something else in her eyes that I do not quite recognize.

"Hikaru," she says slowly.

The lie of the name hangs in the air between us. I am only now beginning to appreciate how many secrets this valley shelters.

"You are welcome to stay here, but," she pauses, as if the words are hard to form, to pull together. "Stonefall believes you will have a welcome from the desert people. The desert tribes keep track of their own. They will know who you are and take you in. Especially," with a significant glance to the door, "if you can recall a part of your father's name."

I meet her gaze steadily. "I'm waiting here for you."

Stormwind turns to collect her cloak from its peg by the door. "Think on it, then. If you decide to leave, remember to take the mirror with you."

"I'm not leaving." Does she think I would abandon her? That what she has done for me carries no weight at all?

"Whatever you choose," she says gently, "stay or leave, keep the mirror by you."

This isn't the time to argue. "Of course," I say. I lift her pack, hold it out to her. "Is there anything you've forgotten?"

"Not that I can think of."

She's wrong. "A charm to keep you safe."

She looks at me strangely, as if I speak of an impossible thing.

"I have the stones you collected. I'll fashion them into wards when we stop to rest."

But in my fractured memories, I know Blackflame. I know that if he fails to convict Stormwind, a circle of ward stones will hardly protect her. "You still need something more.

Something to hide you. Like shadows." My voice cracks over the last word, the memories it holds.

She glances toward the door. Stonefall will be ready momentarily.

"Promise me you'll make something before you reach Fidanya."

For a long moment she hesitates. I wonder what she sees, what part of me and my broken past she has focused on. Then she nods. "I promise. Farewell, Hikaru."

"Farewell," I say, the word rough in my throat.

She makes no move to leave, but stands before me, pale hair pulled back in a severe bun, lined face creased with worry, arms slack at her sides. I wonder when she last bid good-bye to someone like this. I wonder if she ever saw that person again.

"It'll be all right," I tell her, and because it sounds like a lie—an empty phrase that holds no truth because it holds no knowledge of the future—I wrap my arms around her. She stands in my embrace as if she does not know what is expected of her. I laugh into her shoulder and step back. "Come back soon."

"I'll try."

Outside, Stonefall leads his horses over from the goat pen. He straps Stormwind's pack to the spare horse and then they both mount up. She raises her hand in a final, unspoken farewell. I find I have no more words either, and lift my hand in silence. Stonefall watches me as he has this last hour or two, so I turn my hand toward him as well. He dips his head, flicks his reins, and then they are on their way, moving at a brisk walk up the trail.

I stand alone before the cottage, watching until the forest has swallowed them and I am left alone in the only place I know anymore.

I spend the remaining daylight hours gathering dead wood from the forest and carrying it back to the cottage. I'll save chopping it for firewood for another day, when I'm not already fatigued from repairing the roof.

As twilight grows heavy in the valley, the sky lit by far-off shafts of sunlight shining over the mountain peaks, I make my rounds, completing the final chores of the evening. After milking the goats and returning them to their byre, I check the coop for newly laid eggs and round up the chickens for the night. It seems strange that these chores are now mine alone, that every meal will be spent alone, every conversation come to an abrupt end. It feels as though Stormwind must be inside the cottage, or gone foraging for herbs. But she is no more here than my mother is, and only slightly more likely to reappear in my life of her own volition.

I wouldn't normally worry about her return. It would be a given. But it's Blackflame.

While I have lost much of my past, those moments closest to the fire I lit within myself have somehow survived best—as if they were still too fresh and green to burn well. So it is not difficult to recall Blackflame's physical presence, tall and commanding, golden hair and pale blue eyes. I can't—will never—forget the cruel, thin-lipped smile he wore as he brought the fang lord Kol to visit our cages and feed from Alia Degath mere hours after masterminding her parents' deaths.

Layered beneath this memory lies another one, rescued from the ashes. It is all sharp edges, disconnected impressions, but it is carved so deeply into my mind that not even my sunbolt could fully destroy it. Blackflame stands in his courtyard, his eyes hard and yet somehow bored. His words are muffled, but I hear them: *Hotaru Brokensword is dead. Do not come here again.* I did not know it for a lie then, knew only a sickening despair at the thought of my mother's passing, and the smothering sense of his contempt.

Blackflame has no concept of compassion. When he seeks revenge, he plans it well. When he sought to destroy the Degaths, he did not account for the possibility of catching a street thief, and so I managed to escape with the Degath children. Though I was recaptured, they got away.

I have no doubt that he knows Stormwind and will not underestimate her. The only thing about her that he does not know is her connection to me.

MAGICAL WARDS & DEFENSES

Glowstone in hand, I clamber up to the loft and cross to the trunks lining the back wall. Stormwind has been gone since afternoon. Now that it's full dark, she will have stopped for the night, but should still be far enough away that she won't be able to sense my actions.

I kneel before the last trunk in the row. The only one Stormwind usually keeps warded, it contains her magical items and books. Placing my hand on the lid, I feel the faint reverberations of the ward awakening.

There's no subtle way to do this. The ward is designed to block all attempts to open the lock except those made by Stormwind herself, a safeguard put in place before I came to live here. My hands wander over the lid, follow the prickly tingling until it becomes an uncomfortable buzz right above the lock. Resting my left hand over the unmarked surface where Stormwind traced her ward, I breathe in and let myself feel it. *Bound,* I decide, sensing the way the spell turns in on itself. That's easy enough.

I take a moment to raise a shield around myself, drawing on the strength of the wood that houses me, the unseen force of air in motion and still. A flick of my fingers loops the magic around me, the fine hairs on my arms rising at the brush of power. The shield should protect me from any unexpected consequences of my actions. I return my attention to the ward itself, resting a finger on it. I can feel it precisely now, know the shape of it in my mind, and with three sweeps of my finger, I change it: *bound* to *unbound.*

The ward shudders, Stormwind's magic fighting mine. I press my palm over it as if I could meld the two together. *Yes—* that's exactly what I need to do. I trace over the ward again, *bound* into *unbound*, letting my magic pour into the first and then expand into the second, drawing Stormwind's casting with it.

I sit back hard as the ward stutters and then flares bright as a flame before winking out. With a crack, the trunk's panels shift apart, the corners breaking free of each other. The chest disintegrates, falling to pieces before me, no nail holding its place, the wood itself splintering where hidden cracks formed. Within the debris lies the pile of books I'm after.

Well. I hope she was too far away to feel *that*.

I let my shield dissipate and use a spare blanket to gather up the wood. I shake each item from the trunk over the blanket, gently dusting off splinters. There are five books, a number of tightly bound packages I probably have no right to open, and, at the bottom, a cloth-wrapped bundle. As I lift this last one out, the wrapping falls free and I realize I hold the separate parts of a richly made ensemble in my arms.

The shin-length pleated skirt flows black with two wide rows of brightly colored ribbon sewn at the bottom, red and green. The cloth—Northland, perhaps—is soft in my hands, thick and warm. The matching forest-green vest is tailored to be form-fitting. Embroidered flowers and leaves cascade down the front and flow along the hem in an exquisite interplay of reds and yellows, a touch of black and white bringing the design into further relief. Beneath these, I find a simple white blouse with full sleeves. Put together, the dress would be stunning. It's meant for high ceremony, weddings and the like, handed down from mother to daughter.

Something falls free from the blouse as I hold it up and thuds to the floor. Laying the various parts of the dress gently over one of the remaining trunks, I stoop to retrieve the fallen pouch. Through its fabric I can feel the outlines of a book no bigger than my hand—and something else, wide and hard. Without giving myself time for second thoughts, I tug open the pouch. The book appears to be a diary of sorts. I close it quickly, then stare at its leather cover. These words weren't written for me, and whatever the story of this dress, it isn't mine to read, however much I want to know what it says.

I make myself set the book down. Stormwind respected my few silences. I can do the same for her. Still, I slip my fingers back into the pouch and withdraw a large circular brooch that shines gold in the dim light of the loft. Many-petaled flowers follow its rim, each with a small ruby at the center. A far more ornate flower at the brooch's heart holds a ruby nearly as large as my smallest fingernail. The dress may or may not be an heirloom, but this brooch certainly is.

I carefully return the piece to its pouch along with the diary and wrap up the dress once more. I wonder if Stormwind ever wore these clothes herself. If I see her again—*when* I see her again—I'll ask. After all, it's not like I can put the trunk back together again. She'll know what I've done. With a guilty grin, I pack the dress away with its pouch in one of the remaining trunks and carry the books down the ladder to the worktable.

With the fire crackling cheerily in the hearth and the cottage brightened by glowstones, I can almost believe Stormwind is outside, taking a solitary walk, or perhaps gone to gaze into the lake. Almost.

I lay the books out before me. Each concerns a different branch of magic: *The Healer's Compendium, Advanced Elemental Castings, Magical Wards and Defenses, The Transformation of Objects,* and *The Making and Breaking of Bonds.*

I've learned a great deal of healing magic and herbs from Stormwind. I suspect that her original training was as a healer-mage, though she's never said as much. Perhaps it was long ago for her, a part of a life she left behind. At any rate, I don't need more herb lore now.

I flip open *Advanced Elemental Castings* and page through it. I've just finished *Elemental Castings,* its precursor. It took me nearly the whole year to work through the book, my progress agonizingly slow. Stormwind insisted that I perform each spell flawlessly before moving on to the next. Unfortunately, the blaze I welcomed into my core when I cast my sunbolt changed the balance of magical elements in my body. Fire comes naturally. Earth and air are a challenge, water even more so. Still, I made it through, completing the last of the spells this past week. No doubt Stormwind planned to bring out this book in the next few days.

If I had a month, I would read *Advanced Elemental Castings* at once. I would take an additional hour daily for *The Transformation of Objects* and *The Making and Breaking of Bonds.* But I don't know how much time I have, so I reach for *Magical Wards and Defenses.*

I read into the night. The first two chapters cover basic defense spells Stormwind taught me or helped me to remember, and I get through them quickly. I wonder if she sometimes consulted these books while I was outside attending to my chores, for thus far there isn't a spell I *haven't* learned. They are mostly simple defensive sigils and their counterparts—like the protection on the trunk I so masterfully negated just now. Perhaps she used that ward specifically, knowing I'd easily be able to break it should the need arise. I wouldn't be surprised if she did.

The book goes on to describe how to prepare a circle of wards like those surrounding the valley. Or, as I recall from that last day before my sunbolt obliterated the rest of my memories, like the stone prayer beads I set around the vacant building where my friends and I meant to spend the night. Although those wards only contained the power to alert me to betrayal and could not provide any further defense.

I rest my head in my hands. How differently might that night have unfolded had I been a fully trained journeyman by then, as I should have been? If I'd had such a book at my fingertips years ago, if I'd committed it to memory, each spell imprinted in my mind, the soldiers who attacked us might have been easily turned back. We might have escaped all together, betrayer and betrayed.

I needed this book, needed it desperately. And now I may need it again. Except I need to have mastered it already, to have practiced the spells it describes until they come as naturally as breathing. At its first casting, a new-learnt spell can be as clumsy and uncertain as a newborn foal taking its first steps.

We discussed my work each month and negotiated together what I would focus on, but I didn't know about this text. Stormwind didn't tell me—probably for good reason. She was trying to fill the gaps between what I'd studied with my parents and what I'd taught myself. She must have believed I would have another two or three years to learn from her, which would have been plenty of time to memorize this book—all of these books—from cover to cover. Neither of us considered that Blackflame's reach might extend to this valley.

Letting out a shaky breath, I go back to reading, stopping only when my head grows too heavy to continue.

In the morning, after seeing to the chores I can't forego, I raid Stormwind's belongings once more. This time I look through the tightly wrapped bundles I'd relocated from the destroyed trunk. Eventually I find what I need, a set of pouches containing three necklaces. The first two are hardly any use to me at all, being fashioned of gold. A ward stone can hardly be made of metal. But the third necklace is lapis lazuli. The deep blue stone beads lie on my palm, coiled on their cord, and I wonder if I'm thieving.

For now, I need to do this. When Stormwind comes back, I'll return it to her. And if she doesn't...well, perhaps I'll still be able to give it to her. I add the gold necklaces to the pouch containing her diary and brooch and make my way back downstairs, clutching my prize.

With *Magical Wards and Defenses* propped open beside me, I untie the cord from the silver clasp and slide the beads off. They're comparable in size and shape—elongated barrels, thicker at the center and thinner at the edges. Together, they make a truly beautiful necklace, but no one bead stands out from the others, so I take a knife and carve a ring around the center of one of the beads. I'm not quite sure what I'll say to Stormwind about that.

With the first bead marked, I string them back on a different cord nearly six paces in length, tying a knot between each stone to space out their placement. I attach the silver clasp to the ends of the cord, creating a circle within which I can comfortably sit alongside my pack, or even curl up for a nap.

Finally, I set about creating a set of wards. At heart, the spells I'm weaving are no different than the valley's wards, except I don't need a warning as much as a shielding from hostile magic and protection from attackers. I want these beads to create a bubble around me that cannot be penetrated. I don't know if I have the ability to manage this casting or not, but I'll get as close as I can.

I work for nearly two hours layering my enchantments. I cast a simple shielding, strengthening it repeatedly until it can withstand a spell of the highest order. Then I stabilize the boundaries created by the shield to stop physical objects from passing through: arrows and swords and stones. By the time I accomplish this much, my eyes feel dry as dust and I have to blink often to keep my focus clear. There's a faint ringing in my ears from the magic I've expended, and I have a new problem to contend with once I'm rested...the air I breathe within the wards might not naturally replenish itself.

I gather up the cord, looping it around my hand until it's compact enough to stuff back into its pouch. That's enough for now.

After a light lunch, I walk out to the lake and perch on a small boulder, staring out across the rippling waters. How had Stormwind managed out here alone day after day? What was she running from, what was so terrible that she chose to spend her years here in solitude?

I massage my temples, trying to ease the ache spreading behind my eyes. With the gentle autumn sun warming my shoulders and the wind whispering to itself across the lake, I feel sleep softly beckoning. All the magic-working has taken its toll. I stretch out beside the stone, turning my head to gaze out over the shimmering water.

Before long, I slip into a doze, my mind drifting along familiar paths, thinking now of Stormwind, then my mother, then Val. In the way of dreams, I find myself inexplicably somewhere else, my thoughts untroubled.

I stand at the stern of a good-sized ship. Two tall masts with slanted triangular sails rise at my back, the mark of a sea-faring dhow, built to navigate rough waters. Before me lies a city unlike any I've heard tell of before. The buildings are carved into two huge cliffs that face each other, forming a deep gorge above the rolling waves. The city is bounded by low-walled streets and sheltered by soaring cave roofs. The buildings must be built into caverns, though I cannot tell how deep they go. The city might just as easily hold a few thousand as a few hundred residents.

I shift, leaning against the rails. No— not *me*, but the man whose eyes I look through. I hold myself still, hovering beside his awareness, conscious now of the faint pressure of his thoughts, words that bear the sound of his voice: *home* and *barrier* and *trouble brewing*. I know the eyes I see through are amethyst in color, that the body I have slipped into isn't human at all.

I've had dreams like this before, a handful of times. Each time I lost my hold on it before I could be sure of its reality. This time, I intend to stay as long as I can. I make myself small, keeping away from the thoughts that brush past me, light as the wings of moths.

The boards creak behind us. "It always looks better at a distance, doesn't it?" The speaker, a man with light brown hair and peridot green eyes, steps up to the railing beside us. He gazes at the receding city with a mix of humor and contempt.

"Most things do," the breather whose body I share replies blandly, his voice deeply familiar. I pull farther back, try to keep from speaking his name in my mind.

"Bah." The man spits into the water. "I don't know what we expected of them anyway." He turns away. "I'm going under."

Val nods. He glances to the side, and I see that the ship approaches a rocky shoal. As the ship shifts, the captain adjusting its course, a faint ripple crosses the deck. Val looks back at the city—but it's no longer there. Blank cliffs run unbroken along the shore. The canyon is gone, the buildings hidden. The wide-open waters are rocky and unwelcoming now, waves crashing against jagged stones where a moment ago we sailed through calm seas.

Magic. I think the word aloud without meaning to, awed by an enchantment so stable and powerful it can mask a whole city from sight.

I jerk awake as suddenly as if someone slammed a door in my face.

Stunned, I sit up, staring unseeing at the lake before me. The sunlight reflects off the water, burning my eyes. Only a dream. I rub my face, press my fingers into my eye sockets.

Except that I've had such dreams before.

"It's not really possible," I tell the mountain air. It's wishful thinking, the hope that I could maintain some contact with the one other person I remember as well as Stormwind. No magic would allow as simple a connection as these dreams. There are those who learn to spirit walk, but that takes great training and even greater effort. I slip into these dreams, the five or six I've had, as easily as if I were stepping into the lake for a swim. One moment I'm dry, the next, immersed. Besides, if it *were* magic, Stormwind would have discovered me long ago.

"Just dreams," I say to assure myself.

Neither the mountains nor the lake make any answer.

I spend the afternoon on the roof. Yesterday I repaired a third of the north face with its low overhang. Today, working much more quickly and with far less concern for detail, I finish mending the remainder of the north side. Stormwind and I had worked on the south face together, and I take only a few minutes to inspect our repairs. The roof will hold for the winter, whether we're here or not, and I have more pressing concerns.

As evening sets in, I finish the last of my chores and settle in to read *Magical Wards and Defenses*, making note of the sections that might help me enhance my wards. I won't be able to commit even a fraction of what I read to memory, but at least I'll have gained a greater understanding of the various spells, and can select what I want to work on next.

I keep the mirror beside me as I work. Stormwind should have reached the portal at the nearest town, Sonapur, sometime today, but Stonefall will likely take her straight through to the portal to Fidanya. She won't have a room to rest in, or the privacy to contact me, until very late. In all likelihood, she'll wait till tomorrow. Still, I can't help checking the mirror now and then.

Before I retire for the night, I gather up three of our daily-use glowstones, replenish their store of magic, and carry them up the ladder to tuck into my own daypack. Standing there in the magic-brightened cocoon of the loft, the house empty below me and charms and wards in my hand, I can no longer avoid the *why* of what I'm doing.

I don't believe Stormwind will come back. Regardless of her innocence or guilt, Blackflame will not allow the possibility of losing.

There's so much I don't know, but this much is certain to me: Stormwind is gone. Without someone outside of the High Council to break her free, she'll never return.

The only question left is whether I pursue her or follow her instructions to remain here, living alone and teaching myself. And when I can bear the isolation no more, will I go in search of a family I don't know, and from whom I'll always have to keep my talent a secret? How will I live with myself, knowing the choices I've made?

I curl up on my pallet, staring at the darkness until I slip into a dreamless sleep.

I spend the following day improving my string of wards and collecting dead wood from the forest. With our harvest already in, there's little else to worry me other than caring for the animals. I find myself checking the mirror regularly as the day progresses, but no matter how often I look, it offers me nothing more than my own reflection.

As used to solitude as I thought I'd become, the silence left behind in Stormwind's wake feels heavy and smothering. My movements sound overloud in the small confines of the cottage; the walls seem a little too close together. It's funny how a home I considered cozy and comforting has so quickly become an eerie shell, made so only by the departure of a friend.

By the time I slide under my blankets, I know Stormwind should have reached the High Council. Once she was safe in her own room and had set her wards, she should have contacted me. But the mirror has been quiet all evening long. I lie on my side in the darkness, watching the pale blur of my reflection and trying not to worry.

But I have run out of excuses for why, even now, deep in the night, Stormwind has yet to appear in the glass.

A MIRROR IN THE NIGHT

The following day, I teach myself a smaller charm from my now-favorite book: smokers. I bind ash and smoke into a casing formed from an empty nutshell. Given my proclivity for fire, it hardly takes two tries to make one. When I snap it to the ground out by the lakefront, a dense black smoke pours forth in a forty-pace radius from where I stand.

I take a deep, untroubled breath, stretch one arm into darkest night, and begin a count until I can see again. Even with the gentle breeze blowing in over the lake, the smoke lasts surprisingly long. And, as my book had promised, it merely creates a visual barrier. I can't see my own fingertips, but neither my throat nor my eyes react to the fog.

It provides the perfect cover for an escape, and even though it's based in fire, it neither kills nor harms. I can allow myself this. By the time I'm ready to turn in for the night, I have a handful of smokers to add to my daypack.

I've kept the mirror by me all day, carrying it with me even into the goat byre and chicken coop, and now I lay it beside my pallet. It offers me nothing more than a glimpse of my own features. It isn't long before I slip into a land of murky dreams.

I wake to the sound of a voice. "Hikaru?"

I jolt upright, blinking at the bright oval on the floor.

"Hikaru?" The voice is tinny but familiar.

"Mistress Stormwind?" I scramble to pick up the mirror. "Are you well?"

"Yes."

She doesn't look it. Her eyes are shadowed and her skin sags with exhaustion. She seems a different person from the hardy, confident woman with whom I've studied this past year.

"The trial?" I ask.

"It begins tomorrow."

"So soon? Are you ready?"

She shrugs. "As ready as I can be."

That doesn't bode well at all. Wasn't Talon supposed to help her? "What about—"

"I have only a few minutes now," Stormwind says, cutting me off. "There's something I have been meaning to discuss with you regarding your studies. You know that the greatest spells draw on what is around you rather than rote words and stored enchantments."

"Yes."

"The easiest higher order casting for a mage to make is their first. Mine called up a storm. Now I can replicate that casting as easily as snapping my fingers."

"Not mine," I murmur, realizing where she means for this conversation to go. We've discussed my sunbolt before, and I thought Stormwind had accepted that I wouldn't attempt it again. Apparently she can be as stubborn as I am.

Stormwind smiles, but there's nothing happy in it. "You have practiced channeling."

I nod. That's one skill Stormwind drummed into me nearly every day of my studies, to the point that I often dreamed of channeling—water, magic, smoke, goat's milk, or whatever other unexpected material she assigned to me.

"You are as proficient now as most master mages ever become. So yes, you can replicate your sunbolt." Her voice lightens. "In the interest of keeping your hair, however, make sure to channel it."

"I see." I smooth back my hair, feathery soft and surprisingly fine. In the months since I came to Mistress Stormwind's cottage, it has grown back as slowly as moss on a river stone. Now it frames my face, tickling the tops of my ears. But regardless of whether my spell costs me my hair or not, I cannot fathom casting it again. Unlike Stormwind's name-spell, mine can only kill. It *has* killed.

She knows me well enough to gauge the path of my thoughts. "In a time of need, your first casting will come to your fingertips. You must learn what to do with it so that you do not destroy yourself a second time."

"I won't use it."

She purses her lips. "Practice. Start very, very small."

I lean toward the mirror. Stormwind would never suggest I practice my sunbolt without her, not unless…. "How long will your trial run, exactly?"

"A week, perhaps less. Should I not return...."

"Mistress—"

"The cabin is yours. Stay there. The wards will keep you protected until you are ready to leave."

I take a slow breath. "What will your sentence be?"

"Imprisonment, most likely," she replies. "But I may sway the Council. Of the ten regular members, four are strongly in my favor, and two more appear undecided. If I can get five, Talon will give her vote to me."

But she won't get the fifth vote. If they're undecided, Blackflame will find a way to influence them. I have no doubt of it. "You need to leave," I whisper. "This won't be justice. You know that."

"I know. But there's no running now."

Of course there is, I want to cry.

"If I run, I will be admitting my guilt. I will not do that. I am sorry. I meant to see you through your studies."

I shake my head, a sharp, jerky motion. I don't want her apologies, nor do I want the implication that my worst fears will be realized. "You can't accept this."

"I have no other choice." Her eyes bore into me. "I want you to open the fourth trunk and use what you need from there."

I duck my head guiltily. "Uh, yeah. I'll do that. But—"

"I dare not use this mirror again. There are too many people watching. We cannot risk them learning about you."

"Wait." I reach toward the mirror. "I need to know what happens to you."

She glances up, past her own mirror. "Someone's coming. If I can, I will try in three days. Farewell."

"Farewell."

She fades from view, leaving me staring at the mirror. My own face looks back at me, my features shadowy blots on paler skin, all subtleties lost in the darkness of the loft.

Three days, and then what? The future yawns before me, dark and cold and ready to swallow me whole, just as my past stretches out behind me, bleak in its emptiness.

I killed a man, a fang, a *monster*, with the magic that thrums through my veins. I left another to die, himself held prisoner by a demon of a different tenor, when I might have helped him.

Is this what I am, what I will always be? Does Stormwind expect that I'll forget her, her friendship and kindnesses, and go on as if she had not existed? Go on hiding who and what I am, abandoning those I cannot or will not help?

I clasp my hands, resting them on my bent knees. This is not the life I want. Some of it will always be mine; I cannot escape the threat of the Council no matter where I go or what I do. Nor can I change my past. Gazing at the pale outlines of my hands in the darkness, I know I must decide soon just what I'm willing to do—what fears I'm willing to face and what truths I'm willing to fight for.

The next day spreads out long and lonely, with only the necessary chores and my studies to fill them. It seems a long time from dawn to darkness. I keep the mirror nearby throughout the day and lay it beside my pallet at night, even though I don't expect to hear from Stormwind. I fall asleep easily, tired from the worries plaguing me, and slip into a land of murky dreams.

"See anything?"

I wake with a start, my heart hammering in my chest.

"Nothing," a second voice responds. I turn my head, careful to keep my movements small. On the floor beside my pallet, the mirror glows. The voices coming from it are distinctly male.

"There has to be someone there. She wouldn't have brought it along otherwise. Can you get its location?"

Mages. Probably Blackflame's supporters. Biting down on a curse, I cast around, searching for something hard. I'm not about to let a mirror betray me to him again.

"I'm working on it."

No time— not if they're using a locator spell. I slide my blanket off my bed and sweep it over the glass in a single move. Ignoring the muffled exclamation, I flip the blanket-shrouded mirror over and smash it on the brick beside my bed, knocking the little wooden crow statuette aside.

The voice on the other side cuts off mid-sentence.

With trembling hands, I check the black mound of my blanket. The light has gone from within it, the connection broken, but there's a comfort in certainty. I take a shaky breath as my fingers find the sharp edges of the broken glass.

Think, I command myself.

At least one of the men was a mage skilled enough to try to pinpoint my mirror. But was Stormwind's mirror stolen, or has she already been convicted after a single day? And did the mage have enough time to complete his locator spell?

I gather up the blanket and climb down to the main room. It probably doesn't matter if they were able to trace the mirror to this valley. If Blackflame can find out from the High Council where Stormwind made her home, he'll send someone to see what he can find regardless of the spell's results.

At least I have one thing working in my favor: even if Blackflame's men departed the moment Stormwind presented herself, they still won't reach our valley until tomorrow. We're too far from the portal for faster travel than that. I have a little time to do this right.

First I bury the mirror beside the goat byre, the shards still wrapped in my blanket. By the time I stamp down the dirt on top of it, I have a clear plan for leaving. I pause only to trace a protective ward over the broken glass, sealing it from any tracing spells.

Next, the animals. I pour out extra feed for the goats and chickens and open their pens. It's possible predators will get them, but better a chance to graze in the wild than death by starvation.

I race up the short path to the cottage. With a half-thought command, every glowstone in the house blazes to life. In the loft, I grab my daypack with the charms and string of wards already inside. I add a spare set of clothes, the crow statuette, then pause. I'm not sure where I'm running to yet, but…it would be wise to be able to pass for a mage if need be. I retrieve Stormwind's spare set of robes from a trunk, holding them out at shoulder-height. The bottom edge puddles on the floor. Stormwind's a good head taller than I am. No matter. Hems can be adjusted.

I take a final look around and remember the pouch with its brooch and necklaces. I retrieve it, shoving it into my bag with the robes. Stormwind will likely never return here. It makes no sense to leave them behind, and perhaps I'll be able to take them to her. The gold itself might serve her well.

Downstairs, I fetch sewing supplies to shorten the robe. I pack a few days' worth of food and water, then toss in the contents of the coin jar by the window. I run my hands over my hair, trying to think, then race back up the ladder to fetch my comb. Back downstairs, I wrap my knife in a bit of leather and add it to my pack, then lift my cloak down from its peg.

I make myself walk around the cottage one last time and come to a stop in front of the medicinal cabinet. Of course—hadn't Stormwind made me help her pack for a reason? I fill a few empty pouches with herbs for fever, pain, stomach upset. The salves are too heavy to carry, but I take the herbs I might need to make a paste to treat burns and open wounds. That's enough. If I need more help than that, I won't be able to treat myself.

I complete my circuit and come at last to the books. My stomach twists with regret. They're too heavy, and I'm out of time. I gather them all and hide them behind a pile of pots at the back of a cupboard. With mages on the way, the books are probably safer there than within a warded trunk.

I pocket a pair of glowstones and shoulder my pack. It's heavier than I would have liked, but without a clear idea of where I'm going or how long it will take to get there, the extra provisions and medicines may prove lifesaving. The only sentimental item I've included is my wooden crow, and it's too light to make a difference.

Outside, I lock the cottage and trace the sigil on the door until it brightens. Stormwind has layered her enchantments here. This ward triggers three other protective spells. It'll take a high mage to break open the house, and Stormwind will know the moment it happens. It's the one way I have to alert her to what's happening.

I pause as I reach the edge of the forest, turning around to face my home. In the full-bright light of the moon it waits for me, safe and quiet and empty. With the friendly company of the trees at my back and the moonlight silvering the lake, I admit to myself that I don't really know whether Stormwind is truly innocent or not. I do know that Blackflame intends to destroy her, and that's all the motivation I need.

I turn and start into the woods. Somewhere nearby, an owl hoots. I don't want to go racing toward the High Council and Blackflame—not even if my mother's there—but this isn't about what I want.

Stormwind took me in when I had nowhere to go. She trained me when any other mage would have turned me over to the High Council. She gave me—and Val—the benefit of the doubt. This last year, I have been her guest, sheltered by her walls and the spells that protected her valley. The least I can do is trust her and offer her what aid I can.

This time, I'm not running away from my fears.
I'm running straight toward them.

The moon dips low in the sky, its edge skimming the peaks of the surrounding mountains. I've been walking for hours with a glowstone in hand. Even with the full moon, the path is too dark to travel without some light.

Now the sky has begun to lighten, velvet darkness fading at the edges. With dawn hinting at the day to come, I decide to rest. I'll travel faster with an hour or two of sleep to refresh me.

Ahead of me, the forested slope gives way to a scree-strewn mountainside. Better to stop while I still have cover. I make my way carefully down through the trees until I lose sight of the path above me, then find a pine with low-hanging boughs beneath which I can shelter.

I lie down with my pack for a pillow and wrap myself in my cloak against the autumn chill. I could use my wards to protect myself, but if mages truly are riding toward the valley, they're more likely to take note of active spells than a sleeping traveler. I slip the wards into my pocket just in case.

But I'm too wound up to fall asleep, my thoughts flitting from Stormwind to the mages in the mirror to all the things I don't know. I try to slow my breath, still my thoughts. Stormwind taught me to meditate when I first came to stay with her. Under her guidance, I learned to examine the edges of each memory I hold, reaching for what it once connected to, sifting through the ashes in search of color or scent. As I have a hundred times before, I gather them to myself as a miser would his most precious jewels, counting them out one by one.

Here— here is a moment of laughter with a young man whose black and brown hair and sharp teeth hint at his true shape: a tanuki, or raccoon dog. He leans against a carved door painted a vibrant turquoise, his arms folded and his head tilted to the side, brown eyes twinkling with mischief. *Kenta.* Of my few memories of him, this is my favorite, for there's no darkness in it, no fear or desperation.

Here's another man, dark skinned and long fingered,

whose face I only catch in fleeting glimpses. More than his visage, I remember his cloak, black as the night. What I recall of his name suggests how little I knew him: *Ghost.*

Then there's a scattering of other people like a handful of seeds tossed to the ground for the birds to peck up: women with whom I may have shared an apartment, others whom I must have once called friends. Shop owners and street children, the people who filled my days. And from the last of those days, the Degaths.

I remember my last day in Karolene, the chain of events that led up to my sunbolt. These are the memories I do not want, the sorrow and fear and dark choices I made, the deaths I witnessed and allowed. The way I gathered sunlight to myself until it roared within me, a fury of flames that I unleashed upon the fang lord Kol, teaching myself in that moment to take the essence of what surrounds me and kill with it.

These recollections leave a bitter taste at the back of my mouth, and I turn my thoughts away from them. Instead, I draw up the memory of my mother as I saw her in Blackflame's gardens, solitary and peaceful, unaware of my presence. The sight of her had nearly broken me with grief, as had the knowledge that she had abandoned me, chosen Blackflame over me. It was only afterward, in the quiet winter months spent in Stormwind's cottage, that I began to wonder if there was more to her story. She is too great a mage to be held for so long against her will. But has she joined Blackflame to support him—or to undermine him? Nothing I have learned has brought me any closer to understanding her. Still, I hope. I cannot bear not to.

There are a few last memories, moments that I can no longer place in time: wandering a lush, flowered garden with my father tall and gentle beside me. Kneeling before my mother to recite a lesson I no longer recall. Drinking spiced coffee from a blue-rimmed cup in a busy marketplace. Bits and pieces, shards of the whole.

Through Stormwind's tutelage I've recovered this much, and only this much. Most of my memories may never return. There will always be gaps in my knowledge of the past, gaps in who I am. This is the price of my bolt of sunlight, its single flash of irrevocable destruction. As I lie wrapped in my memories, I know that I've gathered as much as I can from the ashes.

Now I must remake myself, drawing upon the lessons my

body retains: the clever fingers of a thief, the quick instincts of a girl growing up on the streets of a strange city. I cannot ever truly know who I was. It's time to discover who I may yet be.

Hoofbeats echo across the mountainside, urgent staccato drumbeats.

I crouch beneath the low-growing boughs of my tree and peer through the needles. The sun has risen high enough to cast its light upon the forested slope, shining bright upon the rocky mountainside further on. The riders high above me slow their horses as they enter the trees, the path more pock-holed and dangerous than the scree-covered trail they just traversed. Foolish of them to have pushed their horses even there. They're in a hurry, and no one hurries down these paths.

I wait, breathing slowly, and catch a glimpse of cloth flapping. Robes? I can't be sure, but I don't need to be. I already know. A handful of locals live on the mountainsides before Stormwind's home, and almost none beyond. These riders want to get to her valley very, very badly. Blackflame must have sent them as soon as he learned where she lived, perhaps urged them on when the mages failed to locate the mirror. I clench my jaw, anger sparking within me. How dare he?

The riders continue on, the sound of their passage overloud in the sudden absence of birdsong. I hold my breath, wound tight with fury. The Council is worth nothing if they allow this—and they do, for how else would Blackflame have discovered Stormwind's home?

I wait until the thud of hooves fades to stillness and the birds begin to speak again, then push myself to my feet. I don't have time for anger right now. I can't afford to be anywhere nearby once they realize I've already left.

Sonapur is the only place with a portal, the only way to Stormwind. A few quick calculations tell me that even if the mages turn back the moment they reach the empty valley, their horses will be too tired to make the return trip at such a brisk pace.

As long as I keep going, I should reach Sonapur before them.

THE BURNT LANDS

I travel through the day, stopping only twice for twenty minutes' rest. In the late morning, I feel the skittering, skin crawling sensation of the ward at the great deodar cedar triggering. Whatever doubts I might have held regarding the riders evaporate at once. Around noon, the wards on the cottage itself flare. I stumble to a stop with a rush of vertigo, the blood running cold in my veins. Then the wards are *gone*, their magic blasted to shreds. I bend over, my hands clutching my knees, shaking as my connection to the spell disintegrates. It takes me a few breaths before I can walk on, my legs not quite steady beneath me.

I reach Sonapur near twilight. Evening flows down into the wide vale, the western mountains silhouetted against the failing light. The great snow-covered peaks far to the north have begun to fade from view. Bright points lie scattered across the plain, twinkling cheerily. The markets will be closing now, the carpet weavers and wool dyers and spinners and shawl makers going home for the night.

Below me, the river I've followed these last few hours widens, pouring into a great lake dotted with lily pads and the faint smudges of lotus flowers. Docks stretch out from the shore, many of them crowded with fishing boats, a few with larger, merrily painted houseboats.

My path descends to the lake and joins a hard-packed dirt road that runs alongside it. At the edge of the forest, I kneel beside a spindly pine tree and trace a sigil upon it. I don't put much magic into it; the brush of cool valley air and the rustle of leaves is enough for my purposes. When I walk on, I leave behind a ward no stronger than a glowstone, charmed to alert me to those who pass down the path behind me. Within a day it will run too low on magic to maintain itself, but a day is all I need.

I follow the road into the town, pulling out my glowstone as night descends. Though Sonapur is settling down, there are still people moving about here. I could easily ask for directions, but instinct tells me the fewer people who remember me, the better. At any rate, I can't get too lost. If memory serves, all the major roads intersect at the great square where the portal stands.

As the road widens, the tightly packed mud-brick buildings with sloped wood-shingled roofs begin to spread out and then are replaced altogether by free-standing homes, multi-storied buildings, and well-made workshops. The dirt road is replaced by cobbles. At the last of the buildings facing the great square I pause, leaning against the wall.

The central area of the square has been designed as a park, with cobbled pathways and benches and a fountain. A row of lampposts bearing glowstones provide ample light to the groups of men seated around game boards of some sort, drinking tea and conversing. They act perfectly normal, but they leave a wide gap between themselves and the boundary wall of the portal, far to the right.

The portal itself is nothing more than a threshold with neither door nor room to call its own. Instead, a few stones on either side suggest a wall that never was, and the stones of the portal rise between them, straight and simple, the clean work of an expert mason long gone. A low wall encircles the structure with carved gates on either side, the far gate opening directly to the road. No doubt the wall itself is mostly for show, the portal protected by wards to keep trespassers at bay.

Inside the enclosure stands a mage, his back to the portal, his cloak hanging open to reveal his robes and the hilt of the sword at his side.

The sentry means that accessing the portal will be somewhat more challenging than I'd thought. I should have expected it, but part of me hoped I would find it unguarded, as it had been when Stormwind and I visited in the spring.

Bolstered by the appearance of a trio of older women strolling the paths and the apparent respect with which the men greet them, I leave the street for the garden. I stop before the first of the food vendors. He pushes a cart with a built-in bowl of coals to keep his wares warm, and for a copper happily fills a tin dish with *chole* for me.

"The guards are new," I say, nodding toward the portal as I take the food.

The man pauses, but doesn't look over his shoulder. "Yes," he says with clear displeasure. "It's mages' trouble, and none of us are happy to see it here. Were you planning on traveling, daughter?"

"No," I lie. "Just passing through." I take a bite of my food. It's delicious, the chickpeas tender and the spices warming me all the way down to my belly. "They don't sound like they're here on behalf of the High Council."

"They're not," the man says. "We've heard of mages being their own problem, but it hasn't touched us here before. These men won't allow anything through, not even a message to the Council itself. Best steer clear of them, daughter."

"Yes," I agree, and wander over to a bench to sit and eat. It's sound advice, but there are more mages on my heels. I'll need to pass through the portal before I get caught between them. Especially if they're Blackflame's lackeys, come to destroy what they can.

The portal is easy enough to study from the tops of the surrounding buildings. The mages below, for all their constant vigilance, never look up. There are two that I can see from here, one on each side of the portal. I sit for a full half hour, observing them and hemming Stormwind's robe. Not once do the guards raise their eyes to the rooftops. Nor do the others who frequent the gardens, the vendors keeping their attention for their customers, the men focused on the games they play.

Once I finish sewing, I take the back stairs down to street level and make my way through quiet thoroughfares and small alleys until I'm far enough from the portal that my magic will be difficult to detect. I scale a low building and settle myself at the center of the flat roof. The streets here are near silent, the residents gone to bed. As long as no one heard me climbing, I doubt I'll be found out.

Retrieving my string of wards, I loop them around myself and close the silver clasp. The spells activate at once, a momentary flicker of magic that recedes into a faint hum barely detectable even to me. I wait, listening for any sound of alarm.

Nothing.

Perhaps this task will be easier than I'd hoped. I set to work on a series of charms, half listening for movement. The shield built into my wards should keep the vibrations of my magical workings from reaching the mages back at the portal. Regardless, nothing I'm making should be a great enough casting to be noticeable. No doubt some of the charms used daily by the locals would draw more attention.

Still, I work as fast as I can. I finish within a quarter of an hour, scoop the charms into my pockets, and disconnect the wards.

It takes me nearly an hour to visit the three rooftops I'd chosen from among the buildings across the garden from the portal. On each I leave a small pile of charms and smokers. By the time I finish, my feet drag and my head feels heavy. I make my way around the garden by back streets, returning to the rooftop I'd used to spy on the portal. From this vantage point, the gardens lie quiet, the last of the vendors packing up their carts and heading home. The mages still guard their gateway, though they no longer stand. Instead, they sit with their backs against the stone, legs stretched out.

Now would be a good time to put my plan into action, but I'm already weary from a full day's travel on almost no sleep. Better to rest a few hours and make my attempt when I have enough energy to run, and keep running. I stretch out, using my pack as a pillow. If the mages who rode to Stormwind's valley return, the ward I set at the pine should alert me with enough time to try the portal before they arrive. I'll have to trust in that.

I wake with a start while the sky is still dark. It takes me a moment to identify the sound that alarmed me. Then I flip on my side and spot a cat prowling through the broken bits of furniture piled along the roof's back wall. Not my ward at all. It takes a little while for my heart to slow.

It's time to move.

The mages are still on guard, sitting with their backs to the stones, though it looks as though the one facing my direction may have nodded off. I'd have to stand beside him to activate the portal, though, which I'm not about to do. Just as well I have a distraction planned.

Downstairs, I press against the wall of a teahouse, closed for the night, and peer around the corner to the portal. No change. I reach out with my mind, letting my magic ride the faint breeze, high and light and easy over the rooftops until, just there, I find the first small pile of charms.

I take a deep breath, listening to the quiet of the night. The first birds have begun to chirp, but the houses remain dark— at least for now.

With a single twist of power, I activate the charms. They explode in rapid-fire succession, sending pinwheels of green and red and orange flame twisting through the sky, their sound ricocheting off the buildings around us. The display might warrant irritation from the mages, but the blanket of black smoke swirling down from the rooftop will assure their prompt attention.

The guards at the portal pivot to stare. A third mage, hidden until now behind the low boundary wall, leaps to his feet, shouting to the other two. A moment later, the pair departs, racing toward the far end of the square. The remaining guard rubs his face and goes to stand before the gateway, facing the direction of the disturbance. I smile tightly. One is better than three.

As the windows of the teahouse brighten, I reach out again, setting off the second set of fireworks and smokers. Dark smoke roils up over the far buildings, lit from within by bursts of heat and light. The remaining mage takes a few steps away from the portal, his back to me.

Already people are pouring out of their houses, men shouting questions as they gain the streets, women pulling their children back inside. I step into the road and move briskly past a knot of men staring up at the fading conflagration, letting those who race forward to offer help speed past me. As I walk, I weave a shield around myself that's faint as the first light of dawn, the flimsiest of protections but something I can easily strengthen.

A few paces from the back gateway to the portal, I reach out a final time, carefully now—so carefully, because the mages will be watching for magic—and set the last stash alight. Screams ring out in the park as smoke engulfs a third rooftop.

A group of men converge on the mage at the portal, shouting at him across the barrier of the enchanted wall. He snarls back at them, one hand on the sword at his side, the other held before him in warning. The men's faces look sallow in the early light, their voices hoarse with anger and panic. I feel a twist of guilt at the fear I'm invoking, but it's too late now to change my course.

Three more steps and I reach the gate to the portal enclosure. I set my hand on it, guessing that the lock will be spelled. Mages would hardly be bothered to keep a key for each portal they wish to travel through. Thankfully, the sigil for *open* glows in my mage sight. I trace it quickly, keeping an eye on the guard.

He shouts at the men, gesturing for them to stay back, his attention so complete he doesn't notice the faint breath of magic as the sigil releases the gate to me. I step inside, leaving the gate open, and pad over to the portal, moving slowly even though I want to run. It's vital that those who see me think I'm not inside the enclosure, that I'm on the other side of the wall. That there's nothing for them to see here.

Gripping a smoker in my hand, I approach the stone sides of the portal, using their bulk to shade me from the mage's sight. I inhale and gather the magic I'll need to activate the portal—the age-old air, pine-scented and river-damp, the growth of moss on the stones underfoot, slow and sure.

"You!" A glance shows me the mage turning toward me, hand extended. Behind him, the men stare at me, mouths agape. "Halt!"

I smack the smoker against the side of the portal, smoke enveloping me at once. *Now.* Sensing the sigil glowing pale blue in the stone, I pour my magic into it as I trace the lines as fast as I can, my eyesight clouded by darkness. *Open*, I command—and it does.

A force smashes into my shield, tearing through it and knocking me sideways against stone. Swallowing a cry, I push myself off the arch and stumble through the portal.

The world disappears. I'm floating, suspended in night, portals shining all around me like distant stars in foreign constellations. I find the one to Fidanya with hardly a thought. The spider-silk path between us beams bright and strong. It has obviously been traveled by more than a few mages recently. And another one about to come in after me, no doubt.

Tightening my focus, I lean forward. The magic of the portal grips me at once, pulling me along until I'm spinning through a vortex of flickering lights—doorways and their pathways racing by, perhaps even other travelers. I've experienced this rush before, a lifetime ago when Blackflame sent Kol and his retinue through a portal to their home. Then, it shimmered past me and I barely caught more than a flash of dizzying lights.

Now, though, I need to concentrate. The mage will likely have entered behind me. Like me, he'll have identified which path was last used. The moment after I step out of the portal, he'll follow me out, and I won't be ready to defend myself. Not against a warrior trained to attack. I need to escape him before then.

As I careen forward, I widen my focus, pressing outward with my mage senses. Three more paths cross mine before my destination. The first hurtles past before I can assess it. The second is bright and shiny—but the last, to my left, glimmers pink so faintly I almost miss it. I swerve onto it with a magic-fueled leap that nearly sends me flying into darkness, the light around me devolving into tangled strands that pull at my body. My bones slam against the sack of my skin as if they might rip through.

I scream into the void, pain obliterating my concentration. Black spots streak across my vision. This is why portals are dangerous. I can feel myself sliding, the route as slippery in my mind's grasp as fine thread.

No. I cling hard to the portal with its ancient path, push back with all my force, ignore the pain, staring wide-eyed past the darkness that blurs my sight. For a single agonizing moment, I teeter on the edge of a nightmare precipice. Then the momentum of my new direction sucks me in, steadying me as it pulls me forward into a new vortex of light twisting around me.

The open portal flashes before me. With a gasp of relief, I tumble through it. But there's no city on the other side of this portal, no crowds to lose myself in or alleys to flee down. There is only sun and dust and the broken walls of a forgotten fortress, silent as a tomb.

I take two shaky steps forward into the debris-strewn courtyard. Agony ripples out from each strained joint, tendons and muscles pulled nearly to snapping.

I gulp down a breath, assess my surroundings. The stone portal stands at the center of an interior courtyard, littered with broken tiles and stones from the surrounding walls of a great fortress. The sun is already bright overhead. The air tastes of dust, hot and bereft of moisture. All around stretches a vast quiet: nothing moves, no bird chirps, neither leaf nor cloth rustles in the wind. This is hardly a welcoming land.

My first concern, however, is the mage following me. I don't want to be standing here if he steps through the portal.

The main entry to this inner courtyard has been made impassable by the collapse of the buildings that must have once towered over it—but there's one other option. Gritting my teeth against the pain, I stumble toward a vaguely door-shaped hole in the wall behind the portal.

Halfway across the open ground, a ripple of magic slips past me, faint but unmistakable.

I turn in time to see the mage stagger into sight. He bends over, hands clasping his knees, eyes squeezed shut. My eyes catch on his boots, barely visible past the fall of his cloak—deep brown, polished to a shine, with a curving symmetrical design cut from light blue leather and sewn over the ankle. Rich boots for a wealthy man.

He gasps, shakes his head. He'll recover enough to search for me any moment now. I'm too close to use a smoker effectively, and anyway he could easily disperse it with a wind. The rubble makes moving silently impossible. I'll have to shield myself and try to talk my way out of trouble. Keeping my gaze on the mage, I reach out with my senses to gather magic to myself.

My breath stutters in my lungs. There's nothing there.

I cast about blindly, closing my eyes as if I might sense magic more easily that way. I focus on the energy that should be pulsing through this land, through the very stone around me, through the scorching air.

Nothing.

With a quiet scrape, jarring in the overwhelming silence, the mage takes a step forward and swivels, surveying what's visible of the courtyard. I swallow hard, eyes wide. He still has weapons he can use—the sword at his side, whatever martial training he's had. I have no time to pull out my string of wards and connect them, and besides, they'd only trap me here. My best weapon is my voice.

"Peace," I croak.

His focus whips to me. He lifts a hand, fingers splayed.

"Peace," I cry, terrified suddenly that he'll find power where I found none. But then his features go slack with shock.

My breath comes out shaky with relief. "There's no magic here."

"What is this place?" His voice is sharp, jagged.

I shrug, grateful that it's only half as painful as I'd expected. "Last left turn before Fidanya."

"What?"

There's really no good way to explain this, but I want to make this man my ally, at least for now. So I keep talking. "I don't really know. What place has no magic? And why would there be a portal here?"

"You used a portal without knowing where you were going?" He squints at me, studying my features. He clearly thinks I'm a complete idiot.

"I changed my mind halfway through," I correct him. He can't possibly think less of me.

"You're a *child*."

"Journeyman."

"What in all the hells were you doing using the portal? And why didn't you ask permission?"

"Since when are the portals regulated against mages? You weren't supposed to be there, and I didn't want to deal with you. I'm trying to get home to my mother." Almost true. Stormwind has been both mentor and friend, the closest thing to a mother I can remember. And my own mother could very well be in Fidanya as well.

The mage snorts. "She lives here?" His voice is heavy with contempt.

"No. I'm only here because you chased me."

"You're a fool." That's really not much of an improvement over being called a child.

"We need to find a way out." The words taste familiar. How many times did I use them in the life I cannot remember? Did I often get into difficult situations? "Whatever this place is, I don't want to spend the night here. Without magic, the portal is no good to us. So…. Peace?"

He nods stiffly. "For now. But I want answers. Soon."

I shrug, bob my head. After all, "soon" can have more than a few interpretations. "There's a door here," I say, gesturing at the hole in the wall behind me. He starts toward me. I wait until he's caught up. I don't dare turn my back on him. He casts a dark look at me, but remains silent as we walk side by side to the opening. The hall beyond it is dark, lit at irregular intervals by what must be more doorways, some brighter than others. The far end shimmers: an exit to the outside.

I step over the threshold and send an apprehensive glance in each direction, finding only the same uneven gloom. The mage lifts his hand and light blooms around us, the glowstone he holds throwing into sharp relief shards of tiles and empty doorways.

"Is that wise?" I ask. Ahead of us, there's a bundle lying on the floor, sharp-edged but too far away to see clearly.

"Wise?" the mage says, drawing out the word.

I wave vaguely. "The glowstone. In a magically dead land? It might draw attention."

"At least then we would have answers."

I bite back my retort. Arguing with him will only slow us down—and the glowstone *will* make it easier to navigate these hallways.

I start forward, my eyes drawn to the thing on the ground. I can't quite make it out. Something pokes out from the bulk of it, reaching across the floor like an errant branch, or dried twigs.

Filled with foreboding, I move closer, straining to identify the thing in the light of the glowstone. When I do, my throat closes up. The shape stretched out before me is nothing more than papery skin curled over brittle bones—a mummified corpse preserved by the endless heat, untouched by nature, its clothing long since dissolved away. Its bones protrude obscenely, each rib tracing a line around its hollow chest, the skin between the pelvic and hip bones so thin that it seems translucent, as if the light were shining through parchment.

My stomach tightens into a ball, heavy as lead. The skull bears no expression, dull teeth showing through leathery lips, the eye sockets vacant. But that hand, outstretched…. A plea. Or a single, hopeless attempt to escape death.

Beside me, the mage breathes a curse.

I retreat slowly, as if walking through water, gasping for

air that's too dense to breathe. I stumble back to the doorway we just passed, the room dim within. I don't enter, but peer through the opening—and there amidst a scattering of debris lit by the unobstructed windows, I spot two more desiccated bodies, their arms entwined in an embrace that suggests love and fear and pain and desperation.

I back away from the door, my eyes roving up and down the hallway. How many rooms are there? And how many—

"They're all dead." The mage stands beside the first corpse, studying it with an eerie calm.

"I guessed," I say, hating the waver in my voice. The reality of a fortress—or palace or whatever—filled with skeletons has my body trembling, even as my mind tells me that the dead can harm no one.

"What else have you guessed?"

I run the details through my mind, trying to put the pieces together. A place without magic, a place where the people are extinct and the life has been sucked out of the earth itself.... "These are the Burnt Lands."

"They are. And you brought us here." The glowstone transforms him into a nightmare of gray and black and silver, fury radiating from his frame as he stands over the corpse.

I make myself meet his gaze steadily. "We need to get out of this building."

He glares at me a moment longer, then turns and steps past the corpse, striding toward the end of the hall. I follow, wrapping my arms across my chest to clutch the straps of my pack. I hold my breath as I step past the body, irrationally terrified of accidentally touching it.

The Burnt Lands. Every apprentice—every child, really, regardless of whether or not they have magical talent—knows about the Great Burning. Four hundred years ago, the mages of the Eleven Kingdoms divided into factions, pitting themselves against each other in a bid for power and wealth. They worked enchantments that unleashed catastrophes over the land, draining whole regions of magic in order to rain fire upon their enemies, even forcing the ground to sink in upon itself, swallowing whole cities. The Great Burning ended with a conflagration of spells and the annihilation of two entire factions of mages.

Not long thereafter, the High Council of Mages was founded to regulate magic and mages in the hopes of preventing such a war from ever happening again. The Burnt Lands are what remain of the great, abandoned regions where the magic was drained, making them barren and unlivable.

The end of the hall opens to what must have once been a wide and fertile garden. The plot is terraced in long low steps with stone paths meandering over the exposed earth or leading down to the next terrace. But the earth itself is desolate. Deep cracks snake across the dirt, some nearly as wide across as my hand. No hint of trees, no brush or shrub. Not even a thorn bush.

A boundary wall encloses both gardens and building. It rises three or four times my height and is as wide as my arm is long, but one section has crumbled to pieces. A wall like this one doesn't crumble of its own accord; something must have knocked it down. Hopefully whatever it was is long gone, as dead as the people left behind here.

The mage starts toward the broken section of wall. I follow, grateful for his silence. But as we reach the edge of the gardens and step down to traverse what might have once been a road, he asks, "Who's your master?"

"We have greater concerns right now," I say. I have no intention of telling him anything about myself.

"Yes, we do. After what you did, traveling between portals and bringing us here, you deserve to have your magic revoked."

His words make me shudder away from him. "That's absurd," I say roughly. "I put no one's life in danger but my own."

"I would never have—"

"There was no reason for you to come after me. The portal is never guarded, and you had no authorization from the Council to be there. You were there to cause trouble. Can you really fault me for wanting to avoid you?"

His hand whips out, closing around my arm with viselike strength. "Don't you dare lecture me, girl. You didn't ask for passage. You're lucky I didn't kill you outright."

I stand stock-still, outrage flaming in my chest until my breath tastes of smoke. This man, this *mage*, is one of Blackflame's associates. He was in Sonapur to keep the portal closed until his friends had raided Stormwind's valley. He is not my ally. He will never be my ally.

"We need to move." My voice is cold and ugly and almost unrecognizable. "We can discuss the rest of this if we get out of here alive." Before he can argue, I jerk my head at the break in the wall. "I see magefire."

He turns toward the wall, then drops my arm to stride

forward. I follow, massaging my bicep, thankful to be walking behind him.

He climbs up onto the tumbled wreckage of the wall, staring out.

From here, the land drops away steeply. The late morning sunlight illuminates the roofs of a great city spread out below us—vast, multi-layered, and completely still. Just past the last of the buildings, a single orb hangs in the air emitting a flickering blue-green light.

As I glance toward the mage, I catch sight of a dark spot moving far out in the distance: a bird. I can't tell if it flies beyond the magefire or above the city, but I'm absurdly grateful to see some sign of life.

The mage clambers over the remaining stones. Dread curls in my stomach as I watch him descend the barren slope toward the silent city. But there's no other place to aim for, and I want to escape this land as fast as I can.

I follow after him warily, the dead earth sliding beneath my feet.

SPELLS OF STONE

We weave past buildings that rise two and three stories high until we reach a wide avenue paved with flat yellow stones, pockmarked with age and scoured by the wind. In a few places the pavers appear to have been pressed down, the surrounding stones riding up at angles, as if some great weight had been dragged along them. The mage walks to the center of the road, his boots tapping softly as he casts up and down its length.

This must have been a major thoroughfare once. Now the buildings that line it gape at us with dark windows. My skin crawls as I stare at the silent structures. Are the people here dead as well, or did they manage to flee this place? And where's all the trash? The broken wagons, whatever might have been abandoned in the wake of an exodus or sudden extinction? People don't—can't—take everything with them when they run. I left Stormwind's home full of clothes and dishes and food, left chickens and goats to fend for themselves. But there's no trace of anything here. Even the entrances stand empty: no doors remain, no shutters to close up the windows, nothing.

No one takes their *doors* with them.

The mage continues down the avenue, ignoring me. My internal compass tells me we're heading roughly toward the magefire. We pass building after building, all of them run down and falling apart, their entries yawning open like hungry mouths. Puffs of dust rise around my boots with each step. Nothing else disturbs the earth, no tracks of wild beasts or birds. The emptiness of the land presses against me like a sheet wrapped a little too snug, making it hard to breathe the magic-less air.

Something scrapes against stone.

The mage's head whips around as he searches for the sound. I stand still, straining to make out any sign of movement. The noise comes again, a heavy scraping somewhere out in the city. The pebbles on the road rattle softly.

"Run," I say, breaking into a jog.

The mage glances uncertainly up and down the road as I reach him. Everything lies quiet.

"Run," I repeat, keeping my voice low. "We really don't want to know what that is."

The pebbles rattle again, the vibrations traveling up our legs. That decides him. He races ahead, his boots thundering on the stone underfoot.

That's not the way to escape a pursuer. I may not recall running from anyone or anything quite like this before, but it's simple and clear: move quietly UNTIL you're found out. But I don't dare shout to the mage to slow down, step lightly—my voice might only hasten whatever chases us.

Being left behind suddenly seems as dangerous as being loud. I speed up, searching for a break between buildings that I can use to part ways with the mage, but they're constructed shoulder to shoulder. My pack thumps rhythmically against my back, reminding me with each slap how much my whole body aches.

There— an alley up ahead. The mage has almost reached it. He barrels forward, then skids to a stop, twisting and lunging back the way he'd come. His face is nearly white, his eyes so wide they look as if they might pop out of his skull. I pivot and begin running hard. I don't need to see what he flees to know I don't want to meet it.

Behind me, stone grinds and shifts as if beneath an immense mass. The mage pants as he races after me, wheezing with terror. I glance over my shoulder, golden morning sunshine illuminating the road behind me, and I falter.

A long gray *thing* ripples around the corner, a line of darkness on the yellow stones. Behind it come others like it, scraping at walls as the creature pulls itself into the avenue. They remind me of squid tentacles, but they're scaly and end in massive, wickedly curved talons. Far more disconcerting than the strangeness of the limbs is the sheer size of them: some are as wide around as a horse. I can't tell how long they are, for I can't quite make out the creature they belong to.

The longest arm snaps toward us and its claw gouges a hole in the road not fifty paces away. The shock of it—the metal-gray sheen, the *thwack* against stone—sends me stumbling forward, unfreezing my muscles.

I sprint down the road, putting all I have into running, my lungs burning. Behind me, the noise of the creature's progress grows into a rumbling, grinding roar. The strange ripples in the pavers I noticed earlier seem not so inexplicable now.

It growls, a deafening sound that reverberates through my body, like nothing I've ever heard before. It may be huge, but it's fast and, I bet, hungry. The mage clutches his side, a step ahead of me now. Nor will I be able to continue this fast much farther. Neither of us can outrun this thing.

I do the one thing I can think of—I leap through the window of the building next to me, shouting for the mage to follow. He wheels around and clambers over the sill a moment later, his breath coming in short, pained gasps as he drops to the floor.

"This way." I pull a glowstone from my pocket and raise it high enough to bring an exit into focus. We barrel through the room toward the hallway. I barely register the eerie emptiness of the place—no cloth, no furniture, no doors—only the shriveled remains of people scattered here and there like fallen autumn leaves.

The creature howls, an ear-splitting sound of fury. Its tentacles scrabble through the window behind us, stabbing into corners in search of its prey. Boots skidding over the gritty floor, I plunge into the central corridor and find salvation: stairs.

I don't say anything, half hoping the mage will choose a different route, but he follows on my heels. I take the stairs two and three at a time, far more worried about the horrific creature behind us.

As we reach the landing, the beast finds the front entry and a mass of tentacles fly down the hall toward us, smashing against the walls and scrabbling up the stairs. I continue up the next flight, the mage panting out curses in a language I don't know. At the end of the hall, I see a window, but it's already filling with tentacles. What *is* this creature?

As I turn to ascend the final set of stairs to the roof, something flashes past the window, bright as the midday sun. *Magic.* I'm not sure what being could work magic in such a place as this, but the pureness of the light gives me hope. I scramble upwards as the tentacles whip down the hall, talons gouging the staircase.

The mage behind me falters, boots sliding. He's barely three steps ahead of the creature. It'll have him in a heartbeat, and he'll die.

And he's only here because of me.

I lunge to grab his arm and haul him to the landing. He fastens his fingers around my wrist, pulling himself out of reach of the claws behind him. They scrape blindly at the bottom of the stairs, ripping up chunks of stone, but they can't get any closer.

"Up," I say, releasing him and turning toward the next step.

He doesn't let go of me.

My gaze snaps to his, fear prickling my fingers and making my legs feel strange. "No," I whisper. "Don't—"

"It needs a meal," the mage says, voice rasping, "and it won't be me." He yanks me off balance. I cry out, jerking away from him and lashing out with my glowstone. I manage to smack him hard across the face, but then his boot comes between my feet. For a sickening moment I teeter on the edge of the stairs.

Get back!

I barely register the words ringing in my mind before the mage shoves me, hard. I swallow a scream, throwing my arms up to shield my head as I fall. I slam down the stairs, bouncing toward the mass of tentacles.

Feet first—get your feet first!

I follow the shouted advice mindlessly, twisting my body as I come to a stop amidst a tangle of three or four great tentacles.

Don't move.

Someone is talking inside my head, and it's not me. Somehow, that's almost worse than lying surrounded by the talons of a nightmare monster. Almost.

I lie still, trying not to give in to panic, to flail my way back up to the landing. I'm desperately aware that my shoulder rests ever so gently against one of the tentacles. They aren't moving either, though. They've gone strangely calm. In the sudden quiet, I can hear the mage's boots thudding across the roof above me. I wonder if the beast can hear them, too, or if it can feel the pounding of my heart through its skin. Or perhaps hear the same voice that's in my head.

Hysteria bubbles up within me. I clamp down on it ferociously, make myself breathe slowly.

The rippling limbs shift, the talons leaving huge gashes as the creature retreats back down the hall. I curl in on myself as a tentacle beside me lifts, but the thing apparently can't see me here, and must not feel me, for the dry, scaly arm slides past and retracts through the window.

More silence, so overwhelming it fills my ears and laps at the edges of my mind. Where's the mage? The beast?

Wait here, counsels my invisible helper. Am I losing my mind? Have I somehow cobbled together a guardian from the people of a past I no longer remember, a conglomerate of voices to scare me witless when I most need to keep my thoughts clear? Or maybe it's someone who knows how to survive murderous mages and impossible monsters. I press my palms to my ears, because even though the speaker makes the silence easier to bear, I don't want to hear him again. I'd rather listen to the over-loud sound of my breathing, the rush of blood in my ears.

Think. Which way should I go? Which way will be safer—up or down? I'd better move, because dealing with two enemies at the same time is much worse than just one. I sit up, taking stock of my body. Everything hurts, but nothing feels broken or sprained. I release my ears to run my hands over myself, checking for cuts I haven't noticed, some terrible damage my brain might have failed to report to me. My ribs ache, and so does my left hip, but beyond that I seem surprisingly unscathed. My pack appears to have protected my back. I reach for the dull oval of my glowstone.

The building shudders. The mage shrieks, the sound of his terror cutting through the air. Three great talons curl through the open doorway above me, slamming into the high ceiling and tearing through it. I dive off the stairs as shattered stones tumble down the steps, a scream lodged in my throat. Tentacles swing overhead, curling around the edge of the floor and digging into the walls.

The mage cries out again, words that have the sound of old magic, though there's nothing here to fuel them. But there should be—sunlight filters through the dust and debris. At least it should have some power left.

Run, the voice in my head orders.

Wait, I respond, and reach a trembling hand out to the sun. I strain with all my senses, reaching out past the tips of my fingers, but there's nothing. So impossible. There has to be *something*. I of all people should be able to touch the fiery potential of sunlight. With my face tilted up and eyes closed,

I search for the force that must be there.

And then I find it—a huge spidery web of magic drawn together at a central mass, pulsing with power, spreading tendrils over the roof of the building, moving and stretching. The beast.

I step forward, concentrating on my vision of the creature. In my mind, it glows in the sea of darkness above me, the innumerable tentacles coalescing in a central body. I see its eyes, round and disc-like, its great beak-like maw nestled at the center of its tentacles, edges sharp as blades. Strands of magic outline each joint, each scale, as if the creature were made solely of energy before being given physical form. The filaments pulse with magic that flows freely along the beast's limbs, the whole in perfect balance.

Except for a single thinner strand where one of the tentacles meets the creature's body.

I hear a faint *whoosh* and the bright burst of light I saw before passes above me once more. With my mage sight, I perceive it as a small ball of brilliance hurtling through the air, side-swiping the monster. I have an ally of some sort, though I have no idea who it is. As the orb's illumination passes, I hear a strange, gurgling cry that may or may not be the monster.

Run now or it'll be too late.

I shake my head. I doubt I'll get more than a half block away from this thing before it hunts me down. Better to fight than run. I have only this moment, this heartbeat.

Focusing on the strands of the creature's illusory web, I reach straight for the thinning thread using all the power left in my body: the river air I can still feel deep in my lungs, the dark blood in my veins, the sunlight stored within my bones. My magic crosses the distance to the beast. With a single, deft twist, I catch the strand and snap it.

A surge of magic rebounds against me. I cry out, staggering back against the stone steps, holding up my hands as if by their simple physical reality, I can push back the power of the beast. Gasping, I fight to find my focus. The monster is not yet undone. There's a scraping sound again, somewhere both far and near, my hearing suddenly unreliable.

Already the beast's magic has begun to weave itself back together. *No.* I catch the loose end of the spell thread and yank with all my might. The beast roars, and the next moment a writhing mass slams through the hole in the roof, talons slicing down to embed themselves in the stairs two paces above me.

I edge away, half-mesmerized by claws as long as my calf. It should have worked. Pull the strand and the spell should have come apart at the seams.

At the seams.

Sewing is something I've learned quite well this past year. Stormwind made me pick out my stitches whenever they weren't straight enough. To open a seam quickly, you need to snip the thread in two places, *then* pull.

I dart forward, shying away from the nearest talon and throwing my arms around the tentacle itself. It's smooth and cool, snakelike. Still holding tight to the loose strand far above me with my magical senses, I dig into the web of enchantments within the tentacle, tearing at it. My fingers slide over the scales, but under my hands, the magic itself ripples, jerks. I clench my teeth and pull harder.

The strand snaps. I pull at it with all my strength. It tightens, then suddenly glides free, a long spider-silk thread glowing blue-white in my mage sight. I pull it close so that it can't retract and it loops around me, filling the hollows within me with stone and dust. My skin hums with it, my ears buzzing.

The spell-beast howls, a sound of rage—and pain. The other limbs jerk away, but the one I hold remains still.

All I've done is break off one piece of the central body. Hunkered down beside the now-motionless tentacle, I wrap my arms around myself and use my senses to reach out to the next one as it writhes away from me. *Reach, twist, snap, and pull.*

Wave after wave of magic released from the beast slams against me. Agony hammers at me from inside my skull. The beast roars again, but the sound is muted, distant. My breath wheezes, shaky and uncertain. I've done too much, absorbed too much of the harsh power that made this creature.

Can you move?

If I had the energy, I'd laugh. Moving seems like an utterly bizarre suggestion right now. I close my eyes and listen for the beast. I can hear the sound of stone scraping, a great echoing thud, and then fainter noises, until all that's left is my own breath rustling in my lungs.

Are you wounded?

What an aggravating voice. It'll probably keep talking until I tell it something.

'M all right, I think in reply. And then, *Too much magic.*

The severed tentacle remains beside me, talon buried deep in the stairs. The long scaly appendage of it, dull gray and lifeless, curves up the staircase and disappears over its edge. A second tentacle, its claw dug into the landing, arcs above me and ends in a jagged line against the too-bright sunlit sky.

I lay my palm on the scales. The surface is rough, gritty, the magic gone from it. I stagger to my feet. When I pull my hand away, bits of rock crumble to the floor, leaving the tentacle's surface pitted and uneven. I've heard of magic that manipulated stone, but I've never imagined it on such a massive level.

Stooping, I retrieve my glowstone, then resettle my pack on my shoulders, wincing at the new bruises I've accumulated. I need to leave before anything else that lives in this cursed place comes hunting me.

Above me, the demolished stairwell brightens. My mage sight tells me it's the friendly ball of magic I sensed earlier. A moment later, a flame curves around the monster's stone tentacle rising high above the stairs and swoops down to the landing. I close my eyes against the onslaught of light.

"Mageling," a voice says, the light dimming.

Through slitted eyes I see a bird standing on the landing. It's at least as large as a peacock, and that's where its likeness to a mere bird ends. Its body flickers with a flame that knows no heat, gold and ruby and sapphire. It's warmth and comfort, beauty and radiance. For a heartbeat I simply stare in awe.

"You did well," the phoenix says. "From what you accomplished, I expected to find a master mage."

I shake my head. "Is he…is the mage dead?" I ask, my voice hoarse. Even as I form the words, I know the answer.

"The beast caught him. There was no helping him."

I rub my arms. I'm glad the mage is dead, deeply grateful I no longer have to fear him, and yet it sickens me. As far as I can remember, in perhaps a year of living, I have caused the death of three people: the fang I left behind in Blackflame's cages; the fang lord Kol upon whom I unleashed my sunbolt; and now this mage, who threw me to my death and so, no doubt, saved me.

Three people. Not knowing the names of two of them makes it a hundred times worse. But I tried to help the mage— it was his choice to push me down the stairs, to race up to his destruction. It wasn't my fault. Except that I snuck through the portal knowing he might follow. I led him here.

"Come," the phoenix says, voice soft. "There are other creatures that wander this place. You must leave now or risk facing them."

I nod jerkily. The phoenix flutters over the nearby tentacle to land beside me. The stairwell is too narrow for him to fly, so instead he descends the stairs on foot, head bobbing, wings extended slightly for balance.

I follow him, grateful for his radiance. My head pounds with the force of the magic I've absorbed. I can feel it thrumming through my veins, buzzing beneath my skin. I keep a hand on the wall, try to focus on the strangeness of this moment, the things I need to understand. Why did the phoenix come to our aid? And why is he leading me out now himself?

At the bottom of the stairs, the phoenix dims his fire and crosses to the now-empty doorway. "Quickly," he says, darting outside. "There is a bridge across the canyon that borders the city. A globe of magefire burns above it."

I nod, stepping carefully over the newly fallen stones and bricks.

"The Burnt Lands end there. You'll be safe once you cross."

I didn't know that for certain, but it was the one thing I was counting on.

"The bridge is—" He turns to gesture with the tip of his wing.

"Northwest," I supply, my voice rough as sandpaper.

The wingtip points down the avenue. "Yes. Keep straight to the plaza, then turn left. You'll see the bridge from there. I'll keep watch from above." He folds his wing. "I am sorry I cannot allow you time to grieve your master. Once you're safe there will be time."

"He wasn't my master," I say, dropping my chin so he doesn't see the shame written on my face. I wasn't grieving for the dead mage. I was mourning myself, what I have become.

I force myself forward at a brisk walk, scanning the debris scattered across the road. Ahead of me, a shiny brown boot leans against a broken stone, its pale blue embellishments spattered with a dark liquid. I slow until I am a pace away and can see the splintered white bone and torn flesh protruding from the top.

I swallow hard to keep from retching.

"What is it?" the phoenix calls sharply, and then he's

beside me, wings spread. "Ah."

I'm shaking. "I should...bury..."

"There is no time. The blood will call to them just as magic does."

"Magic?" I echo, forcing my attention to the bird. It's so much easier to look at him than what's left of the mage.

"Do not use any charms here," the phoenix warns. "That was your first mistake. It creates a beacon for the spell-creatures to follow." He steps past me, turning so that his body obstructs the boot from sight. "I will carry this to a far rooftop, one that they cannot easily reach. Now run, child. We do not have much time."

A FEATHER TO BURN

The plaza must have once been the bustling center—or at least one of the centers—of this great city. A wide cobbled expanse greets my eyes, running longer than it is wide. Broken stonework suggests that there might have been monuments here, or fountains, perhaps a raised stage. Whatever it had been, the plaza and its guard of broken-backed, faceless buildings send chills up my spine. I stick to the edges, terrified of moving to the center of the plaza, even though less rubble litters the cobbles there.

As I reach the wide thoroughfare leading to the bridge, a chorus of howls rise from the far edges of the city. Lilting and eerie, they are filled with the promise of death. If these creatures are anything like the tentacled beast, they will move horrifyingly fast. Hiking my pack higher on my back, I run.

The blue magelight is visible above the bridge now, rising in front of me, but the desert air deceives my senses. I cannot tell how far I am, what distance I have yet to cover. The light does not waver, burning brighter than any fire.

I pace myself to reach it as fast as I can.

Now, in these moments with the dead air searing my lungs and the painful press of magic against the inside of my skin and organs, my thoughts gain a sudden and strange clarity. I catch glimpses of recent memories: Stormwind gazing out over her lake, tall, proud and so very alone; Stonefall greeting me with the words of my father's people, dark eyes understanding more of me than I had known; my mother, dressed in silks, waiting patiently for the unknown to reach out to her.

My mother, whom I thought dead, who might think the same of me. I can't imagine what Blackflame might have done to her when she went to him, all those years ago. Perhaps he convinced her she'd lost everything, everyone she ever loved, as he did me. But she hasn't.

If I live, I will speak with her.

The phoenix shrieks behind me. I glance over my shoulder to see a torrent of shadows pour onto the road some distance back. Individual details are impossible to make out in the shadows thrown by the buildings, but there is no question that they are moving faster than I am.

The phoenix swoops down over the pack, talons outstretched, fire trailing him as if he were an arrow of flame rather than a living creature. One of the creatures answers his attack, twisting away and rising up on its hind legs, clawing at the fire-drenched air. The pack's howls and snarls send terror needling through my body.

I focus all my effort into running, placing one foot in front of the other, again and again, as fast as I can, as if by doing so I might suddenly take flight. There is no other escape from these creatures. The buildings here are too broken to hope that I might shelter on a roof, or jump from one roof to another and so lose the pack. No doorway I have yet seen still holds a door. The bridge is my only hope.

It is not so far now, clearly visible in the morning light, rising beyond the last of the buildings. Built of the same brick as the city, the bridge offers a glimpse of lost majesty: soaring pillars connected by great stone arches, carved with a twisting floral pattern only partly eroded by time and wind. Below the arches, the roadway soars across the canyon, wide and long and, after all these years, still sturdy and unscathed.

The phoenix shrieks again, so close that I nearly choke. They are almost upon me, and I have nothing—

Not nothing.

I whirl, dropping to one knee to steady myself before my mind even registers what I am doing. *Spider silk*, I think, spinning the image into being in my mind's eye, drawing on the thrum of the spell-beast's magic still buzzing beneath my skin. I flick my fingers, focused on the pack leader, so close now I can see the gleam of its eyes, the long dark spines that start at the nape of its neck and run down its back.

A thick, glimmering silver cord flies from my fingertips, spinning across the distance between us. The creature leaps upwards to avoid it, but the cord still brushes its forelegs—and sticks. The end of the cord swings on, yanking the creature off balance and wrapping around one of its hind legs.

It slams against the cobbles, roaring its fury.

My fingers loose another cord, and then, as I find my rhythm, a volley of six or seven more. That is all I have. It will have to be enough. The leader still growls and snarls, two legs so entangled it can no longer move them, its other legs scrabbling for purchase as if it might heave itself up. The second cord has slowed, though not stopped, another nightmare creature. The remaining cords have disappeared into the depths of the pack. I can only hope that they have caught on the creatures, binding them together in confusion.

I make for the bridge once more, dimly registering the flare of light behind me as the phoenix swoops again. The arch rises before me, still a good fifty paces away.

The phoenix shrieks again, and the sickening scratch of claws on stone sounds behind me.

Swerve left! Faster!

I dodge left as commanded, knowing I am still too far from the bridge. I'm not going to make it. But I have to—there is still so much I must make right—

Talons close on my shoulders, sinking into the straps of my pack and gripping me tightly. I scream, trying to twist free as my feet leave the ground.

"Be still!" the phoenix thunders from above me.

I sag with relief, air rushing past my face as the ground drops away. The talons grasp my shoulders tightly, strong enough to bruise but not enough to break the skin. Behind me, the nightmare creatures snarl furiously. The phoenix pumps his wings, straining to keep me out of their reach.

Bend your knees.

I do, trying to raise my feet as high as I can without disturbing the phoenix's flight. Strange how the phoenix's mind voice is so different from his spoken voice.

Finger-length claws slice through the air below my boots. I pull my feet higher, wheezing with terror. And then we are winging through the arch. The air ripples around me, a great, thick barrier of magic that almost takes the place of the air itself. I open my mouth, gasping for a breath that will not come, and then we are through.

The phoenix widens his wings into a controlled glide, descending quickly. Not quite a third of the way across the bridge, my feet touch the ground again. I stumble forward as he releases me, my legs wobbly beneath me, and slam to my knees with a grunt.

I have never before been so grateful to feel stone beneath

my knees. At least, not in the last year. I lean forward on my hands, fighting the urge to giggle hysterically.

The phoenix makes a tight, swooping turn and lands facing me. He tilts his head, bright eyes focused behind me. I glance over my shoulder in time to see one of the shadow beasts throw itself through the archway.

"No!" I cry, stumbling to my feet. But the creature only slams into the magical barrier, needlelike teeth bared and forked black tongue flicking. It rises up on its paws, swiping at the barrier with claws nearly as long as my fingers. But neither its claws nor the sound of its fury breaches what stands between us.

"It cannot pass. You are safe now," the phoenix says.

On the other side of the arch, the rest of the pack stalks back and forth, eyeing us balefully. "What are those things?"

The phoenix steps up beside me, watching the nightmare creatures calmly. "I suspect they were once lycans."

"Lycans?" I echo, disbelieving. They look nothing like wolves, or humans, or anything in between.

"The desert dwellers tell stories of a mage who lived within these lands, and the pack of lycans who swore their loyalty to him. He enslaved them in a spell that twisted and changed their bodies into what you see and destroyed their minds, perhaps even their spirits."

A shudder runs through me. It's possible. With magic, a great deal is possible that should never be done. The High Council was founded primarily to regulate magic so that such crimes would never be committed again. "Do you believe the stories?" I ask.

"I met the mage and the lycans. I can well believe it."

I stare at the phoenix. He's at least four hundred years old, then. What he looks at now he remembers as something else, something that passed away centuries ago. It's almost impossible to fathom, that he can hold so much of the past when I can remember no more than a year of my own life.

He turns toward the other end of the bridge. "Come, there is shade and a place to sit at the far end. I would speak with you."

I follow him across the bridge, wondering what exactly he wants from me. The paved road that leads from the bridge is broken, swept over with dirt and cracked apart by thorn bushes—four hundred years abandoned. The low walls that run along either side of the bridge end at the road, forming large, angled pillars a little taller than I am. The base of each pillar flares out, wider than the rest of it, forming a natural bench.

The phoenix flutters up to sit on one, sheltered from the sun by the pillar's shadow. He is back to his quiet gleams of gold and scarlet, his shadows of cobalt and deep purple. I lower myself to the rough stone of the bench a pace away from him. He's a phoenix, a legendary creature so rare they are more myth than anything. They aren't known for befriending humans—our lives are no more than a candle flame's short flicker compared to theirs.

"You're wary of me," he says, a hint of regret in his voice.

"I am honored to speak with you." That much is true. I'm pretty sure not even First Mage Talon has had the opportunity to sit and chat with a phoenix. But I don't know why he's here, or why he would want to speak with me.

He tips his beak toward me. "You smell of ash."

I stare at him.

"I thought I imagined it before, or mistook it for wood smoke clinging to your clothes. But it is you."

I clear my throat. "I burned myself once, with a spell." I don't want to explain how, to explain that I gathered the magic of the world around me to kill my enemy. I don't want to speak of killing at all.

"I see. And then there is..." He pauses, resettles his wings. "You must have questions."

All I have is questions right now. What did he almost say? How do I possibly get to Fidanya from here? Was it the phoenix in my head or am I going mad? And why does the phoenix care what questions I have?

I lick dry lips. I have water in my pack, but until I know where I can refill my flask, I had better conserve it. I look out over the valley, consider the dead city at our backs.

"What about the bodies?" I ask. "Why were they left behind, but nothing else?" I tick off on my fingers what's missing. "No doors, no trash, no broken bits and pieces. Just stone—and the bodies."

My question seems to please the phoenix. He eyes me brightly. "Humans have a strange sense of honor. The bodies were left behind for those brave enough to venture in and bury them. Everything else was drained of its essence to power the spells cast by the mages who once lived here."

I wrap my arms over my chest. "This wasn't always a desert."

"No. Deserts seem to develop primarily due to human

stupidity," the phoenix says with an edge of contempt. "In this case, the connection is direct." He shrugs his wings. "I am more concerned with what you have done."

Trespassing on the Burnt Lands? I wouldn't have chosen to if I'd known what awaited me. "That portal should have been destroyed," I say testily. "I had no idea it would bring me out here."

"Yet I am glad it did."

Surely I heard wrong. "You're *glad?*"

"Tell me, what did you do to the spell-beast that trapped you in the building?"

I hesitate.

"And how did you find the magic to slow the pack that hunted you?"

I consider the phoenix, his fire-and-night plumage. He helped me. I would not have made it out without him. So, as simply as I can, I tell him how I unraveled one creature's magic and used the part of it that I absorbed to attack the others. After all, there's no reason to tell him I'm not officially a mage.

The phoenix listens without interrupting, nor does he speak when I am finished. Instead, he studies me in silence and then, just as I am beginning to feel unnerved by his regard, he hops down from the bench and paces away to gaze across the canyon toward the Burnt Lands. "Where do you go from here?"

"Fidanya."

He nods. "To report the mage's death. And then?"

I bite my lip. There's no way I can make such a report without implicating myself. The phoenix hasn't realized I'm not a traditionally trained student, that I have something to hide. He certainly has no idea I intend to help my unofficial mentor, regardless of what the Council decrees for her. He might not actually care—I have no way of knowing what his relationship is to the Council—but there's no need to tell him any of that.

"There's something else I must do there," I admit.

"There is work that must be done here," the phoenix says, so softly I wonder if he speaks to himself. I hope he does. I have no interest in going anywhere near the Burnt Lands again. But then he turns back to me. "It is time to try again to...*unravel* the spells that plague these lands."

"Try again?" I echo.

"It has been attempted before, but never with any success.

You," he fixes his bright gaze on me, "*you* have succeeded. So I must ask you to return."

I shake my head. "I'm not going back in there."

"Someone must. A mage such as you, who can break apart the spells that drain the magic from the land and pour it into such creatures as you have seen."

I squint at him, as if that will bring his words into greater focus. "I wondered how the spell-creatures could survive without magic. You mean that they're the reason there *is* no magic?"

"Not precisely." He tilts his head back, studying the barrier from where he stands. "There are spells that stretch across the sky, that root through the earth, spells that have been contained by the boundaries set around the Burnt Lands. Those spells gather the natural magic of all they touch—the sunlight and moonlight falling through them, the wind blowing past—and channel it to the spells that are connected to them. And so, the spell-creatures remain, even after four hundred years."

"Why would anyone make such a thing?"

The bird shrugs his wings as if this were a mystery he has long since given up pondering. "You are human. Perhaps you can understand it."

I look away. The answers are simple, in their way: greed, rage, perhaps even vengeance. I don't know enough of the mages who destroyed the lands at my back to know what passions ruled them, but I don't doubt they are the same passions that govern humans today. They had wanted to destroy their enemies, to assure that they would never rise again. They succeeded.

I gesture weakly behind me. "The magefire above the bridge—how does it keep burning? And how were the barriers you mentioned set up?"

"The barriers took decades to build," the phoenix says. "And they do not block the flow of magic, though the mages who built them tried hard to achieve that. In the end, it was all they could do to contain what had been made. As for the magefire, it was one of the few successful adaptions they made to the spells of the Burnt Lands, channeling some of the magic gathered by the draining spells into the fire rather than the spell-beasts."

"If they did that much, surely they could have—"

"Three of them died in the making of that spell," the phoenix says quietly, cutting me off. "Only now that the spells have begun to…fray does it seem possible that another attempt should be made."

"Perhaps," I allow. "But not by me. I'm not even a full mage."

"You are mage enough."

I have the distinct feeling he doesn't care a whit for human designations of power or rank. "I have things I must do, someone I—" I clear my throat, try again. "I need to make sure a friend is well."

That earns me his full attention. "A friend in Fidanya?"

I nod.

"You said the mage you traveled with was not your master. You have one?"

"I— yes."

The phoenix and I contemplate each other.

I should have mentioned my supposed mistress at once, argued against being able to help him on the basis of my obligations to study. I should be naming her now, explaining all of that. But—

"Would your master return here with you?"

"No," I say. "I doubt it. But I must go to Fidanya."

I owe the phoenix a debt, a life debt. By rights, he can demand I stay here and set to work on the curses that hold the Burnt Lands in their thrall, and I would comply, at least for a time. I ought to—I know I should. But I owe Stormwind something greater than a debt, and I have no idea how she is, if she's well or in danger, free or imprisoned. Until I've done what I can to aid her, neither my heart nor my conscience will let me rest.

The phoenix's feathers glimmer and spark as he considers me, my words, all the things I haven't said. "Of course you must go," he says finally. He dips his head, his beak searching through the feathers at his breast.

When he lifts his head he holds a single iridescent gold feather in his beak. I reach out, cupping my hands beneath it as he lets it drop. It is burnished gold, the very edges shimmering with all the colors of the sunset.

"I will fetch the desert dwellers who roam these lands to guide you to your destination."

I nod.

"When you are done with what you must do, burn that feather and I will come."

I hold my breath to keep from speaking, from arguing. A life debt is a heavy thing. I owe him at least an attempt at what he asks.

"And if you are in need," the phoenix continues, "I will help you."

He opens wide his wings and takes to the air, the heavy beat of his wings sounding in my ears, the brush of warm air across my face raising gooseflesh on my arms.

The feather shivers against my palms, as if I hold the rest of my life in my hands, a delicate and fragile thing.

A DESERT WELCOME

It's late afternoon before the phoenix's aid reaches me. I've spent the intervening couple of hours resting, and have just finished a light meal of bread and cheese when I catch sight of a dark shape moving over the ridge of the hills that line the valley before me. The shape gradually resolves into the loping form of a camel carrying a rider garbed in black.

I push myself to my feet, assessing how injured I am. The same points of pain remind me of their presence: hip, thigh, ribs. But they're bruises, and not as deep as they might have been. I'll keep.

The rider's camel gains the valley and continues toward me at speed, slowing only as it reaches the broken road leading to the bridge. This close, it's clear the rider is a woman: her *thobe* is loose and swaying, heavily embroidered with cross-stitched bands of red and yellow above the bottom hem—interlocking diamonds and triangles that are repeated along the edge of her head scarf and on the front of the bodice. The sides of her *thobe* are open to the hips, and the woman wears loose pants beneath.

Within another minute, the camel has crossed the remaining distance and the rider pulls it to a stop. Setting her foot in the curve of her camel's neck, she swings down, turning to me with a smile. "*Ahlan wa sahlan.*"

It is the greeting of a host to their guest. Though I cannot remember having heard it before, I recognize it, and it stirs something deep within the ashes of my memories. *Family and plain*, she has said, one of the most generous of desert welcomes, treating a guest as if they were returning to both family and an abundant and spacious land.

"I thank you." My words sound strange to me, my tongue

tripping over their form. It is far easier to understand her words than to construct my own. How well had I known my father's language? And how much will come back to me now?

The woman steps forward, reaching out her hands to clasp mine. Her face is somewhat stern, but that may simply be this moment. She has large, expressive eyes, dark as the deepest wood, and bright with pleasure. "I am Huda bint Ahmer of the Bani Saqr. My sister and I are camped an hour's ride north of here. You would bring us great honor if you joined us—we can discuss where your travels will take you, and how we might aid you."

I dip my head. "It would be my honor." And then, belatedly, "I am Hikaru."

If she thinks it strange that I give no family name, no tribe, she makes no indication of it, saying simply, "We are honored."

She has her camel sit down, then straps on my pack and helps me up before climbing up to sit in front of me herself. Huda clicks her tongue and the camel lurches to its feet. I grab hold of her waist as we pitch forward and back, half-certain I'm going to slide off. Huda waits patiently until the camel stands still and I drop my hands.

Thankfully, camels walk more smoothly than they stand. Our mount adeptly makes its way through a scattering of rough stones and around the dusky green branches of thorn bushes. We leave the valley with its forgotten road to the bridge, crossing over low hills and continuing on. There are no visible paths, no stars but the sun in the sky, yet Huda knows precisely where she is going.

I spend the hour's ride mulling over my questions, trying to find the right words in a language I don't consciously recall. I need to get to Fidanya as fast as I can. The more I consider the theft of Stormwind's mirror, the mages that converged on her valley, and the closing of the portal in Sonapur, the less I can make myself believe she could possibly be well. Add to that the easy violence of the mage who followed me here, and I'm completely certain Stormwind has either been falsely convicted and imprisoned, or is in imminent danger of such violence herself.

To cross the desert to Fidanya safely and quickly, I'll need Huda's help. While she's already intimated her willingness, I suspect my requests will be easier to discuss when we're facing each other and I can make gestures and point at things.

Soon enough, we reach the wide valley where Huda and

her sister have made their camp. A herd of nearly sixty goats move in knots across the valley, grazing on the finest of desert grass that grows here, or munching on the tough leaves of the hardy desert bushes. Two more camels wander among the goats, and past them hunches a small black structure—a tent?

"Ya Huda!" a voice calls. A girl races across the sands toward us, her *thobe* hiked up to her knees, her legs flashing brown beneath.

Huda laughs and waves to her sister.

"Sumeyya is still a little young," she explains.

"You brought a guest!" Sumeyya hollers as she nears us.

"Yes, my sister. Shall we welcome her to our camp?"

"Oh!" Sumeyya plows to a stop, face tilted up to stare at me: large brown eyes, a small nose, thin lips currently opened in surprise. "Please! Be welcome! *Ahlan wa sahlan!*"

"I thank you," I say, and I can't help the smile spreading across my face. She must be no more than ten years old, possibly younger. She nearly jigs with excitement, biting her lip and looking toward Huda imploringly.

Huda gives a faint shake of her head. "Go ahead and wake the fire for us, and we will eat together."

Sumeyya dashes off, and Huda urges the camel forward again. Their campsite consists of a small tent constructed of short poles and black cloth, the hard packed dirt beneath covered by a woven blanket. A small campfire set within a rectangle of stones burns before the tent. Sumeyya squats before it, setting a pot of milk against the stones to warm.

The camel lowers itself to the ground in the same unnerving way as it stood, a steeply tilting rocking back and forth I fear will send me tumbling down. Only when I stop clinging to her does Huda hop down and turn to help me dismount.

By the time I'm safely off the creature, Sumeyya has set out a platter heaped with separate mounds of goat cheese and dates, accompanied by a thick, hearty bread.

I take a seat on the blanket beside the fire and Sumeyya immediately offers me a pitcher of water. "For your hands," she says, and I hold my hands out over the side of the blanket while she wets them, then scrub them as best as I can. She pours a little more water to rinse them off, and then does the same for her sister.

As we begin our meal, Sumeyya throws a pleading glance toward her elder sister. But neither sister asks any questions. Of course they won't—this is the due of a traveler. I clear my throat, and Huda looks up at me. As my host, she won't bring up my departure for fear of implying she wants me to leave. So it's my role to ask. "Can you tell me how long to walk to Fidanya from here?"

I'm fairly certain I accidentally used the male form of "you" in addressing her, but neither she nor Sumeyya laugh. "Two days' ride," Huda says. "It will be faster for you by camel than walking."

Is that an offer? My newly remembered language skills are far too uncertain to rely on for nuanced understandings.

Huda tilts her head, clarifies. "The desert is vast. You will need a guide. I will take you there."

"Your sister needs you?" I ask.

Sumeyya grins. "Oh, I have traveled alone with the herd before. There is no worry."

I turn my eyes toward the valley, consider the rise and fall of a land I know nothing about. I could easily lose my way, run out of water. This is not a land that knows forgiveness. Perhaps that is why its people show such kindness. But in Sumeyya's bright smile and open face I catch a memory of another girl, one whose innocence I saw broken: Alia Degath, her small form lying limp and drained in a cage.

"There are...dangers here?"

Huda shakes her head. "We are well within our lands. Even if raiders were so cunning as to find the herd, they would not harm my sister regardless."

Sumeyya nods, and now I see a part of her that her earlier excitement obscured: she is serious, her eyes shrewd, her voice measured. "There is nothing else to fear in these lands that I have not already faced before."

That's somewhat comforting, but I can't push away the weight of my memories. What if something *does* happen? Could I forgive myself then?

"It is our honor," Huda says with a faint tone of reproof.

It seems one doesn't argue with the honor of a desert dweller. I bite my lip, embarrassed by the rush of relief flooding through my breast. I need her help, and I know it as well as she does.

"It is I who am honored," I attempt to say. I must get it close to right, for her demeanor relaxes and she leans back on her hand, her gaze moving to meet her sister's before returning to me.

"If you are willing, I suggest we rest through what remains of the day. The moon is full and we can travel through the night easily."

"Yes," I say, nodding. "I go to a…" I trail off, decide better of speaking of a friend in need. "Important," I say instead, grateful that my language skills make this incoherent statement perfectly acceptable, if not understandable.

"Then we will travel by the fastest route," Huda says.

"Which way?" Sumeyya asks.

"West around the howling caves," Huda tells her sister. "From there it is only one day's ride to our destination."

Sumeyya answers with a note of trepidation, "If you travel further north, the crossing will be shorter."

"But the path overall is longer," Huda argues. "And we will still have to cross."

"There is…danger?" I ask, wishing I had more words at my disposal.

Huda turns to me, and while her expression is somber, her eyes glimmer with some deeper emotion—amusement perhaps, or excitement? "We must pass through another tribe's lands."

"They are friends?" I ask hopefully.

"No." Sumeyya's emphatic response removes all doubt.

"Our enemies have honor," Huda says, tilting her face to look out over the far hills.

I nod, expecting her to go on, but she doesn't. Instead, Sumeyya chortles with understanding and says, "I hope while you are gone I have the honor of meeting another traveler."

"So you may," Huda returns, although she clearly hopes nothing of the sort.

After our meal is done, Huda leads me into the tent, furnishing me with a cushion and a light blanket. I stretch out to rest in the deep shadow thrown by the black cloth overhead, and find that I need the blanket. The tent is surprisingly cool, and I am more tired than I realized. I listen to the faint tap of plates and soft rustle of cloth as the sisters clean up the remains of our meal.

"Did you speak with the phoenix, then?" Sumeyya asks quietly. I open my eyes and listen carefully. The tent walls don't do much to obscure her voice. "I saw him fly down to you, and then you left," she continues. "I knew you'd be back, but I've been waiting on thorns to hear about it!"

Huda laughs gently. "I spoke with him," she affirms. "What will our milk-brother think of that?"

Sumeyya almost squeaks with excitement. "Kareem is going to *weep*. Imagine! The first time in weeks he isn't with us, and we not only see the phoenix, but he actually *spoke* to you! What did he say?"

"Just that he'd brought me a traveler."

"The words!" Sumeyya huffs. "What did he say?"

"He said, 'I bring you a traveler, O Daughter of the Desert.'"

Sumeyya lets out her breath in a sigh of such delight I want to laugh into my pillow.

"To be called a daughter of the desert by the phoenix himself," Sumeyya murmurs, as if this were the greatest possible achievement.

"Well, I'm not sure what else he might have called me," Huda observes. "Other than, 'You with the camel!'"

Sumeyya gurgles with laughter. "And then? You left at once!"

"I told him that—"

"The words!" Sumeyya reminds her sister. "The exact words!"

Huda chuckles. "I said, 'It is my honor to aid a traveler. Where will I find her?'"

I raise my eyes to the tent roof. Even simple nouns have genders in the desert tongue. I must have inadvertently changed the gender of half the things I've mentioned so far.

"And?" Sumeyya presses.

"He said, 'She waits at the bridge to the Burnt Lands. I would that you went to her at once.'"

"So you did!" Sumeyya crows softly, clearly approving of this explanation.

"So I did."

"Oh, I wish I could go with you now."

"I doubt our guest cares to travel as slowly as a herd of goats," Huda observes.

Sumeyya accepts this without argument. Laughing, she says only, "Kareem will *weep*."

I wake to the distant bleating of goats. The little tent lies empty, the changed placement of cushions and blankets against the other side the only indication that Huda and Sumeyya have come and gone again. I check my boot, glad to find the phoenix's feather still safely plastered to the inside, even though I don't want it, want nothing more to do with the Burnt Lands. I am not the mage to unravel the spells that keep the Burnt Lands locked in a void of death and violence. If I were to take on an enemy, it would be Blackflame. Not his nameless predecessors that made such a cursed land.

Admittedly, they probably weren't his direct predecessors, except in political ambition. The Great Burning was led by mages hailing from the Eleven Kingdoms, not the Northlands. Even so, this land, these spells—I do not want to risk my life dismantling them. Perhaps I can find a way to avoid returning until…until I can't avoid it anymore. I sigh. The trouble with being honor bound is you're honor bound. At least I can plan my return, time it, ensure Stormwind is well first, then bring the charms and wards with me that might make the difference between survival and a violent death.

All things to worry about after I know how Stormwind is.

Rising, I duck through the tent's low opening.

Outside, Huda and Sumeyya have packed up all but the essentials of the camp. Huda greets me with a smile, pouring out a cup of warmed goat's milk. The milk is fresh, seasoned and sweetened slightly, though I can't tell what herb was used, or even what sweetener. Honey, perhaps. No doubt desert honey has a different flavor from high mountain honey.

Sumeyya picks up a piece of bread from the plate before us and dunks it in her own cup of milk. Ah. That would explain why there was nothing to eat with the bread. I follow her example, and find the combination delicious.

As I eat, Huda and Sumeyya chat briefly about the routes we will use—which paths Sumeyya will take the herd along, and a few more details of how Huda and I will make our way.

"If you travel two days north, you should be able to meet up with Ruba and her sisters. You could continue with them until I return," Huda suggests to her sister.

Sumeyya agrees, her eyes alight at the prospect.

We finish our meal quickly. Barely twenty minutes later, the girls have packed up the last of their supplies, taking down their tent and making ready for their departure with an ease and efficiency that speaks to a lifetime of nomadic travel. Huda gestures for me to join her at her camel, its saddlebags bulging with provisions. Sumeyya clasps my arms, standing on her toes to kiss my cheeks, and bids me safe travels and peace. I return her farewell, and clamber up on the camel, Huda helping me situate myself before she makes her own farewells.

"I want to know *everything*," Sumeyya tells her sister as they hug.

Huda laughs. "And I will remember it all for you. Keep us in your prayers, little sister."

"And me in yours," returns Sumeyya.

Huda clicks her tongue at her camel and it rocks its way to its feet. We start across the valley, riding toward the setting sun. And even though I cannot recall praying very often, I send up a prayer for these two sisters and the quiet of their lives.

AN ENEMY'S HONOR

We travel steadily through the day and into the darkening night, following no discernible path. Huda guides the camel with perfect confidence as the full moon lights the land, silvering the landscape. The desert is starkly beautiful in a way I did not expect: hills covered with flows of black rock leading down to wide valleys, dunes rising here and there, a scattering of bushes and hardy, wind-twisted trees.

We stop once to stretch our legs, remaining on the camel otherwise. The creature is built for endurance, from its thick hide to its heavy-lidded eyes to its long, loping gait. Huda takes a string of prayer beads from her pocket, clicking through them slowly. I listen to the faint, comforting snick of stone upon stone, and give myself up to the gentle sway of the camel, the cool brush of the desert wind against my face.

Some part of this desert was my father's homeland. Did he grow up here, crossing this land of sand and rock and thorns as Huda has? Or did he hail from a different tribe, far across the sands? For all I know, the girl riding before me could be my cousin.

Until a few days ago, my father had barely existed to me. There was nothing to consider of him except this: I knew he loved me, and that he was dead. But with Stonefall's visit came the startling possibility that through my father I might have family...that the love he bore me might be rekindled in the people he left behind, uncles and aunts and cousins of whom I know nothing. I don't want to leave this land without at least asking. I may not have given myself permission to seek them out—Stormwind may need me too urgently for that—but I can still ask.

"You have many mages here?" As the words leave my

mouth, I realize how abrupt the question sounds.

Huda shakes her head. "No. In our tribe, we have not had a mage come back to us since Sheikha Noora. She returned to God three summers ago."

"Come back?" I echo, since it is easier than pulling together my own words.

"When we find a Promise among our children, we keep them with us until the age of seven. Then, when they leave, they are old enough to understand that they must return to their family and tribe. Mages born in the desert always come back to the desert. It is our way."

Except my father had not. "What if one does not come back?"

Huda considers this. "There was a mage from the lands we will pass through who did not return. Or rather, he came back to say that he could not remain in the desert." Huda shakes her head, but I cannot tell if it is disgust or merely disapproval. "He loved a— a woman not of the desert. And he wished for power among the mages. So he left. His brother was also a mage, and he married as he was meant to, and lives with his tribe now."

I cross my arms over my chest, holding myself. There cannot be that many desert mages who married across cultures and moved up the ranks of mages. "What happened to the one who left?"

"He died. We didn't hear much of that. His family did not mourn him. He was already dead to them."

"Oh," I manage. She twists to glance at me, and I quickly drop my hands to my thighs. "What happened to his wife? Children?"

She shakes her head. "I don't know. They're our enemies, after all. We hear what the wind brings us, the stories shared in markets. Once we knew that they would have one less mage amongst them, we did not ask further."

"Yes," I agree. It makes sense, of course. But the faint hope I nursed, the possibility of a family that would greet me with pleasure, slips into darkness. Even if my father isn't the same mage Huda speaks of, he too didn't return to the desert or marry a desert dweller. He'll be dead to his family as well. There's no one here for me.

Huda looks at me a moment longer, as if she holds a question on the tip of her tongue. Then she turns back to watch the camel slowly pick its way through a flow of rocks. Where they are tall enough to throw shadows, it's almost impossible to see the ground clearly.

It's odd Huda hasn't used a glowstone yet. Or is it? Her tribe doesn't have a mage. Charms must be precious, conserved to last as long as possible.

"Here." I offer my glowstone to Huda. It brightens with light, a gentle star cocooned in my hand. She exclaims with delight, taking it and quickly fixing it into a leather strap that hangs by her knee. It is the work of a moment to pass the strap around the camel's neck and fasten it to the other side of the saddle, so the stone shines from the base of the camel's neck. It casts enough light to ease our passage without creating shadows that might startle the creature.

"Thank you," she says as she sits back, balanced effortlessly on her knees.

"You do not have?" I ask hesitantly. Surely, they should be able to trade easily for so simple a charm.

"Ours are old. We keep them for when we must use them. They are not half as bright as this! In three months' time when we travel north to Wadi Qadeema, we will take them to the mage there to strengthen."

At least I've found one thing I can give her to repay some part of her kindness.

We make camp near dawn. The hills have grown steadily higher, the stone they are built upon jutting out at angles here and there, and the valleys slightly more hospitable to growing things—at least as far as I can tell in the moonlight. As we come around the final hill to our destination, a faint, eerie whistling drifts across the hilltops toward us.

I tense, shifting as I try to make out its direction.

"The howling caves," Huda tells me. "It's just the wind. Nothing to fear."

Her explanation doesn't stop the hair at the back of my neck from prickling. I've seen enough strange things in the last day that such a sound is hardly comforting.

Thankfully, Huda leads us in a different direction from the whistling cries to what is clearly a well-established campsite, with a wide, flat area cleared of rocks and stones, two fire pits, and a well off to the side. The well is small but deep, surrounded by a low wall and covered over by a flat, circular stone. I help Huda push it aside and wait as she lowers her leather bucket down, down, down until it grows heavy in her hand and she lifts it out again. We refill the leather water bags, then offer a drink to the camel, who downs three bucketfuls before moving away.

Huda spreads a blanket on the ground for us and, after a quick meal of bread and dates, we lie down to rest. I glance at her, the keening of the wind sounding faintly in my ears. She raises her eyebrows in question. I offer her a faint smile and roll on my side, facing away.

She has no wards. Of course she doesn't. If magic is so hard to come by as to make glowstones a treasured charm, wards would only be used in the most serious need, and young girls who are merely goatherds may not have access to them at all.

I could use the string of wards I've made, but it would hardly stretch around the whole of the blanket. If I removed the beads from their cord, I'd have to adjust the spells, and Huda would learn my secret.

I close my eyes. *I'm being foolish*, I tell myself firmly. Huda would not rest so easily if she feared for our safety, nor would she choose a dangerous camp.

But it still takes me a while to drift off to sleep, the howling of the wind echoing faintly in my ears.

Huda makes a thin flatbread on a curious, upward-curved pan, her newly made fire crackling merrily. I prop myself up on my arm, blinking at her groggily as the bread slaps against the pan. The sun is high in the sky—late morning or early afternoon? I'm a little too muzzy on my directions to be able to tell. I rub my face, look back at Huda.

"We'll start when you are ready," she tells me. "It's cool enough to travel through the afternoon, and our enemies will be resting then. By evening we should have crossed most of their lands."

I nod, sitting up, and she brings the bread on a platter piled with cheese. We eat quickly, and by the time we're done, I've woken sufficiently to realize she's allowed us barely three or four hours of sleep. I fold the blankets while Huda stows away the food, and in a matter of minutes we are ready to leave.

Huda guides the camel around the side of the hill we had sheltered against, then stops, studying the desert.

"We leave your lands here?" I hazard. I hadn't expected us to camp quite so close to enemy territory.

"Yes," she says, gesturing past the valley before us. "Beyond those hills, our lands end." With a trace of wryness she adds, "The well we used tonight has changed hands between our tribes a few times."

"You're not worried?"

"No," she assures me, but I can read the tension in her shoulders, the tightness with which she grips the reins.

"We can go a different way," I suggest, not at all sure the fastest route is the best anymore.

Huda shakes her head and clicks her tongue at the camel. "There is no need for you to worry," she says, as if that decides it. I study the back of her scarf, wishing I could understand the way her mind works, the way honor works here in the desert. How very strange it seems to hold even a little faith in the honor of your enemies.

"It would be different," Huda says suddenly, "if we were not just two women traveling together. If we had men with us there would be bloodshed. That's why I am grateful my milk-brother was away when you stepped forth from the Burnt Lands. He would have insisted on coming, and then if we met with anyone," she shakes her head. "Someone would surely die."

"But women are safe?" It seems absurd at best—that the men would kill each other and the women might pass through unscathed.

A slight pause. "Yes," she says. "And you, as a traveler and guest, are guaranteed safety. For you there is nothing to fear at all."

We remain vigilant through what's left of the morning. Huda dismounts to study the tracks we come across, checking how fresh they are. Each time we crest a hill, or pass from one valley to the next, we slow so Huda can scan the land before urging the camel forward again.

But halfway across a wide, scrub-brush valley with nowhere to take cover, Huda tenses. "There." She nods toward the hills continuing to the north. "A patrol, I think."

I squint against the early afternoon sun, and make out a line of riders paused at the top of a hill. "They see us," I say flatly.

"Yes."

Huda neither stops our camel nor urges her on. We continue at a walk across the valley. The riders, however, press their camels into a run, expertly navigating the rocky hills. As they reach the valley floor, they begin to whoop and shout, their camels lengthening their stride until they seem to fly across the land.

Huda tightens her grip on the reins, turning the camel's head toward the riders.

"How do they know we are not from their tribe?" I ask, since it's clear Huda has no intention of running.

"I wear the colors of the women of the Bani Saqr," she says, her voice tight. "But they will not attack us."

They sure look like they're attacking. Perhaps it's merely a show of strength, but I still reach out with my senses, gathering the burning energy of the sun falling around me, the dry force of the wind. I wish there were something other than sunlight to draw on. I will have to use it with care, transform it into something less deadly.

The riders fan out as they reach us, reining in their mounts to form a semicircle with us at their center. In the resulting quiet, the shuffle and panting of the camels seems unnaturally loud. A grizzled warrior urges his mount forward from their midst. He is tall, broadly built, with thick hands and shrewd eyes. Over his flowing, sand-colored robes he wears a sword strapped to his side. A quiver of arrows rests by his knee, alongside his bow.

"Peace be upon you," Huda says, her voice clear and carrying. "I guide a traveler to Fidanya. Have you come to add your escort to mine?"

The warrior's eyes flick from Huda to me, taking in my half-desert features, my foreign dress. His men trade uncertain glances. All except for one, a young man whose cloth *kufiyah* sits slightly askew over his brow and whose grin is even more aslant.

"And upon you, peace," the warrior returns, his voice deep and not unfriendly. "To assist a traveler is, indeed, a high honor."

I let my breath out through barely parted lips, easing my hold on my magic but not letting go completely. The men voice their assent, though most don't look too happy about it. Before me, Huda remains still, only her shoulders relaxing a fraction.

The warrior knees his mount forward, riding along one side of the semicircle toward us. "We cannot all accompany you, I fear. But I shall leave you enough guards that no harm may befall you." He reaches the end of the line and turns to study his men. "Who will aid these travelers through our land?"

I am hardly surprised when the young man with the crooked grin sets his camel padding forward three steps. "It will be my honor," he says, his face serious now.

Five other men push their mounts forward almost as one, moving so quickly that I nearly miss the frown that flits over their leader's face. I don't catch their words, layered as they are on top of each others', but I can't miss the meaning. As two more men come forward, the old warrior raises his hand, "Enough, my brothers. An escort of six men will suffice."

He dips his head to Huda. "We are grateful that the women of your tribe do not take up arms," he says, his eyes glinting with—humor? Or respect? "With such bravery as yours, we would surely be driven from our lands."

Huda inclines her head in response, making me wish I could see her face. But she says only, "I am honored."

The young man's grin is back, and more than a few of the other men are smiling as well. Whatever their enmity, they seem to have a good sense of humor.

"I leave you my son, Laith," the warrior says, gesturing to the young man. "And five more of my finest blades." He tells us their names, but I barely manage to catch one before we are on to the next. In the end I can only be sure that the man in his thirties who sits beside Laith, with a narrow nose and fine lips, is called Faris the son of someone.

"Your generosity in aiding travelers is known across the desert sands, and rightly so," Huda says.

The warrior merely dips his head again, wishes us peace, and with a shout to his men, departs at a brisk pace.

Huda turns her regard upon Laith. "We meant to travel on another hour before resting."

I'm pretty sure we meant to travel right through, but I'm more than happy to adjust our plans for a short rest. No doubt Huda's intentions changed the moment she spotted the warriors, and again when she realized we had their escort.

Laith gestures expansively, the memory of his grin still lurking in his eyes. "Then let us travel."

Huda sets our pace, and the warriors break into two groups, Laith and Faris riding ahead while the remaining four follow behind us. They are all armed with curved swords and bows and arrows. Their robes run the gamut from dark brown to sand gold. Unlike Huda's *thobe*, theirs are unadorned, falling in simple elegant lines around them.

"That was Hamza ibn Mansoor himself," Huda murmurs, speaking to me over her shoulder. "He is one of the leaders of his tribe, and one of the greatest warriors of the desert."

"Ah." All this means to me is that we were very, very lucky he didn't take offense at our trespassing.

"And he has left his own son to guide us," Huda adds. I finally place her tone: amazement.

"His son chose," I point out. I suspect from the frown Hamza had so quickly wiped away, he would have been much happier if Laith *hadn't* chosen. I go on, "And you made it clear where their honor lies."

She chuckles, a deeper, throatier sound than I would have expected. "When you have chosen a path, you must walk it with courage."

"Yes," I agree, looking out past her scarf to the backs of the two men on their camels, and beyond them to where Fidanya lies, still hidden behind the desert hills.

We stop for the afternoon at a well dug beneath a high bluff. The shallow caves and wide stone overhangs provide shelter from the heat of the sun. There is plenty of grazing as well—the thorn bushes are now interspersed with other bushes whose smoother branches and wider leaves the camels clearly enjoy.

Huda sets out a blanket for us in a depression in the bluff that, while hardly a cave, provides us with privacy from the men. Laith arrives to check on us first, lugging a bucket of water. We drink from it, refill our leather water bag, and then Laith offers what's left to Huda's camel. It ignores the bucket, having drunk its fill the night before.

"Have you traveled to Fidanya before?" I ask Huda as Laith lifts the bucket once more, ready to return.

"No," she says. "I have heard stories, but I have not been there before."

"Is there something I can tell you?" Laith asks. He keeps

his eyes focused respectfully on the blanket.

"I must find a friend there," I say slowly, searching for the words I need. "But the first night, I will need to stay," I gesture, hand open. The more I hear and speak the desert tongue, the more it comes back to me, but there are definitely still gaping holes.

Laith tilts his head, grinning. "That is no trouble, even if you *are* arriving on the first day of The Festival of Guilds. There are three great caravanserai on the outskirts of Fidanya. Each offers travelers three nights' stay at no cost."

"Three nights?"

"It's tradition. They are not so far from the desert to have forgotten the rights of the traveler."

For which I will be long grateful, I decide. "What is the Festival?"

He blinks, then casts a quick glance at Huda before answering. "It is…three days of celebrating. All the markets are closed, and every trade guild presents itself to the king's palace to offer up tokens of their finest work. They begin their procession from a different direction each day, starting from the east on the first day, the west on the second, and the south on the third. Each guild gives freely of their wares as they make their way to the palace, so the people have no need for the markets." Laith's gaze has turned dreamy, his voice sweet and deep. "In the evenings there are festivities the like of which few cities can boast. There are theaters built at all the great squares, showing plays from all the Eleven Kingdoms. There are fireworks to light up the night, and at midnight, they remember the turning back of the Northlanders."

I frown, racking my memory for any reference to an invasion from the Northlands. "When did the Northlanders come?"

He laughs. "Hundreds of years ago, but they still burn models of fortresses and catapults to celebrate that victory."

"Have you seen the Festival before?" Huda asks from beside me, her curiosity piqued.

"No," Laith says, his voice falling. "My brother has, and told us often of what he saw. I have been to Fidanya before, but never at this time of year." He offers us his crooked grin. "Perhaps in escorting you, I shall finally see some part of the Festival myself."

Huda looks at her pack, delving inside it with complete focus, as if our meal will otherwise escape us. Laith hefts his bucket and returns to the men.

A few minutes later, as Huda sets out dates and cheese for us, Faris appears with a platter heaped high with dates, a different kind of cheese, and rice mixed with spiced meat. As he spies Huda's food, he says, "No, you are our guests now. Let us provide for you."

"Even as our tribes war," she says, looking him straight in the eye.

"Even as our tribes war," he repeats. And then, as she continues to meet his gaze, "Let us be your hosts in truth."

"Our guest may eat," Huda says finally, gesturing toward me, "but it has not been a year since my brother died upon the swords of your tribe. I cannot share your food."

He lowers his head slightly, his eyes darkening. He has lost someone as well. The sickening truth of what it means to be enemies, to speak of war, clutches at my chest, squeezing the air from my lungs.

"I see," he murmurs, and sets the platter down by my side.

I don't know how to accept it. Smiling and nodding seems like a betrayal to Huda; to take it without acknowledgement, exceptionally rude. But, like Laith, Faris simply turns and walks away.

I look down at my hands. These are not my people, not my concern. Except that, in a very real sense, they may be my people. Laith and Faris might actually be my relatives, and Huda—Huda I would want as a friend and sister, if I could choose such a thing. But my choice, now, is to seek out Stormwind. I cannot help each person I come across, least of all when they neither seek my aid nor want my interference.

"Eat," Huda says, pointing to the platter Faris brought. "Do not feel that you cannot eat the food of your host for fear of offending me. You are a traveler, and this enmity is not yours."

I want to tell her that I am sorry about her brother, though his death has nothing to do with me. I want to tell her that I have killed, and brought death, and that I want it all to stop. But she cannot eat the food of her enemies, and we are worlds apart, though we sit upon the same blanket. So I eat, from the platter of her enemies, and from hers as well.

LIGHT & SHADOW

After a brief afternoon rest, we travel on through the remaining hours of the day and into the night. Laith had suggested that we could reach the nearest caravanserai bordering the city around midnight if we kept going. Huda and I traded glances and agreed to this plan once. She has no wish to remain in her enemies' company longer than necessary, and I want to get to Fidanya as fast as possible.

So we ride on by moonlight, the stars our guide, six armed men our escort. A few hours past sunset we crest a low ridge to see a great plain spreading out before us, all traces of the hills vanished. Nearest us, the land lies dark, hidden beneath the undulating shadows of crops. Farther on, bright lights begin to intersperse the fields here and there, and then the lights grow closer together until the far part of the plains seem nothing more than a carpet of light.

It is huge, this city. I had not expected something so populated so close to the desert.

"How is there water for all the plants?" I ask Huda as we descend to the first of the fields.

"Two great rivers flow through this plain," she says. "The king had channels built to spread water to the fields."

"Does he," I start, then hesitate, not sure how to ask my question. "Is he king of the desert?"

She snorts. "He thinks so, but we follow our own laws. We send him a tribute each year, and he leaves us alone."

"Mmm."

She lifts a hand toward the spread of light before us. "One who lives in such a place cannot understand the way of the desert."

Though I have traveled through the desert less than two

days, gazing at the density of light and wealth and humanity concentrated on the plain before us, I think I do see some of what she means.

We reach the caravanserai deep in the night. Lit with a vast quantity of glowstones, the collection of buildings appear bathed in light, the open yard before them bright and cheerful. As tired as I am, I notice only that they are big, clean, and bustling with people. From somewhere nearby, shouts and laughter ring out among strains of music. From farther away comes the occasional boom of an explosion, though no one seems alarmed. All part of the festivities, I expect.

Laith and Faris intercept a young man wearing a long tunic topped by a sleeveless vest, as well as a loose drawstring *selvar* not unlike those worn by the desert folk, except that his have somewhat more folds of cloth centered at his waist, creating a baggier look as a whole. The young man leaves and returns within a few minutes with a young woman to assist Huda and me. She is dressed in much the same style, though the cut of her *selvar* is slightly roomier, if that's possible. Rather than a vest, she wears a sleeved jacket lightly embroidered with stylized flowers.

With her help, we unload our camel and carry Huda's belongings into one of the buildings, leaving the men to see to their own mounts. The woman leads us down a hallway to a locked door behind which are built a series of stone spaces that look like nothing so much as cells barred with iron gates. Staring at them, I feel a chill creep down my spine. I rub my arms, trying to dismiss my fears. I'm just tired. These cages are filled with sacks, trunks, barrels, and all manner of objects, not people.

Huda pulls out what few items she will need, and I shoulder my pack, and the rest the woman locks into an empty storage space, handing Huda the key.

We follow the woman up a flight of stairs to a dormitory. Most of the beds lie empty. Here and there a woman shifts on her pallet, her form swathed in blankets. "We have only three beds left," our guide says as she leads us to the back of the room. "Our guests are at the Festival, but this room will fill up by morning. It is well for you. Your men must sleep in the back courtyard."

Huda presses her lips together, but doesn't offer a correction on our relation to our escort. Instead, she thanks the woman for our quarters and a few minutes later we are both in our pallets.

I open my eyes to find the dormitory half-lit, curtains drawn over the windows. I peek out from behind the heavy cloth at the great semicircular cobbled yard we rode into last night. It lies relatively quiet now, the hour still early. I spot only a pair of horses hitched to a post and a small group of men conversing in a doorway.

When I turn back to the room, Huda is sitting up on her pallet, prayer beads clicking. Perhaps she wasn't asleep at all when I awoke, only lying down with them in hand.

"Did you rest— good?" I whisper. The room is now full of sleepers, every bed taken.

She nods noncommittally, which I take to mean she slept miserably but won't insult our hosts by admitting it. "If you are hungry, I believe our host mentioned a dining…room." Huda says the last word awkwardly, and it takes me a moment to put my finger on why: she isn't used to rooms with specific functions, or to rooms at all. She's used to walls of cloth, open fires, and shared space.

After washing up, we head downstairs and are directed through a great courtyard—apparently not the one where Laith and his friends were given space to sleep—to a dining hall. It is huge, greater than three of Stormwind's cabins put together, with long, low tables running the length of the room, and cushions on the ground to sit upon. The room is mostly empty, but no sooner do we sit than a young girl brings us a tray laden with fresh bread and spiced milk. She returns a few minutes later with a large platter of spiced eggs fried with vegetables, and plates of freshly cut apples and pears.

"What will you do?" I ask Huda as we start our meal, sharing from the platters before us. "How will you go to your lands?"

She looks up from the food, smiles briefly. "You are right, I will not go back with them."

"Then?"

She tilts her head, indicating the room and what lies beyond it. "After the Festival, there should be at least one caravan riding east. I will join it, if I may."

"They would say no?"

"I must be able to pay," she explains. "To ride with a caravan means you are protected by their numbers and guards."

I frown. "It is a lot?"

"I am not worried."

Which tells me nothing. Nor do I have much to offer her, even if she would take it—there had been hardly a handful of coins in Stormwind's coin jar, most of them coppers.

"What of the men?"

"I cannot ride alone with them," Huda says. "They are not my relations. But I am sure they will remain here until I find passage back. It is their honor to do so." She makes a slight gesture, as if brushing away such thoughts. "And you? Will you need direction from here?"

I shake my head. "No." It would be wiser to ask directions of a stranger on the street, someone who will forget me among the masses of faces and people they see each day, than anyone here.

Once we finish, Huda accompanies me to the entrance of the caravanserai. It feels strange to leave her so easily, so suddenly. And without being able to offer her anything in return for what she has done for me. Well, there is one thing, however small. I pull a spare glowstone from my bag and press it into her palm. "Here," I tell her. "It is small, but I hope it brings you light."

She smiles, closing her fingers around it. "There are many kinds of light. The light of friendship can dispel all darkness."

My smile is almost a grimace, for I am not much of a friend to her at all. I have brought her out of her lands and I leave her far from her home, unsure of how to return safely. She touches my arm gently. "I do not know what burden weighs on you, but I wish that it might be lightened."

Her words bring me back to myself. Here I am wallowing in self-pity, when she has gone to such lengths to help me. "I thank you," I say. "And I wish your road— safe and easy."

"And yours." She takes a step back, then suddenly grins. "My sister's wedding will be during the white nights of the next month—the nights of the full moon. If you are able, we would be honored to welcome you as our guest."

"*Sumeyya?*" I ask before I can help myself.

Huda laughs. "No, our elder sister, Zainab. Will you come?"

"I…" A month from now seems as unknowable as where I might be in five or ten years, if I should live so long. "If I am—

can," I stumble. "If I can, I would be honored to attend."

"I look forward to it, for my heart tells me we will meet again." She grasps me by my arms and kisses my cheeks lightly, in the desert tradition.

"Peace be upon you," she tells me, stepping back again.

"And upon you, peace."

The streets are starting to come to life as I make my way into the city. The road from the caravanserai is broad, its large stone pavers lying flat and perfectly aligned. A host of workers sweep and scrub after the night's festivities, pushing along barrels on small carts to collect the debris they find. They must have been at work since dawn, and they still have a great deal of work ahead of them. The main road is relatively well swept, but the smaller cross-streets are littered with scraps, broken flags, and bits of cloth and paper.

The buildings are many-storied, built of yellow stone and brick as the city in the Burnt Lands had been. These buildings, however, are vibrant with life. Clotheslines crisscross the alleyways, strung from windows and balconies. Potted plants overflowing with mint or flowers line the edges of balconies and rest on wide windowsills. Everywhere there are doors and shutters, brightly painted in green and blue and red.

I pause at an intersection with another large road, glancing one way then the other. The buildings are now so tightly packed, the sun not quite high enough to peer over their shoulders, that I'm not certain which direction will take me to the city center—or if that's where I need to go at all. But there, resting against her cleaning cart, stands an older woman with a wide, friendly face and reddened cheeks.

"Hello," I say tentatively in Tradespeak.

She bares her mouth in a gap-toothed grin. "Hello to you! Up early, aren't you, child?"

Her accent is so strong it takes me a breath to parse her words. Then I shrug, smiling slightly. "I've just arrived. I'm supposed to meet my uncle at the Mekteb."

"We've a few. Which one is it you want?"

"Uh. The mages' school?"

"Ha! That's the Mekteb-i Sihir. Follow this road till you

reach the second great square—you won't miss them. The first has stages built for the players, and the second is for the sporting competitions. At the second, take a left and keep going. It'll take you over the river and right past the front gates. Maybe an hour walking from here. Been there before?"

"No."

"The biggest building has six domes. You can't miss it."

"Sounds impressive."

"It is. Very beautiful. We're blessed to have such a great school here. But then," she sweeps her arms out proudly, "we've a great city. It's only natural, wouldn't you say?"

I nod. "I've heard the High Council is here this year as well."

"Oh, aye," she drops her arms, apparently not quite so pleased with that. "That they are."

"Any interesting news of them?"

She snorts. "Get a gaggle of mages together and something interesting is bound to happen, good or bad. Why, just the other day they convicted one of their own of all sorts of terrible charges."

I feign shock, my throat tightening, though it is no worse than I expected. "No! Who was it?"

"A Mistress Stormwood, or the like. Said she was undermining the Council itself, consorting with rogue creatures, and I don't know what else."

"What'll they do with her?"

"Lock her up," my informant answers philosophically. "What else do you do with someone like that? They'll send her off to Gereza Saliti."

My eyes widen. Stormwind mentioned the Gereza once, an island stronghold, the prison itself dug deep into the earth. The prisoners may as well be buried alive, she had said. I swallow hard and hope my reaction looks like a laudable mixture of fear and surprise as I ask, "Then she's still here?"

"Oh, aye. With the Festival, there's too much disturbance to try to move her. They'll wait till it's quiet. At least," she shrugs, "that's what we've heard out here. You never know with those mages. Maybe that's what they're saying so we don't look for her to pass through in the middle of it all."

I chat with her for a few minutes about the Festival itself so that my questions on the Council won't stand out in her memory. She urges me to catch a play or two, and to come out for the midnight "burning of the fortresses," as she terms it.

"If my uncle allows me," I assure her. "I would love to see

such a thing."

"Aye," she agrees. "When I was young, I spent from noon till dawn at the Festival. Mind you, make sure you go with your uncle, or some group as will keep you by their side. The Festival is safe enough, but a girl alone in the night is never a good idea."

I smile my agreement, even though alone is all I've got.

By the time I reach the second square, the city is bustling with people. Children shout and laugh as they chase each other through the crowds. Street vendors push their carts along, selling food to the spectators flocking the morning's competitions. I catch the scent of fresh baked bread, roasting meat, fried fish. From the far side of the square rise the shouts and hoots of the men gathered around a wrestling ring.

I thread my way through the growing crowd and turn down the connecting street, following it to a great river, wide and deep. The bridge over it rises on pillars high enough for low-masted ships to pass below. I squint as the light reflects off the water, try to recall my geography: the great rivers bisecting the city, the desert and the Burnt Lands to the east— and of course, the sea to the south.

I continue across the bridge and barely five minutes later reach the entrance gate to the great domed building of the Mekteb-i Sihir. *The School of Sorcery*. It's a lovely structure, all flying arches and fluted towers, with a great sapphire dome at its center and five lesser domes cascading down around it. Lower buildings stand to either side of it, and I think that there must be even more buildings behind them. A high, white wall surrounds the compound, far enough away from the buildings that there must be gardens within as well.

The grand entrance is gated with iron, an exquisite melding of central flowers and radiating geometrical designs. Today, one of the side gates stands open. A turbaned old man, dark-skinned and bearded, perches on a stool by the gate, a staff in hand. He wears the tan *thobe* of the desert people, and despite his age and non-magical appearance, I have no doubt he's an excellent guard. He wouldn't be there otherwise. I keep my gaze ahead of me as I continue down the street, careful not to give any indication of my interest in the Mekteb.

As I walk, I scan the buildings opposite the school. The third building down from the gate has an open-air stairwell built into its side, opening into a snug little alley. I turn the corner and walk to it, climbing up as if I know exactly where I'm going. The stairwell ends at the top floor, the hallway bisecting the building perfectly empty. I walk down the hall, coming to a stop at a balcony built out from the back. Below me, I'm surprised to see a hidden inner courtyard shared by the buildings that make up its walls. Within the courtyard are benches and walkways, a few straggly trees, what appears to be a vegetable patch, and a plethora of flowers.

More importantly, right next to the balcony a small back stairway goes up to the roof. The door at the top is jammed shut, but a good hard shove opens it—the lock seems to have been broken some time ago. There's not much worth stealing up here, other than clothes drying on their lines. I duck under them, making my way to the front of the building, and settle myself on an overturned bucket by the low boundary wall. From here I have an unobstructed view of the Mekteb's front gate.

Over the next hour, flocks of students leave the school, some in their own clothes, most with their robes worn on top. They greet the guard with smiles or nods, or sometimes not at all, too caught up in their conversations. Now and then, a solitary mage enters the gates. The guard watches them more carefully, but a smile and nod seems to get them through just fine. Do they know the guard, or is there something else about their appearance that makes clear their right of entrance? Is there some brooch or pin all students wear, some bit of embroidery that states their affiliation?

From this distance, I can't tell. But I might not need to worry about it. A good excuse might get me through just as easily. I pull Stormwind's robe from my pack, pull it on over my clothes, and set off to visit the turbaned gatekeeper.

I take the back alleys around to the bridge and start up the road again, keeping an eye out for other mages headed in the same direction. As the gates come into sight, I spot a robed woman ahead of me. I quicken my pace so that I'm only a few feet behind her as we reach the gate.

The guard observes our approach with rheumy eyes.

"Good morning, master," the woman calls in Tradespeak.

"Morning," I echo, nodding.

He nods to the woman, then turns his gaze to me.

"Morning," he agrees, his voice rasping slightly. He watches me expectantly and I find myself slowing down. And immediately curse myself. I should have kept walking.

"Are you here for someone?" he asks.

So he does recognize who belongs.

"I've a message for a master here." I hold up the pouch that once housed all my charms. Now a single glowstone weighs it down. He eyes the slightly bulging pouch thoughtfully, then looks me over. "My mistress wasn't able to come herself," I add as he frowns at my boots. Did I step in something?

He raises his gaze to me. "Your mistress?"

I don't miss a beat. "Mistress Sunbolt." It's a mage name by the sound of it, but not one he'll likely have heard before. Even Mistress Stormwind could think of no other mage who had earned such a name.

"Hmm. And the master you're to see?"

"Master Stonefall."

"Ah yes." The old man tugs absently at his turban. "He's here. Have you been in before?"

"No, sir."

"Rehan," he calls, glancing past me to the far side of the gateway. "Rehan!"

A sloe-eyed young girl with the golden skin of the locals and a pair of dark brown braids bouncing down her back comes running toward us, broom in hand. The dustpan lies abandoned some paces behind her on the path that runs alongside the boundary wall. "Yes, Master Jabir?" She asks.

"Take this young lady to Master Stonefall's rooms. You know where they are?"

"Couldn't find 'em unless they called my name," she says cheerfully.

"White Raven Hall, fourth floor, by the Seven Claw stairwell."

"Right," she says. "White Raven Hall. Come along, miss."

I follow the girl down a long, paved road leading toward the main building. Closer to the domed building, the road is bounded by two long, rectangular pools, fountains playing in their midst. But before we reach them, my guide turns off and follows a cobbled pathway leading us around the main building.

We come out at the corner of a long garden lined by tall buildings on either side. Built out from the buildings are domed arcades offering a shaded walkway to the students through the hot summer months. The garden itself is carefully manicured, scattered with benches and fountains. A peacock struts along one of the walks, its jewel tones surprisingly dull compared to the phoenix's colors.

The grounds are filled with young men and women, some as young as six or seven, newly identified promises, and some as old as I, ready to leave for their journeyman studies. The arcades where we walk are busy, students shouting greetings to each other and standing in knots. Rehan threads her way past them, and few if any take notice of either of us.

"This way," Rehan calls, darting through a set of great wooden doors. Above them, a carving of white marble ravens adorns the lintel. Inside, we continue past a stairwell with its railing carved with feathers before coming to what can only be the Seven Claw stairwell, the stone banister supported by thin white marbles rails. Each rail ends in a carved raven's foot sporting seven onyx claws.

It is so uncanny a sight, so realistic and yet fantastical, I slow to a stop. This is a school of mysteries and magic, and the home of the High Council. Once I go up these stairs, I cannot be sure what will follow.

"He's at the top," Rehan says cheerfully, and starts up the stairs. I make myself follow after her, the stairs curving round and round as if we climb a tower, though the stairs regularly open up to another landing. Wide windows follow the line of the stairs up, giving us a view of the gardens from ever-higher perspectives.

At the final landing, the girl comes to a stop before a pedestal on which a stone raven perches. "Master Stonefall," she says.

The raven flutters his alabaster feathers and glances over his shoulder before croaking, "Fifth door on the right. Watch your step!"

I study the raven in fascination but, having provided this direction, it lapses back into stone. The girl has already moved ahead. I follow after her, keeping an eye out for tripping hazards, but there's nothing of concern underfoot.

"Is that all it does?" I ask, glancing back at the raven.

"The raven? Oh yes, they just give directions. People got tired of never knowing who was where, what with the students moving rooms every year, and offices getting shifted about and all that. Here we are."

She comes to a stop before a wooden door. A clawed raven's foot holds a round iron knocker. At least this raven's foot has the right number of toes.

"Thank you." I say. "I haven't really any coin to give. I'm very sorry."

She laughs sweetly. "Oh no, miss, that's very kind of you, but I couldn't take anything anyway. Jabir would have my head."

I give her a questioning look.

"At the gate," she provides helpfully. "Our resident Guardian."

"Guardian?" I ask. "You mean the guard?"

"Oh no, Jabir's a Guardian. They're old creatures. Some say they were around when the phoenix itself was first born. He's been with the Mekteb for longer than anyone can remember."

I hesitate, my unease deepening. "What powers does a Guardian have?"

Rehan grins. "He can tell a lie as clearly as if you wore a banner proclaiming it. He can tell if your intention is honest or corrupt. And if he ever has to defend the Mekteb, he's a force to be reckoned with. Even the first mage of the High Council wouldn't cross Jabir."

"I see," I say faintly, wondering why Jabir let me through at all.

With a wink she is off, disappearing with a soft patter down the stairwell.

He must have sensed the half-truths behind what I was saying. Perhaps he knew I didn't mean any harm. Regardless, he let me through and I have no intention of wasting time pondering it. I lift the iron knocker and let it fall. As the dull thud reverberates down the hall, the wooden door creaks open slightly.

"Master Stonefall?" I call uncertainly, considering the cracked opening. Faintly, I hear a rustle from the room. I push the door open, calling out again. The room lies in silence. It is a study of sorts, a desk against the far wall by the window, papers and books piled on it, additional bookshelves against a wall, mostly empty, and an array of weapons hung upon the other wall—swords, daggers, a pair of small axes, a set of javelins, and a variety of crossbows.

"Master Stonefall?" I call again, stepping in, and trip over something in the way. I catch myself before I come down on the—man.

I scramble to kneel beside the fallen figure, gently turning him on his back. Stonefall's face seems unnaturally pale beneath his desert-tan complexion, his features tightened with pain. Today he wears the long, plain *thobe* of the desert people, its soft brown marred with a few small streaks of deep red. Dark eyes flicker open to focus on me as I call his name again.

"Master Stonefall? Where are you hurt?"

His hand scrabbles at his stomach, where a splotch of dark blood slowly spreads. I use my knife to cut open the cloth, revealing a small puncture wound, its edges ragged. The skin around it is black already, the wound itself bubbling with dark blood. His hands jerk, the fingers tightening into claws, and something clatters to the floor: a long, black dart with a barbed tip.

"Who do I call?" I ask, my voice shaking. He opens his mouth but no sound comes out. In the time it would take me to run back to Jabir, explain what I have found, and return with help, Stonefall could easily die. I look around the study frantically. Surely there must be something here, some herbs, some charm for poison. I make a quick circuit of the room, shoving papers away, searching for anything, *anything*. But there's nothing of any use—feathers, a mortar and pestle, herbs I don't immediately recognize, a metal brooch, threads of varying hues, and the weapons.

I jerk open my pack, then desperately pat down my pockets—and find the glowstone. I bite my lip, staring down at the dying man, then back at the charm. I don't know what I'm doing, but I have to try. Stonefall grips my hand as I kneel beside him, his breath wheezing.

"I'm going to try something. I'm not sure how well it will work. Is that all right?"

He nods once, his eyes so dilated I can hardly see any brown left. I place the glowstone beside the wound and lay my hands on either side of it, framing the discolored skin. I gather together all that I recall of the last months, drawing on the cool mountain air, the warmth of our goats and the clucking of our hens, the shaded trails and fleeting glimpses of mountain ibex, the company of squirrels and sparrows, and slowly I begin to feel the beat of the man's heart, feel the poison sliding through his bloodstream.

I call to it with the voice of living things, with the memory of Stormwind's smile, the crunch of fresh apples, the rustle of leaves in the wind, and I feel the poison move toward me, turning back by what paths it can find. I call to it with the beat of my own heart, with the ebb and flow of blood through my veins, and it bubbles up from the wound, sickly yellow, trickling toward my hands. *Life light,* I think, remembering a crow from a tower room long ago, and the glowstone shines as brightly as a star. I channel the poison into it, watching as the fluid seeps into the stone, brightening as it burns away.

My hands tremble as the last of the poison surfaces, mixed with a dark black blood, thick and viscous. The stone absorbs this as well, the blood crusting on its surface. The puncture wound remains, for there is no magic that can mend flesh. But it's clean now, and should heal well.

Vaguely, I hear voices in the hall. Stonefall's hand rises and catches my wrist. I look at him blearily. "Hide," he whispers. "Now."

I look around, blinking to clear my vision. "Where?"

"The next room…Stormwind's pack is in the wardrobe. Use her charm." The voices are nearly upon us, raised in alarm. "Hurry!"

I jump up and stumble past him to the second room, my shoulder thumping into the doorframe. Lurching through, I shove the door shut and race across the room to the tall wardrobe, throwing its doors open. Stormwind's pack is set carefully at the bottom. I pull it open with shaking fingers, shoving the closet doors shut with my hip. A charm, a charm, I tell myself, rifling through her clothes.

In the first room, I can hear voices now, the soft, pain-ridden voice of Stonefall, and those of the men and women with him. My fingers close on the fabric of Stormwind's charms pouch. I yank it out and drop down against the wall, in the shadow of the closet. From here, I'm shielded from immediate sight, but anyone who steps in will find me. With nothing but the bed, the wardrobe and a nightstand, there are precious few places to hide, and everyone will check under the bed. I need whatever charm Stonefall thought would hide me.

I spill the contents of the pouch into my lap, shoving the ward stones to the side, and see something glinting beneath the seeker charm she had packed: a ring made of a twist of wire and dark thread, a single black bead gleaming at the top.

Someone pushes the room door open, footsteps thudding through. I shove my finger through the ring and hold perfectly still.

Silence.

I wait, holding my breath, and listen to the tap of shoes moving slowly around the room. I watch in icy panic as a mage comes to the foot of the bed, then stoops to look beneath it. There's nowhere to run, no way past the mages in the other room. Whatever this charm was supposed to do—

The mage straightens and scans the room again, his eyes pausing on the wardrobe and then gliding right over me.

I stare him straight in the face, unable to believe it as he looks around one last time and then turns to leave.

"There's no one here," he says, closing the door behind him.

I glance down at my hand, expecting to see the wire ring, but my eyes slide away. I find myself looking at the tiled floor. I try again, by my gaze slips sideways past a vague grayness to the wall. I blink once, then rest my pounding head against the wardrobe.

Stormwind had promised to make a charm of shadows, something to keep herself safe.

She kept her word.

STONEFALL

I gather up the charms on my lap and ease my pack around to slip them in, keeping my eyes averted so as not to strain the shadow charm. It's strange to work by feel, but at last I think I've got them all in. Then I crawl over to the bed, taking my pack with me. If my charm uses shadows, then it will work best where they are deepest. Plus, I don't want to get stepped on. Whether or not people can see me, they'll know I'm there if they trip over me.

Thankfully, whoever cleans Stonefall's rooms swept under the bed recently. Once I'm sure I've pulled my bag and robes fully under the bed with me, I let myself breathe and consider where I am.

Which is to say, hiding under the bed of a rogue-hunter and high mage. After magically drawing poison from that same mage's wound in the middle of a school of sorcery. That also happens to be the current home of the High Council of Mages.

I stare sightlessly at the tightly strung rope underpinnings of the bed. Stupid. Stupid stupid *stupid*. How could I have used magic in the middle of the Mekteb? On a mage? One who met me before and now knows that I've been hiding a magical talent?

Whatever he thinks, he offered me an escape. Unless I can find another way out from under the bed, I'll have to face him in order to get away. At least I can be grateful for small things…. Embracing his desert heritage as he does, Stonefall will have his honor to think of. He owes me his life, and in return I intend to gain his help getting out alive.

The voices from the connecting room grow louder, and then bodies fill the doorway. Four sets of leather slippers enter, two of them crowded around the third, and the other hurrying ahead to the bed. I'm not surprised that third set is the plainest of them all. Stonefall did not strike me as the type to want metallic embroidery and tassels all over his shoes.

The ropes holding up the mattress creak as Stonefall eases himself down. I lie perfectly still, listening to the muted conversation. No, he doesn't require anything. A guard outside the door is fine, but he does not wish to be disturbed. No, for the final time, he didn't recognize the mage who'd helped him. Nor did he recognize his attacker.

"At all?" presses one of the mages. Her voice is the calmest of the lot, steady and cool.

"I have an idea of who sent him," Stonefall tells her. "But without proof, I would hardly speak of it."

"I understand."

"A healer should be here within a few moments," one of the other mages says.

"I am fine," Stonefall assures them. "Go back to your work. With the door guarded, I doubt my attacker will return."

After a little additional urging, the mages depart. The cool-voiced mage offers one last time to remain in the outer room, but Stonefall refuses. They shut first one door, then the other, their voices growing fainter as they proceed down the hall.

The room lies quiet. It seems wisest to let Stonefall decide when it's safe to speak. I use the time to figure out what I will say to him when the time comes. I run through various explanations, but the best ones are the closest to the truth. I need Stonefall to tell me what really happened to Stormwind, and where she is now. There is even the smallest possibility that, as her friend, he will help me reach her. Because, unless she confessed to murder, I will not sit by and let her be sent to Gereza Saliti.

"You're under the bed," Stonefall says.

I frown. "How did you know?" It's a little strange to have this conversation around the mattress.

"I have no trouble focusing on any part of the room, and you wouldn't have been so foolish as to hide in the wardrobe."

The idea never occurred to me, though if it had, I probably would have dismissed it at once. The space is too tight, and a bunch of clothes pressed around an unseen shadow would have made a mage stop and think, no doubt.

"How did you know about the charm?" I ask.

"Stormwind made it before we traveled through the portal.

I knew it was still in her charm pouch."

"What is it, exactly?"

"A look-away charm. It cloaks the wearer in shadows and turns away the eyes of those around them."

I run my fingers over the thin wire, the single bead. Look-away. An apt name.

Faintly, someone knocks.

"That will be the healer," Stonefall says. "Stay where you are."

I raise my eyes to the mattress and grin. I didn't really plan to introduce myself, even to a peaceable healer.

Stonefall calls for the healer to enter. She comes through at once, walking swiftly. Her shoes are a dark blue with pale blue embroidered flowers and leaves curving over the top. She is efficient, quietly and quickly assessing her patient to ensure he is past the point of danger.

"This is the dart," Stonefall tells her when she finishes examining him.

"I'll have to test it," she says. I can't quite place the musical lilt of her accent. "Perhaps we can learn something from the type of poison used. Now, tell me about the spell that saved you."

"The, ah, mage called up memories of her life to draw the poison away."

"*Memories?*" the woman echoes, her tone astonished. "She could not have been a healer then."

"No," he agrees. "She then channeled the poison into this."

There's a short silence. The healer, I imagine, is studying the glowstone I used.

"Unconventional," she says with a hint of approval, "but it clearly worked."

"For which I am grateful."

Did he say that for me or her? Or both of us?

The healer prescribes Stonefall an herbal tisane and a day's rest and leaves as quietly as she came.

Stonefall waits until the outer room's door clicks shut, and then murmurs, "Come out. There's no one here but me."

I slip the look-away off my finger to preserve its magic as long as possible and work my way out. It is exceptionally embarrassing to have to wiggle out from under someone's bed while they're peering over the edge at you. I sit up, run one hand through my rumpled hair, and attempt to look dignified as I finish sliding out my legs and clamber to my feet. Master Stonefall rests on his bed, propped against a pile of pillows, his face slightly sallow beneath his natural tan. His features are smooth, the faint hint of crow's feet by his eyes the only sign that he feels any strain now.

We eye each other for a long moment.

"She said you were her servant." His voice is quiet, measured, like the gentle tread of a hunter approaching his prey. My mind flashes to his wall of weapons, to the array of blades he'd worn when he'd come to fetch Stormwind. He's a rogue hunter, and I must look a lot like a rogue right now.

I shrug. "I do help out around the house."

A slight line appears between his eyes. Apparently humor will not do me any favors right now.

"Indeed. That was an impressive casting you made. One of the mages who came sits on the Council. He said he felt it halfway through the building."

I feel the blood drain from my face. "The High Council?"

His eyes glint as he dips his chin. "He could tell as well as I that it wasn't any of our students. Or mages."

It doesn't even occur to me to lie, to try to deny his words. I know enough of magic and the safeguards Stormwind kept in place for me to realize he must be telling the truth. "How?" I ask instead. His answer might at least help me disguise my magic in future.

"The casting itself was very unusual. To use memories as a basis for a spell is…uncommon."

"You saw the memories?" I ask, interrupting him.

"I believe so," he says, and continues unperturbed. "Then you channeled the poison, as if it needed to be contained." He turns over a smooth gray object in his palm. With a start, I recognize my glowstone, its light diminished.

"I was calling to the poison, and it was coming to me. I needed somewhere to put it. The glowstone was all I had."

He raises his eyebrows. "Most mages would have burned the poison away."

"I don't know about most mages, but I didn't want to accidentally burn you." There is a very, very small possibility that he'll mistake me for— what? A journeyman? Certainly not a full mage. Which raises the question of why Stormwind was harboring a student in secret. I have no doubt he'll get to it.

"Ah." He studies me for a moment, then continues, "Every apprentice also learns to add just a faint touch, their own signature, to their work. It builds accountability and becomes so habitual that a journeyman of your skill would have included it without realizing it." He meets my gaze, his voice disturbingly calm. "Unlike 'most mages,' you have no signature."

I watch him silently, focusing on keeping my breath even, my expression neutral. I can think of no lie, no half-truth, that would explain all he knows of me. But there's no one else here, and he offered me refuge, so I have some reason to believe he will not turn me over to the High Council. At least not immediately.

He sighs. "Come and sit," he says, gesturing to a chair beside his bed. "For Stormwind's sake, I would hear what you would tell me, including why you came to my rooms when you did."

To take the chair will mean being within easy reach of him, and much farther from the door. But he is a master mage. The distance that remains between us now would hardly make a difference. I walk stiffly to the chair and perch on its edge.

"Water?" Stonefall gestures to a pitcher and three small ceramic cups on the bedside table.

I shake my head.

"You don't trust me," he says, eyes crinkling.

I shrug, glance at the water again. "If you wished to hold me here, you wouldn't need to drug me. No doubt you have a spell that could bind me to this chair until you released me, or something of the sort."

The faint trace of humor leaves his face, and he is a rogue hunter once more, shrewd, dangerous. "Yes."

I think of Huda, refusing to share the food of her enemies, and find myself reaching for the pitcher. I pour out two cups, handing one to Stonefall. He takes it, sipping once as if to show me the water is harmless. I don't need to see it. I take a sip, study the movement of the water in the cup. This conversation, these moments—I will need to navigate them carefully. And I don't yet understand Stonefall well enough to gauge how to approach him.

"Why did you seek me out?" he asks, breaking the silence between us.

I consider my cup, the simple white inside, the turquoise and cobalt flowers flowing around the sides, then look back up at him, echoing his own words. "For Stormwind's sake."

His brow furrows. He's clearly taken aback. "You came here to learn what happened to her."

"Yes."

"Did you trust so much in my friendship with Stormwind

that you thought I would not report you to the High Council?"

"I didn't intend to use any magic here." I eye him warily. "Who shot you, anyway?"

He waves his hand, dismissing the question. "You're dressed as a mage. What was I supposed to think?"

I glance down at my robes and almost laugh. "That was just to get in. These aren't even mine." I lift the hem, showing him where I'd turned up the extra cloth. "They're Stormwind's."

He chuckles. "A mage hiding in mage's robes. The perfect disguise."

"It worked well enough to get in here, though I doubt it will help if I'm caught." Which I kind of am right now.

"No," Stonefall agrees. He seems on the verge of saying something, then purses his lips.

"Tell me what happened to Mistress Stormwind," I say.

He nods, but he doesn't look at me as he speaks, his gaze distant. "She faced charges of treason against the High Council. She was found guilty and will be sent to Gereza Saliti, to remain there until she dies."

"I've heard that already. What was she actually convicted of?"

He counts them off. "Conspiracy to overthrow the High Council, conspiracy to assassinate the first mage of the High Council, perjury under oath, and failure to renew her oaths of allegiance."

The charge of developing alliances with creatures inimical to the High Council seems to have been dropped, but the rest still stand. I shake my head. "That's absurd."

His dark eyes fasten on me in cool appraisal. "She was found guilty and sentenced accordingly."

"By whom?" I ask, matching his tone. "Blackflame?"

Stonefall's expression hardly flickers. "Blackflame is not on the High Council."

"Then he has a very long arm."

"That he does. However, he missed the one charge that would have been accurate: training a student in secret."

"How do you know she didn't register my apprenticeship?"

"You're an *apprentice*?"

Oh, hell. He thought I was a journeyman. I *wanted* him to think I was a journeyman. "Whatever—register my journeyman-ship," I flounder.

He stares at me. He knows. And he's not at all sure what he thinks of me.

"I'll leave now," I say.

"I wouldn't, if I were you. There are guards posted by my door to prevent a second attack. For all that they are there for my protection, I think they are much more interested in meeting you."

"The windows?" I set my cup down and rise, moving toward the windows.

"Guards below them by now, and far too many mages passing by to try anything so foolish as climbing out."

I let my hand drop from the curtain and turn back to him. "Do you speak truth?"

He turns the gray glowstone over in his hand, studying it. "I owe you a life debt. That is not something my people take lightly. I will not endanger you."

That doesn't mean he won't keep me here by trickery, though. But I'm losing focus on why I came here. I'll find a way out. The question is whether Brigit Stormwind will. I need to find out what help I can finagle from Stonefall.

I take a deep breath and plunge ahead, "You wanted to know why I came here, to you, instead of finding out Stormwind's fate from afar. Do you believe she's innocent of the charges brought against her?"

Stonefall doesn't answer at once. When he does, his words are hardly comforting. "I believe her largely innocent, yes. But this is Stormwind we speak of. You know her past, you know how close she kept her secrets. Perhaps some of what she was charged with was based in truth." He pins me with a hard gaze. "Certainly to train an unregistered apprentice, to *hide* a magical talent, would be considered treason among mages."

"Then they should have charged her with training me."

I don't know Stormwind's past as Stonefall thinks I do. I have no idea who she was before she secluded herself in her mountain valley, keeping company with no one and nothing but her secrets, until I came along. By then, silence had become her way of life, her secrets so strong a shield that even if I wanted to, I could not have broken them open to learn what lay beneath. No, I don't know if she's innocent.

But I doubt that her innocence, or guilt, had anything to do with her sentencing.

"Was it a fair trial?" I ask.

Stonefall doesn't answer.

"They could have imprisoned her in her valley. She hardly

ever left it anyway. Why not declare that her prison?"

He laughs, a sound that carries both humor and sorrow. "There's no revenge in that. It wouldn't suffice."

I think of Blackflame, what I know of him. It's easy enough to forgive him what I've forgotten, what I can't recover from the ashes of my memory. It wasn't that hard to stay with Stormwind and ignore his existence, unconcerned with what he might be doing because he had faded from my reality. But I've known Stormwind for a year, and while she has her secrets, I know she doesn't deserve the sentence he has visited upon her.

I take a slow breath. "Where is Stormwind right now?"

Stonefall tilts his head, watching me shrewdly. "She's being held here."

"Here where?"

A silence. "I'll answer three questions, and that is all. Then you must leave."

He knows exactly why I'm here. I take a moment to gather my thoughts, then ask again, "Where is she being held?"

"Shahmaran Hall. There are old holding cells in the basement. The lycan guard has cordoned off the stairs down, and allows no one and nothing entrance. Stormwind herself has been placed under a binding spell."

"A what?"

He grimaces. "It is the worst sort of spell. Under it, she will experience incredible pain should she attempt a spell of her own. Should she persist, it could kill her."

There are much worse punishments, I think. After all, it merely means that a mage becomes the equivalent of the average person until the spell can be lifted.

"Is she chained?" I ask, remembering my imprisonment with Val.

"Yes."

"You have to tell me more than that. If she's chained, who has the keys?"

He sighs. "The lycan guard might. First Mage Talon certainly does. She's most likely keeping them in her rooms." He hesitates. "Susulu Hall."

I bite my lip, trying to think of the wisest third question I could ask. There are so many things I don't know, no one thing seems more vital than three others. In the end, though, knowing how much time I have trumps everything else. "When will she be moved?"

"She has three more days here while the arrangements are

made." He smiles faintly. "There are no portals at the Gereza, after all. Even without the Festival of Guilds to contend with, it would take that long."

Three days isn't much time, but it's significantly better than, say, three days too late.

Stonefall clears his throat. "You'll be in direct opposition to the ruling of the High Council."

"It's wrong."

"It's the High Council," Stonefall says, his voice soft, persuasive. "To oppose them as a mage is to declare yourself a traitor. Is that what you want?"

"I don't think this is about what anyone other than Blackflame wants. I'm not worried about him."

"Then you're dead." For a moment, I think it's a promise he intends to follow through on himself. But he remains at ease, propped up in his bed.

"We're all dead," I tell him. "Some more than others."

He leans forward. "Listen to me. I tell you this because you have risked a great deal in coming here, and you risked more in aiding me when I could not help myself. Leave. Leave now, and never return. You cannot help Stormwind, and you cannot oppose the High Council. If you are caught, which you will be, you will lose your freedom, and perhaps your mind. Whatever Stormwind was thinking when she took you on, she would not want such a future for you."

I don't know what future I want. Without knowing my past, I'm drifting, unsure of where to go or what to do next. But I reserve the right to choose my own future. And I think Stormwind has the right to a just trial. Failing that, I'll stand by her as she stood by me. If she favors imprisonment, then let her do it on her own terms, away in her mountain valley. Not that she can return there now—whatever life she has after this will either be as a fugitive or as a prisoner on the Council's terms.

But Stonefall is right about one thing. Stormwind would be furious if she knew I was here. I nod. "I understand the risks."

He doesn't immediately answer. I glance toward the door. With Stormwind's charm, I'll be able to walk past the guards, but I'll need a reason for the door to open and shut of its own accord. In a word, I'll need Stonefall.

"You shouldn't do this," Stonefall says.

I shrug. I know he's right, but that doesn't change anything.

He sighs. "You're opposing the High Council, but you may

also undermine it. Blackflame won't be pleased if Stormwind escapes, and he'll hold Talon responsible."

"She's first mage of the High Council, right?" Surely she's protected herself from him?

"Yes. And she's no supporter of his."

Abruptly, Stonefall stiffens, listening. In the other room, a door clicks shut.

"Hurry," he whispers. But it's already too late. As I rush toward the bed, my hand desperately seeking the shadow charm in my pocket, the connecting door swings open and a man steps in.

"Mistress Sunbolt," Jabir says as I plow to a stop beside the bed. "I trust you delivered your glowstone in time."

I exhale with relief. "Guardian Jabir." I touch the fingers of my right hand to my heart. "I never claimed to be more than an apprentice...but you are right, the glowstone was quite useful."

"Jabir?" Stonefall says, utterly bewildered. "You know this woman?"

The old man smiles. "The mageling had some strange story about needing to deliver a glowstone to you. Her intentions seemed honorable so I let her through. I am certainly glad of it." To me he says, "It was well done."

"You knew I was lying."

"There was some truth in each thing you said," he observes. "And you carry the favor of the phoenix in your boot."

Ah. That explains the look he gave my feet back at the gates.

"The phoenix?" Stonefall echoes.

"I...came through the Burnt Lands." Remembering that nightmare place, anger sparks within me. "Why is the portal there still open? I sought a portal near Fidanya, and that was the closest. It's a death trap. It should have been closed ages ago."

"It's marked," Stonefall says. "The color of the path is tinged with red, to warn travelers away. To close it from the other side would be near impossible. The dangers of the land itself, and the lack of magic to work with.... How did you escape?"

"I ran." The words are hard, flat. I had not realized that I was angry at all, but now I'm furious that the portal still stands open. "Another mage came after me. One of Blackflame's hirelings sent to track down any of Stormwind's allies."

"What?" Stonefall and Jabir demand simultaneously.

"Most of them rode to her valley—I'm pretty sure they destroyed her house. I made it to Sonapur and found they'd put a guard on the portal. I created a diversion and got past them—but one followed me."

"Into the Burnt Lands?" Stonefall asks.

"Yes. But," I raise a hand, let it fall. "He didn't make it out. One of the spell-beasts caught him." My stomach twists as I remember the fine leather boot lying in the road, splintered bone protruding from its top. "I never learned his name."

Jabir asks, "And the phoenix?"

"He helped me escape."

"Why the feather?" Jabir presses.

I rub my hand over my mouth. "He thinks I can unravel the enchantments that hold the Burnt Lands."

"You're an *apprentice*," Stonefall snaps.

"Tell us why," Jabir says. "Why would he think a mageling would succeed where whole teams of mages have failed?"

I look him straight in the eye. "Because I unraveled a part of a spell-creature as it attacked the building I sheltered in, the one that killed the mage."

Stonefall leans back against his pillows, closes his eyes. He looks drawn, exhausted. Jabir, however, looks somehow younger, his old eyes almost gleaming, and the wrinkles around his mouth deepening as if he holds back a smile. "Indeed," he murmurs. "Indeed."

Stonefall opens his eyes, fixing Jabir with a hard look. "Master Jabir," he says. "The young lady has attracted a good deal of attention with her working here today. It will not go well with her if she is found."

"It is my duty to guard the Mekteb and its mages," Jabir replies. "Today a mage was attacked as I sat by. I am not pleased." I have the distinct feeling that, of the three of us, Jabir is the most powerful. He meets Stonefall's gaze calmly. "Who attacked you?"

"A hooded person," Stonefall says. "A man, I think. He did not speak."

Jabir crosses the room and rests his hand on Stonefall's forehead. "Show me."

Stonefall closes his eyes, and Jabir's hand slides down to cover them. Stonefall flinches, takes a faint, gasping breath, and then goes still. For a long, long moment, they remain frozen, and then Jabir drops his hand. Stonefall wipes the sweat from his upper lip with a shaking hand.

"A mage," Jabir says, voice soft with anger. "Though he wished to be thought a common assassin, using that dart. At least you fought him. With that wound, he'll be easier to identify."

"He'll hide in a corner licking his wounds till he's better," Stonefall says with disgust. "He was no more than a dog doing his master's bidding."

Jabir clicks his tongue. "The politics of the Mekteb have grown dark indeed."

"Not the Mekteb," Stonefall counters. "The High Council."

"You had best leave as soon as you are able. I'll put a ward on your rooms. Should anyone enter with an intention to cause harm, I will know it." He moves toward the door.

"What of the girl?" Stonefall points his chin at me. "She cannot stay here in safety."

Jabir eyes me thoughtfully. "She is a free mage, yes?"

"I serve my mistress," I say, wondering at the term *free mage*.

"And who would that be, truly?"

I've already told him so much, I may as well tell him this. "Mistress Stormwind."

"Ah, yes. Poor Mistress Stormwind. I remember her well. She's one of only a few high mages who never knowingly compromised her principles."

"Then you...don't believe the verdict is just?" I press, feeling a thousand times better already.

"I believe that mages are people," he says quietly. "And that makes them very dangerous to each other, and to the lands. My loyalty lies with this school, and with this land. But if I were loyal to one such as Stormwind," he raises his brows, "then I would not accept such a verdict."

"Jabir, she's half-trained and already in danger simply by being here," Stonefall says.

Jabir shrugs, moving toward the door. "When you are ready to leave, mageling, I will be sure to look in a different direction."

"Thank you," I manage.

He glances at Stonefall. "With your permission, once I've set the wards on your rooms, I will dismiss the guards."

Stonefall nods. With a dip of his head toward me, Jabir departs.

I take a step after him, toward the door, even though the guards are still there. My steps are so light I'm almost dancing. A way out. I have a way out. I know where the keys are. I know where Stormwind is. There are still quite a few more details to work out, but—

"You're planning your own death," Stonefall says behind me.

I turn to face him. "I know," I agree amiably, since it's easier than arguing.

"You don't," he snarls. I back up a step, surprised at the ferocity of his words. "Even if you both should escape, the Council will hunt you until they find you. And when they discover what you are—it will not go well for you."

"What am I?" I ask carefully.

"A rogue," he says. "And that is what I hunt."

I remember his wall of weapons with a sinking sensation. But if there were that many rogue mages, surely there'd be a lot more talk about them. "How many rogue mages are there?" I ask warily.

He shakes his head, as if reading my thoughts. "Very few. I primarily hunt rogue creatures: fangs that break their agreements with the Council, or won't agree in the first place; lycans who go feral; various other creatures that cause trouble; breathers. If you escape, I have no doubt I will be one of the mages sent after you."

Which means I'm getting help from the man who will hunt me down. "At least I've told you all about me. That should make it easier to track me."

"This is *not* a joke."

"I know that," I reply, and the anger I felt earlier sparks to fire inside of me. "Do you know how I came to Stormwind? I lived in Karolene. A *rogue mage* by the name of Blackflame took me prisoner because I was trying to help a noble family escape him. His men caught us all, killed the lord and lady, and took their children and me back to him. He kept us in a set of cages in the basement of his house. He let a *rogue fang* named Kol feed off the youngest, a little girl, and agreed to give me to Kol as payment for a favor. Kol got me, even though I managed to help the others escape, and he locked me in a tower room with a breather. And do you know what?"

Stonefall shakes his head once, his eyes intent on me.

"That *breather* and I escaped together. That breather risked his life to help me when Kol caught up with us. And when I killed Kol with a spell, that breather nursed me back to life and delivered me to Stormwind to be trained. So don't tell me I don't know about danger, or running, or hiding. And don't tell me about rogues. You don't know *anything* about rogues if you think all breathers are rogues, yet you call Blackflame a mage."

I take a deep breath and hold it to keep from ranting further. The silence after my words is deafening.

Stonefall makes no move, his dark eyes steady on me, his expression completely inscrutable. Then he nods once, to himself, and says, "What of the Shadow League?"

I start, staring at him. What can he possibly know about that? About my connections to them? "They're in Karolene," I manage.

"Not since your friends came here."

"My friends? What are you talking about?"

"The Degaths."

I open my mouth, close it again.

"You just told me your story," Stonefall observes mildly.

"I didn't name them." Even in my anger, I'd been careful to only call them a noble family. I'd named Blackflame and Kol without concern, though.

"No," he agrees. "What you don't know is that when the Degaths escaped, they came here. The High Council had just arrived, and they immediately petitioned for Blackflame to be removed from his post in Karolene, citing what they claimed had passed."

"What they *claimed*?"

He holds up a hand to stay my protest. "In addition to laying their parents' deaths at Blackflame's feet, they showed the half-healed wounds the youngest daughter had on her neck, and claimed it was given to her by a rogue fang lord named Kol. I was sent to investigate him."

My hands tighten into fists around the cloth of my robes. "You went."

"I did," he agrees. "I took three mages with me, because fangs rarely attain power without support from their own. We found a burial ditch of bloodless corpses, and more than a few children with neck wounds. So we broke apart the clan he had gathered in his fortress. We also found the place where he died. It had the memory of sunshine and ash seared into it. A spell that, had the one who cast it survived, might be a called a *sunbolt*."

And I, in my foolishness, gave Jabir that name. And he used it for me, in front of Stonefall.

"The Degaths called you a thief and a hero, but not a mage. Your magic was unsigned then as it is now. Your stories line up very well. Except," Stonefall holds his words for a heartbeat, "you should be dead."

I glance away. "It was close."

"It never occurred us that the breather who escaped at the same time might take care of you."

"Because all breathers are rogues."

A pause.

"Perhaps not," Stonefall allows.

I stare.

He gestures abruptly to the wardrobe. "Stormwind's pack is in there. I suggest you take what you need from it and leave the Mekteb."

He has to tell me to leave. That's his only choice. The smartest thing I can do is pretend to comply. I retrieve Stormwind's pack and go through it quickly—I already have the charms. I find little else she might need if I break her out. Spare clothes will be the least of her worries, and easily stolen at that. The herbs, on the other hand…I transfer the pouches and jars to my pack, nestling them among my clothes. My fingers brush the cool wood of the crow statuette as I tug at my spare skirt. Val would probably be as displeased with my actions as Stormwind. I bite back a grin and make sure the little wooden figure is well protected before closing up my pack and returning Stormwind's to the wardrobe.

"Take this as well." Stonefall offers me a new glowstone. "Wear the look-away and wait here until I've been gone a quarter hour. If Jabir hasn't gotten rid of the lycans already, I'll demand they escort me. That will be your chance."

"All right." I add the stone to my pouch of charms. "Is it easy for mages to sense this at work?" I ask, turning the wire ring of the look-away over in my fingers. It's such a slight charm to hold such power.

"Not particularly. Once it takes effect, there's almost no sign of magic at work."

That's something, then. I slip it on and sit down to wait, my back against the wardrobe.

INVISIBILITY

Leaving Stonefall's rooms is as easy as opening the door and stepping out, the look-away charm on my finger. I pad down the hall, past the alabaster raven to the Seven Claw Stairwell. As I reach the ground floor, an older woman in mage's robes sweeps past as if I were not there at all.

Suppressing a grin, I turn toward the exit and stop. The double wooden doors before me stand closed. I need to leave the building unobserved, which leaves me very few options. I take the best of them and stand to the side and wait.

Just as I'm beginning to think no one will ever decide to use the doors again, a student comes down the stairs and heads for the doors. I fall in behind him, careful to step lightly, and slip away. My breath freezes in my lungs. His gaze flickers over the wall and back to the door, now closed. Does he sense me somehow?

My breath begins to burn in my lungs, but I don't dare let it out. If he reaches out an arm, he'll find me....

With a frown, he turns away, heading up the arcade. I exhale softly and step back to lean against the wall.

It's early afternoon, the sun still high in the sky. No more than two hours have passed since I first entered the Mekteb. Now, however, the students walking down the arcade dart glances at those they pass—and there are few indeed who walk alone. The gardens seem conspicuously empty, until I spot the forms of two white-turbaned guards pacing a central pathway, their leather and velvet armor and sheathed swords hardly comforting.

I cannot see their faces clearly, from here, but I don't need to—I know they are members of the lycan guard, sworn to protect the High Council. Even though they have nothing to do with the monsters of my past, I cannot banish the memory of James attacking me in his demi-form, human but for a wolf's head. I take a shaky breath, push away my memories. It's up to me to keep myself safe now. Panicking will not help.

Word has spread about the attack on Stonefall and the presence of a rogue mage at the school. Everyone is looking for me. I need to find a way to disappear fast, and a shadow-charm, however handy it may be, will eventually attract attention. I need something more subtle than magic to keep me safe.

I remain pressed against the wall, observing the movement of mages, servants, and the guards on patrol. The servants are mostly locals, though some appear to have come here from elsewhere. The students clearly hail from all Eleven Kingdoms, their skins ranging from darkest cocoa to golden bronze. I fall into step behind a trio of girls as they pass me, talking cheerfully of the play they intend to watch this afternoon. They provide the perfect cover for my footsteps, should we happen to pass any lycans.

I follow them down a path to a second row of buildings facing another garden, and right into another building—a dormitory, it seems, where they intend to collect the rest of their friends. I slip off the charm in an empty stairwell. I can do this, I tell myself firmly, and walk confidently out, heading down the covered arcades and ignoring the occasional curious glance. A mage in mage's disguise. It works perfectly, at least for the places where mages are expected to be.

But I need more than that. I need invisibility, and that's precisely what I intend to find. I stride past an armory, two or three buildings that appear to be workshops, and finally spot what I'm looking for. There, near the currently closed rear gate, stand two humble-looking buildings: the servants' quarters. I pass the first one with barely a glance. A group of young men in servants' attire lounge about the front door. The second building will be the women's quarters.

Sliding on the look-away as I turn the far corner, I follow the back wall of shuttered windows until I reach an open window. I wait there, listening. After a few minutes there's a faint rustle. I move on. Through the second open window, I catch the sound of a whispered conversation. The third offers up a silent room. A quick peek over the windowsill shows me a closed door, four beds of which two remain unmade, and a pile of rumpled clothes beside a pair of wooden storage trunks. Ten minutes later, I have a set of servants' clothing—

the same white *selvar* and long, dark-green tunic the serving girl Rehan wore. The tunic's a bit loose about my shoulders and wide around my middle, but who am I to complain? If anyone asks, I'm new and still need to alter my clothes to fit better.

I stuff my robes and tunic into my now bulging pack and wrap it up in my skirt, tucking the resulting bundle under my arm. I don't want to leave it anywhere. Hiding it in plain sight seems the best option.

The look-away in my pocket, I head back to the center of campus. Even carrying my bundle, hardly anyone spares me a glance. Certainly I draw less notice than I did as a mage. I lower my head to hide my smile, and walk quietly through the Mekteb.

One can only hope everything else will go as smoothly.

I follow the paths between the outer buildings, keeping an eye out for a likely servant. With the Festival fully underway by now, the grounds are clearing out. Only a few groups of students stand about, waiting for their friends to finally get ready. There are very few adults visible beyond the guards. But the servants continue going about their duties. I want one who will look kindly on me and not question my ignorance.

As I reach a path running between two buildings I spot an elderly servant trundling toward me, pushing a handcart filled with dirty linens.

I offer him a hesitant smile. "Excuse me," I say in Tradespeak.

He slows to a stop. "Yes?"

I drop my gaze to the ground, shifting my weight from one foot to the other. "I'm very sorry, it's just— I'm new and I'm supposed to go to Susulu Hall and I don't remember which one it is."

"Ah," he says, glancing at my bundle and dismissing it as nothing more than a delivery or the like. "No trouble, that. The buildings all look the same till you know what to look for. Watch the floors under the arcades." He gestures to the building at our side. "This here is Zilant Hall. A Zilant is a long-tailed dragon with wings. So what did the tile layers put underfoot? A mosaic with a zilant."

"So a susulu…" I say hesitantly.

"One of the water people—the mosaic'll show you a woman with a fish tail." He massages one of his shoulders. "For Äbädä Hall, you'll see an old woman in among some trees and birds and such. Best they could do for a forest spirit, it seems. Shahmaran Hall, of course, is the snake queen."

"Oh, thank you!" I don't have to pretend the rush of gratitude I feel.

He returns my smile. "You're welcome." He points down the pathway. "Susulu is the second building down from the Great Hall. You'd best run along and get your work done. We've only a couple hours left before it's our holiday, too."

It's all I can do to keep my smile in place. Two hours? Not that I begrudge the servants getting time off as well, but…

"Thank you," I repeat, and set off at a brisk pace.

An hour or two should at least give me enough time to scout out where First Mage Talon's rooms are. Unfortunately, I doubt I'll be able to manufacture a pretext to get into her rooms until tomorrow if I'm supposed to be off work so soon.

I cut across the main garden toward Susulu Hall. To my left, the domed building rises in all its glory—the Great Hall, as the servant called it—where the High Council has meeting rooms for the duration of their stay. While I've always known that the High Council travels each year to a different land, being tied to no one Kingdom, I didn't consider what this would mean in terms of where they met. What do they do in other kingdoms, where there are no schools to welcome them?

A group of Promises hurry past me, their robes flying, their voices hushed with excitement, barely noticing me in my servant's garb. It seems too…innocent and young a place for something as serious as the High Council. Then again, for me the idea of the High Council has always been indelibly linked to fear of discovery. These students have nothing to fear. What would it have been like to come here? What if my parents had declared my Promise instead of hiding me?

Utterly pointless reflections, these. I wouldn't be the same person, or have known Stormwind, or burned myself to a cinder or any of a hundred other things. My father would still be dead, and my mother would still have gone to Blackflame, seeking his help. But I would have been safe here, and Blackflame wouldn't have cut me off from her. Couldn't have, because I would have had the Mekteb's mages to help me separate facts from lies, and my mother could have found me here easily when she wished.

But she could have found me in Karolene regardless, if she'd tried, just as I found her from Stormwind's valley. She didn't, and it's this truth that has caught at me every time I pulled up her reflection in the crystal clear waters of the lake. Was she protecting me in some way, or was she glad to be rid of me?

The path ahead curves around a fountain. Crouched among the bushes that grow alongside the far side a trio of boys gather around something on the ground. They keep looking up, over their shoulders, talking to each other in explosive whispers. One of them spots me and grins, surprising me from my train of thought, but he looks away again just as quickly. As I near them, a small black thing flies out of the bushes straight toward me.

Skreeeeeeeeeeeeeeee!

I shout, diving to the side as it screeches past. It turns at the touch of a slight breeze, sailing high over the gardens and slamming into the stone face of the building behind us. With a barely audible whine, it bounces down off the arcade.

I lie on the ground, my ears filled with its echo, and remember...being cornered. I know this memory, but in this moment it is fresher, more detailed than what I pulled from the ashes under Stormwind's guidance.... Guards with black armbands surrounded me, and then another such charm shrieked past us, distracting them. I close my eyes, not caring that I'm lying in the middle of a path at a mage-ridden school of sorcery. I slide into the memory, running pell-mell through a busy marketplace, down back alleys between stalls, and then bursting through the back of a fruit stand, the old woman there offering to hide me, a young boy on the other side of the counter watching wide-eyed as I climbed into a crate of green coconuts, the close darkness of my hiding place. And that's all.

I take a shuddering breath and push myself to my feet, even though I want nothing more than to stay in that memory, catch hold of each detail while it pulses fresh in my mind. The boys shout with laughter, the bushes they hid in shaking and rustling as they give voice to their amusement. I catch a scattering of noise as those journeymen and apprentices along the arcades realize what has happened, laughing behind upraised hands.

I grab my pack and bundle it up again as the boys mock

the way I'd cried out. If I could, I'd march over there and throttle them. My plan was to walk unnoticed through the grounds. Instead, I'm the center of attention. All I can do now is make as little fuss as possible, and get *away*.

I get no more than three feet down the path before a guard in leather armor rounds the corner of the fountain at a sprint, his boots crunching against the gravel. I plow to a halt. His gaze cuts between me and the boys, taking in the scene at once. He raises his hand to me, palm out in a silent command to wait, and crosses to the bushes. Catching the nearest two boys by their ears, he brings them to their feet with yelps of pain. The remaining boy scrambles up, his laughter wiped away by surprise.

"You'll be apologizing to the young miss now," the lycan orders.

"Apologize?" says the elder of the two boys he holds, as surprised as I am. He cannot be more than thirteen, though from the way he tries to brace his feet and hold up his nose, despite his captive ear, he thinks himself a grown man. "To a servant?"

"No," the guard says. "To the young woman you insulted. I'm not concerned with her occupation." The third boy backs away. "You as well," he says sharply. "Don't think I don't have your scent by now."

The boy hurries toward me, followed up by the guard still holding his two flinching captives. He is built tall and lithe, with a long thin face and tawny brown wolf's eyes. I would estimate him to be perhaps twenty-five, certainly no more than thirty years. He smiles as he meets my gaze, his teeth preternaturally sharp.

I look away, my heart pounding, my mouth going dry. He looks nothing like James, and yet I cannot think past the memory of the wolf-headed man who attacked me in Kol's tower, the way Val had breathed from him, aging him decades in a matter of moments. How terrified and *grateful* I'd been to watch James die.

The boys come to a stop some feet away. "Sorry, miss," one of them mumbles.

"All of you," the lycan says, and the boys at his left yelps. I almost feel sorry for their ears.

I nod at the chorus of apologies that rise up.

"And you won't do it again," he prods, letting the two boys go. They back away, the third with them, shaking their heads emphatically. "Because if I hear of anything happening, I'll know who to look for," the lycan adds, giving them a sharp-toothed smile.

"No sir," one of the boys gibbers. "We'll be good, we will."

The lycan nods, and the boys bolt down the path. The other witnesses who so enjoyed my fright have gone on their way by now. But there are four more lycan guards standing silently a few paces away.

"All right, miss?" the lycan asks.

I jump. "I— yes, fine," I mumble, terribly aware of the keenness of his gaze, the silence of his movements. And the fact that I am surrounded by guards.

The lycan nods at the other guards, and they move off at once. He must outrank them. "Will you allow me to walk you where you're going?" He gestures vaguely toward the garden, the buildings on the other side.

"Susulu Hall," I say, trying not to clutch my pack too tightly. Hopefully, the skirt is doing a good enough job of hiding it—checking would only draw his attention.

"Of course." He starts forward and I fall into step with him. This is bad. I was supposed to be the invisible serving girl going about my business. Now I have a high-ranking lycan escort. Could I be any more conspicuous?

"Have you been working long at the Mekteb?" he asks as we leave the garden. We cross a wide cobbled walk and step under an arcade. The mosaic beneath this arcade is all blues and greens, sea creatures twining along the edges. At the center swim water maidens, their long hair spread about them.

"Just started," I mutter, keeping my head bent. He's probably taken a good look at my face by now, but the less he remembers, the better. In fact, the more I sound like an embarrassed maidservant, the better.

"Ah," he says knowingly. "That explains why you're wearing someone else's clothes."

I stumble slightly. His hand whips out, steadying me. I go still at his touch.

"And why you're afraid of me."

I pull my arm free, glaring straight ahead at the doors of the hall. "I'm not afraid."

"She has a voice," he says, eyes twinkling. I feel myself flushing and have to purse my lips from replying. I'm supposed to be a no-one. The less I give him, the better.

"We don't bite, you know," he adds.

No, I don't know, I think, but I don't say it. He thinks me harmless, and I want him to forget me as soon as possible.

"I must go. I'm late," I tell him, keeping my voice steady.

"Then go." He dips his head and takes his leave, grinning.

A MAP OF THE WORLD

I roam the building until I find a young woman polishing the second floor stair railing. She's dressed in the same garb I am, though the ends of her sleeves have two embroidered diamonds, as white as her *selvar*.

"Oh, hello," I say with undisguised relief. "Can you help me? I'm new and I'm supposed to help with the cleaning, but I've gotten turned around."

"You're supposed to be cleaning here?" Frown lines crease her forehead.

"I think so," I say with a grin and shrug. "Yesterday was my first day, and everything's a bit of a jumble. Can I help you?"

The girl brightens, any concern for whether I'm in the right place evaporating. "Sure. I'm Esra."

"Rehan," I reply, happily stealing the name of Jabir's helper.

Esra takes me to a supply closet, and is only slightly surprised when I ask if I can leave my bundle there while I clean. "I don't have a room yet," I explain. "Once the Festival is over they'll find me a place."

"Oh yes," she says knowingly. "There are always a few servants who miss work and lose their positions. You'll have a room within a couple days."

She outfits me with a bucket and brush, and sets me to scrubbing stairs. I start near her, and within a few minutes I have her chatting about working at the Mekteb—and then about the shocking events of the day, and what she found out from her friends a little while ago.

"A rogue mage, can you believe it? Must have been a mage, rather than a wild Promise, to have everyone in such an uproar. Walked right in here and healed a high mage and then walked right back out." She sits back on her heels and shakes her head. "The Council wanted to shut down the whole campus, but Headmistress Jeweltongue wouldn't have it."

"Why not?" I ask curiously.

"Because it's the Council," Esra mutters under her breath. I ease back on my heels as well, waiting expectantly. "They've been causing trouble all year. Anyhow, Jeweltongue said the mage was probably long gone, and all a lockdown would do is strand most of the students outside the walls, and she couldn't do that. She's posted extra guards and mages at all the entrances instead."

"So they're still letting people out?"

"Last I heard." Esra flexes her fingers, then picks up her brush again. "Least ways, *I* don't intend to miss the Festival over some mage who goes about unexpectedly healing people. There's much worse in the world, you know."

I have to agree with that. "Are there other ways out?"

She sighs. "Not with all the trouble we've had today. But they'll get an earful from me if they don't let us out!"

By the time we reach the third floor, my arms ache, my fingers feel like they're going to fall off, and we have finally reached what I came here for.

"What's that?" I ask, pointing my brush at the single arched doorway at the top of the stairs, the wooden door a work of wonder, carved with flowers and trees, animals of all sorts peeking out from behind them. I blink as a monkey drops down from the branches of a tree, sending up a flurry of butterflies that come to rest on the leaves carved across the top of the door.

"First Mage Talon's rooms," Esra says. "She had that done her first week here."

There is no way I would dare try to enter on my own. As much as I need to get in, as little time as I have, I can't risk doing something stupid and getting caught. It's likely warded against all attempts at entry, both magical and mundane. I'll have to find another way in.

"It's beautiful," I say, and bend down to scrub the next stair. "I bet she has some amazing things. Wish I could clean in there."

Esra laughs in agreement. "She's very particular. Only Housekeeper Yilmaz is allowed to clean her rooms. And they're always locked when she's not in, so it's not like we can just peek in."

I make a face. "Are all the mages that picky? I can't imagine they each have a housekeeper assigned."

"No, just First Mage Talon and Arch Mage Blackflame."

My fingers convulse on the scrubbing brush. "Blackflame?" I echo. "I've heard of him."

"Haven't we all," she agrees. "He's down a floor. He won't let anyone into his rooms, though. Brought a servant with him to do his cleaning. And his own source slave."

I flinch.

She nods, though she can't know what I'm thinking. "It makes the apprentices really nervous to see source slaves walking around. Although, for the most part, this one stays in his rooms."

"What do they look like?" I ask, against my better judgement. "What's so different about them?"

"There's something about their eyes," Esra whispers. "And of course they have those tattoos on their arms, the ones that bind them."

"What about their eyes?" I press. I already know about the ink spells used to bind source slaves' magic so that they can only funnel it to their masters. Stormwind made sure I understood that much. But she never mentioned anything about eyes.

"I don't know how to describe it. You'll see," Esra says with a slight shudder.

I nod, but I hope I won't. I don't want to know what my eyes might look like if I get caught.

Once we finish, we stow away our cleaning supplies in the large basement closet and I collect my skirt-wrapped bundle.

"Are you going out to the Festival?" Esra asks as she stretches her back, hands on her hips.

"Not tonight." There is no way I'd risk going through even the servants' gate today, no matter how helpful it might be to speak with the Degaths. At her look of disbelief, I add, "I promised my uncle I'd go straight back to his house. He might let me go out with my cousins a bit."

"*Might?*"

I shrug. But if I want Esra's help getting out at some point, now is the time to ask for it. "I'm hoping to go out tomorrow night anyhow. I, uh…"

"Yes?" She looks at me expectantly.

I duck my head. "I have a friend I was hoping to meet."

Esra snorts with laughter. "Let me guess, your uncle has no idea?"

"Well, he's very protective," I say, figuring that if I did have an uncle out there, he would not at all be pleased with what I'm up to. "But if I can get a place to stay here tomorrow night, then he won't have to worry about it."

She glances at my pack, then turns toward the hall. I fall into step with her. "Well, if you still don't have a room tomorrow, maybe you can share mine. I'll talk to the girls I room with."

"Really?"

She meets my surprise with an open smile. "Yeah."

Guilt twists in my gut at how I'm using her, how easy it would be to take further advantage of her friendship. I hope she never finds out who I really am. "Thanks," I say with a strained smile. "Do you start here first thing in the morning?"

She nods. "All day, every day. I'll be here at first bell. What about you? Are you split between buildings?"

"I'm not sure. I guess I'll find out in the morning." I grin.

"Well, I hope you're here. It will be a huge help."

"What about Housekeeper Yilmaz?" I ask. "I thought you said she cleans too?"

"Oh no! She only cleans First Mage Talon's rooms. Housekeepers hardly ever clean. They keep order, make sure everything gets done. They're the ones who handle the mages directly most of the time. Yilmaz is in charge of three buildings."

Which might explain why I haven't met her yet. "Three!"

"Yes— she has Susulu, Äbädä, and Neme."

I nod, filing away the names, though I doubt I'll need them. "Do housekeepers live in the servants' quarters as well?"

She raises her brows. "Not in a hundred years. Housekeepers can choose to live in the city, or in one of the buildings they're assigned to. Yilmaz has her own rooms downstairs—two rooms!" Esra pauses at the side door leading out to a path between the buildings. "One day, I'm going to have the same thing."

"I think you will." I really hope she does.

"I definitely will," she says. "Coming?"

"Actually, I think I'd better go back and, um, wash up," I

say with a touch of awkwardness. "I'll see you tomorrow."

She grins, departing with a cheery wave.

I head down to the basement. The supply closet here is larger than the ones located on each floor, and has a small washroom next to it for servants. I wash up first, then slip into the supply closet, pulling the door shut behind me. Somewhere on this floor are Yilmaz's rooms, and I don't want to accidentally run into her quite yet. Nor do I want my growling stomach to give me away at the wrong time. I slip out my glowstone, set it on a shelf, and dig out the last of the cheese I'd packed. It's hard and salty, the flavor stronger than I like, but I have to eat something and it won't keep much longer.

As I eat, I consider what I need to do this evening. My best hope of getting the key to Stormwind's shackles is tomorrow morning, using Yilmaz to get into Talon's rooms. But I also need to learn all I can about where Stormwind is being held, which means I need to visit Shahmaran Hall right now—as a servant, before anyone realizes that there shouldn't be any servants walking around anymore.

I pop the last of the cheese into my mouth, and slip the glowstone into my pocket. A brief listen at the door tells me the coast is clear. Letting myself out, I make for the stairs.

The campus is calm and quiet now, the sun dipping past the roofs of the buildings. It's difficult to believe that it was only this morning that I stepped into Stonefall's rooms. There are still guards everywhere, but they aren't patrolling anymore. Instead, they're stationed at different points, keeping watch. They no longer expect to catch their rogue sneaking about, it seems.

I walk briskly along the arcades, nodding to the guards I pass as I reach them, and otherwise keeping my gaze decidedly elsewhere. I check the tiles beneath my feet at each building. I don't exactly know what Shahmaran, the snake queen, looks like, but I expect I'll recognize her when I see her.

I reach the end of the walk without seeing anything likely, and cross to the two buildings that run along the bottom of the garden. Lots of strange people and animals appear in the floor tiles, but no snakes and no queens. I start back up the other side, walking toward the Grand Hall now, parallel to where I'd come down, hoping to God the guards haven't noticed my circuit and aren't wondering what I'm doing.

Shahmaran turns out to be the building directly across the gardens from Susulu Hall, and two buildings over from where Stonefall lives in White Raven Hall.

When I reach the door, the nearest guard tilts his head, studying me. He looks vaguely familiar.

"Took the long way around, eh?" the other guard says.

"I…got a bit turned around," I admit. "I'm new and, um, I couldn't remember which one was Shahmaran," I gesture to the tiled image of a beautiful woman with a crown on her head, and, from the waist down, a coiling serpent tail.

I glance back at the guards, and realize where I know the first guard from. "Also, there were some boys in the garden earlier today who played a trick on me. I didn't really want to chance going through there again."

The guard nods, a single decisive dip of his head. "Saw that. It doesn't happen often, as I understand it. Even when we're not around, the school won't stand for it. The boys have been reported and the Mekteb's Headmistress will deal with them." He offers a friendly smile. "Well, go on then. You'll want to finish up your work so you can get to the Festival."

I grin with relief. "Thank you."

The building lies mostly empty, the faint snatches of a conversation drifting down the hall to me. The main doors open to the center of the building, with a wide hall extending out to the left and the right. There are stairs at both ends, though only the one to my right appears to go down to the basement. I move away from the voices, heading to the stairs I'll need. The doors are mostly open, giving me quick peeks at the classrooms within—bright, cheerful spaces, each with a great central oval table surrounded by chairs, the walls lined with shelves filled with books, and jars, and even what might be charms on display.

At the end of the hall I find a slimmer wooden door, and with a rush of relief I open it to find a supply closet. I stow away my pack and arm myself with a bucket of soapy water, a scrubbing brush, and a drying cloth.

I walk my bucket of soapy water down every hall, working my way up. On the second floor, a long stretch of unbroken wall has been decorated with a mosaic map of the Eleven Kingdoms. I pause to study it, using the edge of my drying cloth to shine a few tiles as I look it over. The map is not very detailed—it's hard to capture fine detail with mosaic. But to my right lie the eastern Kingdoms, each with its name, ruler, and the arch mage that serves it painted on in smooth black strokes. In the middle, the desert stretches long and golden, the Burnt Lands in their midst a darker brown without any label.

I inch along, trailing my cloth over the mosaic, reading the names of the various arch mages, the lands they serve. The ink must be spelled to change as the appointments and rulers change, for not one of them appears to be inaccurate. I pause, tilt my head, for there is Karolene to the south with its sprinkling of smaller islands in the ocean. It looks small, surprisingly tiny compared to the great Kingdoms of the mainlands arcing down around it. Beside the central island is written, "Karolene, Regent Siwatu, Arch Mage Blackflame."

My hand tightens into a fist around the cloth. *Regent?* Is the sultan dead? And what about his crown prince? There was one—I thought there was one, at least.

I push away from the wall, tamping down on my agitation. I know so little. I barely know who I was back then. What can I possibly know of the political situation? Still, that line of writing, those lines together, strike me as wrong.

Faintly, I hear the tap of feet on the stairs behind me. I make myself walk on. Up the opposite stairs, the third floor lies empty and silent, the doors closed. I walk it anyway, find nothing of note. I take the stairs up to the roof. The door at the top remains unlocked, and from the benches and potted plants on the rooftop, it's clear that the space is often used. From here, the many domes of the Great Hall look vast and beautiful, glittering in the late afternoon light. To their left, I can see past the far boundary walls to the city itself, the buildings crowded together but still well cared for here. To my right, the rest of the campus stretches out, the myriad rooftops cutting each other off from sight.

I walk the rooftop garden slowly, keeping away from the edge so I'm not spotted from below. Freeing Stormwind and then bolting for an exit won't work—not with the number of guards already at the gates and the likelihood that a magical alarm will alert them before we ever reach them. A rooftop escape, I decide, chewing at my lip. It will have to be the roof. After all, no one ever looks up.

Getting her off the roof will be a trick. I haven't learned any transformation spells as yet, nor can Stormwind turn herself into a sparrow and flit away unobserved—not with a binding spell on her. I'll need a way to lift her to safety somehow. Looking out over the rooftop, I know suddenly and clearly exactly what I can do. I just don't want to do it.

Every step of this plan seems to steal away a little bit more of what future I have left to me.

I rub my face, move back to look at the rooftop door. Before I worry about leaving the rooftop, I'll need to get Stormwind here in the first place. I run my fingers over the lock, the doorframe. I'd prefer to have a key to it, or better yet, charm it so that it won't lock properly. But I don't dare use my magic so flagrantly—at least, not until I'm on the run and don't care anymore. Not the best of plans, to say the least. If I can find a skeleton key, I'll most certainly steal it.

But this may be my only opportunity to adjust the lock. I pull the door shut and squat beside it in the semidarkness of the stairwell. Resting my hand against it, I study it with my mage sight.

I find two sigils, central points of magic. One, at the center of the door itself, seems to be a protection against breakage and use of force. It's simply cast, as though the mage who set it never imagined anyone would want to remove it. I place my palm over it, take a deep breath, and gently channel the magic out of it, draining it of its power. It's so small, it flickers out without mishap. If I could have used such a trick with Stormwind's trunk, I would have.

The sigil on the lock, however, is designed to protect, and will activate other spells if its magic is interrupted. It's dormant right now, but the more I assess it, the more it worries me. It's designed to seal the door shut through magic and the physical lock mechanism itself. It's also connected to the protective sigils glimmering on the walls. As I reach out with my magical senses, I realize they're interwoven with larger spells that could very well cloak the entire building and connect to a network that covers the entire campus.

Whatever I do to the one sigil will echo back to the whole tapestry of spells, like a thread snagging in a fine fabric. People are already on alert. One snag, and it will be all I can do to escape right now.

I'll just have to be careful. At least, with my senses open, I can feel a continuous tremor of magic in the air, as mages and students and their charms use and release magic across campus. They are small things, nothing great being done at the moment, but it's enough of a steady rumble to hide what I do. I hope.

I grind the heels of my hands into my eye sockets. I can do this. Kneeling before the door, I frame the invisible sigil with my fingers and study it. The only way it would be activated is if someone activated the spells protecting the building—in the case of an emergency. Otherwise, it remains dormant, allowing anyone who wishes to visit the garden.

I almost laugh, realizing the simplest solution. I don't need to destroy the sigil. I need to keep it dormant. To do that, I need to adjust the weave of spells around it.

For a handful of slow, deep breaths I observe the magic, the occasional tiny pulse of energy that flows through the strands, the connections between this sigil and the others, the thicker ropes of the protective spells woven through the building itself.

Three strands of magic. I'll have to adjust three any way I look at it. I wait until the next faint pulse of energy passes and then lift a hand, reaching out with my senses to trace one of the strands. I feed a little drop of magic into it and lengthen the strand, looping it around the central sigil. Now it encircles the sigil as a whole and touches on the two other strands that connect to the sigil.

I take a steadying breath and reach for the two strands anchored to the sigil. I channel a whisper of magic into them right where they touch the sigil, envisioning a tree branch naturally forking, coaxing the strands until they each unfurl a new thread, bright and long enough to reach the loop I created. The edges glimmer blue, and with the lightest brush of my fingertips, I fuse the strands to the loop.

The next pulse will come any moment. Grasping the strands where they attach to the sigil, I ease them free, using the finest touch of magic to separate them, keen as a blade. The spare threads waver, even as the pulse of magic starts across the wall toward me. *No.* I fold the threads back to the loop, smoothing them down with a flick of my fingers before snatching my hands away. My heart hammers in my chest.

The strands flow over each other. As the pulse reaches them, the loop absorbs their magic, sealing the sigil in a vacuum. The pulse sparkles along the strands, following the newly created loop and continuing on, leaving the sigil at its center untouched. I've done it.

With only slightly shaky hands, I gather up my cleaning supplies and start down the stairs. By the time I reach the ground floor, it has fallen silent. I still have one more thing to do. I may have made myself a way out, but I still need a way in. I move to the open doors of the classrooms that look out the back of the building, peeking in each until I find one whose windows are partially blocked by bushes.

Stepping inside, I swing the door shut behind me. I wait for a full minute beside the door, listening for footsteps, for sounds of alarm as someone goes to investigate what I'd done to the rooftop door. The hallway lies silent. Thank God for the Festival. Had the classrooms been filled, all of this would have been impossible.

I cross the room, skirting the large central table surrounded by chairs, a pile of books and a basket of charms at its center, and head for the window with the largest bush planted outside it. These windows are filled with panes of antique glass: heavy, thick stuff that slightly distorts the world beyond. Velvet curtains hang on either side of each window. I reach out tentatively, moving my hand from sill to glass and back again, and find variations on the same two sigils: one for the breakage of the glass, and the other to seal the window shut as a defensive mechanism.

I flex my fingers, and with a small smile, set to work. It only takes a moment to drain the sigil against breaking. Like its counterpart on the door, it isn't connected to any of the other protections, and so its disappearance won't be detected. Then I kneel by the window, frame the sigil on the windowsill that will seal the window as a whole, and wait for the next magical pulse to pass by. I follow the same process as I did with the door's sigil upstairs. It's easier to adjust the strands this time around, though that doesn't keep my heart from pounding.

Finished, I push myself to my knees shakily, collect my bucket, and head for the door. The hallway remains quiet. It seems...absurd. But no one is expecting Stormwind to run. She came of her own volition; no doubt she presented herself as an honorable prisoner. She *is* honorable. But she'll run given the chance. The trial is over, as unjust as it was, and she has nothing left to prove.

As for the guards, they have no reason to connect the rogue mage who healed Stonefall with Stormwind's presence. Still, I need to leave, and quickly, in case some slight tremor of what I've done raises interest. But there's one last place I need to see before I go: the basement.

I take the stairs down, clutching my bucket. At the landing, I make myself start humming. Below, the hallway continues along the length of the building to where it ends. There's no sign of guards—no indication that Stormwind is being kept here at all.

Did Stonefall lie to me? Everything I've done today was built on the premise that he told the truth. Keeping my steps light, I swing my scrubbing brush, humming all the while. I have a pretense to keep up, regardless of what I find.

Doorways, more doorways, and then an intersecting hallway, an underground annex. Relief rushes through me as I reach it. A pair of guards stationed at the stairwell at its end blink at me, tilting their heads, curious but unworried, for they'd heard the lightness in my step, the happy sound of my wordless song.

"Oh!" I say brightly. "I'm so sorry."

I reverse course, pausing only to trade my bucket for my pack, and leave by a side door, nodding to the guards there as I stride down the path.

SEEKER

I spend the remaining hours of the day on the roof of the servants' quarters. Nearly all the servants have already departed for the Festival when I arrive. The girls still lingering on their way out cast me curious glances as I walk briskly through the halls and up the stairs, but a smile and a nod suffice to get me past without any questions. The rooftop is a mix of open use space, cluttered with old benches retired from the rooftops of finer buildings, and rows upon rows of laundry lines, about half of which are filled.

I make my way to the back corner, well hidden behind the laundry, and there I stay. I eat a bit of the dried, spiced goat meat I brought with me, and rest my back against the low wall that encloses the roof and think about what I'm trying to do, and how I'm going to do it. There are no easy answers, no one simple plan. There are so many factors that will have to fall into place for Stormwind to have any chance of escaping.

The only thing I can do is run contrary to every expectation the lycans and mages who hold her captive will have. If they expect her to run away through the campus, she must depart right over their heads. In fact, they'll expect her to run at once, just as the mages who came to Stonefall's aid thought I must have fled already when I was hiding all the time in his room.

If I can find a way to hide her for even an hour or two within the building itself, getting her away will be that much easier. I'll also need a place for us to go, and a way to protect Stormwind from being traced. My string of wards might work at first, but eventually we'll need something stronger that she can walk with. I'm going to need help—as much as I can do, I don't think I can manage all this alone. But before I go seeking allies, I need the key to Stormwind's shackles.

Taking out the herbs I have with me, I sort through them. Half are meant to be taken orally, through tisanes or mixed into a broth. But a few are for physical applications, and they might not agree with a person if ingested, which would serve my purposes admirably. Unfortunately, the best of my options is also the bitterest.

Rising, I slip on the look-away and go back downstairs, ghosting through the halls, checking for unlocked doors. At each door I pause and listen, then bend down to peek beneath the crack, checking for light. The rooms on the third and highest floor are larger than those on the ground floor, and house only two occupants per room. These must be the servants at the top of the pecking order, one step down from housekeepers. They certainly have more clothes and finer belongings than what I'd seen in the ground-floor rooms earlier today.

From one room I filch a small ceramic bowl, nicely painted and filled with bits and pieces of things. I leave the contents behind and keep looking, until, in the second-to-last room, I find a tray of baked sweets on a table—flaky pastry with a layer of chopped nuts at the center, doused in a sugary syrup and carefully covered with a clean cloth. Perfect. The syrup is so heavy it's unlikely Housekeeper Yilmaz will notice the dusting of herbs I'll add in between the layers. After all, if Yilmaz is used to cleaning Talon's rooms on her own, she'll need some reason to take me in with her tomorrow. Tainted sweets is the best I can come up with.

I arrange almost a third of them in the bowl I'd taken, then cover the tray once more, murmuring an apology to the true owner. Then I take myself back upstairs to hide behind the laundry lines for the rest of the night.

Esra greets me with unaffected pleasure the following morning. "You're back! I was hoping you would be."

I smile. "So was I. But I'm not quite sure of anything still—I couldn't find the housekeeper I spoke with yesterday. Perhaps I should talk to Housekeeper Yilmaz?"

Esra's expression falls, but she nods. "You probably should." She gestures toward the stairs down. "She hasn't come up yet. You could try knocking. Hers is the third door on the right."

I'd already discovered which rooms were Yilmaz's early this morning, when I'd left her a present on her doorstep. Now I shift uncomfortably and suggest, "Why don't I help clean until she comes up?"

"Fine by me," Esra says. "It's a lighter day today—we get off at lunch! No room cleanings, either, only the halls, the stairs, and the windows. Any preference?"

"Halls?"

Esra blinks, and then says, "Are you sure you don't want the windows? They're easier."

They are, but I want to keep an unobtrusive watch on the stairs, not get caught cleaning the windows in the stairwell, or end up too far away to notice Yilmaz going up to Talon's rooms. Assuming she'll clean them today.

"But that's hardly fair to you," I say with forced lightness. "You take the windows, I'll do the halls, and maybe we can split the stairs."

Esra grins and hands me the local version of a broom—the bristles bunched together and tied into a thick, short handle. "Can't argue with that!"

I take the broom and set off down the hall. Without an actual stick attached to the broom, I have to squat to sweep the long bristles across the floor. But my work goes very quickly thanks to the longer reach of the bristles. Once I finish the ground floor, I go up to the second and sweep there as well, pausing to listen every time I hear footsteps.

I am beginning to despair of Yilmaz showing up at all when I hear a slow, heavy tread on the stairs. I take my broom to the hall closet, then move quietly back to the stairs, arriving in time to see the broad back and tightly braided hair of the housekeeper as she turns up the landing. She very nearly drags herself up the stairs, one thick hand gripping the railing tightly.

I follow behind her on silent feet, listening as she gains the landing before Talon's door. Then I patter up behind her.

She leans against the railing, clutching the banister tightly. Catching sight of me, she frowns, eyes burning in an otherwise unnaturally pasty face.

"Mistress Yilmaz?" I come to a stop three steps below her.

"What do you want?"

I flinch at the growl in her voice. She must be feeling terrible. I should have put only a few pastries in the bowl. But

I didn't think she'd eat more than a couple so early in the morning, and I didn't want to give her a half-empty bowl.... At least the herbs I'd used only cause temporary discomfort. By this afternoon she should feel better.

"Well?"

"I— ah, I'm new, and I was told yesterday I could work in Susulu Hall, but—"

"What? Who told you that?"

"I don't know," I stammer, ducking my head. I have to keep my story consistent with the one I told Esra, which only gives me so much wiggle room. "A housekeeper, but I've forgotten her name, and so I cleaned here yesterday with Esra, and today too, but I wanted to check if you were expecting me here."

"No, I'm not."

I let my features fall. "If it's all right—could I please clean here today?"

"And what would you do? Esra is more than able to do her work herself."

For all Esra's happiness to have a cleaning companion, I don't doubt this. She's both efficient and hard working. But it isn't Esra's work I want to do. "Perhaps I might help you?"

"What help could you possibly be? What are you—third level?" Her eyes fall to my sleeves, "Fourth level!"

"Apologies, mistress." I duck my head, realizing belatedly what the embroidered diamonds mean.

I hear a faint gurgle, and Mistress Yilmaz stifles a groan, her head sinking.

"Are you well, mistress?"

She squeezes her eyes shut. "I feel like one of those poor rats the students practice their tricks on."

"Please let me be of service," I plead. Hopefully, reframing my request from offering help—as one might a peer—to serving a mistress will appease her. "I'm sure by tomorrow, with the Festival over, someone will figure out where I should really be."

She considers me, then casts a glance toward Talon's room, one hand massaging her stomach.

"Oh," I gasp on cue, standing on my tiptoes and staring at Talon's door with unabashed awe. Since yesterday, a vine has wrapped its way up the tree, and a snake hangs from one of its branches, its tongue flicking. The butterflies have alighted on the leaves, wings spread open and pulsing slowly.

"First time, eh?" Mistress Yilmaz says, sounding almost

kind.

"It's amazing," I breathe.

She grunts and heaves herself up the remaining stairs to the door. As I hover on the stairs, she pulls a ring of keys from her pocket. A thin chain connects it to a great metal brooch pinned to her skirt. She flips through an array of keys of all different shapes and sizes, some as black as night, some as gold as the sun. As she passes a striped one with a cat's head, it gives a muffled meow.

"You ever cleaned for someone before?" She finds the right key and slides it into the lock.

"Oh yes. I worked for a merchant before this, but they fell on hard times. I did all their cleaning for them, and even some cooking."

She grunts, leaning heavily against the doorframe. "Go on, then."

I offer her my most pitiful look. "I don't suppose…I might be able to— to clean for you?" My eyes dart to the wondrous door and the room beyond it and then back to her.

"What? Should I let a fourth rank servant into First Mage Talon's own rooms?"

I feel my face fall, and drop my eyes in dejection. *Stupid!* I should have asked about the diamonds yesterday and stolen a uniform from a higher-ranked servant. I've lost the better part of a day. I only have through tomorrow before Stormwind will be moved to Gereza Saliti. And I won't be able to try this approach again—unless I can draw out that mix of pity and amusement Yilmaz showed me when I first saw the enchanted door.

"Forgive me," I mumble, hunching my shoulders, as if I know how very pitiful I am, how pathetic my yearnings. And that her commands are to be respected. "The door was so lovely. It must be beautiful inside. I shouldn't have presumed."

I pad slowly down the stairs, head bent in dejection. There's no need to rush. After all, I *want* Yilmaz to call me back. If she doesn't, she'll be safely locked within the First Mage's rooms for the next hour or two. I'll have to wait for her to leave before I try another tactic. Perhaps, now that I know where Yilmaz keeps her key ring, I can try to steal it from her.

"Hey now, girl," she calls after me. "Where'll you be working today?"

"Me?" I turn to her in pretended confusion. "I don't know.

If you don't want me, I don't know what I'll do till tomorrow."

She considers this darkly, then nods decisively. "Then you can do a bit of work for me." She jerks her head toward the doorway.

"Oh! Thank you!" I dash up the stairs, a grin splitting my face.

She eyes me, her expression severe. "You must be very careful not to disturb anything. Do only what I tell you to do."

"Yes, mistress," I reply, coming to a stop and nodding meekly. I follow her in, paying close attention to her directives. We enter a spacious sitting room, furnished with chairs carved from a dark wood, brocade cushions softening their seats. Scrolls depicting scenes from different lands hang from the walls: here a great snow-capped mountain with steep cliffs and scraggly pines, there a sheltering grove, an ornately decorated temple at its center. I peel my gaze away from them, make myself focus as Mistress Yilmaz sets me to dusting the room before she goes on to the next room herself.

I slip my hand into my pocket, wrapping my fingers around the branched end of Stormwind's seeker charm. I have more than a few charms with me, but the seeker is easy enough to find by touch, made of a twig as it is. "I seek the key to Brigit Stormwind's shackles," I murmur. The seeker vibrates in my hand, and then tugs my fingers toward the door leading to the next room. It will have to wait then. I resume my work, cleaning and plumping the cushions with a vengeance.

When I'm done, I step into the next room, a study, only to find Mistress Yilmaz seated at the desk with her arms wrapped around her stomach. "Mistress?" I ask softly. "What shall I do next?"

"This room," she says hoarsely. "Wipe down the bookshelves. Pick up any paper you see and wipe under it, and then put it back exactly as you found it. Exactly. Anything else that needs straightening you may straighten."

"Yes, mistress." I bob my head and start on the far end of the room. The study is a fascinating place, filled to the brim with charms and ingredients for spells, some of which are quite rare. Crammed between two books I find a bottle of salamander eyes. Caught in a glass globe that has rolled into the corner flutters a strange, winged creature, its body glimmering and whirling so fast I cannot make out what it is, though I am sure it's no bird.

Nowhere do I see where the first mage might have secreted a set of keys. Whenever I turn so that Mistress Yilmaz cannot see my hand, I check the seeker charm. Each time, it jumps in my grasp, pressing against the cloth of my tunic toward the other side of the room. I cannot tell, though, if it means the door there, or the desk at which Mistress Yilmaz sits. When I peek at her as I organize and dust off a side table cluttered with jars of herbs, I find her staring down at the desk, unmoving.

I make my way through the room until I reach her at her desk. The seeker very nearly jumps out of my hand when I check it. "Mistress?" I ask with a touch of hesitancy. "Shall I dust the desk as well?"

"What?" Mistress Yilmaz looks up, her eyes glazed. I push down on my guilt. I'll have regrets no matter what course of action I take. I can't think about it right now.

"The desk," I repeat, gesturing toward it with my rag.

"Oh no, not even I may touch the desk. The first mage herself takes care of that."

My heart sinks as I gaze at Mistress Yilmaz's elbows pressed hard against the dark-grained wood. She sends me into the third room, a private sitting room, and from there the bedroom. I dust and wipe and set to order everything in sight, opening the curtains, carrying out the tea tray, and so on. I carefully lift a book off the bed, moving it to the floor so that I can straighten the sheets and blanket. A line catches my eye as I set it down: *those bound under such spell can make no casting of their own.*

I drop to my knees, crouching over the book, and quickly skim the page. It describes the binding spell, its characteristics, and its one small flaw: *However, it is still within their ability to activate another's casting, stored within a separate object such as a charm. As such, great care should be taken to remove all charms from the vicinity of where a rogue mage is imprisoned.*

I get to my feet and make the bed, my hands tingling with excitement. I double-check the book as I return it to the bed, to make sure I have read it right. The words remain exactly the same. With my hand in my pocket grasping the seeker, I float back out to Mistress Yilmaz, barely bothered when she sends me out to fetch a broom from a small, half-hidden hall closet, and sweep out all the rooms. By the time I finish sweeping, some of my elation has worn off, for Mistress Yilmaz still sits at the desk. As I return the broom to the hall closet, I hear a faint sound behind me.

"You're a good girl," Yilmaz says, stepping heavily into the hall and pulling the door shut. "Hard worker. Come to me tomorrow, and I'll put in a word for you, for the third level. And I'll see you get placed with a good housekeeper." She fumbles with her key ring. "But not today."

I watch with despair as she turns the key in the lock. So close. I'd been so close.

"Help me down the stairs, now," she says as I continue to stand by the broom closet. I cross to her and she grips my shoulder, taking each step one at a time. There are a lot of steps between the third floor and the basement.

"There," she says when we finally reach the bottom.

"Thank you, mistress," I say, trying to look appropriately grateful. I may not have gotten the key, but at least I've learned the one shortcoming of a binding spell. She pats my shoulder and shuffles down the hall toward her door.

She's planning to rest—which means I might be able to get Talon's key from her now. "Mistress, let me walk with you."

"What?" she asks blearily.

"Just to make sure I know where to come tomorrow," I say hopefully. "And you can lean on me."

"Anyone can tell you where to find me," she grumbles, but she takes my arm and gives me a good bit of her weight anyhow.

I walk her to her rooms, straight through the outer sitting room and to her bed. "Why don't you lie down?" I urge her. "I'll help you with your shoes."

She lets me lower her to her bed. I nearly stagger with the sudden relief from her weight. She lies down on her side, leaving me to heave her legs up onto the bed. I slip off her shoes and place them beside her bed. Her eyes are already closed. Deftly, I unpin the brooch by her pocket and slide out the key ring.

She catches my wrist, her eyes flying open. "What do you think you're doing?"

"I— I was only going to put it beside you," I stutter. "So you'll be comfortable. Right here." I move my arm to the bedside table, her hand still attached, and set the key ring on the table.

"Ah," she says, releasing my wrist.

From the stand beside the door, I fetch the pitcher of water and tin cup and pour her a drink. The water will help flush the herbs from her system. "Have a sip, Mistress Yilmaz," I suggest, coming to kneel beside her. "It might help you feel better."

"What is it?" she asks, her hand already reaching for it.

"Just water," I assure her. "Have a sip or two and see how it settles."

She leverages herself up and takes a few sips, water trickling down her chin. She hands it back to me wordlessly and collapses on her back. By the time I refill the cup and set it beside the key ring, her eyes are closed and her breathing has slowed.

Perhaps, if she falls asleep fully right now, I can slip out with the key ring in hand. So I take a silent step back, slide the look-away charm on my finger, and wait as she drifts deeper into sleep.

While I wait, I slip my hand into my pocket to release the seeker charm. I'll need to refocus it on identifying the key to First Mage Talon's rooms. I can't afford to run off with the whole key ring in case Yilmaz wakes up and looks for it—at least, I can't take it for more than a few minutes. The seeker pulls steadily in my grasp, and I realize suddenly that it is not pressing *up* but *forward*. I stare at the key ring sitting on the bedside table with its collection of strange keys, take a step forward. The seeker jerks toward it, making my pocket bulge.

The key I sought wasn't in the desk at all. It was with the housekeeper as she sat at the desk.

A glance at Yilmaz tells me she's as deeply asleep as someone with a stomachache can be—out but not too deeply. I scoop up the key ring, sliding it into my pocket and moving on silent feet to the door. When I glance back at Yilmaz, her eyes are slitted open, staring straight through me.

I wait, my blood thrumming in my veins. Her eyes drift shut again. Sending up a prayer of thanks, I let myself out, leaving the bedroom door cracked open.

Quickly, now. Quickly.

I hurry to the servants' washing room, bolting the door behind me. A quick opening of my mages' senses tells me there are a few charms at work around me, a faint magical buzz in the air that means one more charm, even a strong one, will hardly draw notice. I pull off the look-away and sit down cross-legged on the tiled floor. Hastily arranging my string of wards around me in a circle, I close the silver clasp. The shield built into the wards snaps into place around me.

I let out a breath and slip the key ring from my pocket, depositing it on my lap. Holding the seeker tight in my hand, I use it to nudge each key. The cat key, farther down the ring, hisses at me. I glance at the door. The shield may hold in any magical reverberations, but it isn't soundproof. I move on, but the seeker continues to vibrate, seeking, until I reach the cat's head key. It sends a little tingle up my hand and goes completely still as I touch it to the key. The cat's head opens its mouth to yowl. I hastily shove my thumb into its mouth, and it bites down *hard*.

Swallowing a cry, I yank my poor thumb free and shove the seeker's stem into its mouth instead. It growls like a dog and works its jaw, shredding the stick with its tiny metal teeth. I press the stick in tightly, and work the key free of the ring, leaving behind a few drops of blood and some shredded pieces of my poor charm. With a muttered curse, I fling the key head-first toward the can of washing water on the floor beside me. Unfortunately, it rebounds off my shield and smacks me in the leg, yowling plaintively.

I spread my hand over the key and reach for its magic, desperate to shut it up. The key pulses with energy but…it isn't connected to anything. It's just a cat's head key that won't quiet down. The spell is concentrated on the head itself, and on instinct I pet it, scratching it behind the ears with a touch of magic.

The yowl lessens to a purr.

Really?

Still massaging the back of its head, I lift the key gently, assessing it. With a careful stroke, I slip two loops of magic together, rub the key as if it were the cat's tummy, and the thing falls asleep.

Of all the lizard-brained ways to build in an alarm.

I stick my bleeding thumb in my mouth and glare at the infernal key. It takes me a few moments to clean up, carefully wiping up the blood and dusting off the splinters from my seeker charm. While not destroyed, the stem of the charm is significantly mangled. I whisper an apology to it and set it down beside me.

Then I take another key from my pocket—the one key I own: the key to Stormwind's cottage. I slide it on to the key ring in place of the cat's head key. I need only a small glamor, a touch to the cat's nose—it wrinkles it slightly—and then to the cottage's key. The key wavers in my sight, until I look at not one sleeping cat's head key but two. A small spell indeed for such a great deception.

I pocket the original cat's head key along with the seeker, unclasp my wards, and let myself out of the washroom. The hall lies silent. I need to leave at once, but first, I must return the key ring. Wearing the look-away, I sneak back into Yilmaz's rooms and leave the key ring on her bedside table.

She grunts slightly as the keys clink together, and then settles once more. Back in the hall, I slide off the look-away and head for the stairs.

I did it. I have the key, I know the shortcomings of Stormwind's binding spell. It's a good beginning, but it isn't a plan by a far cry. Because even if I can get her the key, and then distract the guards long enough for her to slip out and to the rooftop, I still need a place for her to go, and a way to protect her from being traced. Without either of those, she may as well stay where she is. We'd be caught within hours.

My feet slow on the stairs as I worry over my options, but they all come back to the same truth I'd faced last night on the rooftop: I need help. I have to find the Degaths, see if there is some part of the Shadow League here that will help me.

As I reach the top of the stairs, I hear the sound of voices descending, footsteps in the stairwell above me.

"That servant was supposed to stay close." A man's voice, irritated.

"I'll see to it he does in future," a woman replies, her voice cool, the words touched with the faint lilt of the eastern Kingdoms.

"Indeed."

Both voices are terribly familiar. I plow to a stop two stairs from the ground floor, as a pair of mages descend the final steps to the hallway. I know them, know them both—

Blackflame rounds the corner, moving toward the building's side exit. Seeing him is like watching a dream waver between fiction and truth, memory and reality. He is exactly as I remember, tall and imposing, with a mane of golden hair that falls about his shoulders in thick waves and frames a face as cold and dangerous as steel. "You there," he says sharply, spotting me. "Go up to my rooms. I need the front room cleaned."

I drop my gaze to the stone steps, nod jerkily. The woman beside Blackflame has gone completely still. I don't look at her. Can't. I've seen her face a half-dozen times in Stormwind's lake, but now I can't raise my eyes to her. Because even though everything would change if she actually recognized me, I want her to— I so desperately want her to cross the distance between us and reach out her hand to me, speak my name.

So I don't look.

"Yes, master," I say instead, voice hoarse. I dip a clumsy curtsy, still balanced on the stairs.

"Stay with her," Blackflame says to my mother.

"Yes," she says distantly. "This way, girl." She gestures up the stairs.

Blackflame departs with a muttered word to my mother, striding past without another glance. I follow Hotaru Brokensword as she sweeps elegantly upstairs, her kimono rippling over the steps behind her.

"There," Brokensword says as I hesitate in the doorway. She points to a pool of vomit by the far window.

Any hopes that she might truly have recognized me die away. It's been five years. I've grown from child to woman, and even if she still thinks me alive, she would never expect to see me here, in servants' clothing.

I glance around the room once, taking in the opulent furnishings, the luxurious tapestries hanging on the walls—a Northland tradition. Tapestries make a room hot in a country like this; at least they do ten months of the year. A young man no older than I sits hunched against the wall to my left, knees pulled up to his chest and face turned away. He wears a charcoal gray pants and tunic set, the sleeves cut short to bare his arms. From the elbow down they are covered in great black, crisscrossing lines, as if he had once tangled his arms in a burning web.

Source slave.

"Girl," my mother says, an edge to her voice. "You're here to clean."

I jerk my attention back to her. "Yes, mistress. Let me fetch some cloths from the closet."

"Be quick."

I hurry to the supply closet down the hall, grabbing a bucket half-filled with soapy water and a stack of cleaning cloths.

I let myself back into the room quietly. The boy still huddles against the wall, though now he clutches a blanket around himself, trembling. Perhaps he was trembling before too, but the shaking of the blanket can't be missed. I nod to him and cross the room to the vomit. It's his, of course. No doubt he tried to get to the window, but didn't make it in time. What spell did Blackflame cast, that he would make his source slave sick to achieve it? Why didn't I sense anything while I cleaned and went about stealing keys? But the room must be warded, of course. And Blackflame doesn't care how the boy feels, so long as he serves his purpose.

As I clean, the boy watches me, his eyes dark and…almost blank. From the set of his jaw, I know he's in pain. But he makes no sound, only watches me. My mother has disappeared into the connecting room.

I finish drying the floor and bundle up the dirty cloths together. Crossing the room, I pause at the door. I can't just leave.

"Are you— will you be all right?" I ask, pitching my voice low.

He tilts his head, looks at me. No. No, he won't. He doesn't say the words, doesn't need to, and he's not going to lie either.

"Is there anything I can do?"

His lips twitch, somewhere between a smile and a grimace. "No," he whispers. "What I need you cannot give me."

Freedom. Safety. Kindness.

I stand by the door, and now I'm shaking again, impotent with fury and sorrow and helplessness. I'm here to help Stormwind. But what about this boy, this source slave? He can't survive long. He's being used too brutally. But who else will help him? He knows I can't— or won't. He knows he's alone and trapped, his future clearly laid out, stark and ugly and short.

Brokensword steps through the connecting door. "Are you done?"

I jerk my gaze to her, then look down. I don't recognize her anymore, this woman who would allow a source slave—a *boy*—to be used so cruelly. This woman who kept my Promise secret, knowing that I might one day pay the price this boy has, and yet shows him neither mercy nor compassion. An eternity ago in the Burnt Lands, I promised myself I would speak to her if I could. But now? Now I have no words for her, cannot begin to comprehend the chasm that lies between us.

"Very good," she says. I remain beside the door, rooted there by the truths of this room. "You may go," she says, gesturing sharply.

I glance toward the boy. He watches me with his old, old

eyes. I don't dare address him again under my mother's eye. Instead, I step out, closing the door behind me with clumsy fingers.

I move to the supply closet in a daze, leaving the dirty cloths bundled together on the ground. I take the stairs down, go out the side entrance. The sun shines brightly outside. It is barely noon, and students congregate in groups, laughing and calling to each other as they prepare to leave the Mekteb for the Festival.

Blackflame has long since disappeared to wherever he is going. Upstairs, my mother will go about her duties, whatever they may be, while the boy sits shivering against the wall.

I start along the path, walking blindly, my legs quivering slightly beneath my weight, as if they were not made of muscle and bone at all, but something softer, weaker. My breath comes in quick, hard gasps.

Why am I so upset? She's here. With him. The last time I saw her, she was walking in Blackflame's gardens, unaware that he had imprisoned me. Now she's come to Fidanya with him. I thought she didn't see him for what he is, that she stood beside him and supported him and trusted him because he'd tricked her somehow. But I was only deceiving myself. Brokensword is no fool. She sees Blackflame for precisely what he is, and she joined him. She cares no more for me than she does the source slave—the source slave that could have been me. Fury courses through me with a suddenness that leaves me shaking in a completely different way. I want to scream at her. How *could* she?

I've wanted to speak with her for so long, thinking that she would remind me of who I am...that she could help me ground myself in the life I used to have, reclaim those parts of me I lost when I killed Kol. But I'll never get those pieces back, and my mother can't help me. Not when she has lost the person *she* was five years ago, before my father died and she left me to fend for myself.

I will not let seeing her shake me so. The woman I just met isn't my mother anymore. She birthed me, and mothered me, and then left me. I've been reborn of fire now, mothered by magic and ashes, and I do not need her anymore.

OLD FRIENDS

"Rehan! Wait!"

I don't register her voice until Esra is almost upon me. I blink at her uncertainly as she puffs to a stop before me. "Sorry," I say.

"Did something happen? I saw you come down and go out the door in a rush…. Are you crying?"

"No, of course not." I swipe at my eyes and find them surprisingly damp.

Her face softens and she touches my arm. "What happened?"

"I— um…Arch Mage Blackflame wanted me to clean up a mess in his rooms."

"He did?" Esra frowns. "I thought he brought his own servant for that!"

"Couldn't find him, I guess. Anyway, I saw the source slave. Blackflame used him too hard for a spell and he threw up."

Esra purses her lips, looks down at the ground. "I'm sorry," she says finally. "You'll get used to it in time. Mages have their own rules, and they do things their way. As much as they say we're all the same, they don't really seem to believe it."

I cross my arms over my chest. "No," I agree.

"Come." She tugs my elbow until she can thread her arm through mine. "Walk back with me. I left my things out. I'll get everything put away and we'll go out to the Festival together, find something to laugh about."

We walk back to Susulu Hall together and gather the bucket and scrubbing brush Esra left in the middle of the hall, taking them downstairs to store in the basement closet. I collect my pack while Esra sets the closet in order.

"Did you talk to her?" Esra gestures toward Yilmaz's door.

I nod. "She didn't know anything about me. Said I could work here today and we'd sort it out tomorrow."

Esra makes a face. "I hope they sort you back here again."

I smile, but my heart isn't in this deception. Part of me wishes I could work with Esra, and another part wishes I could walk upstairs, take the source slave by the hand, and start running again. The rest of me is just so very tired. I say only, "I hope so."

As we leave Susulu Hall, Esra nods to my pack still bundled in my old skirt. "You don't have a room yet, either?"

"No."

"Did you tell your uncle you'd be staying here?"

I blink, remember the lies I'd told her yesterday, the groundwork I'd laid so I might be able to visit the Degaths. "I was hoping to," I say tentatively.

"When do you need to meet your friend?"

I squint at the sky, as if gauging the time from the sun. "About an hour?"

Esra laughs. "Then let's go!"

We change our clothes in her room, Esra opting for a crimson tunic and saffron yellow *selvar*. I pull on my spare tunic and skirt set, eliciting a sideways look from her. She is kind enough not to remark on either their dull colors or their utterly foreign appearance.

"Do you want to leave your pack with me?"

It would certainly be easier, but there are too many things I can't afford to have stolen. I already know how easy it is to steal from here. "Will it be safe? It's all I have."

Esra's features darken. "Someone was talking about a few things disappearing from the upstairs rooms this morning—nothing too valuable, but I don't know. I keep the door locked, but if one of my roommates forgets...."

"I'll carry it."

Esra nods.

Ready, we meet up with a number of Esra's friends waiting on the cushions of a small common area. There are trays of cheese and flatbreads set out on a low table to the side. After a round of pleasantries and introductions, and a quick bite to eat while we wait for two more girls to arrive, we set forth. It's a short walk to the back gate, easily visible from the building itself. A mage sits on a throne-like cushioned chair to the side of the gate, a cloth sunshade erected over him. He glances over our group disinterestedly. I pretend not to notice, instead asking Esra what her favorite part of the Festival is.

She's in the middle of telling me about the performances she hopes to catch tonight when one of the four lycan guards posted by the gate steps forward, pointing at me. "You, there. I haven't seen you before."

Our little group jerks to a halt. I smile, focusing on keeping my breathing calm. "Oh, I'm Rehan."

"She's new," Esra volunteers. "Works with me in Susulu Hall."

I nod in agreement, hoping to God the guard can't sense my tension, the sudden dampness of my palms. His eyes flick to the pack slung over my shoulder. It seemed wisest to hide it in plain sight, but now I'm not so sure. The other servants shift closer to me, training their gazes on the guard expectantly. There's no question in their minds that I'm one of them.

"That's right," one of the other guards says. "I saw Osman Bey walking her there—yesterday, was it?"

I flash a grateful smile to the guard who'd spoken and nod in agreement, silently blessing the boys and their prank.

"Why've you got your pack with you?" the first guard asks.

"She doesn't have a room yet," Esra says. "But she'll probably stay with me tonight."

That puts his remaining doubts to rest. "I'll let our next shift know to expect your return," he says, gesturing us through.

I grin at Esra. She beams at me, her eyes alight with innocent anticipation for the Festival and its delights.

I stay with the group for a good half hour, following along as we cross the river and circumvent the western edge of the Grand Bazaar, closed for the day, its winding alleys lying quiet. It seems to be the only quiet place in the city.

Street performers are out, juggling and doing acrobatics, and in the first square we pass, a wrestling match is about to begin. The wrestlers' skin gleams with the oils they've used to help slide out of their opponents' grip. They stretch, jump, and kick to warm up, then lift their voices in increasingly vociferous prayers that both ask for aid and describe how they will lay low their enemies. A couple of the girls in our group slow their steps to watch, but they get pulled along as we continue on.

We reach a broad avenue and come to a halt behind a wall of people shouting and cheering. Beyond them, huge rolling platforms pulled by multiple teams of oxen pass by. Each platform bears a giant wooden model of a brightly painted building or fortress, and from their rooftops and snug balconies and walls brightly clad men and women wave to the crowds, tossing out handfuls of items.

"Are those the fortresses that get burned?" I ask Esra as she waves her arms at the next building rolling our way.

"What? Goodness, no, this is part of the parade of guilds." She throws me a laughing look. "This is— oh!"

She jumps higher as a handful of items fly through the air, her hand darting in front of the man's before her. "Got it," she cries, ignoring his irritated glance. "See, look! These are the jewelry guilds. They've made loads and loads of things to share as they go through the city to the king's palace."

She holds a pair of earrings made of bright metal wire and strung with glass beads. "It's not silver or anything, but it will be pretty to wear now and then, don't you think?"

"They're just throwing them to people?"

"Uh-huh." Esra pockets the earrings and rises on her tiptoes to watch the next great wagon rolling toward us. "That's half the Festival. Didn't you know? The guilds from each part of the city parade through on their assigned day, giving away what they've made right on up until they reach the gates of the palace to pay their yearly tribute."

A cheer goes up as another guild member gestures toward us, holding up a handful of rings.

"I love this day," Esra says happily, stretching up on her tiptoes again.

"Yeah." Most of the other serving girls have fanned out along the edges of the crowd, waiting for their chance to catch a trinket. I slant a glance at the sky. "I'd better go. When will you head back to the Mekteb?"

"Before midnight," Esra says, making a face. "We're supposed to be back before the burning of the forts."

"You'll stay out as long as you can, then?"

"Of course." She sighs as the man with the rings heaves

them to the left of us. "What about you?"

"Probably."

"If you get back early, wait in the common room for me. I'll come get you so you can share my room."

"Thanks."

Esra waves me off with a grin. I peel away from the crowd, heading toward the nearest big street. It takes me a few tries and a couple of coppers to get directions to the Degaths' residence, but the directions are clear and seem honest, taking into account the route of today's parade. They deliver me into one of the wealthier neighborhoods of the city in a little less than an hour. Here, the road with its wide cobbled sidewalks and shade-giving trees lies mostly empty.

There are guards posted at the end of one of the streets. I meekly request directions of them, and after a question or two they direct me the final few turns to my destination.

Old Lord Degath must have managed his affairs very well. His heirs live in a great villa, the boundary walls covered in a colorful tiled mosaic of repeating geometric patterns. I come to a stop across the street, studying the house.

Whether or not they remember me well enough to recognize me, what am I really hoping from them? They're nobles. They didn't know the first thing about survival when we last met. I thought of them as children at the time—the Degath children, because they were the children of Lord and Lady Degath, but also because they hardly acted like adults at the time. Even though Saira was easily my age or a year older, and Tarek older than she, their initial bickering and silliness in the face of danger led me to consider them children. Only Alia had really been a child.

Now that they've lost their parents, and weathered Saira's betrayal—if she is even still with them—what will they be like? The house before me suggests that they matured quickly, grew older and wiser in the space of days or weeks. Perhaps they have an older retainer or family steward who provided them with the counsel they needed to manage their wealth wisely and consider their political strategies. And no such advisor worth his salt would counsel them to help me. Nor do I think they know the first thing about actually effecting an escape.

That kind of thing had been the Shadow League's work.

I run my hands through my hair, pat it back down again. All I can risk asking them—or telling them—is that I need the Shadow League.

Crossing the road, I knock at the gate. A moment later, the gatekeeper opens a small rectangular peephole, his dark eyebrows furrowing beneath a vibrant forest green turban. He says something in the local tongue, eyeing my faded and creased clothing with disdain.

"I require a few words with Lord Degath," I say coolly in Tradespeak. "Is he in?"

A pause. "Who asks?"

"Hitomi. Of Karolene."

He waits. After a moment, when it becomes clear that I've elaborated all I plan to, he mutters a suggestion that I wait on the bench and slides the cover over the peephole. I settle myself on the stone bench and rehearse possible conversations in my mind until he returns.

"Miss Hitomi," the gatekeeper says, swinging open a small door built into the larger gate and waving me toward a another green-turbaned man, this one armed. His tunic and *selvar* are pristine, the cloth lacking even the finest wrinkle. Compared to him, I look like I've crawled out of the gutter. "This way."

The carriageway circles around a wide pleasure garden, a tiled fountain at its center. A myriad of flowering bushes line a paved walk that crosses to the fountain and continues to the villa. The house itself is a grand structure, at least three levels, with wide open windows—missing the latticework I remember from Karolene. A central balcony on the second level is built into the building itself, making a floor of the first level's roof. I scan the building, checking the windows. In one, a figure stands in shadow. A slight movement on the balcony draws my eye. The door stands open, and I could almost swear I saw the swish of robes disappearing within.

It would make sense for the Degaths to bring a mage into their service. And wise of them to be careful of unknown visitors. Especially a visitor claiming to be the girl who they believed died a year ago helping them escape from Blackflame.

The guard leads me through a richly appointed foyer and into an empty sitting room. "His lordship will be with you shortly," he tells me, and departs at once.

I stand, staring around the room, feeling more at home than I ever did at Stormwind's. I was comfortable there, and it never occurred to me until this moment that I had not been completely at ease. But this—the stiff rectangular cushions lining the wall, the slightly plumper cushions scattered below them, embroidered in a multitude of colors—this speaks of home in a language deeper than words. I turn slowly, my eyes traveling over the carpets lying two and three deep, the low wooden tables inlaid with brass, the ornate lanterns hanging by long chains from the ceiling.

I don't remember these things precisely. I suspect I rarely spent time in such rich surroundings, but the comfort of sitting on the floor feels suddenly and completely *right*. I sink onto the carpets, leaning my head back against the wall cushions, and close my eyes. Sandalwood scents the air, faint and yet warm as the sunlight falling through the windows.

I want to go home. And I don't even know where that it is, or if it exists.

I open my eyes, glare fiercely at my hands on my lap. This isn't the time to get all mush-brained over echoes of things past. I'm here, with troubles that aren't going to blow away with the first puff of a breeze. I have a key, a charm, the beginnings of a plan, and half of an idea of a way out. And a fractured memory that affords me this: I've never been the best of planners.

I straighten my back, take a few slow, calming breaths. I put all thoughts of the homes I once had and lost behind me, and let myself drift into the resulting lull. The cushions against my back are firm and supportive, the faint brush of magic against my skin—utterly unexpected. I focus on the walls, then the hanging glowstone lanterns, and the faint, pulsing magic beneath the carpets themselves. Magic is woven into the very walls of the room, into every permanent surface, like a series of interconnected spiderwebs, and at the center of each web shines a sigil.

I'm sitting in a trap. I flinch back reflexively, pulling in my senses, and the room remains still around me. But that doesn't change what I'd glimpsed: sigils of protection and defense surrounding me. This isn't just any sitting room, it's the one where the Degaths meet those they're unsure of, their enemies. It's the one they invite mages into, because the very protections held by the walls would throw the mages' spells back on them. It's brilliant, and absolutely terrifying.

"Hitomi of Karolene."

My eyes snap to the door. Tarek Degath stands at the entry. I have no idea how long he's been there. I rise to my feet and offer him a slight bow, the fingers of my right hand touching my heart. "Lord Degath."

He is head and shoulders taller than I am, still slim and

clean-shaven as I remember. He wears the traditional dress of Karolene, his clothes of the formal cut, a long flowing robe, the neckline embroidered with circles and swirls that flow partially down the front, loose-cut pants peeking out from below, and an embroidered cap. The fall of the cloth merely accentuates his elegance.

"We have met," Tarek says. It isn't a question, except that his expression tells me he wants an answer.

"A lifetime ago," I agree. "We were taken prisoner together and I helped you and your sisters escape."

"But you yourself did not."

"No. I was given to Kol, as was their agreement."

Tarek takes a step or two into the room, comes to a stop. He's still wary of me, ghost that I must seem to him. "We learned as much, but that was all. When the High Council sent their mages to investigate—far too late, but still—they informed us that you must have died."

I shrug, half-smiling. "Fortunately for me, they were wrong. I escaped, but I lost a great deal: most of my memory, my health. I didn't remember Karolene for…." I think back. "Months."

"And yet you remember us?"

"Of all the memories I have, I remember most clearly the events leading up to the spell that took my memory."

He nods slowly. "Then you remember that I betrayed my family."

"Y-you?" I stutter.

He looks at me, unblinking.

"No, it was Lady Saira. She and Blackflame spoke—I remember that. It had nothing to do with you."

He tilts his head, his expression unreadable. "Well, you know that much, but so do Blackflame and his supporters. Why should I not consider you," he waves one hand to the side, half-dismissing me, "another trick sent by Blackflame, meant to finish the work he began a year ago? Can you give me some reason to trust you now?"

And there's the crux of the matter. What can I tell him that hasn't already come out from the stories they told, the petitions they made, the investigation they launched to find me. *To find me.* I stare at him. When Stonefall told me, the truth of it hadn't registered. The weight of it. The Degaths demanded an investigation, pushed the High Council itself to track down Kol. Of course they wanted to bring him to justice for what he did to Alia, but they had hoped to help me as well.

157

Now I've come back from the dead, and Tarek can't believe it. Nor do I know how I can convince him. The dead don't rise.

"You have no reason for me to trust you?" Tarek asks, his voice quiet.

I shake my head. "I'm sorry," I say. "I shouldn't have come. But someone told me you were here, and I thought you might still have some connection to…my old friends."

"You need help," Tarek says abruptly.

I feel suddenly small. As if I came here to use him—which I did. "It's not help you can give me directly."

His gaze is as sharp as a diamond blade. "I will not endanger my family."

"And you don't trust me. I don't blame you," I say, holding up a hand. "It's that there is someone I need to help, and I don't know anyone else here. I only arrived two nights ago. There's a great deal I can do, but I can't do it all on my own."

Something in his face shifts, and then he laughs, a quiet, disbelieving chuckle. "You're still saving people."

I shrug, embarrassed by his amusement, unsure of his words. I'm not really saving *people*, just one person whom I care about very much. Has that somehow convinced him of my identity? "I'm no hero," I say stiffly.

He shakes his head, gestures to the cushions. "Please, sit."

I do, and he takes a seat a alongside the wall, turned to face me. "I remember you well. You look different now—hollowed out, but…"

"But?"

"Stronger," he admits, shrugging away the contradiction. "You couldn't pass for a young man anymore."

Is that a compliment? It hardly feels like one.

"Your face is etched in my mind. I doubt I'll ever forget you. To us, and especially to Alia, you were—*are* a hero."

"She's well, then?" I ask quickly. The image of her lying crumpled in her cell, drained to within a breath of her life, has haunted my dreams often over the last year.

"She's recovered," Tarek says. "She's not the same, of course, grown older, more serious. But we've all changed."

It would be hard to remain an innocent child after such an experience.

"I'm sorry," I say, even though it isn't my fault. Even though the fault lies with his other sister, Saira, and the betrayal she agreed to in a foolish bid to out-politic her father and gain Blackflame's support. And, ultimately, it lies with Blackflame himself.

He shrugs. "We're alive and," a gesture to the room, "well. If I could bring my parents back, I would. But some things cannot be undone."

No, they can't. I know that well enough.

"Why didn't you send word to your friends?" he asks. "We would have heard from them, if they learned you'd survived. We asked to be told."

I look away, letting my gaze wander over the cushions, the carpets. Why didn't I contact them? Why did I focus solely on my mother? "I didn't remember them at first," I admit. "I was weak for a long time after I escaped. Finding a way to contact them from where I was, without bringing attention to them— it seemed dangerous. Not worth the risk."

He stares at me. "You didn't think they'd care?"

"I was already dead to them. They would have grieved and moved on by the time I remembered anything at all."

Tarek leans back against the cushions. "I think you misjudge the depth of your friendships."

I don't have an answer to that. I feel suddenly sick with myself. All those months studying in Stormwind's valley, spying on my mother and sifting through my memories, and I never considered that I was being selfish. Not that I should have left, or even that I could have contacted my friends among the Shadow League easily without sharing a blood tie, but surely I could have found some way to send word that I had survived and moved on? That our decisions, Saira's betrayal, did not actually mean my death.

"Allow me to offer you tea," Tarek says, "And refreshments." A serving girl, hovering at the entry, takes this as permission to enter and crosses to us. She sets a silver tea tray down on the low octagonal table between us. The tray is filled to its edges with a teapot, small drinking bowls, and plates of pastries, dried fruits, and nuts. The girl serves us quietly and efficiently.

Tarek sips once from his cup, waiting until she disappears from view. "The help that you need," he says slowly. "Who does it relate to?"

I consider my possibilities. I need help, am almost desperate for it. But involving the Degaths would be monumentally stupid. They are still a noble household, and still standing against Blackflame with all the legitimate power at their disposal. And as the Ghost said when we first set out to save them, a resistance against Blackflame requires the voices of those with the power to speak, as a complement to the work of the Shadow League itself. Whether or not the Shadow League exists here is irrelevant. I have no doubt it's still at work in Karolene.

"It's better that I tell you as little as possible," I say finally. "I was hoping there might be a group of people here...like those who helped your family in Karolene. Those are the people I need."

"Then you are willing to leave unsatisfied?"

No. I bite my lip hard. He doesn't trust me. There's no hope of involving him. Which means his words aren't an offer of help but a thinly veiled invitation to leave. I force a smile and set my tea cup down. "I was never unwilling to leave, but I do thank you for your hospitality."

He raises a hand. "Stay, finish your tea at least." And then, "Will you not tell me where you went after you escaped Kol?"

"I was taken in by a healer living in a rural valley. I spent most of the last year with her. She made me her apprentice once I was well enough to help her."

He laughs, a genuine, deep-throated laugh. "I wouldn't have imagined a street thief settling into being a country healer's apprentice."

"Why not?" I ask, irked. "I wasn't a street thief by choice. I did that to survive."

"And healing? Was that a matter of survival as well?"

Is he mocking me? I take a deep breath, make myself answer. "In its way, yes. It was also a means to making a living, rather than simply scraping by day after day." Stormwind *had* insisted I learn a great deal of herbs and healing. I could easily pass as a healer's assistant at this point—or even a rather mediocre healer—selling my knowledge to keep myself while still hiding my talent.

Tarek looks slightly abashed, but his gaze doesn't waver. "Then it's this healer who's in trouble."

I underestimated him, his ability to parse conversations and strategize. Or perhaps I didn't think clearly enough about meeting him, about who he has become in the year since I broke him free from his cage and sent him fleeing through Blackflame's gardens to safety. "I thought you couldn't endanger your family."

"No," he agrees. He sets down his cup and rises, waiting expectantly for me to stand. I don't know what other argument I can make, what I can do without directly involving the Degaths. And they've already suffered enough losses. I could demand that they help me—Tarek has enough honor to know that he owes me his life, his family's lives. But I can't do that, and he won't offer it himself.

I follow him out the door, leaving behind my half-drunk tea and half-eaten pastries with a twinge of regret. I should have eaten faster. It's the best meal I've seen since the caravanserai.

From the foyer, I can hear more clearly the faint noise that had teased the edge of my hearing in the room: a girl's laugh, and the sharp bark of a dog. Tarek opens the front door, stepping to the side and holding it for me.

"I am sorry I can offer you nothing more," he says as I step through.

I nod, my eyes going to the two young women on the garden path. The elder wears a housedress, a long flowing gown of bright yellow, embroidered with red flowers, bell sleeves serving to emphasize her delicate wrists and long, tapered fingers. A matching scarf wraps around her head in a crown, setting off her long neck and the elegant line of her shoulders. The younger is on the cusp of womanhood, her form still small and her clothes simpler, though equally bright— orange and yellow and white.

"Alia?" I whisper just loud enough for Tarek to hear, as my gaze finds her neck, the pale scars barely visible as she looks toward me. I beam at her, happy suddenly in a way I forgot I could be, my feet light and my heart singing. This girl is vibrantly alive, laughter on her lips and eyes dancing, as unlike the girl in my memory as the living are to the dead. She looks up, and her face stills as she catches sight of me. She tilts her head, glances at her sister, voicing a question.

The dog at their side huffs softly and trots toward me. It's a somewhat fluffy golden creature, with perky triangular ears and dark fur around its eyes. Its legs, also darker, appear slim under the puffy fur of its body. My brow furrows as I study it, taking in the ringed tail, the bright eyes.

The women follow after the dog. As they near, the elder, who can only be Lady Saira Degath, says, "Hitomi?"

I dip my head, raising my hand toward my heart, and then the dog launches himself at me—except he isn't a dog. I take half a step back, yelping in surprise, as the dog-man grasps my arms with a shout, his face coming into focus as a man's barely a hand away from my own. I stumble, and if Tarek's hands hadn't whipped out to steady me, we would have gone down in a heap.

"Hitomi!" The dog-man, now fully transformed, shouts,

still gripping my arms. He's surprisingly strong, given how slim and short he appears.

"Y-yes...." I make myself focus on him.

"Well," I hear Saira say to her brother. "I guess it really is her."

I know this man, his bright brown eyes, his shaggy chestnut hair mingled with black. I know him both as a man and a dog...no. Not just any dog. A black-masked tanuki. "Kenta?" I say, my voice uncertain.

He laughs and steps back. He isn't wearing a shirt, and all that passes for pants are a pair of tight leather—half-pants? Leather is the easiest material for a shifter to take with them when they shift, and it takes some time for younger shifters to do even that. I'm grateful he managed that much.

"Thank you," Kenta says, glancing quickly at Tarek. "I almost didn't believe your note, but I shouldn't have doubted it."

"I am only glad you received it and came so quickly."

Kenta nods, turns his attention back to me, his lips parted in a smile that shows two rows of almost human-looking white teeth, the tips slightly sharper than they should be. "We thought you dead. Why didn't you send word?"

I shake my head, still staring at him.

"Come in and put on some clothes," Tarek says from beside me, "so my sisters can stop admiring the floor and look at you again."

Kenta laughs, reaches out to grasp my shoulders. I startle, not at all ready to be hugged by an unclothed man I barely remember. His fingers just brush my shoulder before he drops his hands, still chuckling. "Just making sure you're not a ghost."

"No," I assure him.

"You *are* certain it's her," Saira says from behind him.

I glance over his shoulder at her, but Saira is studiously looking at the ground to avoid the sight of her barely clothed friend. Alia, however, watches me solemnly, eyes unwavering. She no longer looks a child at all.

"Absolutely." Kenta taps his nose. "I know my friends' scents. It's not something mages have managed to glamor yet."

"Good thing you're a tanuki," Tarek says, gesturing us back to the sitting room. "And forgive me, Hitomi, for not welcoming you more warmly at first. You understand my concerns."

"Perfectly."

Kenta steps away to rifle through a carved wooden trunk set against the wall. A moment later, he swings a sage green kimono around his shoulders, sliding his arms through the wide sleeves and wrapping an earth brown obi around his waist to hold the folds in place. He turns to us and bows with a flourish, while I consider the implications of his keeping a spare set of clothes here.

"And now," Tarek says, still waiting at the door with his sisters, "we will leave you to talk." He nods toward me, "The room is warded, so no word you speak will pass these walls."

"I thank you," I say.

"It is the least we can do," Tarek says. "I hope we will meet again when the troubles that occupy you are past."

"I look forward to it." It seems as likely as my attending Huda's sister's wedding in the desert in a month's time, but I can at least pretend I have such hopes.

Tarek bows slightly and withdraws a step, waiting to close the door for his sisters. Saira hesitates in the doorway. I cannot read her expression, the hollow weight of her gaze. She betrayed her family once, and the Shadow League, and while her parents are gone, I wonder what she thinks now, seeing me apparently returned from the dead. She has aged in a way that has nothing to do with the passing of the days. Her eyes are deeply shadowed, the light in them more like darkness than anything. Without a smile on her lips, she seems adrift, bereft. I wonder how hard it was for her to find a place in her family again, whether her siblings will ever truly forgive her.

"Lady Saira," I say hesitantly.

"I am...grateful that you found us," she says, her words awkward in the space between us. With a jerky nod, she departs, her slippers whispering to silence as she hurries away.

Tarek reaches to shut the door, his expression cool and still.

"Thank you," Alia says suddenly, one hand out to stop the door. "And I'm sorry."

I look at her in confusion. "What for?"

"Kol would never have noticed you if you hadn't tried to protect me."

Tarek's features tighten, but he does not look at me. A year, I realize. A year she has lived, blaming herself for my death. I make myself smile, though it is a small, sad thing. "But I am glad he did, my lady. If he hadn't, I would have remained in Blackflame's power, and he would have killed me long before

163

anyone else could have helped me. So you see, together we traded that future for one I could escape."

Alia stares at me, her lips parting, closing again as she struggles to find words.

"I thank you for that," I tell her. "And I would do it again a hundred times, no matter the consequence. But...I am so very glad to see you well."

She smiles tremulously. "I am glad to see you, too."

I dip my head, touch my hand to my heart. To my surprise, she returns the gesture, as if we were of equal standing.

"Please come see us again," she says.

"I will try," I promise.

Tarek smiles at me with unexpected warmth. Then he ushers Alia out and closes the door, leaving me alone with Kenta.

FLIGHT OF THE PHOENIX

Kenta waits beside the tea tray, gold-flecked eyes intent on me. He's tied his hair back with a leather cord, and he looks completely different now from the laughing, carefree man of a few minutes past.

I clear my throat. "Tea?"

He grins, a slight upward curve of one side of his mouth. "Of course."

Was it a memory of me that made him smile, or something else? Perhaps I used to love food...or I was always hungry. It's unsettling to be in the company of someone who knows me better—knows better who I was and what my life was like in Karolene—than I do myself.

Kenta pours himself a cup while I sit. "Will you tell me?"

I reclaim my plate, remembering the regret with which I'd left it. This time, I'll finish everything on it, even though my stomach feels as hard and small as a stone. In a moment. First, I take a sip of my tea, now barely warm.

I tell him what he already knows: how we'd been taken to Blackflame's home, and then how I'd picked the locks to help the Degaths escape Blackflame's cages only to be caught again. I stumble to a stop, remembering that first glimpse of my mother—my shock at seeing her alive, the surreal vision of her across a decorative lotus pond.

"What happened?" Kenta asks. His words are not just the curious pressing of an acquaintance, but the gentle inquiry of a friend.

"I saw my mother there," I admit. I cannot bring myself to speak of this morning, of how I last saw her, cold and callously uncaring, a source slave that could have been me huddled against the wall beside her.

He closes his eyes for a heartbeat. "I thought she was dead."

I nod. "So did I. But she was alive and well, and she didn't see me." I shift, smooth out my skirts. Against the embroidered cushions and the vibrant colors of the carpet, they appear mottled gray, creased and stained, threadbare in spots. I focus on a snagged thread, teasing it with my fingers as I go on. "Blackflame gave me to Kol. Some kind of trade to cover a minor debt, I guess. You know he has a portal hidden in the gardens?" I glance up. For the first time since my recovery, the fact that I know this detail strikes me as important.

Kenta's gaze sharpens. "We suspected. Did they use it?"

"Yes, it looked like a—" I try to fix its image in my mind's eye, make sure I haven't somehow changed it by my remembering. "An archway with a gate. Nothing fancy. I don't remember much of it."

Kenta nods.

"They took me through, and the next day Kol gave me to a breather he held prisoner."

Kenta nods again, as if he expected this, though his eyes burn with anger.

I hold up a hand, letting the loose thread go. "The breather and I, we made a pact and escaped together."

"A pact?"

"I picked the locks. He dealt with the guards."

Kenta lets his breath out with a soft laugh. "You always land on your feet."

Not quite. "We escaped, but Kol caught up with us. The breather fought him and…we managed to kill him. But I was badly hurt, almost died."

"The mages who went to investigate claimed that Kol was burned to death, that there was nothing left of him but a memory of a spell." He watches me steadily.

I shudder. What an apt description of what I was after casting my sunbolt: a memory of a spell. "There's not much more to tell. I lost most of my memories, barely knew who I was. It took me a long time to remember much of anything. That's part of why I never contacted you." I rush on before he can question me, "The breather kept me alive long enough to deliver me to a healer. She took me in, and trained me once I was well enough to learn."

Kenta blinks. "As a healer?"

"Yes. She's a healer-mage herself."

Kenta's eyes narrow slightly. "And she took you on because…?"

"Because Blackflame orphaned me at least once over, and because a breather brought me to her. Breathers don't usually approach mages for help, so it meant a lot, what he did."

Kenta remains still a long moment, studying me. I can't read his expression. "She must be a very unusual person."

"She is. And she's also why I'm here now. She's been unjustly imprisoned and I mean to get her free."

Kenta's smile is a feral thing, sharp and dangerous, all the more unsettling for its sudden appearance. "Then I will help you. What's her name?"

"Brigit Stormwind."

His mouth drops open. *"What?"*

I nod, unsure of his reaction. He knows something of her. Is it only the news of the trial that must be the talk of the city, or something more?

He rubs his face, then says, voice flat, "She's the one who helped you."

I answer as if it were a question. "Yes."

He starts to speak and then checks himself. This clearly isn't anything close to what he expected. I don't want lose his support. I may not remember him very well, but he was part of the Shadow League. There are things he will care about regardless.

I lean toward him. "The conviction has nothing to do with justice."

"I know that," Kenta says. "Nothing involving Blackflame ever does. But— *Stormwind?* Have you considered the ramifications for the High Council if she escapes? And what would happen to you if you were caught helping her?"

"I know the risks," I say with as much quiet firmness as I can muster. "I just need a little help from the outside. I expect to carry most of the direct risks myself. As for the High Council—they'll handle the politics."

"Indeed," he says dryly. "Tell me your plan."

Ten minutes later, Kenta sits back and closes his eyes.

"I don't need much," I say uncertainly.

He speaks with his eyes still closed. "You're proposing to break a convicted mage out of a cell guarded by the most highly trained lycan guard in the Eleven Kingdoms, and located under the feet of the High Council itself."

"Yes, but—"

"And you propose to do this by tricking them into letting

her out themselves and then whisking her away over their heads."

"Pretty much," I admit. "I just need a few allies to help me get the remaining pieces in place. And a place for her to go."

He studies me through slitted eyelids. I can almost hear the thoughts running through his head as he processes this last point. "You think she would join the League?"

"I don't know. She might, she might not. She certainly has every reason to support the Shadow League, especially if you help her now and call it your work with them."

Kenta crosses his legs and leans forward, elbows on his knees. "Even if it is possible, are you sure it's worth the risk?"

I answer without hesitation. "Yes. Just as I thought it was worth the risk to help the Degaths escape Karolene. Listen, I can't control what Stormwind does if we get her out, but I've spent the last year with her, and I can guarantee that she won't make us regret helping her. I also know that what Blackflame has done, drumming up these charges and having her falsely convicted, is precisely the sort of thing we used to fight against. She's innocent. Even the Mekteb's Guardian thinks so."

Kenta's eyes darken. "The Mekteb's Guardian? You spoke with him about this?"

"I didn't intend to, but I didn't have much choice in the end. He said he's willing to let us slip by."

Slowly, so slowly it unnerves me, his lips twist into that same dangerous smile, sharp teeth bared. "The guard will move her the day after tomorrow, you said?"

"As far as I know."

"And once you get her to the rooftop? What then?"

"I have an idea—someone who can help. But I didn't want to call on him before I was sure of the rest."

Kenta nods. "Tomorrow will be a quiet day in the city, and a busy one at the Mekteb. Not a good day to plan an escape."

I can understand if Kenta can't help. I'm asking him to fight for someone he's never met. But I can't give up on Stormwind myself. So I say only, "I understand."

"Oh, I'm not letting you walk into danger alone again," Kenta says. "We'll see how quickly you can persuade your other ally. If you can get him in the next couple of hours, we do it tonight."

I nearly choke. *"Tonight?"*

"Most of the campus, including the mages, will be out celebrating. Hardly anyone in the city will notice the alarms raised over the noise of the Festival, at least not at first." Kenta rubs his hands together, cracking his knuckles. "With the streets full of revelers, and the skies full of fireworks, the lycan guard will be hard-pressed to spot your escape, let alone follow."

"That's all good," I agree. "But it's afternoon already."

"Then we'd better move fast."

We leave the Degaths' home via the service road that runs past the rear stables. Using the shortcuts Kenta knows, we leave behind the grand houses with their wide sidewalks in a matter of minutes, exchanging them for tight, mazelike streets cutting between three- and four-story stone buildings.

"How long have you been here?" I ask as we thread our way through the crowded streets.

"About a month," Kenta says. "Once we realized Blackflame planned to stay here longer than a week or two, the Ghost sent me to keep an eye on him."

"He came to press charges against Stormwind," I say.

Kenta nods. "That's about all he's been up to as far as I can tell."

"So there isn't anything like the Shadow League here?"

He smiles ruefully. "No. The king appears to be a good one, or at least not bad enough to incite rebellion, and the arch mage assigned here isn't one of Blackflame's supporters. She seems to embrace her position as servant of the people and counsel to the king."

We reach a wider thoroughfare, crowded with people bustling between the squares and plazas where the afternoon festivities await. A whiff of baked bread and spiced meat stops me in my track. The pastries were all very well and good, but the scent of real food has me almost drooling.

"What *is* that?" I ask, trying to figure out where the smell is coming from.

Kenta laughs. "Lunch is on me. But we'll walk with it."

He leads me straight to a street vendor, his push cart laden with puffy flat breads, meats grilling over an improvised fire in a metal container. The vendor empties a skewer of beef kebabs over a flatbread, tops it with fresh cut onions, tomatoes, lettuce, and a dollop of seasoned yogurt sauce, and rolls it up for the young woman in front of us.

The smell is delicious, and surprisingly strong. My thoughts, half on the kebab roll and half on planning Stormwind's escape, *click.*

"Kenta," I say as he finishes giving the man our order and steps back beside me.

"Mm?"

"The onions and garlic." I gesture to small piles of both stacked on the cart. "How do they smell to you?"

He shrugs. "Not bad at all."

"What if they're roasting, or fresh cut? Would it make it harder to pick up another scent?" Because if they do even a little, then with a magical nudge they should work wonders for masking a scent trail.

Kenta slants me a measuring look. The corner of his mouth crooks up. "I expect so. Shall I buy a few?"

I grin back at him, my mind running through other charms I might make. "Yes. I might need some ash and some nut shells as well."

"Ash I can supply you with. Nuts we should find along the way."

As the man finishes making our rolls, Kenta steps forward to chat with him, coins in hand. When we set off again, I've added two heads of garlic and three small onions to my pack.

"Good?" Kenta asks as sink my teeth into the roll.

"Amazing," I manage through a mouthful of half-chewed kebab.

"Some things never change," he murmurs.

I swallow down my bite. "They don't?"

He sidesteps an elderly couple chatting in the middle of the road. "How much do you remember about— Karolene?"

"Very little," I admit. "I remember what happened leading up to Kol very well. I remember Saira's betrayal, I remember you and the Ghost and…Rafiki. Beyond that, I have only bits and pieces. Images, a few words or phrases."

"That's all?" Kenta asks, his words faint with shock.

"It took me a month or two to remember my mother's name," I explain as we turn down another street. "Stormwind tried to help me to remember more, but at this point, I think I've recovered what I can."

"I…see. It won't come back then, will it? Your memory?"

Into the comfortable rush of people and movement around us, I let out the truth I am just starting to come to terms with.

"No. Most of it won't. I'm still recovering pieces, but there was a part of me that burned with Kol. Not everything can rise from ash again."

It's strange thinking that Kenta could know me, know what I've done, better than I do myself, when I hardly know him at all. "Will you—" I begin and then stop.

He cocks an eyebrow.

"Tell me about Karolene," I suggest, which is not at all what I meant to ask. I glance away, toward a juggler and his whirling blades, barely visible beyond the heads of a circle of onlookers.

I want to know who I was in Karolene, but for the first time I'm beginning to understand why Val wouldn't tell me what he knew of my life. Kenta knows me—through his own eyes. Not knowing myself, I might invent a false history for myself built on his words.

"There's an uplifting topic," Kenta mutters. "What would you like to know? The sultan died of a debilitating illness some months ago. Blackflame kindly helped appoint a regent until the heir can be located. Until he came here, Blackflame was at the palace every other day to provide his own counsel as well."

A debilitating illness—as my father had, wasting away no matter what cures my mother brought him. Wasting away because it wasn't an illness he suffered from, but poison. I clear my throat, try to focus. "Didn't the sultan have an heir? Some prince or the other?"

"Of course. The crown prince. You've forgotten his name, haven't you? No matter; he's disappeared. Gone into hiding, if you ask the Ghost."

"Not like the other people who disappear?"

Kenta smirks. "No. Blackflame was desperate to find him, and our informants were clear he didn't know where the prince went."

"There have been other changes as well," he goes on. "Blackflame has almost completely replaced his guard with northmen. The new tax laws favor northern traders, which means we have more of them coming through every day to the detriment of some of our own traders."

I'd forgotten these people, forgotten that Blackflame was more than a name that haunts my dreams, a voice that took my mother from me. All this time that I've been living safely in the mountains, he has tightened his hold over Karolene. And people are suffering.

"You said you wanted nuts?" Kenta nods toward an elderly woman roasting nuts alongside the next building.

"In their shells." It might look a little too odd if we offered to buy empty shells.

"Right." He darts ahead to speak with the woman. By the time I catch up, he's handing over a copper in exchange for an old, worn pouch of nuts.

"That enough?" he asks, handing it to me.

"Plenty."

"Then let's go."

Kenta leads the way through a few more narrow alleyways to a stairwell built along the side of a building. We reach the roof as I pop the last of my roll into my mouth. Kenta comes to a stop toward the back, blocked from view by multiple lines of washing strung from poles. "This look all right?"

I nod. It's empty and quiet, and not too near any major streets. A few rooftops away, a half dozen brightly colored kites swoop through the air, riding the salty breeze, their ribbon tails fluttering behind them. A scarlet kite suddenly jerks free, swooping erratically before disappearing below the rooftops. A faint cheer rises from the kite fliers. "What are they doing?"

"Kite fighting," Kenta explains, half-eaten sandwich in one hand. "They try to bring down the other kites, or break them free from their owner. Last kite left is the winner."

Nothing to worry about, then. I sit down and work off my boot. The feather I scrape from the inside sole is mashed and ratty, but still holds a gleam of gold.

Seeing it in my hand, Kenta asks, "What exactly will you owe this friend of yours?"

"Nothing I don't owe him already," I admit. "I'll merely owe it sooner." It helps to think of it in those terms.

"You're sure about this?"

I consider the feather, the glint of gold. No, I'm not sure. Burning this feather means that after I help Stormwind, I return to the Burnt Lands. It means that I must make an attempt at breaking apart ancient enchantments I know nothing about, spells that could very well kill me in their unraveling.

Stormwind wouldn't want this. She didn't want me to come here and she would never want such a future for me. No more than I want a prison for hers.

"It's all right if you don't do this."

It's a relief to look away from the feather, to Kenta.

"There's no other way past the guards. She can't just walk out of there. They'll follow her trail, her scent. Garlic and onions might mask her passing for a few moments, but she's not going to be able to walk out of the Mekteb."

"What about you? Or is this friend of yours going to fly you both out?"

"He'll fly me out if he wants me to help him," I reply grimly. Although the phoenix making two trips is hardly a good idea. I sigh. "Or I can walk out, wearing mages robes. There will be enough mages combing the campus that they might not realize who I am until I'm gone." That strategy has worked well enough so far.

Kenta shakes his head. "The campus will be closed off. No one will be going through the gates."

I nod, look out to the kites fluttering through the air. Beyond them, a flock of birds rises and falls, a smudge of black trailing over the far rooftops. Would that I could shift myself into bird form, as Talon must be able to. But that's far beyond anything I can master in the next hour or two. "Then I wait them out, dressed as a servant."

So many uncertainties.

Kenta shifts. "As far as I can tell, Stormwind went to her trial willingly. She chose her path. Make sure you want to choose this future for yourself, before you call whomever that feather will bring. Let me know when you decide." He ducks beneath the clotheslines, continuing on until he's lost from view on the other side of the roof.

I *want* him to tell me not to do this, to be the one who points out that it's suicide, or just plain stupid. Hearing the words is different from knowing them, and as long as I'm only telling myself these things, I can brush them aside. But Kenta is relying on me to consider the risks, choose wisely.

Wisdom tells me that only sorrow lies down this path. I cannot see a way for both Stormwind and I to escape unscathed. I close my eyes, clutching the feather tightly. I remember Stormwind standing in the doorway of her cottage, bidding me farewell, not knowing how to hug me back. She realized, then, that her life was finished. That she would never return—to the cottage, to teaching me, to the companionship we shared this last year as mentor and student. As friends.

I open my eyes and glare down at the feather. She sheltered me, protected me, and trained me, in part because of what Blackflame did to me. I will not let her go without a fight. If I am caught and lose my magic, so be it. And if we escape and

I must face the Burnt Lands, then I will face them.

Huda's words echo in my mind, whispering on the wind that blows across the rooftop. *When you have chosen a path, you must walk it with courage.*

Lifting the feather high, I call on the fire that lies dormant in my bones, sending a single spark through my fingertips.

The feather catches as if it were a torch, flaring up in a scorching ball of yellow and blue. I snatch my hand away with a yelp. It remains floating in the air, burning and burning and burning.

"Kenta," I call. The clotheslines rustle as he moves toward me.

At the sight of the floating fire, he lets out a low whistle. "Some feather."

The fire drifts downward, lessening as it descends until it touches the floor and goes out. All that remains is a single thread of ash. I nudge it with a fingertip and it disintegrates against my nail.

Kenta kneels before me, his kimono accenting the line of his thighs, the wiry strength of his shoulders. I don't even know this man. His ease with me, the certainty with which he chose to help, tells me we were friends once, knew each other well. But the person that I am now he knows no better than I can claim to know him.

"When we were betrayed," I say, my voice rough, awkward. "In that building. You and the Ghost hid. I remember that."

His eyes narrow slightly, his jaw tightening.

"Do you remember how?" I ask.

"You hid us. The soldiers walked up to us, looked up at the burnt-out stairwell, and left. They never saw us."

"Shadows." The word is almost a whisper, as if I dare not speak this truth aloud even here, with just the wind and sun and a dozen lines of clean laundry to witness it.

"Yes."

Relief rushes through me. "Then you know."

"I would have guessed regardless. Even the Degaths know. You killed Kol with a magic so strong that the High Council found its traces months afterward. By all accounts, only you and the breather escaped. Breathers don't have magic—not the kind that can cast spells."

"I...see," I manage. For the first time, burning myself to a cinder actually seems like it was a good idea. The High Council didn't look any further for me, assuming I was dead.

"I'm glad you know," I tell Kenta. "It makes things easier now." I wave toward my bag with its assortment of onions and garlic and empty shells. "I'm going to make some charms to distract the lycan guard. I'll need that ash you said you had, too."

"Are you sure it's safe to practice your magic here?" Kenta asks.

I shrug. "It's unlikely that there are mages living in this part of town—it's too poor. And on a day like this, they'd have no reason to come here. I'll shield myself. With the number of charms in use, no one should notice. I won't be using much magic."

He makes no answer.

"We still need to figure out how to get her the key and charm," I say to distract him. We've already discussed this once at the Degaths' home, but part of me is hoping that Kenta lit on an idea on the walk here.

He grins, that light returning to his eyes. "You figured out someone cleans Talon's rooms," he teases.

"The lycans will hardly allow an unknown servant in to clean Stormwind's cell," I point out. "Especially not when most of the servants have the afternoon off for the Festival."

"No," Kenta agrees, still grinning. He lifts what's left of his sandwich in the air. "But surely they must feed her."

Kenta fetches me a bowl of ash from his rooms below, then departs once more to see to our preparations, cat's head key and the look-away charm in his pocket. I set to work on the remaining charms I must make. They're easy enough, adaptations of ones I've made before, and I work through them quickly. Barely half an hour later, as I finish the last of them, I squint against the brightening sunlight.

Brightening?

I leap to my feet, dumping my new charms onto the rooftop as I shield my eyes from the glare of a second sun. A ball of golden flame shoots across the sky, trailing an afterimage of shadow behind it. In the space of a breath, it covers the remaining distance to my rooftop, hurtling downward at an impossible speed.

I clench my teeth around a shout and squeeze my eyes shut. My back brushes the shield wall created by my string of wards. I hold still, knowing it will protect me. Ropes snap in rapid succession, a whiff of burnt things teasing my nostrils, and the light goes out.

"Well," the phoenix says, "I am happy to see you are not in immediate danger."

I lower my arms from my face, blinking to dispel the dark spots floating across my vision. The phoenix stands a few paces away, completely unruffled. Behind him, the laundry lines lie in a tangled, half-burnt mess, steam and smoke rising from them in equal measure. At least half the clothes are scorched past saving.

A dull commotion rumbles up from the streets below.

"There is something you need, is there not?" the phoenix says.

If his tone had been smug, his words gloating, I might have pulled back, at least for a moment. But his tone is detached, professional, as if we were discussing bartering animals. The thought sends a shudder through my body, a memory I cannot quite place.

I kneel to unclasp my ward string and look the phoenix in the eye. "I have a question for you. A deal. If you agree, then I'll come with you as soon as this is over."

The phoenix bobs his head. "Tell me."

RAISING THE ALARM

We spend a full half hour discussing Stormwind and the escape plan. The phoenix isn't altogether pleased, and he probably wouldn't have been fully swayed had I not mentioned Jabir's complicity. It's ironic, really, because the Mekteb's guardian let me enter—and offered me a way out—in large part because of the phoenix feather I carried. But eventually, the phoenix agrees.

The High Council seems to matter to him only in as much as it keeps another Burning at bay. His willingness to do what I ask to get me back to the Burnt Lands immediately makes me wonder how fleeting our lives feel to him.

"And you will stay a season," he says after he has heard me out.

"I cannot stay in any one place that long."

"You ask a great deal for less than three months of work," the phoenix says.

"Three months will be long enough for their hunters to find me. I'll stay a month, and return again a year later for a second month."

He shakes his head. "It will take you a month just to begin your work. Two months together, and I will offer you shelter from their hunters should you require it."

Shelter seems an impossible thing, but if the phoenix believes he can do it, it would be foolish to refuse. And I do owe him. I lick dry lips, knowing I have precious little bargaining power. "Very well."

Kenta arrives in plenty of time to meet the phoenix, having seen his light in the sky and hurried back. Together, we agree on a location to fly Stormwind to—a rooftop neither too close nor too far from the Mekteb, where Kenta will be waiting.

"It is better if you can make your own way out." The phoenix plucks another feather from his breast and drops it before me. "But burn this if you find yourself in trouble."

I hide it in my boot once more. When the phoenix departs, he merely spreads his wings and flies, looking not unlike the peacocks that grace the city and Mekteb.

"Your secret ally is a phoenix," Kenta says, staring after him. "I can't even…*what* will you owe him?"

"Some spell work," I say vaguely.

Kenta gives me a hard look, then sighs. "Come on, or the bread will burn."

I follow him downstairs and into a surprisingly barren room, containing only a sleeping mat, a large leather pack, a low table cluttered with bowls and cups, and a worn cushion on the floor beside it. A covered iron pot is nestled in the coals of the room's small stone fireplace, more coals heaped on the pot lid.

He opens the improvised oven with iron tongs and lifts out a single baked roll. "Looks good," he says as he sets it to cool on a cloth by the fireplace. "Give it a moment and we'll be ready to go."

"What took you so long to come up, if you were here all along?"

"I went to get one more thing we'll need." He slips a ring from his pocket. It's bright gold with a huge blue stone that is most assuredly fake. "There are quite a few theatre troupes visiting the city right now. It took me two tries to find one that would sell me a costume."

"But you don't need—"

He slips the ring on. The glamor it carries ripples over him, transforming him into a copper-skinned, dark-haired man in maroon robes.

"—That."

"You didn't think I was going to let you walk back in there alone, did you?"

178

I did, actually. I need him working on the outside. If he comes, that drives the stakes far higher than I'd like them to be. I shake my head. "I'm not risking your life."

"No," he agrees easily. "I am. You're going to need my help to start with." He gestures toward the bread. Baked within it lie the cat's head key, the look-away, and a tightly-rolled note with the words, *Open your shackles, wear the ring, wait.* "You won't be able to add that to Stormwind's dinner tray by yourself without drawing notice."

"This could be your life. You don't have to do this."

"No, I don't." He picks up the bread, still steaming hot, and tosses it into a cloth shoulder bag.

"Kenta—" We don't have time to argue. I need to take the bread and get back to the Mekteb before we miss Stormwind's dinnertime altogether.

He glances over his shoulder. His robes are the dark red of old blood in the dim light of the room. His eyes narrow as he notices my expression. "You're not going to change my mind, Hitomi. Not if you're going ahead with this plan yourself."

I don't know what is driving him, and don't want to take this risk…but he's right. It's his choice. And it will be much easier getting Stormwind the bread if I have help. "If you're coming, you can't wear that glamor until you're inside the gates. The guards will catch it—they have mages posted at all the gates right now."

"Not a problem." He slides the ring off his finger and pockets it, then passes me the bread bag.

My mind flies ahead, trying to work through this new factor in our plan. "The guards are expecting me at the back gate. If you can come up with a pretext for entering from the main gate, we can meet up inside Shahmaran Hall."

Kenta frowns, rubs his hand over his mouth, and smirks. "Delivery for a lady friend. Mistress Flicker."

"Who?"

"One of Blackflame's supporters. Do you have any jewelry I can pretend to take to her?"

"I have nothing of the—" I break off, remembering the necklaces I took from Stormwind's trunk.

Kenta raises an eyebrow.

"It's not mine, it's Stormwind's."

"Even better. If I don't mention names, I'll be telling the truth."

I swing my pack around and dig out the pouch with the chains. "You'll need the truth to get past Jabir. If you say you're going to deliver something, you better plan to do it."

Kenta takes the necklace I hand him. "I'll figure it out."

As I shove my belongings back down into my pack, my fingers brush the crow carving. It's smooth and slightly cool to the touch, and seeing it gives me a certain amount of hope for what's to come. But I wouldn't want to lose it inside the Mekteb..."Do you think I could— could leave a few things with you? In case I can't bring anything out with me?"

Kenta goes still, a tightness around his eyes. My words have hit him hard, though I'm not sure why. We both know the risks we're running right now.

"Yes," he says. His voice is low, almost hollow. "You can."

Working quickly, I transfer what I need to the bread bag— my servants' attire, the mage's robe, the charms. I leave most of my belongings in my pack, rifling through them once to make sure I haven't missed anything. Rising, I hold my pack out to Kenta. "Thanks."

He takes it as if it were incredibly fragile, setting it gently next to his own. I wait as he stands there, but he doesn't turn back around.

We need to go. "Is something wrong?" I ask softly.

He shakes his head and walks to the door. "You won't remember," he says. "But you've done this before."

"Done what?"

"Left me with your most prized possessions, and an emergency stash of coins." He flicks a glance at me, expressionless. "In Karolene. You didn't fully trust that your things wouldn't get stolen from the place where you lived. It was supposed to be a temporary measure."

He steps outside. I follow him into the hallway, bread bag in hand. As he locks up, I ask, "Do you still have them?"

He turns his head to look at me, so close that, if either of us shifted, our arms would touch. The laughter is gone from his eyes. "Yes. In Karolene."

He starts down the stairs without another word.

Returning to the Mekteb is impressively anticlimactic. The same guards are on duty and merely wave me through. I change back into my servants' garb in the women's quarters and head off to Shahmaran Hall. The campus is all but empty, a single servant passing in front of a building far in front of me. There are still guards about, though now they are stationed at only a few strategic locations. They must consider the threat of the rogue mage well past. They certainly afford me no more than a passing glance.

The sun is beginning to dip behind the buildings. I walk quickly, the fear that we've already missed Stormwind's dinner delivery hurrying my footsteps.

As I reach the side entrance of Shahmaran Hall, one of the guards on duty says with sympathy, "Working late?"

I huff with pretend frustration. "Just a few last things that *must* be done."

He chuckles. "At least you get the evening off."

"True," I say, and duck into the building.

Inside, I stash my bundle in the supply closet, keeping only the bread in hand. I leave a couple of charms strategically placed at the crack beneath the door, and slip into an empty classroom to wait. If Kenta makes it in—if he can even find Shahmaran Hall and get past the guards—then he will find me here. Otherwise, it's up to me to waylay the servant.

I try not to fidget as I watch the doorway for movement and consider what story I can use, what sleight of hand, to get the bread to Stormwind without harming the servant or raising suspicion.

Footsteps in the hall. I tense, listening. They're measured, deliberate. Not the servant then—servants would want to make the delivery quickly, the sooner to finish and be off to the Festival.

I press my back against the wall. A shadow darkens the doorway. It could be Kenta, but—

"Hikaru?"

I sag with relief. "Hey," I whisper, glad Kenta remembered to use the name I'd given him.

"Anyone come through yet?" he asks.

"No."

"I'll wait at the end, then."

"Last classroom is still open."

"Good." He continues down the hall, footsteps pausing toward the end.

I move to where I can see through the doorway, take one curious peek down the hall. Kenta turns from inspecting the classroom and begins pacing back and forth before the stairwell that leads to the lower levels of Shahmaran Hall, hands clasped behind his back. With the gold ring on his finger, he looks for all the world like a professor of magic distracted by the thought of some theorem or incantation.

I ease back once more, sliding off my boots and leaning against the wall, my eyes on the doorway. I try not to think about the classroom behind me, what it would be like to join other students at the central table with its collection of magical objects and charms. What it would be like to learn openly and freely with others, or simply to have so much knowledge at one's disposal.

A shadow flickers past. With a silent curse, I hurry forward to peer out. A serving boy trots along carrying a tray in his hands. Kenta calls out to the boy, sounding genuinely pleased to have found someone who could help him.

The boy protests unhappily—he's supposed to deliver the tray at once.

"To whom?" Kenta asks, peeved. "They can't wait five minutes for their dinner?"

"It's for the prisoner, master," the boy says. "I'm not supposed to stop along the way."

"What! That traitor gets her soup hot and I have to wait for help?" Kenta blusters. I have to bite my lip to keep from laughing. "Put that down right there—it will be perfectly fine—and help me a moment. At once! Come along."

The boy sets down the tray and follows Kenta into a classroom, glancing nervously behind him. I wait until they are in, then hurry the thirty or so paces to the tray, my socked feet whispering across the stone floor. In addition to the cup of soup Kenta had protested, the tray holds a plate with a silver cover, and a square of cloth wrapped around two thick slices of bread. I lift the cover to find curried meat and rice. I shove the rice over a bit, squeeze the bun we'd baked onto the plate, and cover it once more.

I retreat to my classroom, my breath loud in my ears. I had planned to use a glamor, a single-word spell, to disguise the bun as whatever sort of bread might be on the tray. But this way it's hidden from the servant's eyes, and I don't have to risk any spells. There are fewer magical repercussions echoing through the building tonight—almost none, which means very little "noise" to hide my spellwork behind. As long as the servant doesn't take off the cover and notice it, as long as the lycans don't think it strange that there are two servings of bread on the tray....

I exhale slowly, press my back against the wall. Nothing to

be done about it now.

Kneeling, I check to make sure the new phoenix feather is still safe and then work my boots back on. Kenta's voice gains volume as he returns to the hallway, sending the boy off to deliver his precious soup to the traitor. The boy's hurried footsteps recede to silence. I listen as Kenta strides up the hall. He steps into the classroom, moving to stand against the wall beside the door. He glances at me, his features relaxing as I nod.

We wait until the serving boy hurries past again, his hands empty. Kenta, watching my face, must see my relief, for he grins and slips the glamour ring from his finger. Then he raises his brows and waggles them at me.

"Nothing yet," he drawls, keeping his voice low. He sounds utterly relaxed, half-amused, as if we were discussing the exploits of a mutual friend.

"I should hope not." An alarm now would mean we'd been found out before the food ever got to Stormwind. "Unless they decide to keep it quiet," I add.

"Always the optimist," Kenta mutters, and then laughs, a soft, stifled sound.

I eye him askance. "What are you laughing about?"

"You," he says, shoulders shaking. "At least, the you I remember. Never mind. Where will you go now?"

"I've got that planned," I reply, knowing better than to share details that might hurt either of us, should one of us get caught. "You need to leave before they close the gates."

He nods, a jerk of his chin, his eyes moving to the window. "You know the building."

"Yes." On our way to here, we walked past the building where Kenta will meet the phoenix, a few city blocks from the gates. I also memorized the directions to his rented room. If I end up leaving separately from Stormwind, I'll be able to find them.

But Kenta still stands against the wall, his gaze on the gardens visible through the window. There is no trace of laughter in his eyes now. "Kenta," I say gently, "whatever happens, I made these choices. I don't want you to regret them."

"It'll take a miracle for you to walk out of here." Kenta almost snarls the words as he turns his gaze on me. "I told myself I wouldn't sit by and let you do that again, back when it first happened, before we thought you dead. This afternoon, I thought I could help you, walk with you as I promised myself. Now I'm going to break my word."

"You're not—"

"I am."

"It wouldn't make sense for you to stay," I point out. "You can't touch the wards and there's no reason for both of us to risk our lives. Someone has to meet the phoenix."

"I know the *reasons*." His voice verges on a growl. "It doesn't change the fact that I'm breaking my word."

I bite my lip to keep from arguing. He finally faces me, and in the failing light, I see the pain in his eyes. And I finally understand why he has helped me so much now; he still has not forgiven himself for my "death," for the sacrifice I made to save him and the Ghost. Just as Alia has not forgiven herself. We are all carrying so much hurt.

I say the only thing I can think of. "I'm sorry."

He snorts. "Even if it was your fault, I wouldn't blame you." He shakes his head, takes a step, and turns back to me. "Tomi?"

I nod, the nickname—so foreign, so completely *right*—settling into me.

"Get out alive."

Once Kenta departs, I take the stairs down, coming to a stop at the first closed door—classroom or storage room, I can't say. I slip a charm or three into the crack beneath the doors, turn tail, and leave, up the stairs and out of the building.

I spend the next hour closed up inside the servants' washroom in the basement of the next building over. After changing into my old clothes and pulling on Stormwind's mage robes, I sit on the floor and wait. From down here, it's almost impossible to tell what's happening in the rest of the Mekteb. I remain where I am until I hear a high wail that raises the hair on the back of my neck, making me cringe. It's certainly not the sort of siren one could ignore.

I make my way upstairs as the wail repeats. Outside, the glowstones under the arcades and throughout the gardens have burst into sun-like brilliance, driving out every shadow. Against their brightness, the forms of the lycan guards—dozens of them—show clear and frightening. They move systematically and fast, small groups combing through the gardens while others search the surrounding buildings.

As I stand at the doorway, two mages race down the stairs, taking the hallway at a run.

"What's going on?" I ask them, stepping back as they approach.

The foremost mage slows, assessing me with a quick, shrewd glance. "Who are you?"

"Journeyman Zainab Tanaka," I say helpfully. It had seemed as good a name as any while I sat waiting in the washroom. "Is it the rogue mage again?"

"No," the second mage says, glancing past me to the doors. "It's Mage Stormwind."

I blink at them. "What?"

"She escaped," the first mage snaps, starting forward. "We haven't time to talk. If you want to help, come along. You can at least be useful keeping the apprentices from leaving their buildings."

I follow after them. "I've experience in tracking," I say, having no intention whatsoever of getting shut up with a bunch of frightened children. I have work to do.

"We'll see," the mage says.

Outside, I trail after the mages as they move to intercept a team of lycans coming down the arcade. They call out a greeting, demanding information.

The lead lycan slows to speak with us, gesturing his men to continue on. "We're expanding the search to the outer buildings. Join one of patrols. The mage may still be dangerous. If you catch up with her, call for reinforcements. Don't attempt to engage her. We don't know what she's capable of."

"She's a high mage gone rogue," retorts the first mage. "She's capable of a great deal."

"Only if she managed to break the binding spell holding her," the lycan says. "There's still a chance we will catch her on campus. If she makes it to the city, it will be…difficult."

"How long has she been missing?" The first mage demands.

"Anywhere from ten minutes to an hour. We need to move quickly to find her."

The mages nod in agreement, and start forward once more. I follow them, parting ways with the guard and continuing around the corner of the building to the path there. At which point, I say, "I'm going to check for students here," and duck into the side entrance of the next building—White Raven Hall.

The mages say something to my back, but I let the door close behind me without answer. The hallway lies empty. Good. I count to five hundred, then slip back out. The mages are long gone, the path between the buildings momentarily empty, the search already widening out, just as I'd hoped. I jog along the path, then turn up the back of the building, following the paths toward the back of Shahmaran Hall.

As I move, I catch glimpses of the boundary wall through the gaps in the next set of buildings. A reddish cloud rises above the walls, two or three times its height, so thick that it completely obscures the distant lantern- and glowstone-lit buildings. In actual depth it might be no more than a pace or two across, but from here it appears impenetrable. Without reaching out with my mage senses to assess it, I can't know its exact nature. I would guess it was originally designed to keep the campus safe from outsiders, rather than to keep people in. I wonder if the mages involved have adjusted it, or if raising it was merely a visible way of alerting the campus and city. Either way, I won't be climbing any walls to get out.

As I near Shahmaran Hall, I cut across the flower beds and paths, headed for the window I separated from the building's magical defenses. With the glowstones shining brighter than lanterns, the bushes below the window offer scant cover. Not good.

Another search party composed of two mages and two lycans rounds the far corner of the building as I stand before the windows. On impulse, I raise a hand, drawing their attention. The lycans break into a sprint, the mages hurrying after them.

"I don't know if it means anything," I tell them as they reach me, gesturing toward the window. "I was assessing the spells on the building—I couldn't understand how she got out."

The elder mage, a stocky middle-aged man, wheezes up to us, clearly displeased at having to run after the guards. "Who are you?" he demands. "Why are you here alone?"

"Journeyman Zainab Tanaka," I say easily. "And I'm searching for the prisoner, or an explanation, or both." He blinks, taken aback. It's amazing what a name and an attitude of entitlement does to make a person appear legitimate.

The lead lycan takes a step forward. "You've found something?"

"This window," I gesture at it again. "The spells have been

tampered with. If someone opened this window after the alarm was raised, it wouldn't matter. It's been…cut off, for lack of a better word."

The mages exchange a single, horrified glance and step closer to the window. The second lycan follows them, no doubt to check for a scent. I turn to the first lycan who remains by me. "I've never heard of anything, but is there a magic that can hide or change a person's scent?"

"We didn't think so," he replies darkly.

"You don't scent her out here?"

He shakes his head. "We've already searched the building for her scent, and done a round out here. Nothing."

"I'd like to go inside, look at the windows from there, maybe take a look at her cell."

The lycan turns his full gaze on me. I wait, trusting the fact that I've shown them something they missed. He'll humor me, I expect, because they're already grasping at straws.

"You think you'll find something?"

I shrug. "I don't know. But I'd like to look."

"Bekir," the lycan barks to the second guard. "I'll escort this mage around front, then rejoin you." He jerks his head at the muttering mages, one of whom lifts a hand to assess the window. "See what they say."

The second mage, a short man with a graying beard, shoots us an annoyed look. "You expect a journeyman to find more?"

The lycan raises his brows. "She's found more than anyone else, hasn't she? Or has the spell not been tampered with?"

"It's changed," the stocky mage says heavily. "But I don't know that girl and neither do you. And she's only a journeyman. If there's more to be found, you'll need a mage. We're coming with you."

The lycan shrugs and turns on his heel, striding back the way they came. I have to trot to keep up. The mages mutter with irritation as they hurry after us, Bekir bringing up the rear. We continue around to the front of the building, passing under the arcade to the main doors guarded by four lycans and two more mages.

"Kemal." A lycan guard raises a hand in greeting.

With a sharp gesture toward me, my escort says, "She found a flaw in the protective spells on the building. She and the mages want to assess the building's spells from the inside."

One of the mages on guard at the door frowns at me. "What difference does it make? Stormwind's already escaped."

I fix him with a cold look. "We need to know if anyone is helping her. If we can learn how she escaped, we may have a better idea of how to search for her."

The stocky mage pushes past me. "As a high mage, I have every right to enter this building if I think it will forward the search."

The mage on guard draws himself up. "And what do you think you'll find? We've already been through the building twice."

"Yet you missed the window that was no longer connected to the ward spells encircling this building. We are looking for subtle magic here, things that might be overlooked." The stocky mage all but sneers at the guard mage.

"Fine," he capitulates, glowering. And then, to the lycans by his side. "Let them in."

One of the guards takes a key from his belt and unlocks the door. I sense a ripple in the wards around the building—the key is spelled to work with the defenses, allowing its holder to pass through without trouble. Now that's a key I could've used.

When we step inside Shahmaran Hall, the mages hesitate, unsure which way to go. The lycans who brought us in, Kemal and Bekir, watch them in silence.

"The window will be this way," I say, stepping forward. The halls are brightly lit, eerily silent. The noise of our passing fills my ears. I lead them down the hall, pausing at the door before the one I want. I can feel the lycans' gaze on my back, measuring my actions. I peek in, then shake my head and continue on to the next one. Stepping in, I move quickly across the room and press my hand against the window, my robe brushing over the sill.

"Move back, *journeyman*," the stocky mage blusters. "Allow a full mage to assess that, if you please."

I step back with a stiff nod, glowering at the ground. But I've accomplished what I've needed to. Any moment now, the lycans will realize they need to search for scents here. They won't be surprised to find mine, the fresh covering the old.

I move to stand by the lycans. "Was there anything unusual about the escape?"

Kemal presses his lips together, shakes his head. "We cannot figure out how she got past us, but she wasn't there when we went to retrieve her dinner tray."

"It looks like she might have climbed out here, perhaps

even before the alarm was raised. I can't say how she got past the guards. Or how she masked her scent." I pause thoughtfully, keep my voice low as I go on. "I'd like to see the room where you were holding her, check if there's anything there that's been tampered with, or any sign of spells."

Kemal exchanges a glance with Bekir, then nods. I return my focus to the mages, wondering what else they hope to find on this side of the window that they didn't see from the other side. After another minute or so, they complete their assessment.

"This should be reported to First Mage Talon," the stocky mage says.

The lycans dip their heads.

I lower my gaze to the floor, trying to look bored as my thoughts race. I don't want any more mages in Shahmaran Hall than are already here. Nor do I want anyone else to focus their attention here before I've gotten Stormwind out.

"Will you want to send a messenger?" Kemal asks.

The stocky mage eyes him with disdain. "Hardly. She will want a full explanation of what has been done. I will go to her myself."

"I'll remain behind to fix this," the gray-bearded mage says, gesturing to the window.

"Bekir will escort you," Kemal says, nodding to the stocky mage. "I'll stay here with the other two."

The stocky mage slides me a glance. He expects me to argue, because I was the one who "found" the flaw. I frown at him. "But—"

"That will do nicely," he interrupts. With a dismissive nod, he strides from the room, Bekir following after him.

"You can reseal this window?" Kemal asks the gray-bearded mage.

"Of course I can."

"Wouldn't it be better to keep it as it is, and post a guard here, until it can be assessed by the First Mage? She might be curious to see it herself."

Graybeard hesitates, clearly torn between what he'd promised the stocky mage, and Kemal's practicality. "I said that I would."

"Perhaps," Kemal says, with fraying patience, "it would behoove us all if you took another look at the prisoner's cell, now that we have some idea what she might have done."

"Ah, yes. That would be wise," Graybeard says, then draws himself up. "If you would lead the way."

Kemal tilts his head. "First, allow me to fetch a guard for the window."

Graybeard frowns. "Of course."

With a slight bow that strikes me as sarcastic, Kemal departs.

I wander to another window, scanning the grounds. A patrol hurries past a building across the way, and that is all. The remaining patrols have moved farther out. Smoke still hangs in the air over the far walls, outlining the tops of the surrounding buildings. Scarlet flares rise up, hanging in the sky above in crimson streaks before gradually dissipating. I squint, trying to make out a shadow passing above them.

"What is *that?*" I point as the shadow comes into focus. A great creature with a long, barbed tail and huge leather wings flies above the walls, swinging its head slowly back and forth as it scans the ground. Oh God, I hope I'm hallucinating. Getting past a *dragon*—I can't quite imagine how we'll do that.

"Oh, that's Jabir, the Mekteb's Guardian. Didn't you know?"

I shake my head numbly, remembering Rehan happily explaining *if he ever has to defend the Mekteb, he's a force to be reckoned with*. She hadn't been jesting.

The dragon disappears beyond my view.

Jabir promised to look the other way, I remind myself. Only now do I realize what a great favor that is.

LOOK AWAY

Kemal returns with a pair of lycan guards and the mage from the front door, who finds it impossible to believe that we might detect anything unknown in Stormwind's cell.

"We're just taking a look," Graybeard says, peeved. "Why don't you see if there's anything else about the window we've missed?"

The guard mage gives him a haughty glance and stalks over to the window. Kemal gestures for us to follow and leads us down the stairs and around the corner to the short hall with its final stairwell. He raises his hand in greeting to the two lycans still posted at the head of the stairs.

Over their velvet and leather armor, they wear an array of weapons—swords sheathed in curving scabbards, twin sets of long-bladed daggers. The one on the right even has a small crossbow attached to his belt. At least neither one is the lycan who made the boys apologize to me in the gardens. Meeting him here, when I'm dressed as a mage rather than a servant would necessitate drastic measures. Measures I'm not sure I'm willing to take.

The lycans look to Kemal as we near them.

"We've discovered a flaw in the building's protections, a window that would have let the prisoner out even if the spells on the building were already triggered. We'd like to double check the protections on the holding cell."

"Go ahead," the one of them says, waving us down.

There are more shadows in the subterranean hall below than I expected, perhaps due to the lack of glowstones. There's a single sconce built into the wall, and a glowstone-lit lantern on the ground. The hall itself has four doors. The first stands open, and a quick glimpse shows it to be a guard room.

Kemal leads us to the door beside the lantern. It's built of thick wood, reinforced with iron bands.

"Let's see, then," Graybeard says, pulling the door open and stepping inside. Kemal glances at me, then follows after. I stand to the side, careful to leave plenty of space for a person to pass through, and study the door.

A single touch lights its sigil to my mage's senses. It glows a soft blue, a series of paintbrush-like strokes and curves overlaying each other, all overwriting the name "Stormwind." I frown, studying the sigil itself, not sure I recognize it. If I had finished my studies, if I weren't somewhere between apprentice and journeyman, I would probably know it. But common sense tells me that the sigil is designed to stop Stormwind herself from opening the door. It would still allow a lycan guard to deliver a meal without requiring the aid of a mage. With the sigil on the door, Stormwind wouldn't have been able to pass through even if she was still within.

But the strangest thing about these spells, the sigil that anchors them, is that they open with the door. Now, with the door wide open while Graybeard inspects the inside of the cell, a pathway has been created through the sigil's enchantment. The strands of magic reaching from the door to the other sigils impressed on the walls within create a tunnel of sorts. It's about as likely to keep her from escaping as giving the cat's head key to a servant would have kept it from being discovered. Which is to say, not at all.

I study the sigil a moment longer, but as far as I can tell, opening the door from the outside was all that needed to be done. Poor Kenta. He really could have done this himself.

"Do you see something?" Kemal asks softly. He stands just inside, back against the cell wall, where he can keep an eye on me and the other mage, who is currently poking at Stormwind's discarded shackle.

I realize belatedly that my surprise must have shown. Nothing for it but to admit it, then. "This is interesting. Who set it?"

"Arch Mage Talon and two others. Is something wrong?"

"No," I assure him. "It's simply not what I expected. I'm sure they know more of these things than I do."

I step through and walk to the center of the room. The cell is tight, hardly six paces in either direction, without any windows. There must be a spell in place to keep the air fresh, or the room would grow suffocating within an hour or two.

Against the back wall lies a bedroll and two precisely folded blankets. On the ground, beside the shackle, rests a dinner tray, the cup fallen on its side, a few last grains of rice drying on the plate. Some part of me registers the shiny metal of the shackle, bright as silver, and quails.

I push my memories of another cell, high up in a tower, firmly into the darkest corner of my mind, and cast another glance around the apparently empty room. No sign of Stormwind. She must be holding her breath, hidden from sight by the look-away charm. Unless she stepped out while I studied the door.

I slide my fingers into my pocket, feel the shape of a few charms, the slip of paper with instructions for her to go to the roof. But I need to be sure she's gotten out first.

"This was opened without magic," Graybeard announces, gesturing to the shackle.

"She picked the lock?" I ask, walking over to inspect it.

He shakes his head. "No, it's warded against anything but the key that fits it."

I turn to Kemal. "Who has the key?"

"Arch Mage Talon, I believe." His expression is closed. Interesting. Does he know it went missing but isn't at leave to say so?

I frown, tap the shackles with my finger. It's the closest I can get to making myself handle them. "Well, there must be another way to unlock them because they sure are open."

The mage grunts in response, then turns to survey the rest of the room. If Stormwind is still in here, I don't want him to notice. Time to go.

"I don't see anything else unusual," I say, pretending to look over the cell one last time. With a shrug, I head out the door. After a moment, Kemal and the mage join me in the hall. I hunker down before the door and study the lock. There should be more than enough space for Stormwind to step out, press herself against the wall of the hallway. It's the best I can offer.

"What happened to the door's key?" I ask Kemal.

"We turned it over to the mages who first responded to our alarm, Master Stonefall and Mistress Ravenflight."

Stonefall. Of course he would be involved. "The door was locked when she disappeared?"

"Yes."

"Mmm." I rise to my feet and give the door a soft push. It doesn't quite close, a thin crack of darkness still visible, as I'd hoped. Just in case.

Kemal starts for the stairs, Graybeard a half-step behind him. With the prisoner gone, they don't care if the door is shut now or not. I follow after, letting myself fall farther behind by degrees, so that I am starting up the stairs as they reach the landing.

I pull a mix of charms from my pocket, along with the tightly rolled message, and hold them behind my back, walking slowly. *Please*, I pray. *Please let her have gotten out.*

Cool fingers pluck the charms from my hand, startling me even though I was hoping for them. Gratitude swells within me. She's out. Safe. And we're almost free.

I move ahead, continuing up to Kemal and the guards posted there.

"—nothing you haven't already found," Graybeard finishes telling them.

I shake my head in agreement as the lycans glance down at me. There's no way Stormwind will be able to walk past these guards without their scenting her. It's time for a distraction. I reach out with my mage senses to the charms I'd stashed along the connecting hallway. As one of the lycans responds to Graybeard, I find the charm I want.

Skreeeeeeeeeeeeeeeee!

The lycans whirl toward the high-pitched shriek and set off at a sprint down the hall. Graybeard shouts, stumbling backwards. I can't wait for him to decide what to do. I jog past him, careful to keep far enough back from the guards that they might not notice the sound of an extra set of footsteps behind mine. I can't hear her over the beating of my heart, but that doesn't mean their more sensitive ears won't.

As they reach the corner, the screecher is already winding down. I use my magic to break the smoker I'd pressed into the crack beneath the same door. Graybeard shouts again somewhere behind me. The lycans move silently, swords drawn.

"Check the rooms here," Kemal orders, yellow gaze sweeping the hall ahead. "We were below and passed no one on our way up."

Just like that, the hallway clears, the other lycans thumping their hands against the wall until they find doors to push open. I reach out with my senses and activate the last charm I'd hidden here: a stinker. It will take a moment, but the smell should help mask Stormwind's passing.

"Young mage," Kemal says as I reach him. "Do you sense

anything?"

"They feel like the charms students use for pranks. There's nothing greater than that at work."

"Pranks?" stammers Graybeard, finally catching up with us. He grips the sides of his robes with his fists, his face pale. "Students?"

"Don't you think?" I ask him as the color rushes back to his face.

He mutters an oath, and raises his hand. Any moment now, he'll call up a wind to disperse the smoke.

Kemal barely spares the man a glance. Instead, he turns to me. "Get upstairs and tell the guards at the door there's been a disturbance."

I step into darkness, one hand out to touch the wall. The smoke is like a wall of night. No amount of blinking clears my sight. A hand curls into the cloth of my robe, gripping it lightly from the back: Stormwind.

Smiling fiercely, I keep going, moving quickly. My fingertips bump over a doorjamb, and then reconnect with the wall on the other side. I stride briskly along, my fingers jumping over another empty doorway, and then, as a breeze begins to pick up in the hallway, the last one before the stairs.

Behind us, a lycan curses, the distinct stench of garlic and onions rising on the breeze. I hope to God the smell is enough to cover the scent of Stormwind's passing. It can't be much farther now. There were only three doorways on each side of the hall.

I stub my toe against the bottom stair. Wincing, I step up and wave my hand along the wall until I find the snakelike railing, the iron scales cool against my palm. We just have to make it up the stairs. The breeze quickens, smoke roiling around us, the world beginning to take shape in shades of gray. I take the stairs as fast as I can in the twilight.

Almost there. Almost there. Almost—

I slow to a walk on the landing, pressing against the railing as a half dozen lycans race down the steps, blades drawn and eyes burning.

Something, or rather *someone*, stumbles into me from behind, then eases back.

"There," I say, pointing down to the hall. "A disturbance— felt like charms at work."

"Go," the one in the lead says, and the other five race on. But he doesn't. Instead, he approaches me slowly, moving with sinuous grace until he's less than an arm's length away, his lean face wary now, cold. This close, I can see him clearly, his eyes amber and gold, and utterly focused on me. "You."

It's the same lycan I met in the garden. I press back, feel Stormwind ease herself down the step behind me. The smell of garlic and onions is nowhere near as strong as I would have liked right now.

He sniffs once, breathing deeply, his nostrils flaring. "Tell me, girl, why are you here, smelling of the rogue mage and wearing journeymen's robes?"

This time there is nothing of humor in his eye. I know instinctively that he won't believe any story I might tell him. He won't let me go. I don't let myself look up the stairs with their passage to the roof and freedom. They may as well be back in our valley in the mountains. I can't outrun him, can't fight my way free. And, remembering his kindness in the garden, his sense of courtesy, of justice that has nothing to do with class or rank, I know I can't kill him. I'll have to find some other way.

At least I can try an explanation.

"I was dressed as a servant on orders," I say calmly. "I am a mage, and went down to the prisoner's cell with Kemal to check it. The disturbance began on our way back up."

His hand closes on my wrist before I even realize he has moved. "You're in league with the rogue, aren't you?" His eyes narrow with fury.

Fight him.

I start at the sound of the voice in my head. The phoenix? But it doesn't sound like his voice, though there's something familiar about it....

"You are," the lycan snarls.

Stormwind tenses behind me. I shake my head, push away the thought of the voice. Now is not the time to worry about voices in my head that know nothing of my ability to fight. "No," I say. "I don't have anything to do with rogues."

"To think I gave those boys a lesson in manners for *you*. I should have known you for a liar."

Behind my back, I hear the faintest of taps and smoke blooms, bursting into the landing and filling the stairwell. The lycan curses, his grip tightening to bruising intensity. I twist hard, trying to drop to my knees, but he yanks me forward. I stumble in the darkness. If I can just break his grip—

"To me!" the lycan shouts, drawing the attention of the lycans amid the growing confusion below us.

Fight him, the voice in my head orders. But I don't know

how. My best chance is to find some spell, perhaps just a burst of power to push him back—

Move!

My mind stumbles to the side as if it has been pushed away, to an empty space beside myself. I watch through eyes I no longer control as I expertly twist my arm, breaking the lycan's hold. The force that has taken over my body sends me surging forward, my fist pistoning out to catch the lycan square in the jaw. He reels back, disappearing into darkness.

Up, I try to shout, though my mouth no longer belongs to me, the being that breathes in my body answering me not at all. Except that it seems to hear my thoughts, for my hand reaches out, closing on the cold iron railing, and my feet race upwards, skimming over the steps faster than seems quite right. I can only hope that Stormwind is following behind me.

I break through the upper edge of the smoke as a half dozen lycans tear down the hall toward me.

"Stop her!" the lycan below me shouts. He sounds like he's gaining ground.

Smoker in my pocket, I tell the thing that has possessed me. *Break it.*

My hand reaches into my pocket, closes on three charms, and smashes them all against the railing. And then I'm racing around the top of the stairs and sprinting up the next flight, my vision consumed by blackness and my sense of smell overpowered by the stench of garlic and onions, so strong it obliterates all other scents. Just as well I'd thought to put a few of each charm in both my pockets.

A lycan pounds up the steps behind me while the rest sound like they're heading back toward the main entry to make sure I haven't slipped past them. Stormwind will hardly be able to follow in my footsteps. I'm leading a guard after me, and the phoenix cannot carry us both at the same time.

At the top of the steps go straight, I order. There's another stairwell at the end of the hall. I might even be able to make it down again and out the unprotected window. Or up a flight to the roof. Anything to confuse them.

The force that controls my body complies and I race ahead. My heart beats frantically, slamming against my ribs. Each breath tears through my throat. I'm moving too fast, the doors flying past me. I can't run this swiftly—no human can. How is this even possible?

Without any suggestion from me, my hand finds another smoker, pitching it hard against the wall I pass. Are the lycans behind me? I can't tell, can barely hear anything beyond the roaring of blood in my ears.

Something slices across my upper arm. I twist, skidding across the polished stone of the hall, my breath coming in a strange, gasping cry that breaks off before it makes almost any sound at all. A crossbow bolt skitters across the floor, another shattering as it hits the stone at a sharper angle. I hold completely still, eyes trained on the smoke behind me.

Pain. I understand it in a detached, unreal way as my body climbs carefully to its feet. Whoever hit me must be nothing short of amazing. They'd shot through a wall of smoke, using the sound of my running to guide them.

A slick wetness trickles down my right arm, and I know in an academic, almost theoretical way, that the pain from my wound is a burning thing. I feel only a whisper of it, like a ghost wound I cannot quite confirm.

"Stop."

The speaker materializes from the smoke: the same lycan as before, crossbow trained on me.

"Hands in front of you," he says, walking steadily toward me. At his back, the smoker still darkens the hall, the day-bright glowstones barely penetrating its shadow.

My hands move in front of me. Am I giving up? Granted, I don't think even the thing that has taken hold of my body can move faster than a quarrel shot from a crossbow. At least not when it is barely five paces away.

When the lycan reaches me, he grabs my good hand and lowers the crossbow. I barely register the scream of pain through my body as I clench my right fist and slam it into his chest, ripping my left hand free as I step into the blow. Drops of blood splatter on his leather armor, but it's my blood, dripping down the hand that struck him. He staggers backward, mouth gaping, the crossbow clattering across the floor.

I follow up with a round kick to his torso, which he partially blocks, and I'm already whipping forward, left hand driving at his face. He raises his arm, blocking my fist, and somehow I expected this, expected him to raise his guard too high. The fingers of my other hand flick out and nimbly pluck the dagger from his belt as I whirl past him.

No!

But my body doesn't mind me. I drop down, attempting to knock the lycan's legs out from under him as he pivots to keep me in his sight. He stumbles, avoiding me. I regain my feet, moving fluidly. He snarls, his fists jabbing at me. I block the first with my left arm, dagger coming up to slice at his arm. He grunts, eyes widening as the dagger scrapes against his leather armguard—he hadn't even realized I stole his blade.

I block his second fist with my right hand, my arm shuddering, muscles screaming. Then I whip sideways and kick hard. I feel my heel connect with his thigh, the shock reverberating through my boot and up my leg.

He stumbles again, and I step into the opening, my good hand with the dagger coming up in what will be a killing strike.

No! I grab my hand with my mind, and for a moment I'm frozen there, the dagger a hair's breadth from the lycan's throat, my body not yet mine to order. "*No*," I scream again, unsure if it is with my mind or mouth or both. And then I'm firmly back in control, whirling and slamming my hand with its dagger against the wall with all my strength. Again, and again, until the fingers sealed around the hilt lose their grip, the dagger clattering to the floor.

I bend over my hand, gasping, aware of pain tracing the lines of the bones in my hand, the far greater pain of the partially ripped muscle and shredded flesh of my upper arm. I squeeze my eyes shut, chest heaving.

When I open them again, it's to the sight a sword blade hanging in the air just below my throat.

The lycan moves with brutal efficiency, catching my good wrist and twisting my arm behind me, his sword never wavering. Not that swords are much good in such close combat, but his dagger's on the ground where I dropped it. He doesn't trust me enough to retrieve it right now.

He pushes me face-first into the wall, pinning me there with my arm. I need to get away. I reach out with my mage's senses, fear and pain sharpening my thoughts, and what I find is stone, heavy and ready to fall, ready to burn as lava burns, smoke and fire and ash. I find bones that wait for flames as kindling does, find air that dreams of death.

No, I beg, my sunbolt smoldering within me, burning the tips of my fingers. *Not this. Never this.*

Claws dig into the skin of my wrist as he keeps me pinned to the wall. *Claws*, I think, struggling to focus, to push away the magic I dare not use. Is he fighting a change? Lycans don't have claws in their human form.

"What are you?" he demands.

Dead, I almost say. It won't matter to him. What he wants to know—how I'd been able to fight him, why I'd acted as if my hand were possessed—is not an answer I can give him.

He snarls with frustration. A cord loops tight around my wrist. Then he grabs my other wrist and pulls it back. If he is gentler, I don't notice, agony rippling along my arm. I try to swallow my pain, but I hear it anyhow, a faint screech trapped in my chest.

A hand grasps the hair at the back of my head. I feel the brush of claw tips against my scalp as the lycan twists my face to his. "Do you know where she is?"

He waits until my breath returns, weak and raspy. "No," I say, letting my gaze wander away from him. I can barely hear my own voice past the pounding in my ears. A blackness that has nothing to do with smokers roils at the edge of my vision. I can't be wounded that badly. Perhaps it's the wound combined with the strain of housing whatever it was that took me over.

His fingers tighten on my hair and I try not to flinch. Every movement hurts, not just my arm.

"You're lying," he says softly.

I consider him, the steady burn of his eyes easier to look at than the shifting smoke. "I hope she is free," I tell him. "But I don't know."

He opens his mouth to speak and then pauses, looking down the hall.

Four shapes step free from the gradually dissipating black fog, blades gleaming. Lycans. I need to focus. With every moment, I slip a little farther from any chance of escape. If only I had finished my studies and had a hundred more defensive spells at my fingertips, spells that have nothing to do with fire. If only my parents had not hidden my Promise, if my mother had not left me to the streets.... My mother. Brokensword.

What are swords but the ore of the earth, forged by flame? I form the spell quickly, drawing on the fire at my fingertips, the strength of the stone walls calling to me, the layers of magic lying thick in the air of this building. Clenching my eyes shut with the effort, I send out my spell, a hundred seeking tendrils, like the finest of vines reaching through the air. Instead of earth, they seek iron, and when they find it, they encircle it, growing thick and strong until the metal snaps. Through the rushing dark behind my eyelids, I hear the sudden ringing crack of swords and daggers shattering, broken blades clanging as they hit the floor.

Now. This is my chance. I twist sideways, dragging my hands free of the lycan's grip.

With a muttered oath, he reverses the hilt he still holds and slams the butt against my head.

I collapse sideways, streaks of light crossing my vision. I take a gasping, shuddering breath as his hand closes on my wrists again.

Through eyesight that is both too dark and too bright, I see letters on the wall beside my cheek: Karolene. I'm pressed against the map of the world, leaving a smeary trail of blood across the sea. I stare numbly at the writing, as if the ink itself might somehow rescue me, call me back to a home I no longer remember.

I slide into darkness with my cheek still pressed against the wall.

FIRE & STONE

I open my eyes to a strange land. Peacocks perch in baobab trees, whistling merrily. Their long, shining tail feathers fan out in display, a thousand lidless eyes glimmering in the sunlight. Below them, baboons play at dice, squatting in the dirt and chittering at each other as the dice roll. I walk among the trees, pausing to watch two baboons break off their game in a show of anger, shrieking and scooping up handfuls of dirt to toss at each other. The other baboons, enthralled by their own games, ignore the tussle.

"Hitomi."

I pivot toward the voice, but I can make out little beyond the trees. Above, the peacocks burst into synchronized song, then separate into a series of complementary harmonies, as if their lovely voices had been trained to replace the instruments of a great symphony. I tilt my head, considering. Something is not quite right.

"Peacocks don't sing," I tell the swell of melody and harmony.

The music ceases.

It doesn't trail off, as the players of a musical troupe might if unexpectedly interrupted, some stopping before others. It simply ends, wholly and completely, as if it had never been. The baboon fight falters before stumbling to a standstill behind me.

Every last baboon turns to look at me. Then they bare their teeth.

Uh oh.

"Hitomi."

I swallow hard and slowly back toward the voice, hoping to God it's not some other baboon. Or someone worse than that.

A baboon lets loose a blood-curdling yell, taking a step after me. Another baboon answers. Then they're all screaming, nearly human shrieks of fury blistering my ears as they jump up and down. Suddenly, one of them charges.

I bolt, dodging around a tree trunk, darting past another one, the roar of furious monkeys rising behind me like a lethal wave. I'm going to die. I'm going to be ripped to pieces by gambling baboons.

"*Hitomi.*"

"Where are you?" I cry. I plunge over a low rise, breaking free of the baobab trees.

Val stands beside a river, a golden plain stretched out behind him. He is exactly as I remember him, midnight hair tied back, pale face grimly serious, violet eyes bright and dangerous as two gems. I really hope a breather can take on a troop of vigilante monkeys. I have my doubts.

"Run," I shout as I near him.

His brow creases. "Stop."

Is he insane? "Run!" I repeat, putting all the force of my breath into the word.

As I reach him, my focus already on the river we'll need to cross, he swerves in front of me, one arm reaching across my chest and spinning me around, throwing off my balance completely. I flail, knocking his arm away, and land hard on my side.

For a moment, I just lie there, trying to catch my breath, my cheek pressed against the rich earth.

"Hitomi," Val says for the umpteenth time, reaching a hand out to help me up as I lie wheezing on the ground.

I scramble to my feet, ignoring the hand. "The baboons—"

I pause, blinking. The baobab trees are gone. Instead, the same golden plain that stretches out from the opposite bank of the river lies before me as well.

"Baboons?" Val repeats.

"And—" I stop, clicking my jaw together before I can add *peacocks*. "Um," I look around, half-expecting the baboons to jump out of a ditch. "There were…where exactly are we?" I ask Val, finally registering his presence for what it means. "And what are *you* doing here?"

He shakes his head, a quick, hard movement. "What were you doing back there in the Mekteb? And why in all the hells did you stop fighting that lycan?"

"I—" I stare at him, the pieces of the puzzle falling into

place. The voice in my head. My body knowing how to fight, moving faster than humans are built to, answering someone else's commands. "*We* were going to kill him."

Val's face is a study in restrained fury. "And now he will take you to your death. You do realize you're a prisoner of the High Council now? How do you think you're going to get out of this...." He pauses, searching for the right word.

I could provide a few: Alive? With my mind intact? Free?

"Safely," he finishes.

"I don't know," I admit. "But I don't think my safety is worth another man's life."

"You don't even know his name. He's nothing to you."

"What difference does a name make?" I snap. "He's still a person."

Val doesn't answer. He gives me a long, inscrutable look. Then he turns away, walking slowly toward the river, the anger seeping out of his broad shoulders.

Should I say something else? I'm not sorry for pulling back, for having the presence of mind to stop before Val used my body to kill the lycan. I'm not sure I could have lived with that. The lycan is not what Kol was, and his death still haunts me. No matter what I think of the High Council, the lycan was only doing what he thought was right. Which means I have to be prepared to die for his life. It's not a particularly good trade-off, and I didn't have time to consider the ramifications in detail, but it's done now.

"You haven't changed," Val says, breaking the silence between us. He stands at the river's edge, watching the waters, his words carried back to me on a breath of wind.

"Neither have you," I quip. He hasn't aged a hair since I last saw him. But as a breather, he wouldn't have, not when each breath he takes from another being grants him new life. A decade means about as much to breathers as a year does to humans.

From the rise and fall of his shoulders, I expect he just sighed again.

"You haven't explained why you're here yet. Or where we are." Or how he took over my body.

"This is a dream," he replies. "I came to speak with you."

"A dream?" I echo. That would explain why I've already forgotten the fall I took. It doesn't hurt one bit.

Val turns on his heel to face me. I'd forgotten how tall he is, forgotten the inhuman grace with which he moves, forgotten those eyes. I'm no longer sure I should meet them as naively as I did a year ago when he was my only ally, and then when he was all I had of my memory.

I wonder what he sees when he looks at me.

"Why did you come to the High Council?" he asks, calm again. "You were to study with Stormwind."

Ah. Maybe he's merely peeved that I appear to have abandoned the apprenticeship he assured me. "I did. She was called before the High Council to face charges drummed up by Blackflame. They're imprisoning her at Gereza Saliti."

If anything, Val looks more frustrated. "I suppose you were rescuing her."

I flush like a scolded child before her schoolmaster. "I came to see if I could help—"

"You're an *apprentice*. Not a thrice-cursed high mage like her. If she can't take care of herself, it's not up to you to save her."

"It is if no one else will," I retort.

We glare at each other.

"Where is she now?" he demands.

"Escaped, I hope." If she opened the note I gave her, and followed its instructions to get to the roof—if she wasn't caught along the way.

"And what will happen to you?"

"I don't know." I pause, studying Val. "Why do you care? When you left, you made it clear I'd never see you again. But here you are. How is this even possible? If this dream is real, if that fight was real, then what about all those other moments..." I trail off, thinking of the times I've found myself by his side, even if only for a few seconds. At least half a dozen times in the last year.

His eyes slide away from mine.

"What?" I press. "Is this spirit walking? Because it's all I can think of and it doesn't make much sense. Spirit walking doesn't give you the ability to take over someone else's body."

He rubs his chin, then looks back at me, his eyes deepening to indigo with an emotion I can't begin to interpret. He opens his mouth, hesitates, says, "I gave you a breath."

"You...." I stare at him, trying to understand. He's a breather. He takes breath—the life force of other creatures— to survive. How could he *give* me a breath?

"After you killed Kol with your sunbolt. You were hardly more than a burned-out shell. I thought you were dead, but then you took a breath. I knew you wouldn't take another one, you couldn't, so...I gave you a breath."

I can't think of what to say, how to understand this. He gave me the lives and breaths of other people, and *that's* how I survived? On their stolen years? "No," I manage, the word so small it nearly gets lost between us.

"It meant that you were able to hold on long enough for your body to begin to heal." Val's gaze burns into me. "It also means that no matter what we do now, we share a bond. Even if we do not want it, try to distance ourselves from it, in a moment of need, it will be there."

I latch onto this. It is so much easier to deal with than accepting what taking a breath means. "That's how— when I was fighting…"

"Yes."

"And…in the Burnt Lands? That voice in my head was you?"

"Yes." His voice remains toneless, but the word itself is enough to shake me.

I run my hands through my hair, pulling hard, as if that will help me straighten my thoughts out. "Does it fade, this bond?"

"No. That's why we do it so rarely."

"Right." This time, I'm the one to look away. I can't gather my thoughts while listening to him turn the last year of my life upside down with his velvet voice. "How rarely?" I ask, to say something.

"Since the Great Burning, perhaps twice."

"*What?*"

"It is neither safe nor wise for us to develop bonds with humans. Not when your mages hunt us as they do. And then…it is hard to watch your bond die." The words are gentle, a quiet reminder that he may only age a few years by the time I'm in my dotage. Should I live so long. The High Council won't kill me outright, I remind myself. Though I'm not sure that being bonded to a madwoman or a slave would work out well for Val. Not that I prefer either option myself.

"So why?" I ask, trying not to sound ungrateful. "Why did you give me a breath?" I push down the ants-crawling feeling that skitters beneath my skin when I think how my life has been paid for in the lost years of other people. Even if they were Kol's guards. Even if they meant to kill me.

Val's boots crunch in the dirt as he crosses to me, head tilted. "Do you remember the tower room? The agreement you made with me?"

I nod.

"You could have escaped alone, and you would have had a better chance of getting away. But you gave that up to free me, knowing I might turn on you. When the dogs found you in the forest, you led Kol away from the cave where I hid. And finally, when you saw that I would lose my fight with Kol, you killed him. You could have waited, but instead you acted when I needed your help, and nearly destroyed yourself. You gave your life thrice over for me. You, a mageling, and I, a breather."

"I told you I wasn't that kind of mage," I whisper, my throat hoarse, aching. I hear the lie in my words even as I speak them. I claimed that I hadn't learned how to kill—and then I annihilated Kol, leaving nothing but a scattering of ash.

Val smiles faintly, aware of the irony. "I know. And I could not let you die for your kindness."

Is that what it was? Or did something else drive me? Guilt, perhaps, at what I left behind me in Karolene? I shake my head. "I don't think I'm as good as all that."

Val doesn't argue. Instead, he says, "I don't regret it."

I stare at him, unable to wrap my mind around all he has said.

"Even though you have the annoying habit of nearly getting yourself killed for other people on a regular basis."

"Mm." I don't know what words to use. A breath. My life is mine because it was sustained by others' lives—directly. I remember how Val breathed from James, and wonder suddenly, sickeningly, if part of James lives in me.

"I have to go," Val says abruptly, glancing to the sky and then back at me. "I've held you here long enough."

He steps back, and the world around us wavers. It's enough to jerk me back to the moment.

"Wait," I say, my voice sharp. His gaze snaps to me. "Three things. Can I call you if I need you?"

"Of course. Reach out for me, use my name, and I will hear you. What else?"

"If I'm in trouble again, ask me before you take me over. Just in case I have a plan, or there's something I can do." Or I don't want to risk what he might do.

Val nods. Behind him, the plains have faded into a murky brown haze, the river turning dark. He spreads out his fingers, his arms at his sides. It looks as though he is pressing back against the changes behind him, holding them at bay.

"And the other thing?"

"I'm sorry," I admit. "For what's going to happen to me."

His eyes narrow. "If they give you a choice, become a source slave. Do what you can to convince them it's the best option."

A fine dust begins to rise between us. I shake my head, raising my voice to reach him. "If the mage they give me to is anything like Blackflame, I'll be funneling my magic to a monster." And I won't survive the year.

"You can escape slavery," he says as the darkness behind him expands, wraps around us. "Madness is a much greater struggle to overcome."

I wake to the sound of voices. Through cracked eyelids I make out two sets of feet by the door: the slippered feet of a mage, and the booted feet of a guard. The room lies half in shadow, lit by a glowstone carried by the guard. Which means…what? A cell, perhaps?

The slippered feet cross to me quickly. They are blue leather embroidered with lighter blue flowers. I've seen them before. The associated voice says, "You did not bind the wound?"

"I asked the mages to check her before they left."

I don't know what he's referring to, but I know that voice. I consider the effort required to fully open my eyes and lift my head enough to see the guard, and decide against it. It's probably the guard who caught me. I don't really want to look into his eyes right now anyway.

"I expected more from you, Osman Bey," the mage says with quiet reproof. Her voice has a slight musical lilt to it, even now when she's displeased.

I squint at the mage as she kneels before me, setting down a bag beside her. Blue leather shoes, that voice—she's the same healer that came to check on Stonefall. She leans forward, brushing the hair out of my eyes. She is middle-aged, her face round, eyes framed by wire spectacles, a thick gray braid hanging over her shoulder. She meets my gaze in silence, her expression closed.

"My apologies, Mistress Brightsong. I should have seen to her myself," the lycan, Osman Bey, says from behind her.

The mage makes no response. She transfers her gaze to my

back, gently resting her hand against my unwounded shoulder. A strange, electric tingling runs through my blood, questing through my veins, sliding over my muscles and bones. I keep my eyes open, watching the healer mage. So, as the current of her magic delves into my body, I see the moment when her eyes begin to widen, her lips thinning out as she presses them together.

"She's lost a good amount of blood. Her pupils aren't dilating as they should. I expect she's in shock. And her hands are still bound. Far too tightly." Brightsong rounds on the guard, anger buzzing in her voice. "Cut them free at once."

"She may still be dangerous," Osman Bey says. He shuts the door behind him before coming to kneel beside the mage. I can feel his fingers on my wrist, but I can no longer feel my hands. It is strange, to think of my fingers and yet have no sense of them.

"Indeed?" Brightsong levels a cutting gaze at the lycan. "Tell me, Osman Bey, for a young mage marked by fire and stone as she is, did she rain fire upon you when you caught her? Did she open the floor beneath your feet, or topple walls on you? Or did she merely light half your brothers on fire with a single flick of her fingers, using their bones as fuel?"

Fire and stone? I try to focus on this: fire *and* stone. The fire written inside of me is from my sunbolt, but what could she mean by stone? The only stone-related spells I've had any exposure to…were in the Burnt Lands. Dully, I remember the backlash of magic from the tentacled spell-creature as I unraveled its enchantments, the way it washed over me and through me, filled me until I felt as though my body could no longer hold me. *Stone.*

The lycan shifts, drawing my attention back to the room. "No. None of those things," he says, a faint note of uncertainty in his voice.

"Then she will not harm us now. Cut her free."

I catch the glint of a dagger from the corner of my eye, and then Brightsong takes my good arm, my left, and lays it on the ground beside me. Then there are hands on my right arm, carefully lifting away blood-stiff fabric. I press my lips together on a scream as the clots rip free from my wound. The muffled, swallowed sound of my cry fills the small room.

"Water," Brightsong says, the word a command. "For drinking, and a kettle of warm water to clean her arm. At once."

Osman Bey rises, moves away. The door opens and closes.

I lie still, feeling a slow fire beginning in my hands, my fingers, as they come back to life.

"I am sorry," Brightsong says quietly. "I don't dare lay a sleep on you, give you anything too strong—or you might slip away entirely. I will numb the area but it will not take away all sensation. You will have to bear some pain."

She lays her hand upon my arm, and this time coolness radiates out, soothing and sweet. In the quiet it brings, I can feel the scrapes on my elbows, the tingling pain in my hands, the bruises growing along the lines of my fingers where I slammed them against the wall, the egg-shaped lump over my ear where Osman Bey hit me. But all of these are small, minor nuisances in comparison to the pain Brightsong has taken away.

She sings as she works, weaving the beauty of her voice together with her magic to staunch the new trickle of blood. Her song swells strong and clear as she burns away any infection or contaminants, then turns deep and gentle as she holds a hand over the open wound, letting her magic wash over it. I latch onto the sound of her song, using it to anchor me against the whisper of pain I can feel through the numbing magic she used.

"The muscle is partially torn," Brightsong breaks her song to tell me. "To heal properly, it must be sealed back together again. The bolt missed your tendons and arteries. You are very blessed."

As her magic seals first muscle and then tissue together, I try to focus on the idea that life is a much better thing for me than death. Tears leak out the corners of my eyes as the pain digs its claws in, piercing through the numbing magic. Her song is steady and true, thrumming through me, but I am waking to realities that it cannot touch. My failure, my capture, means that all those who aided me I may now betray. Stonefall. Jabir. The Degaths. At least Kenta may escape. I can only hope Stormwind got away.

"There," she says, sitting back. "I'll see to your head and hand once we have you settled in the infirmary. Osman Bey." She transforms his name into an order.

"I would advise against it." His voice floats down over me, thickening in my ears like thistledown. "She should be...we can guard against escape."

Brightsong's voice flickers in and out of my hearing. Perhaps she laid a sleep on me, or perhaps this is what pain and blood loss does. "If you...unlikely...prisoner then?"

My eyes drift shut as Osman Bey answers. I catch a couple words through the thickening air: wards, Council.

My breath rustles through my lungs, creating an ebb and flow of pain that finally gives way to emptiness.

TALON

I wake to the scent of lemon, bright and fresh and invigorating. Multi-hued light fills my room, a window somewhere to my side throwing shards of red and blue and yellow on the wall before me. I breathe slowly, aware without shifting of the pain slumbering within me.

I lie on my back, face turned to a blank wall. With each breath, the muscles of my shoulder and arm shift, pain flickering along my right arm. It feels as though someone took a coal and traced a line of fire across my arm. And the whole of my body *aches*, no doubt the result of being pushed by Val to move beyond its natural ability.

I try, discreetly, to look past the foot of my bed without lifting my neck very much. The pain shifts, flaring up, and I freeze, my eyes coming to focus on the door barely visible above the blankets folded at my feet. A pair of lycans stands guard, facing me.

I don't recognize them, at least not immediately. They regard me wordlessly, then one of them turns and leaves the room. I lay my head against the pillow, breathing shallowly. I can't move my right arm—it must be immobilized to keep my wound still—but I can move my fingers easily enough. My other arm is laid out straight, my hand resting on a pillow or towel of some sort. When I try to move those fingers, new flickers of pain make themselves known, far less painful but distinctly there. My hand feels stiff, awkward. I cannot quite form a fist.

I let my eyes drift shut and take stock of my situation. I have one good hand attached to a wounded arm. I won't be able to pick locks. I might not be able to stand if I've lost too much blood. Balancing and all. I squeeze my eyes tight, trying to focus my thoughts. It's daylight. If Stormwind is still free, then she should be safe. I can't escape now, but I doubt that anything too serious will be done to me while I appear so weak. At least not at once. I need to wait and plan.

I hear the faint sound of the door opening, footsteps approaching.

"You're sure she woke?" a woman's voice asks.

"Aye," one of the lycans responds.

"Did she speak?"

"No," the other says.

A finger brushes my cheek. I jerk involuntarily, then grit my teeth against the resulting shock of pain. When I force my eyes open, the same healer mage who first treated me is studying me, eyes shadowed and a deep line forming between her brows.

"I'm glad you've woken." Her voice is cool, wholly neutral. "I am Mistress Brightsong, head healer-mage of the Mekteb. I need you to drink a potion that will help your body replenish lost blood. I have a second for the pain, if you wish it, and some broth to feed the rest of you." I watch her mouth moving. It seems like a great many things to do. "We're going to help you sit up."

Sitting up, I feel terribly exposed before my lycan guards. I wear only a light tunic with its right sleeve cut away, and a pair of drawstring pants I don't recognize. Feeding myself is out of the question, for my good hand is attached to my badly injured arm, now bound in a sling to protect it. My left hand is swollen and colored a lovely variegated purple and blue from when I beat it against the wall.

Brightsong offers me the blood loss potion first, then the broth, with two pieces of bread dipped in it to add substance, and then the second potion. And two glasses of water at my request. It takes an exhaustive amount of effort to down it all.

"What...time?" I ask when I am done, my voice rough despite all the liquids.

Brightsong tilts her head, her gaze steady on my face. "Late afternoon."

"Where?" I have vague memories of being shifted, voices speaking over me. I knew I was being moved and I didn't care where at the time. But I don't recognize this place.

"The infirmary. Our mages have placed wards on the room and you are under continual guard. I would not recommend attempting to leave."

I'm not sure I can even stand right now. "The prisoner?"

Her jaw tightens. "That is not for me to discuss."

"No," agrees a voice from the door. "That would be for me to discuss."

I swing my head ponderously toward the speaker, knowing who I will see: Osman Bey. With his velvet and leather armor and array of blades, he looks right at home between the two guards. And the three of them seem completely out of place in this bright, cheery room. The sight of him, with his golden eyes glittering in the light, sharp and hard as glass, rips away the muffled sense of security I'd managed to wrap around myself.

He steps forward, nodding to Brightsong. The right side of his jaw is bruised nearly purple. I stare at it as he says, "I'll require a few words with her."

"Of course," she says, stepping aside. "She's weak, though, and should not move at this point. You will refrain from hurting or upsetting her."

Osman Bey turns his head to regard her as he passes. I can't see his expression, but Brightsong returns his look with that same unnervingly neutral mask.

He sits on the stool Brightsong vacated, pulled even with my pillow. "I am Osman Bey, captain of the Lycan Guard," he says, his tone cold. "What is your name?"

Captain. I should have guessed it from how he ordered the other lycans away the first time I met him in the garden.

I don't want to lie to him, but refusing to answer won't do me any good. "Zainab," I say finally.

"Family name? Or mage name?"

I shake my head.

His eyes narrow. "I expect it's irrelevant. What were you doing in Shahmaran Hall?"

I close my mouth on my answer, bite my lip gently to remind myself to think. I don't know how much he knows, or if they've caught Stormwind. I can't give away anything. "Just looking," I say slowly. "Did you catch her?"

Osman Bey shakes his head once. "No."

Thank God.

He leans forward, intent on me. "Do you know where she went?"

"No." Not once the phoenix took her to Kenta.

"But you were there to help her."

I almost smile. They still haven't figured out how we did it. "Yes," I tell him. This is a secret I can't keep. I was seen by too many people, and the Council will get the truth from me one way or the other. But, really, I admit it because he told me about Stormwind. It's only fair that I give him one truth in return.

His face hardens. "Why?"

There is something odd in his tone, an emotion half-hidden beneath his tightly coiled anger. But he's not really ready to listen, and I'm not willing to lie. "I already told you," I say finally.

His gaze narrows as he tries to recall our past conversations, the words I used when he caught me.

I let my head loll back against the pillows, the weight of my exhaustion pulling at me. Better to let him think I've simply had enough of talking for now.

"If you can provide any information on the whereabouts of the fugitive, the Council may be lenient with you."

We both know that's a lie. I don't bother answering.

He sits back, glances toward Brightsong. She raises her eyebrows, expression still cool. With a sigh, Osman Bey rises from his stool. At the door, he looks back once, frustrated but uncertain, and then he is gone.

Brightsong helps me lie down again before departing.

He has honor, I remind myself, cheek pressed against the pillow. Only a man with honor would force those boys to show respect for a servant. If he asks again why I came to help Stormwind, perhaps I will answer. If he's ready to hear me.

The wards on my room are complex, layered, and keyed to me. I reach out to touch the walls—a somewhat awkward feat given my wounds, the placement of the bed, and the watchful eyes of my guards. The magical lines that flare up are anchored through sigils and wards on each wall, all of them formed of pure energy except for the one nearly two arms' lengths above my bed. It has been inked on the wall with dark, uneven brush strokes. I can't tell much without actually touching it, but I don't like the look of it at all, not its shape, and certainly not its brownish-black color.

I *can* tell that I don't have the mastery required to reshape the wards enough to get past them. At least one is designed to turn back on me any magic I might release—a safeguard against my attacking the guards. The door's lock is warded against prying, though the sigil on the door itself looks similar to what was used on Stormwind's cell. Apparently, they haven't yet recognized its inherent weakness. Unfortunately, there's always at least one guard in my room with me. With wards blocking even the simplest sleep spell, I have no chance whatsoever of getting past them and through the door. And certainly no chance of walking out an open door unobserved.

If I escape at all, it will not be from this room. Which means I must plan for the worst possibility of all: that I won't escape on my own. I have no way of knowing what Kenta is doing, or if he will attempt to reach me. Perhaps he's been counting on my using the phoenix feather, but my boots are neither on my feet nor anywhere I can see in the room. Asking the guards about my boots would merely assure that they'd find the feather now if they missed it before.

I stare at the ceiling and work through my options again and again, looking for anything I might have missed. By the time Brightsong brings me another potion and more food, I still have as few ideas as I started with.

I greet her quietly, pushing myself up to lean against the pillows, and realize I need to get to a washroom.

Brightsong sets down her tray, regarding me carefully. "Will you need to relieve yourself before eating?"

I nod, my face heating. I'm not sure if I'm strong enough to leave the bed yet—I might be able to manage, but I don't believe for a minute that they'll leave me alone in the room to try.

Brightsong nods and gestures to the lycans. They've changed shift since I first woke, and my new guards include a female lycan. The male steps out at once. The female comes forward to help me out of bed. Brightsong pulls out a shallow pan of sorts from beneath the bed and steps back.

When I decided to break Stormwind free I gave up my right to dignity, to privacy, to a great deal of things I've taken for granted. I make myself do what I must, urinating into a bowl beside my bed, so shaky I need the lycan's help, while Brightsong watches me in a detached, professional manner. Neither the lycan nor Brightsong makes any comment, sparing me from further humiliation.

Once I am done and returned to the bed, the second guard is called back in. My arm feels worlds better, which is to say that it flares with pain only when I move. When I am still, it does not burn. The bruises on my hand seem significantly improved as well.

"I used a few standard spells to break up the clotting and flush out the dead blood," Brightsong tells me when I mention it. She offers me a spoon of a hearty meat and vegetable soup. I wonder if she thinks I might use the spoon as a weapon, or if she really doesn't believe I can feed myself yet. "We've been trying to control the swelling in your arm. No doubt that's benefited your hand. It should heal well on its own—you didn't bruise the bones, just the flesh. You should have its use again within a few days."

"My arm?"

"It's mending very well. The muscle will be tight and weak where it was torn. I'll teach you some strengthening exercises, stretches to maintain full movement." She hesitates. "There are a few small spells that may also help, if done regularly." I look up, but her gaze drops down to the bowl. She knows as well as I that I can't expect to be cared for so well. There's no knowing where I'll be in a few days. The High Council won't wait much longer before putting me to trial, and after that—I'll either be dead, mad, or a source slave, with no one to do little healing spells for me regularly.

Still, I'm grateful for her intentions. "Thank you."

"It is my duty to aid you," she says, the lines of her shoulder tight. Perhaps her help isn't voluntary. I can't assume she doesn't consider me a criminal and a rogue mage. She's just a very good healer.

There's a faint knock at the door. Brightsong turns toward it with evident relief. "Come in."

My guards stand at attention—clearly expecting someone important to enter. I straighten in the bed, ignoring the burst of pain from my arm, and run a clumsy hand over my hair. It feels tangled and badly knotted around the shrinking lump over my right ear. Granted, I have greater worries.

Osman Bey swings open the door. He is still dressed in the light armor he wore the last time he was here, the bruise on his jawline now a livid purple. Perhaps he's been too busy to bother with healing spells. He eyes, shadowed with fatigue, run over me without meeting mine. He scans the rest of the room, then nods to whomever he escorts.

A woman enters. She is short but well proportioned, her face wide with rounded cheeks and full lips, and her hands slim. By the color of her skin, dark as the deepest of woods, I would guess her to be from Karolene or one of the mainland Kingdoms near it. A colorful cloth wrap covers her hair, matching the hint of fabric visible beneath her sweeping emerald robes. She carries herself with authority, elegance, and a deep confidence in her own abilities.

"Do you know who I am?" Her voice rings out clear and true in the small room. She is used to being heard, and being answered.

I shake my head.

"My mage-name is Talon. Until this morning, I presided over the High Council."

I meet her gaze, trying not to show my surprise—either that Arch Mage Talon herself has come to visit me, or that she has lost her position as first mage of the Council.

She glances over her shoulder. "Stonefall. Is this the girl?"

My chest tightens with shock. *Stonefall?* He should have left by now, escaped before I can betray the help he gave me.

He steps into the room, his earth brown desert robes rustling. He stops at the foot of my bed, studying my face. I gaze back at him, keeping my expression blank. Whatever his strategy now, he *did* help me before. I won't endanger him by speaking.

"Yes," he says, in a voice that brooks no argument. "This is the girl who drew the poison from my wound and saved my life." He ignores Brightsong's start of surprise, the slight indrawn breath from one of the lycans. "It seems I owe her a debt."

A debt I consider already repaid, but he's decided to use it to appeal to Talon's sense of honor. I don't understand why, but I'm grateful nonetheless.

Talon nods as if he merely provided confirmation of something she already knew. "Describe the spell that was cast," she commands me.

Proving I aided a mage can only help my case. My voice comes out creaky and weak. "I lured the poison out of his wound with memories of my own life. Poison is…drawn to life. Then I channeled it into a glowstone to contain it."

Stonefall slips the dulled glowstone from his pocket and passes it to Talon. Osman Bey tilts his head, keenly observant. She takes it, turning it over in her hand. "And then you ran," she finishes for me.

I shrug and immediately regret the ensuing flash of pain. "I am not a student here, nor one of your mages. I did not expect to be welcomed by either the Mekteb or the High Council."

"You saved the life of 'one of our mages' and expected

punishment?"

"The High Council is not known for leniency," I observe. "I could not know how you would deal with me, whether you would allow me further training, or strip me of my magic." Also, I'd come for Stormwind, not Stonefall.

Talon looks to Stonefall. "Close the door."

It's already closed, but that's not what she means. Stonefall lets himself out of the room and gestures for the guards and healer to follow. Osman Bey hesitates, waiting until the others have left, but an inquiring look from Talon answers his doubts.

As the door clicks shut, Talon takes the stool beside me. With a flick of her fingers, she smacks a charm against the side table. A faint pressure builds in my ears. I discreetly stretch my jaw one way and then the other to make my ears pop.

"There," she says with satisfaction. "We may speak in privacy now."

Curious.

"What is your name?" she asks.

"Zainab."

"Who trained you?"

"I can't tell you."

"Because we are not known for leniency?" she hazards.

I smile faintly.

"Another question, then. Why did you come here? Was it for Brigit Stormwind?"

I've already admitted this to Osman Bey, but Talon will want more than a single word answer. Though, if I have to tell someone the truth, then why not the person who offered Stormwind so much help in escaping, albeit passively?

"Yes," I say. "I knew she was innocent of the charges brought against her. I could not let her be imprisoned unjustly."

"And you cared enough to come here, knowing we weren't likely to deal with you kindly?" Talon asks, unconvinced.

"I came because she needed help, and because I wished to know how you and Stonefall failed. I knew she considered you both among her allies. I went first to Stonefall and found him dying. I helped him, knowing the Council would seek me for it. Since then, the greatest help I've had in aiding Mistress Stormwind has been your own."

"My own?" Talon echoes. It's an invitation. Perhaps, if she knows how she's implicated, she'll help me somehow now.

"You left the book describing the binding spell open for

219

any to read," I say. "So I learned she could use charms. You gave the key to her shackle to a housekeeper, leaving it essentially unguarded. And," I say with dawning comprehension, "you accepted the lycans' word that she disappeared when you knew she could not leave the cell while the ward remained in place, the door closed. You gave me the time I needed to reach the cell and let her out. You wanted her to escape as much as I did."

For a long moment, Mistress Talon simply looks at me, her gaze as dark and hard as obsidian. "Yes," she says, "I did. But I was not expecting you."

"Who were you expecting?"

"It hardly matters," she replies curtly.

"Then you really did want someone to free Stormwind?" I ask, not quite believing her words.

She tilts her head in admission. "Though I had not counted on how much support Arch Mage Blackflame has garnered on the Council."

I don't want to know. Looking at her, I remember Stonefall's warnings, as well as Kenta's voice cautioning me about the ramifications of undermining the Council. I have to force myself to ask. "What happened?"

"The Council demanded my immediate resignation at this morning's meeting," Talon replies. "They appointed Arch Mage Blackflame to preside over the Council for the remainder of my term."

"They— what?" I falter. *Blackflame?* In charge of the Council?

What have I *done?*

"Although I would like to help you, I no longer have the power to do so. In the morning, Blackflame will call you before the Council to be tried and sentenced. By then you should be well enough to attend."

I force myself to focus on her words. She has almost as much of a stake in my future now as I do. "If they use a truth spell, all that you've done will come out."

"There is no question about that," Talon replies. She takes a small, round—bead?—from her pocket and offers it to me. "The only question is how deep your sense of honor runs."

The bead rests innocently in the pale center of her palm, like the seed of a strange fruit. I make no move to take it, raising my eyes to hers.

"How many people will you betray to imprisonment when the truth spell is laid on you?" Talon's voice is quiet, inexorable. "It won't be just me. Stonefall must have at least helped you escape from his rooms after your casting. And there will be others—there must be, for you to have succeeded in freeing Stormwind. How many people will be destroyed by your words?"

Too many. Even one would be too many. I gesture with my chin to the dark yellow bead, unwilling to stretch out a hand. "What is it?"

"Certain death."

She rises, pushes my sheets back, and slides the pill into the pocket of my drawstring pants. My hands lie frozen on the bed. It isn't until she turns her back to me, moving toward the door, that I find my voice.

"Is this what you demanded of the people you expected to help her?"

Talon pauses, turns. "If they failed, yes. There is no other way around a truth spell."

"Then you're no better than Blackflame."

Talon raises her eyebrows in cool surprise. "On the contrary. You chose this path. At no point did I press you or anyone else to walk it. This," her wave encompasses the room, and me, and all my future, "is the consequence you must bear."

I shake my head, denying her words even as I hear the truth in them.

"I am sorry," she says. The weight of her voice surprises me, the depth of emotion it suggests. In the glowstone-lit room, her dark face appears sallow, the shadows beneath her eyes suddenly darker, deeper. "If I could help you some other way, I would. After the Council takes the truth from you, they will likely order you stripped of your powers. You have proven yourself too dangerous to be allowed to keep your magic, even marked and bound as a source slave. That tablet," —she dips her head— "would be a mercy to yourself as well."

She's right, in a terrible, gut-wrenching way. No one survives having their powers stripped from them, not in mind, and rarely in good health. With my mind and body broken, what future will I have? The Council doesn't exactly take care of those they strip. Orphans like me would be given a pouch of coins and shown the door, as if we have any chance of making our way in the world after being reduced to a husk.

"You understand?" Talon asks softly.

"No," I say flatly. "I don't understand how you could allow any of this. You were the *first mage* of the Council. You allowed Blackflame to be appointed as arch mage. You let him bully a conviction out of the Council. And now you step meekly aside and expect me to kill myself? You're much, much worse than he is. At least he makes no pretense to justice or fairness. How can you not outright oppose him?"

Talon's dark eyes fairly burn with ire. "Do you think you know everything? Go east of here and see what a mage war would bring this land! Blackflame is more than capable of starting another Burning. It is better to leave him his power for twenty or thirty years than to risk that."

"How many people do you think will he destroy in that time?" I demand.

"Not as many as would die in a Burning," she snaps.

"Then stop him before he brings about another Burning," I say. "*Stop him.*"

"Enough." Talon's voice cracks through the room, reverberating with power. "I will do as I see fit. If you have any honor, you will keep your allies from paying the price of your stupidity." She pauses at the door. "Think on it very, very carefully."

I make no answer, don't trust myself to words. It is all I can do not to snatch the tablet from my pocket and throw it at her. No wonder Blackflame has risen so easily to power. I lean back and stare at the ceiling as she departs, wishing I were anyone but myself. Wishing my parents had declared my talent, and trained me to fight, and raised me so that I could do what the other mages here dare not risk.

A VISIT IN THE NIGHT

I wake from a fitful doze to the sound of the door opening, my mind full of echoes of the Burnt Lands, monsters prowling down broken alleyways, the husks of people long dead still reaching out for mercy, a single leather boot splattered with blood. At the faint tap of departing footsteps and the sound of the door clicking shut, I gingerly raise my head to look.

Osman Bey stands before the closed door. The sight of him chases the whispers of my dreams from my mind. I push myself up, my hands fisted in the blanket. He crosses the room without a word and takes a seat on the stool beside my bed.

"You're not going to attack?" Osman Bey's voice is quiet, almost jesting, but his eyes gleam in the pale light of the dimmed glowstones.

"You came in alone, thinking I would?" I reply, my voice shaky.

"The guards are waiting right outside in case I call." He says it so seriously, as if I were truly a threat. It's disconcerting to be considered so dangerous. And worrying that he dismissed his men in the first place, late at night, when Brightsong is unlikely to be nearby.

"We already fought." I try to sound easy, unperturbed, but my voice is still thin and uncertain. "You won."

"Did I?"

I flick a glance to the shuttered window, the darkness visible through the cracks. It's far too late at night for word games, or casual visits. "Why are you still on duty?" I ask, trying to gather my thoughts. "It seems like every time I open my eyes, you're here."

"So it does." He slides off the stool and turns away.

That's odd. Why would he dismiss the guards only to have so pointless a conversation? And why did I waste it? I should have—

He pivots and lunges forward, grabbing me by my tunic. I throw my left hand upward in a futile attempt to block his oncoming fist—but it doesn't connect. Instead, he fingers lock around my wrist and yank it down, away from my face.

We stare at each other, the sound of my breath loud and uneven in the space between us. I hate it, the sound of my fear, so I take the residual terror pumping through my veins and turn it into fury.

"Aren't you brave," I grind out, ignoring the tightness of his grip around my wrist. "Do you make it a habit to attack prisoners when they can't fight back? I thought you had a sense of honor."

He eases back, releasing my wrist, the line of his shoulders slackening. Is he actually embarrassed? "You really can't fight, can you?"

"This room is covered in sigils. I would be an idiot—"

"I mean *fight*. You don't have the instincts of a fighter. Your block would hardly have stopped a slap."

My cheeks burn with mortification.

"How did you fight me last night?" He demands. "I've never met a human who moved as quickly as you, with such finely honed instincts."

This is why he keeps coming back, what he wants to know. It's not something I can give him, at least not fully. But he already knows.

"It wasn't you, was it?"

I shake my head.

"Then why did you stop the thing in you that was fighting me?"

"For the same reason I didn't shower you with fire and stone. I didn't want to kill you."

Osman Bey's gaze rises to the wall, the dark sigil above my head, then drops back to me. "You'd just helped a prisoner escape. You must have known you'd end up here if you were caught. With a magical talent that hasn't been sanctioned by the High Council, you've got even less hope of…"

He doesn't know how to finish. Neither do I. But I can still answer him.

"I didn't think my freedom should come at the cost of other people's lives."

"I see," Osman Bey says quietly, and I realize suddenly

that he might. Despite his pretended attack, he is the same lycan who spoke of respect for servants in the gardens and walked me to my destination.

I need to focus on him now, need to consider what a lycan with a strong sense of honor would do if he realized that his cause was unjust. He is both my least likely ally and my best hope.

"Have you ever been to the Burnt Lands?" I blurt out.

He tilts his head, golden eyes narrowing with confusion. "No. That is not a place to visit."

"I came here through them. There was a pack of creatures that hunted me there: four-legged, furred beasts with forked tongues and spikes down their backs."

A silence stretches between us. Perhaps I've given away too much—that I traveled through the desert to reach the city, that I went where no one in their right mind would go.

"Yes," he says tonelessly.

I'm taking the wrong approach. I shake my head. "Never mind. There was something more you came here for." It is more a statement than a question.

He looks toward the door but doesn't rise. He knows too much—he's seen me in two different roles, heard another piece or two what I've done, and he can't arrange all the bits of the puzzle to his satisfaction.

"Why were you in servants' garb that day?" he asks, as I knew he must.

"I felt like cleaning," I say lightly, which draws a frown from him. "Arch Mage Talon's rooms," I clarify.

"You—?"

"Yes."

He absorbs this, then asks abruptly, "She knows?"

"I expect so. I all but told her."

"She hasn't ordered a guard on her rooms."

"Osman Bey. You're asking the wrong questions. It doesn't really matter whether I was able to free Stormwind because Talon left the one book I most needed open in her rooms, knowing that whoever came to help Stormwind would look there. Or because the key to Stormwind's shackles was being carried around the Mekteb unguarded. The question isn't *how* I got Stormwind free. The question is *why*."

"You expect me to believe that Arch Mage Talon made it easy for you to free Stormwind?" he scoffs.

I look down to my bruised hand cradled on my lap, the digits puffy and discolored, the blues now fading to green and yellow. I don't know how to help him see, or even if I should. He's sworn his sword to the High Council. Even if I convince him that they're in the wrong, what's the likelihood that he'll not only turn away from them, but flout their authority and help me? Then again, what do I have to lose?

"Not easy," I tell him. "But possible, yes."

"Talon would not betray the High Council," Osman Bey says.

"She wouldn't betray what they stand for. But what if they'd already betrayed themselves, betrayed her?" Or, I add silently, what if neither of us has any idea what she's really like?

The planes of his face are hard, his mouth a grim line as he considers my words. But he is considering them. This is as ready as he will ever be to hear what I have to say.

"Talon allowed for the chance for someone to help Stormwind for one simple reason: Stormwind is innocent."

"Why would I believe you?"

He needs proof, something tangible, real. It hardly takes a heartbeat to decide. I slip my bruised hand into my pocket and clumsily extract Talon's gift to me. "Smell this." I hold it out to him. "Tell me whose scent you detect."

He offers me his palm and I drop the pill into it, knowing that I won't get it back. My shoulders sag with relief as I lower my hand. I don't even mind the associated twinge of pain from my arm.

He sniffs once, eyes on me, and stiffens. He sniffs again, looking down at the pill. "What is this?"

"She said it was poison."

"Talon gave you *poison?*"

"I know enough of what she did to allow Stormwind's escape that she'll be implicated if I speak tomorrow. That," I nod my chin toward the pill, "is to give me the option of dying with what she calls 'honor.'"

He understands at once. "Because of the truth spell."

"I would implicate a lot of people," I agree. "Stonefall, because he closed his eyes and told me to run after I aided him. Jabir, the Mekteb's guardian, because he allowed me passage onto the grounds."

Osman Bey waves that away. "No doubt you tricked your way past him."

"We spoke," I reply. "He knew at least part of why I was here."

"No," Osman Bey says. "That's— Jabir would not

endanger the Mekteb, or its standing with the Council."

"Consider his sense of honor. Consider that the Council betrayed its own. And consider that I did my best to hurt no one in helping Stormwind. You—that fight—that was the worst of it. And I am sorry for it."

He does not respond immediately, and in that moment I remember and regret Housekeeper Yilmaz's stomachache as well.

"Jabir believes Stormwind is innocent?" Osman Bey's words are weighted, careful, as if a dozen lives hang in the balance.

"Yes." My voice comes out softer than I expected. I swallow hard. "She was imprisoned because Blackflame wished it, not because she broke any laws or betrayed any oaths. You should ask Jabir before the trial tomorrow."

"And this pill." He uncurls his fingers from around it. "You intend to take it in the morning?"

"Not if you walk out of here with it," I say, attempting lightness, but even I can hear the plea in my words. "I don't want to betray them," I admit. "And my future—the best I can hope for is that they'll make me a source slave."

He sits before me, the dull yellow pill a blot on his palm. He does not speak, and I cannot stand the weight of the silence bearing down on me.

"Do you have any idea what it feels like, to hope for something like that?" I ask unsteadily. I am trembling, though whether from fear or exhaustion or the gentle pain that never goes away, I cannot say. "Magic is so much a part of me, it's my blood and life. I've fought to hold on to it since I was a child. And now I'm hoping that they'll take it from me, bind me to them and use me, and I'll be grateful for it, even though it will eventually kill me."

I look sightlessly toward the shuttered windows, wondering how I can make him see. "Imagine someone could take your true form from you, your wolf form, and control it. Imagine that, even if it was because you did something to uphold your honor, even if you'd do that thing again if you had to, you will still lose who you are."

I gesture vaguely to the walls and the world beyond the wards that encircle me, my hand a mottled blur. "Tomorrow, one way or another, a part of me will die. That pill, it's a coward's way out. I want to take it because I'm not really sure I can survive what the Council will decree for me. And I don't want to bring harm to those who aided me, those who stand against what Blackflame is doing."

I take a deep breath, let it out slowly, make myself wait for his response.

"I've heard tales of Arch Mage Blackflame." It's a neutral statement, telling me nothing. I could worry that he's already in Blackflame's pay, but I can't afford to consider it. So I don't. Plus, he's nothing like the few memories I have of Blackflame's mercenaries.

"I used to live in Karolene. People disappear without a trace. His mercenaries kill in broad daylight." I shrug my uninjured shoulder. "He has a torture chamber in the basement of his home."

Osman Bey's eyebrows rise slightly.

"I've been held there," I say simply. "But you need not believe me. Seek out the Degath family. They're here in Fidanya. They were once a noble family of Karolene. They can tell you."

"I've heard of them as well."

I nod. I am so very, very tired. I've done what I can. Tomorrow will come, and each day after that, whether I have breath or mind or heart to see it. Whether or not Osman Bey believes me, I cannot imagine he will make his decision before the morning. I will face this trial one way or the other.

He rises and slips the pill back into my pocket. I watch him with the same numb disbelief as I did Talon.

"I won't make your choice for you. I believe she gave it to you. It is not for me to take it away."

I close my eyes, wanting to weep. I don't want this choice.

He moves to the door, pauses there. "I will ask," he says, his words soft in the room, and lets himself out.

Lying sleepless through the quiet hours of the night gives me time to consider all the things I don't want to: what my bond with Val really means; whether the breath he gave me has changed me as deeply as my sunbolt did; how my life is built upon the deaths of others. All this time I have tried not to kill again, tried not to take what I should not, and now I find that my very essence may be formed around the stolen lives of others. As long as I consider it, I can find no way around this truth, no way past it.

Then there is the question of the trial, who I will betray and what price they will pay, and what will become of me afterwards. I cannot doubt that Osman Bey's question will be repeated by the Council: how did I fight so well? With a truth spell as potent as the Huq spell, I will be forced to answer and my bond with Val will be uncovered.

Lying with my cheek pressed against the pillow, I almost laugh. *Developing alliances with creatures inimical to the High Council.* Stormwind stood trial for such a charge, and it doesn't even begin to touch on what my bond with Val may be.

The trial will happen tomorrow unless I kill myself first. There is a small chance I might escape before it, but I expect I will be closely guarded by both lycans and mages. If I can find the phoenix feather and burn it, then that will be my best option for calling in help. Though the phoenix, if he is in contact with Kenta, should have a good idea of what's happening to me already. The feather will merely pinpoint my location for him, make it easy for him to rescue me or not, as he sees fit.

The sentence, once decided, will no doubt be carried out immediately. The Council would hardly give me time to escape now that I've destroyed their faith in their ability to keep prisoners safely contained.

I must either find a way to evade the consequences of the Huq spell, or accept that the chance of escape before my sentence is carried out is very, very small. I do not want to bring down a building, or rain fire on my captors, as Brightsong put it. Smaller spells will hardly take out a contingent of guards as well as mages. And that leaves me with no alternative from the bleak future of a madwoman, source slave, or corpse.

No matter how I turn things over in my mind, I can find no other possibility.

I will simply have to stay alert. If I see a chance to run, I must take it no matter what. If there are no such opportunities, then this is the future I chose when I left Stormwind's valley, and again when I summoned the phoenix. Each person who helped me made their own choices in their own time. Talon, when she created an avenue for Stormwind's escape. Stonefall, when he answered my questions and let me go, knowing why I came. Jabir, when he named me a free mage and allowed me passage. They've had time since I was caught to plan for their future, to escape before I am forced to name them.

If Talon's plan was to demand my suicide, then she'll simply have to learn to live with her disappointment.

But as much as I try to absolve myself of all responsibility, I can still see Stonefall's face in my mind's eye as he offered to answer three questions, can still hear Jabir's voice as he promised not to notice when I left the Mekteb. I can still feel the certainty that hummed through me, as if I could not possibly betray them.

TRUTH SPELL

Brightsong brings my breakfast early in the morning, setting the tray beside me before bustling out again. It's the first time she has allowed me to feed myself.

While I eat, she oversees a pair of servants who bring in a low tub, two buckets of water, and a small stool they set within the tub. She sets a stack of clean clothes at the foot of my bed and waits for me to finish.

It is another level of humiliation to be guarded through my bath, though at least it is only Brightsong and the female lycan once more. Brightsong *tsks* her tongue at me as I struggle with my tunic, and assists me out of my clothes and through the process of bathing with an efficiency that speaks to years of experience. At least at the end my hair is washed, the last of the blood scrubbed from my body.

Brightsong bundles me into my new clothes without a word. The tunic she brought is an elegant charcoal gray with white cord sewn in a floral design down the front as well as around the cuffs. Knot and loop closures made of the same cord allow the tunic to open down the front—which explains why I am being offered such a beautiful item: lifting my arm enough to fit into a closed tunic would have been near impossible. The accompanying *selvar* is a simple utilitarian white, but its color works with the embroidery. I will be going to my trial dressed in the richest clothes I've worn in a year.

In a pile on the ground beside me lie my discarded clothes, and with them, the pill Talon gave me. I make no attempt to recover it. Instead, I turn to Brightsong with the one question she might be able to answer for me.

"I was wondering," I say. "When you checked me, you found fire and stone. Was there anything else you noticed?"

Her expression stiffens. "Isn't that enough?"

"It's already too much," I agree, trying not to sound cheerful. Perhaps the breath Val gave me didn't change me as deeply as I'd feared.

"You are about to be tried before the High Council." The quietness of her voice does not belie the ruthlessness of her words. "If I were you, I would focus on finding a way through the next few hours so that, when next we speak, you are still able to ask me questions."

I have nothing to say in answer.

She gathers my discarded clothes and moves to the door, and there she stops. "You saved the life of a high mage here," she says finally, without looking at me. "Be sure that you mention it before the Council."

"I will."

A guard knocks at the door, calling through to inform us that my escort has arrived.

"A minute," Brightsong says, surprising me. She faces me, my clothes cradled in her arms. "I tried to argue that you were too weak to go through with this so soon." There is a darkness to her steady gaze, as if she struggles with regret. I hadn't realized how conflicted she finds herself by my situation. "The Council would question you in hopes of gaining a lead on where Mage Stormwind has gone."

She's apologizing. "I understand," I say, offering her a faint smile. "Will you be there?"

"No. Only those who are known to have encountered you will attend the hearing."

Ah. It could have been a completely closed trial, but the Council may need help asking the right questions. A Huq spell may demand the truth, but you don't have to give what you're not asked for. A helpful loophole, except that I can't count on the Council not asking for information I don't want to give. I will have to flood them with my story in hopes of leading them away from details I'd rather not reveal.

Brightsong glances toward the female lycan, who waits without comment beside the door. I have yet to hear her voice.

"See how well you can stand," Brightsong says.

I have no intention of being carried. If I can take three steps to a bath, I can make it to my trial. I stand up once more. My body answers a little better for the stretching I've done. It's my wounded arm I'll have to be careful with, for each step sends a slight twinge through my muscles. For now it will be bearable. By the end of the trial—well, I'll worry about it then.

The female lycan swings the door open. No less than a dozen lycans and six mages wait for me in the hall. The lycans are heavily armed. Their hands rest on the hilts of their weapons and they watch me with complete attention. The mages are somewhat less cool. Their expressions range from grim to wary to anxious. I keep my gaze lowered as I step into the hallway, knowing that if I look subdued that should at least calm the more anxious among them. A fidgety mage with a deadly spell hovering about their fingertips is hardly a good thing.

"I am High Mage Ravenflight." I look up to meet the assessing eyes of a tall mage who carries herself with the natural grace of a warrior. Perhaps she and Stonefall work together on occasion. I could easily imagine her as a rogue hunter. She continues, "I will head your escort today. Please refrain from any sudden movements, and do not speak until we have entered the hearing room."

I nod and start forward, my escort falling into place around me. Nearly half walk ahead of me and the rest behind me, but for Ravenflight to my left. We descend the stairs slowly, mostly because I take them one step at a time, leaning heavily on the railing. Brightsong gave me only a partial dose of the pain potion to help me keep my thoughts clear. Moving slowly jostles my injured arm less.

I reach the bottom of the stairs, pause to gather my courage.

"Do you require help?" With her black hair, brown eyes, and golden-brown skin, she has the look of the people of the western Kingdoms.

I take stock of my body. I am slightly out of breath, but okay. I shake my head.

We continue out the door and I realize why my escort is so large. The whole of the Mekteb has come out to see me walk to my trial. The gardens overflow with students of every age, the far arcades packed with people. Even the windows of the buildings opposite are filled with curious faces. How foolish of me to think a mistake on the part of my escort might allow me to escape.

"Keep walking," Ravenflight says as my guards knot around me, creating a tight circle two or three people deep in every direction.

At first, the crowd remains relatively quiet. But as we continue down the arcade, and they catch glimpses of me past my escort, a low rumble begins to rise.

"It's a girl! And young, too!"

"What is she, a camel rider?"

"*She* tricked the guard? She's no more than a child—"

"Can't tell where she's from—"

"Mixed blood—and desert at that."

"Where'd she get those clothes?"

"*That's* who got past the lycan guard? They must be—"

I clench my teeth. *I am not too young, my blood too mixed, to be intelligent.* What kind of school *is* this?

"Easy," Ravenflight murmurs, her expression even more grim. "No use getting angry."

Maybe not, but that doesn't mean I *shouldn't* be upset with those I walk past. How could I have imagined that, were my life different, I would have found a place here? Among people who think that my age or breeding are signs of what I lack?

For the first time, I am truly grateful that my parents kept me from this. I expected the world to be set against me, and I was prepared for it. If I'd grown up here, been taught to accept these prejudices and based my expectations for myself on them, would I be anything like the person I am now?

I complete my walk to the Great Hall in a reverie of outrage and unexpected insight. But my temper steadies as we enter the building where I'm to be tried. From the vast, soaring spaces and stained glass to the tiled mosaics rising up the wall and the calligraphy scrolling around the high domes, the grand entry is breathtaking. At the center of the entry, a great water clock tells time, a work of genius to measure out the minutes and hours of the day, its marriage of beauty and function a thing of wonder.

The entryway opens into a great open space where the chant of a holy man reciting a prayer resounds. We bypass the prayer space, walking through a side door into a long hallway, and proceeding to a door halfway down.

Across from the door waits my mother. The shock of seeing her drains the last of my temper, leaving me numb. She wears jade-hued mage's robes, a lovely, shifting green that remains completely unadorned. Beneath them, the pale cream edge of her kimono throws the color into greater relief. Her neck is long and curved, her hair upswept so that her profile is elegance itself. She watches us approach without expression, but I can tell the moment she recognizes me: the slight hardening of her jaw, the crystalline stillness in which she stands.

She knows who I am. Five years' separation, the time it

took me to grow from child to woman, protected me at our last meeting. But my features still reflect both her and the man who was my father, and word would have traveled very fast after my capture. It was her name-spell I used at the last.

As we turn to enter the doorway, Hotaru Brokensword lowers her gaze, dropping her chin slightly, to all appearances a respectful, meek woman. I doubt any of my escort recognize it for what I do—a greeting, and perhaps also a farewell. I look away because I cannot return her courtesy without arousing interest, and because I don't yet know what to make of it. Nor am I sure I want to return it.

The Council's meeting room is meant to intimidate as much as the Great Hall is meant to inspire awe and wonder. The ceiling here is high but nothing like the entryway, the walls covered in another mosaic so complex that my eyes merely gloss over it. What intimidates are the two great curved tables, set facing each other upon a low platform, like the two crescents of an impossible moon curved toward each other. Between their far tips, a third table sits, just large enough to accommodate the first mage while lending him the prestige of pride of place.

The bottom tips of the crescent tables are spaced farther apart, allowing the Council an easy view of the rest of the room. My guards escort me past a set of brocade-cushioned benches to a seat placed at the very bottom of the tables, facing the first mage's place of honor. As I walk, I catch sight of Jabir standing quietly to the side, rheumy eyes giving nothing away. Stonefall, who should have long since fled, has taken a seat on one of the benches, his eyes on the Council tables. I recognize the two mages who were on the patrol I joined, the stocky mage glaring. On the other side are Osman Bey and the two lycans who escorted me to Stormwind's cell. Kemal watches me through narrowed eyes, radiating fury. Osman Bey, on the other hand, keeps his gaze trained on the front of the room, giving no indication that he's noticed my entry. Talon is conspicuously absent.

My chair sports wooden armrests and a cushioned back and seat. I ease myself down, careful not to jar my elbow against the armrest. A few of the Council members stand about behind their tables conversing.

I don't have long to wait. Within a few minutes, a rustle of robes heralds the arrival of the remaining members of the Council. I stare straight ahead as they walk up the aisle behind me.

The first two mages pass me without a glance, caught up in a quiet discussion. The one mage I do not recognize, but the other I would know anywhere: Blackflame.

Today, he wears ceremonial robes, black as the night with gold embroidery rimming the front and the ends of his sleeves, complimenting the bright yellow of his hair. As he walks, the robes sway about him so perfectly I wonder if he's charmed them.

He is beautiful and powerful and considers me nothing more than a nuisance, and a convenient excuse for taking over the Council. It would almost be worth releasing the fire I carry in my bones at him in a second sunbolt, even if it destroyed me. Just as well the room is no doubt warded against every form of aggressive magic imaginable, and such an attack would never reach him. I'm glad not to have the choice.

He takes his seat at the center table and motions to a mage who sits far to my right, papers spread before him. A scribe, I think. A small metal stand sculpted to look like a bird in flight sits before him, a silver bell hanging from its beak. The mage taps the bell once with an ornate hammer. As the silvery note fills the air, I feel a faint brush of magic against my cheeks. I strain my senses, trying to discern what the spell has accomplished, but I can't be sure. It might be that the doors are sealed, or that the room itself is sealed against any type of spying, magical or physical. It feels as though we are, somehow, floating free, untethered to the rest of the world.

Blackflame leans back in his chair, fixing his icy blue eyes on me. The other mages have already seated themselves and likewise turn their gaze to me. I look back silently, waiting. When he finally speaks, though, Blackflame addresses the Council. "It is our duty today to question the prisoner before us in hopes of understanding exactly how Mage Stormwind escaped, and to learn any details that may allow us to recapture her. We must also decide on the future of this…wild Promise, as it were."

Promise? Interesting how I was a rogue mage when I healed Stonefall, and now I am nothing more than a half-trained talent to be done away with.

Blackflame gestures toward me. "I suggest we proceed with a truth spell and begin our questioning, as discussed yesterday, unless there are any objections."

Most of the mages shake their heads. None of them speak. My heart thunders in my chest, my fingertips tingling with fear. If I weren't sitting, I might have stumbled from this sudden weakness. It's all going to come out now. Everything. Every secret I have, spilled before Blackflame....

A smile flickers at the edges of my lips as I stare up at him. Not quite a year ago, the Degaths petitioned the Council to remove Blackflame. Their request was denied. There was no proof, only allegations, and neither party would submit to a truth spell. Blackflame has his secrets too, and I hold several of them. I grin at him, a feral, hungry smile, as three of the mages who escorted me step forward to form a triangle around me, one to either side of me and the third behind my chair. Blackflame may finish me today, but I can bring him down a step or two before that.

One of the arch mages to my left rises, skirting the table and stopping directly in front of me. He makes the fourth point, transforming the triangle into a diamond with me at its center. My smile fades when I raise my gaze to his. He is tall and slim, skin slightly bronzed, with dark hair falling past his shoulders. His starry black eyes could swallow you whole and leave you wandering the dark landscape of your soul for an eternity.

I go still, forcing myself not to look away. He isn't human, or any other kind of humanlike creature I've met. Possibly he's one of the so-called *Pari*, or Fae, who live far to the west. If so, he probably doesn't even need the other mages that surround me to feed his spell.

"I am Arch Mage Nightblade." He speaks carefully, as if trying to fix his name in my memory and calm me at the same time. Perhaps he is. His voice holds the velvet darkness of summer nights, the deep-throated beauty of an impossible songbird. It is a hellish thing to hear, knowing what he's about to do to me.

My hands, curled together in my lap, clutch each other in a death grip. Nightblade. It can't mean anything as simple as a dagger made of darkness—Fae mages prefer names that are more puzzles than anything. Whatever he can do must be a great deal worse than a shadow blade.

"The spell will not harm you in its casting. If you attempt to refuse to answer, or lie, you will experience pain." He says the word delicately. "It is best to comply with the spell. Do you understand?"

I nod. I focus on the stiffness of my fingers to keep me grounded, the thin slices of pain that are my nails pressing into my skin. Now would be a good time to discover a secret weapon I never knew I had. Something subtle enough to escape the notice of eleven arch mages, and strong enough to overcome a truth spell.

Something like a bond with a breather.

Val, I call out, closing my eyes as the mages begin their casting. He makes no answer. How long will it take for him to notice? I take a shaky breath as the hum of power builds around me, flowing through the mages to the arch mage before me. *Val, please! I need you here now!*

Nightblade touches my forehead, drawing a sigil there that holds such potency I cannot even breathe, my lungs frozen, my heart stuttering.

VALERIUS!

The sigil sinks into me, glittering in my bloodstream and shining in the darkness behind my eyelids. A flash of light that holds no heat, that is in fact bitterly cold, blinds me. Then the frigid brightness wraps around my bones, melds itself to the inside of my head.

"It is done," Nightblade says quietly. There's the faint rustle of robes as the mages around me retire to their seats.

Val, I think, one final, hopeless time.

I'm not doing it right, don't have any idea what I'm doing. Perhaps the seal on the room won't even let him in.

"Very well," Blackflame says, voice pleasant and utterly unperturbed.

I keep my eyes closed partly to spite him, and partly to give myself a moment longer, however futile evasion may be now.

"What is your name, girl?"

I open my eyes, aware of a slow pressure building in my ears, a tingling that has nothing to do with fear dancing over my skin.

Val—

Yes. What is this? His voice is terse, abrupt, and possibly the most wonderful thing I have ever heard. The pressure in my ears expands to my throat, wraps itself my lungs.

A trial. I can't tell them my name. Please, can you—

"Your name," Blackflame reiterates, no longer amused.

The tingling becomes needles of ice, shooting through my skin to pierce my bones, my organs.

I take a gasping breath, and can keep silent no longer. "Hi—"

My voice breaks off mid-name, and there is that same, strange sense of internal displacement, of being sent stumbling sideways while my body stays in place. Faintly, I can hear myself coughing, but mostly I am aware of the sudden cessation of pain. And then my voice says, "Hibachi."

Blackflame, all the arch mages, stare at me.

Fire-bowl? What kind of name is that?

Your new family name, Val returns, sounding slightly strained. *You have to admit, it's rather fitting.*

"That is your full name?" Blackflame asks. "You would do well to answer our questions to the fullest extent possible."

Val tilts my head up, so that we look down my nose at the First Mage of the High Council. "Kiki Hibachi. But you may call me by the mage name I earned a year ago: Sunbolt."

A ripple of surprise washes through the room. A few of the mages lean toward each other, muttering questions, and at least three glance uncertainly at Blackflame.

You're how old and the best you can do is Kiki Fire-bowl? I ask Val as we watch the Council's reaction. *Is Kiki even a real name?*

His answer is slow in coming, as if he has to first gather himself. *I'm sure it is somewhere. I didn't exactly have time to plan it.*

I can't fault him there. *Thank you for coming,* I say belatedly.

My pleasure.

No doubt he can hear the laughter in my thoughts as I ask, *Can you stay?*

I'll try. We should stick as close to the truth as possible now.

Agreed. I don't want to trip over a lie and clue the Council in to the fact that I've escaped their truth spell.

Blackflame clears his throat, drawing the mages' attention back to him.

They will ask about your sunbolt, Val says. *I hope you wanted that.*

To tell the Council what Blackflame did? Absolutely.

I can sense his amusement as he answers, *I thought so.*

Blackflame fixes me with his pale gaze. "Our focus today is to understand your actions over the last week in freeing Brigit Stormwind, and what you know of where she has gone."

Well? Val prompts.

I have no idea where she is, I respond truthfully.

Val repeats my words aloud. The mage to Blackflame's right leans forward, eyes narrowing. She is short and stocky, with the olive complexion and dark hair of the north-central Kingdoms. Her hair is cut short and styled so that it stands up in little spikes all around her head. It's a style that suits her bearing. "Surely you have some idea? A guess?"

"It was too dangerous," Val says, echoing the words I give

him. The sound of my voice is slightly strained as he goes on. "I knew I might get caught."

The mages confer with each other, voices murmuring, and then Blackflame waves them quiet. "You must have had an initial plan. Where were you going when you were caught? And where was Mistress Stormwind at that time?"

"I was going to the roof," we explain. "And Stormwind was right behind me. Since I was caught and she was not, I can only assume she eventually got out."

The spiky-haired mage gapes at me. "She was *what?*"

"Behind me. She stayed in the cell until I went in to fetch her."

The whole of the Council stares at me.

Congratulations, Val murmurs. *I don't think too many people have managed to utterly confound the High Council of Mages before.*

Thanks.

In the silence that has spread after my words, Arch Mage Nightblade drums his fingers against the wooden table in a staccato drumroll. "You mean that she hid from sight within the cell until you opened the door and allowed her to pass through the wards there."

"Yes."

"That's impossible," one of the other mages stammers. "We inspected her cell—the shackles were open, there was no sign of her, and she was *bound*. She could not cast a spell to hide herself."

"She could still use charms, and she did. That's all she did."

Nightblade watches me intently. "What charms?"

"A look-away while she was in the cell. After that— perhaps a smoker or two. And a stinker." At least, if I had to give my garlic-and-onions charm a name, that one seems relatively self-explanatory.

"What about once you reached the roof? How did you intend to leave the Mekteb? You must have had an ally if you don't know where she went from there."

"The phoenix agreed to carry us out," I admit. They already have his feather; acknowledging his interest in me may actually do more to save my life than anything else.

"The...*phoenix?*" It's one of the other arch mages, his look of bewilderment mirrored by his colleagues.

Blackflame leans forward. "The phoenix of the Burnt Lands was going to fly you to safety? Or—" He hesitates, though there cannot be that many other phoenixes in the world.

"Yes, that one."

If I stunned the Council to silence before, now I've shaken them out of it.

"That's absurd," Blackflame says, just as a mage to his right sputters, "By what right—"

"We have agreements—"

"I demand an explanation of this! The phoenix has never—"

"Perhaps," Nightblade says, his voice cutting through the rising tide of outrage, "you should start your explanations at the beginning."

This is precisely the opportunity I've been hoping for. "The beginning is a bit further back, Master Nightblade. I'll have to start a year ago, with the sunbolt I mentioned, if you wish to understand the whole of my connection to Stormwind and what I have done to help her."

The mages around the table watch me with varying levels of disapproval, but at least they're listening again. Without even a glance toward Blackflame, Nightblade nods. Ah, he's not a supporter, then.

"I lived in Karolene until about a year ago, when a warrant for the execution of Lord and Lady Degath was issued." Val pauses, giving a moment for the words to sink in. Blackflame goes still, staring at me, really and truly looking at my face. I hope he remembers it. "As part of the Shadow League, I volunteered to help the family escape Karolene before the warrant could be carried out. Unfortunately, Arch Mage Blackflame convinced Saira Degath that, if she helped him catch the leader of the Shadow League, he would allow her family to go free, and no doubt win his favor."

"This has no bearing on the current investigation," Blackflame says, each word hard and cold.

"I'm under a truth spell, and I say it does," Val says for me. "Whatever I testify is only what I believe to be true. You've nothing to fear if you haven't done wrong."

"You will answer only those questions—"

"I will *not*." The anger in my voice surprises me, not the least because it accurately reflects my own feelings. Val must be able to sense me very well. I go on relaying my story as quickly as I can, before Blackflame truly does stop me. "I was there, in the empty building we took refuge in, when the sultan's soldiers burst through the doors and cut down Lord and Lady Degath. I used my magic to hide the true Ghost in the shadows, but I could not reach the Degaths in time."

Blackflame surges to his feet. "Enough!" His face is pale with fury, blue eyes burning with cold.

My voice slices through the rising murmurs of the other mages. "I was taken prisoner with the younger Degaths, and *we were brought to your home.*"

Blackflame slams his fist against the table. "Be silent!" He turns on Nightblade in white-lipped rage, "The truth spell is flawed."

Nightblade rises from his seat, facing Blackflame calmly. "Is it? Allow me to check." He gestures to one of the mages across from him, the one who had stammered out an argument against Stormwind's method of escape. "Bastion, so there is no doubt, I invite you to check the spell with me."

Arch Mage Bastion acquiesces, and they descend from their respective tables and approach me.

Val, will they be able to sense you?

Possibly.

Not the answer I want. *Should you go?*

If they ask you your name, to check the spell, you won't be able to answer with what you've already given them. Just wait. The mages come to a stop before us. *And take your body back in the meantime. I'll hang about at the back of your skull.*

With a nearly tangible *snap* I'm back in my body, and it hurts. Pain tingles along my nerves, my body desperately heavy. I have to focus on breathing slowly, steadily. But I shouldn't hurt this much. Last time Val took me over, the pain I felt was from the muscles I strained in my fight with Osman Bey, and from my wound. This is different.

"Miss Hibachi," Nightblade says, calling my attention back to him. "We will put our fingers on the sigil on your forehead. It should not hurt."

I look down at my lap, too afraid to speak with the truth spell pressing upon me. They touch my forehead together. The spell dances through my blood, the sigil on my forehead so icy it feels as though it might cut right through my skin and into bone.

Bastion steps back, Nightblade letting his hand drop barely a moment later.

"Well?" he asks Bastion.

"It's fine," he admits gruffly. "Fully formed and well cast. I can find no flaw."

"There is no flaw in the casting," Nightblade agrees.

The moment he turns his eyes to the Council, his body still blocking my view, Val murmurs, *Shall I?*

Yes. Is everything— all right? It feels different.

Everything is fine, Val assures me, and by the time the two mages seat themselves, I am back to being a spectator in my own body.

"So far," Blackflame says, cold blue eyes trained on me, "you have not mentioned any allies. You could not have accomplished so much alone. Who helped you?"

"No," Nightblade says, his voice measured as always. Yet the word cuts across the space. "Let us finish hearing the previous answer."

Answer Blackflame's question, Val counsels me. I give him the words I need to prove that the truth spell is still forcing answers from me. "I helped myself for as far as I've told you. I'm sure you'll have the rest from me shortly."

"Such a story has no relevance to the current trial," Blackflame tells Nightblade, ignoring me.

Nightblade tilts his head, eyelids dropping a fraction. "I was placed in charge of the commission that investigated the charges brought forward by young Lord Degath. Since none of the parties involved consented to a truth spell, and all depended on the words of those involved, the commission was disbanded. It is my duty, now that a witness stands before us under a truth spell, to assure that the story is heard. Especially," he smiles amiably, "when the witness claims that it relates to the case on which she is being tried as well."

Over the course of this speech, Blackflame's face has grown hard as stone, until his features look as if they were cut into his face. "Do you think it your duty to undermine the First Mage of the Council?"

"On the contrary, it is the duty of the First Mage of the Council to assure that no Council member, nor mage sworn to us, misuses their magic or power such that they murder innocent civilians. Nor should our arch mages be involved in political maneuvers for their own or others' ambition in the Kingdoms they serve. *That* is the true role and purpose of the High Council." Nightblade gestures toward me with a long-fingered hand. "It is your duty before it is mine to hear out this girl."

"She knows nothing. The warrant issued on the Degaths was for treason, which should make clear the danger they posed. They armed themselves and fought the sultan's soldiers—not mine. The soldiers had to defend themselves.

That is how Lord and Lady Degath died. The sultan had agreed to house them in my residence rather than the city prison as a safeguard for them. We have discussed all this."

"And we will discuss it again," Nightblade agrees with a bland smile. "Let us now hear from the girl on the points of contention between yourself and the new Lord Degath, which she may be able to enlighten us on." He tilts his head, dark hair cascading over his shoulder, and asks me, "What happened after you were taken to Arch Mage Blackflame's residence?"

If I controlled my body, I would be smiling now. I never thought I'd look forward to speaking to the Council, but I am looking forward to this. I may be about to lose my magic or my mind, but I now have the chance to tell a story that could cost Blackflame dearly. I don't intend to waste it.

TRIAL

I tell my story with every detail I can recall, from the way the soldiers obeyed Blackflame when they delivered us to his courtyard, to the way he taunted Saira for trusting him, to the imprisonment and execution he promised Tarek. I describe the cages we were locked in, to which Nightblade says, "You are quite sure that the Degaths were not placed under guard in a guest suite?"

"Cages," I tell him, Val making the word snap through the room. "In the basement, with a torture table at the center of the room and implements on the wall. I have not forgotten any of it."

"According to the Degaths, a fang lord named Kol visited them there. Arch Mage Blackflame tells us that he had nothing to do with Lord Kol, and that whatever incident they are referring to must have occurred after they escaped his guard."

Blackflame does not speak, but I see such hatred glittering in his eyes that I know he will find a way to make me pay for all of this. It should be quite easy for him, but that doesn't stop me. "He lied. He escorted Lord Kol down to the cages himself, and traded me to him to pay a debt. Then he ordered Alia Degath's cage opened so Lord Kol could mesmerize her and feed from her until she collapsed. The rest of us were made to watch."

Nightblade nods as if I have offered up some interesting bit of trivia, but there is no mistaking the uncertainty mingled with disbelief on the faces of most of the other mages.

"Lord Kol is not known to have traveled to Karolene at that time," Nightblade observes. "He did not pass through the portal there, nor was he a traveler on the ships in port. How do you explain his presence, and your departure with him, then?"

Blackflame goes still. Ah, so here's a secret the High Council hasn't caught wind of yet.

"Arch Mage Blackflame has a portal in his garden. We went through that." Val manages to make me sound wholly oblivious to the import of my words.

"That's impossible." It's another arch mage, tall and well built, with dark skin and a slight scar running down his cheek. "Portals are exceptionally difficult to create. One does not simply have a portal enchanted in the garden, as if it were an everyday charm."

Val shrugs my shoulders. "I don't know about that. I know what it looked like and I know we went through it. Kol did not have to go into the city at all."

"That explains quite a bit," another arch mage says in a quiet voice. She hasn't spoken before, and it's only as Blackflame slides her a dark look that I realize she is one of the few who doesn't support him.

"Interesting," Nightblade says over the rising murmur. "Go on, then."

I continue my story. The Council has heard much of it from the Degaths, as well as Blackflame's version of events, but their knowledge of my story ends with my departure with Kol. They don't know the role Val played in my escape. This I give them, along with the story of my sunbolt, though I make no mention of our bond. Instead, I focus on the damage I'd sustained, the loss of my memory, and Val's decision to take me to Stormwind.

"The breather demanded shelter by the Laws of Old from her, and she unwillingly granted it. He asked her to take care of me, help me recover my strength and memories, and train me. She agreed to let me stay, and he left before the three days were through."

Bastion sits forward. "You mean that Mistress Stormwind took you on as her apprentice?"

"Not precisely. She understood that I must have had some training in order to cast my sunbolt. Without my memories, I couldn't tell her who trained me. I believe she made some discreet inquiries to try to locate my master or mistress. She found nothing, nor did my memory improve. At first, she merely assessed me and worked to assure I would do neither myself nor others harm. As it became clear that I was trained, she decided to fill in the holes in what I recalled of my training and bring me before the High Council to be assessed and formally apprenticed once I was ready."

Bastion shakes his head. "She trained a wild Promise beyond the purview of the High Council."

"Oh, I don't think you could refer to my magic as wild by any means. *Free* perhaps, but not wild. As far as I can tell, the one thing you could have justly sentenced Stormwind for was for taking too long in reporting both my existence and her work with me, neither of which she intended to keep silent about much longer."

You're not making friends with that statement, Val says, his mental voice thin with fatigue.

If I thought I could make friends, I wouldn't have outed Blackflame in front of the Council that voted him into power. I hesitate, wondering about the pain I'd felt, the sound of Val's voice in my mind. *You're sure you're all right?*

Yes.

"That is a curious claim indeed," Blackflame says, breaking the silence he has held since allowing my testimony. "Free, not wild. You remember Karolene, or you could not speak of the Degaths. Yet you do not recall your master?"

"No."

"Who harbored you there, then? Who did you live with, and how did you continue your studies?"

His eyes gleam with anticipation. He thinks he will find what he needs to tear me down, destroy me. But it's because of him I was alone in Karolene, which makes this answer both easy and truthful.

"No one. To the best of my knowledge, I was trained as a child. I remember living on the streets in Karolene, renting a place in a shared apartment when I could afford it. I believed my family long dead."

"Your family, the Hibachis," Blackflame says.

"Yes."

Blackflame motions to the scribe. "Have the records checked for an apprentice with the family name Hibachi, born in the last fifteen or twenty years."

The scribe nods.

Don't worry, Val says as I clamp down on my panic. *You lost your memory. Just because you can't explain their lack of records doesn't mean you're lying. There are other explanations for differences in family names.*

True. I have time to come up with whatever explanations I'll need, assuming I survive long enough for it to be an issue at all.

"And so," Nightblade says, "you were studying with Stormwind when she was summoned before the High Council."

"Yes."

Blackflame frowns, his eyes cold and steady on my face. I doubt he will ever forget what I look like after this. I can only hope that my testimony will take him out of the Council as quickly as my actions brought him in.

Nightblade gestures for me to continue, and I launch into a somewhat edited retelling of the last week. Although I would like to leave it out, I have no choice but to describe my journey through the portal and the mage who followed me. I have no doubt that the Council members, if they wish to look into it, will easily uncover that story. I don't dare leave it out, but I do make sure that I don't give it willingly, instead giving just enough detail to trigger the questions that would force me to tell all under the truth spell.

We have the Council's full attention as we describe the first spell-creature. The mage's death—including his attempt to throw me to the monster—meets with a progressively more grim reception.

This time, it is Nightblade who requests the scribe to inquire into the identity of the mage, and the closing of the portal at Sonapur. As well as any information on the identity of the mages who rode to Stormwind's valley.

Finished, he asks, "How did you escape the Burnt Lands from there?"

"The phoenix," I explain, and describe my conversation with the phoenix and the rest of my flight to the bridge.

"So that's how you first met him," the spiky-haired mage says.

"Yes."

"But why would he give you his feather? Or agree to help you again at all?" the scar-faced mage asks.

And here is the gamble I must take, the hope that they will find me intriguing enough to keep as a source slave rather than destroy outright. "He saved my life. In return, he wanted me to attempt to unravel the enchantments that hold the Burnt Lands in their grip."

"You?" Bastion says derisively. "A half-trained mage barely old enough to—"

"This would be the first time in two hundred years a mage has 'unraveled' any of the enchantments holding the Burnt Lands in their thrall," Nightblade observes. "That the phoenix thinks this young mage capable of greater feats should give us pause."

"It gives me great pause," Bastion replies. "She holds no allegiance to us, undermines our authority, frees our prisoners—to hear that she is exceptionally talented and capable of what *we* are not? No, I do not think that a good thing at all."

"No, it isn't," agrees another mage. "*If* this girl has such power, she can hardly be allowed to wield it as she has thus far, without any respect for the Council."

Nightblade raises his hand in a calming gesture, earning an infuriated look from the mage. "Let us hear the rest of her story and keep our deliberations for after." He nods to me. "Did you promise to return to the phoenix at that time?"

"No. He gave me his feather and told me to burn it when I chose to return. He left me and sent some of the desert dwellers to guide me out of the desert." I continue on, skimming over my journey to the city, making no mention of Huda's or Laith's names or their tribes. Nor do the arch mages appear to care about such details. I get as far as my arrival in Fidanya when Blackflame calls a short recess for lunch.

It's interesting to see the shifts in dynamic on the Council as he speaks. His words are precise, confident, and cool, as if he has no doubt as to his power or place. But there's no question that something has changed in the room with my telling; Blackflame departs alone. He does not look for company as he leaves the table, nor does anyone hurry forward to join him.

As the remaining arch mages file from the room, Nightblade approaches to adjust the truth spell.

Here, Val says, returning my body to me. Pain ripples through every muscle, my very organs strangely heavy within me. My sight blurs, refusing to clear even when I press my eyes shut and open them again.

"I will not remove the sigil," Nightblade explains as I try to focus on the floor. His fingers rise to touch my forehead. "It will remain dormant for now. I will reawaken it when we reconvene."

I close my eyes and wait for the numbing cold of the truth spell to fade, leaving only a slight cold spot on my forehead. Nightblade drops his hand. It takes me a moment to open my eyes, and another breath or two to marshal my forces enough to look up to him.

"Are you well?"

I look at him for so long, the golden-pale skin, the night-star eyes, the depth of magic of him, that I almost forget his question. He tilts his head, watching me back. Finally I nod, because I cannot think of what to say.

"You have an hour. I suggest you eat and rest. I expect the trial to continue into the evening."

I nod again.

Once he departs, my escort comes up around me, Ravenflight at their front. I wonder if they waited at the back of the room through the trial, or were sent outside.

Can you stand? Val asks.

I think so, but I'm not quite certain. I look up at Ravenflight. "I might have trouble standing," I say, my voice hoarse. "Please don't be surprised."

She frowns slightly, nods. I heave myself to my feet, wavering until she moves forward and offers me her arm as a support. I take it gratefully.

All right? Val asks.

I think, I say as I start forward, my knees shaky beneath me. *I really rather think we are not supposed to do this sort of thing for so long. My body doesn't feel right.*

A pause.

No, Val agrees. And then, *I need to return to my own body. Call me when they reconvene. I'll be ready.*

Thank you.

I can only hope Val's body has fared better by itself than mine has with both of us. Surely it would be fine? What would the ramifications be of leaving it for hours on end?

My grip tightens on Ravenflight's arm.

"Easy," she murmurs.

I force myself to unclench my fingers. There's nothing to be done right now.

My escort guides me to the next room where two trays filled with food have been set out on a long low table along one wall. It's a room for more relaxed meetings. Low sofas line the walls, interspersed here and there with small carved wooden tables inlaid with mother-of-pearl. I take a seat on the sofa against the back wall, eat what is given me, and close my eyes when I am done, letting my head rest against the wall.

No one speaks. I can't tell how much they heard, nor do I want to risk speaking now that we have left the protections of the Council room. I wouldn't have much to ask regardless.

Eyes closed, I puzzle through the unexpected pain I am left with in the wake of Val's help this time. I consider the possibilities, remember the strain in Val's mental voice as he spoke with me. With a sudden, sickening clarity, I recall Nightblade saying, "You will experience pain."

My eyes snap open. The spell didn't fail, as I thought. It took, and Val is the one paying the price of each lie I tell. A good deal of what I've said has been true, but not all of it. My testimony has been interspersed with lies to keep my heritage secret, to keep the Degaths safe. The bulk of my secrets still lie ahead of me. The Degath's aid, Kenta's help and the building where he makes his home....

"Are you well?"

I look up blankly. Ravenflight stands before me.

"Are you well?" she repeats.

I nod. "Fine."

"You're shaking."

I am. I take a breath, try to still my body. It doesn't quite work.

"Just tired," I tell her.

She nods and moves to stand against the wall beside my sofa, my own personal sentinel.

I close my eyes, trying to still my shaking and focus on what I will do. Before I'm halfway ready for it, a servant knocks at the door to request our presence in the hearing room. The walk back is physically easier, my spirit resting comfortably in my body, the strange heaviness mostly past and the pain no more than a ghostly memory.

Once we enter the room with its protections, I call out to Val again. He arrives as the last of the arch mages take their seats, Nightblade coming around to awaken the truth spell. I drop my gaze and close my eyes, bracing for the mage's touch upon my forehead.

All well? I ask Val, trying to keep my mind's voice calm, unworried.

Well enough.

It's hitting you, isn't it? I ask. *The truth spell?*

How can it?

I don't know how the spell works, but he's telling lies for me. *If it's hitting my body, you must feel it,* I point out. And he must be shielding me from his emotions somehow as well, for I haven't sensed the pain at all.

I'm fine.

I don't believe him, don't believe the very terseness of his response.

I steel myself as Nightblade traces the truth sigil, the

searing cold of the enchantment enveloping me once more as it reawakens.

Ready? Val asks, sounding more himself.

No. Tell me if it's hitting you, or I'm keeping control right now.

Hitomi, don't be a fool. They'll destroy your allies if you speak, won't they? Is that what you want?

He knows the answer to that.

Move over, he says, his tone wry.

Despite my reservations, my consciousness slides easily to the side this time.

At the crescent tables, Nightblade takes his seat.

Tell me how bad it is.

I can feel it, Val admits. *But I don't believe I feel even half of its true power. I can get you through this.*

Blackflame calls the Council to order. In the hard lines of his jaw, the cold glitter of his eyes, I know what he intends. As I have done my best to destroy him in the last few hours, so he will now see me undone through my own testimony. He'll also discover and punish as many of my allies as he can find.

And Val will suffer for every lie I tell to keep my allies safe. Because of what? The life debts he thinks he owes me?

Val, you don't owe me this much. I think the words before I can help myself, even though I know I need his help now. Even though I would beg him to help me if he weren't offering.

I think you and I are past owing each other debts by now, don't you?

Are we? I'm not at all sure I won't feel beholden to Val for what he's doing for me today.

Blackflame gestures to me. "We closed the last session with your departure from the caravanserai. Did you come straight to the Mekteb from there?"

"Yes." At least that is a truth. I will try to spare Val what lies I can.

"How did you enter undetected?"

"I didn't," we say. "I came to the front gate and asked the guard there for entry. I told him I had a delivery for Master Stonefall from my mistress. I didn't believe Master Jabir to be anything more than a mage. He considered my request and granted me passage."

Blackflame raises his brows, looking past me to where Jabir sits. "*Master* Jabir," he says, with a hint of mockery. "Did you not recognize anything of concern in this girl?"

Jabir clears his throat, his robes rustling as he stands. "I noted a great many things about the girl, including the fact that she carried the favor of the desert phoenix. Although she did not tell me the complete truth, I sensed no danger in her intentions."

"No danger," snaps one of the arch mages. "Surely you sensed her magic?"

"She was dressed as a mage. It did not seem unusual."

They haven't questioned him yet.

No, agrees Val. *I think they most wanted to find out where Stormwind had gone, which only you could tell them.*

That means Jabir hasn't yet admitted to giving me free rein to aid Stormwind—an admission that could cost him his post, and one he doesn't have to make.

"I didn't have very clear intentions at that point," we say, Val overriding the spiky-haired mage's attempt to speak. "I wasn't sure what I would do until after I found Master Stonefall dying. Once I healed him, he told me to hide in his bedchamber. He owed me his life, and in return he offered me a few minutes' protection. I wore my look-away charm and stayed there until everyone left. Master Stonefall demanded to know why I came to the Mekteb and what I wanted of him. I told him the truth. I came seeking word of Mistress Stormwind. He told me of her sentencing, and counseled me to leave. He told me that, should I cause any trouble, he would likely be sent to hunt me."

"Did Master Stonefall offer you no further support?" Blackflame demands.

Oh hell. The look-away itself, from Stormwind's pack. The Degaths—

He did, didn't he? Val asks. But he already knows.

"Did he say he did?" I hear myself ask. Val is buying me time, but I'll still have to answer the question. Stonefall chose this path, but I don't want it to cost him his future.

Val, I don't want to hurt you.

He ignores my protest, the furrowed brows and uncertainty on the faces before us giving him all the answer he needs.

"No." My voice rasps, as if the truth spell were pressing on my throat. Perhaps it is. "He didn't really offer any help."

Keep going before they ask more, Val says. *As much truth as you can, and what lies will save the people you need to protect. Otherwise, I'll have to make up lies for you and that may not go so well.*

253

So I do.

"I asked Stonefall's help in leaving his room, since there was a guard posted in the hallway. He agreed, as final payment of the life debt he incurred. He left his rooms and made sure the guards were dismissed. I left after their departure."

An arch mage with an angular face and shrewd eyes leans forward. "You merely walked out of White Raven Hall, despite the guards and the patrols, and no one took any note of you?"

"I was dressed as a mage and my age allowed me to pass as a student. To leave the building, I used the same charm I gave Stormwind—the look-away. Once I was outside, I took it off. No one noticed."

"This is outrageous," another mage mutters.

Blackflame looks to Stonefall. "You not only allowed but *helped* a rogue mage to walk out of your rooms?"

"I warned her to leave the Mekteb. I saw no sign that she used her magic for ill, nor did she argue with my warnings. I hunt declared rogues. The girl saved my life and seemed more concerned with fairness and justice than any rogue I have met."

"Is that how you judge rogues? You wait until they do something in your presence?" Blackflame flicks his fingers, dismissing any response Stonefall might have made. "Did you really think the rogue mage who showed up in your chambers would leave because you told her to?"

A pause. "I thought I may have persuaded her to leave the campus at least for a time. I doubted she would be able to get in again."

Is that why he told me about the Degaths? Or is he merely reinterpreting our conversation? Clearly, though, the Council hasn't questioned him about my visit either, or he would have named the Degaths right now. He knows very well that I've subverted the truth spell and he's helping me protect them. Just as he makes no mention of Jabir's visit to his room either.

Relief rushes through me. Until that moment, I didn't realize how worried I was that Stonefall's sense of honor would move him to confess his truths and uncover my ability to lie through the truth spell. But honor is a tricky thing. Stormwind's unjust imprisonment, and now my trial for aiding in her escape, might call to his sense of honor as strongly as speaking the truth, and fewer people will suffer for it. With his silence, Jabir avoids admitting his agreement to allow a prisoner's escape, and the Degaths are left uninvolved altogether.

"It seems the Council may need to revisit your appointment as a hunter," Blackflame observes blandly and turns his attention back to me. "Where did you go from White Raven Hall?"

"I found out that Arch Mage Talon had the keys to Stormwind's shackles. I decided to get into her rooms to look for them."

"How did you learn that?" Bastion asks.

Another lie. "I heard a group of students discussing Stormwind and joined the conversation. And no," I add at his look, "I don't know their names."

I can't tell if the mages note the strain in my voice, if it registers at all. I go on, explaining with complete truth how I'd stolen servants' clothing, been waylaid in the gardens by the boys with their screecher, and so met Osman Bey for the first time. I know very well that Osman Bey will have reported all that he knew of me at the time of my capture. I don't dare leave out any interaction with him or the other lycans.

Blackflame leans forward, expression contemptuous. "Osman Bey, you knew there was a rogue mage loose on the campus and you didn't suspect a servant you had never seen before?"

"Why should he?" I cut in before Osman Bey can answer. "You did not suspect me yourself."

"What?" Blackflame demands.

"I had the key to Stormwind's shackles in my pocket when I came up the stairs of Shahmaran Hall, and you saw me. You sent me to your rooms to clean the mess your source slave made when you used him too hard. Do you remember? I can't imagine what spell you cast to drain him so, but the boy was so weak he was propped against the wall, shivering and unable to speak. You must remember. You sent me up with Hotaru Brokensword."

Blackflame makes a choking sound, his face flushing. "You—"

"If you did not suspect me to be anything other than what I presented myself to be, you certainly should not blame anyone else, not Master Jabir, not Master Stonefall, not the housekeepers or servants or guards."

Nightblade tilts his head, eyes glinting with an amused approval.

"I did not suspect her," Osman Bey says from the back of

the room, "because she wore servants' clothing and claimed to be new. Every month we have seen new servants join the Mekteb. It is not our duty to monitor the servants. They are employed by the Mekteb, not the Council."

"Mistress Jeweltongue," Blackflame says, his composure icing over once more. "It seems you are unaware of the dangers posed to your students by your lax approach to security."

"On the contrary, Master Blackflame," a woman replies, her voice growing closer as she rises and walks up the aisle behind me. "Our Mekteb has enjoyed decades of peace, and it is our students' and servants' right to move freely on campus as well as into the city. It was the Council's decision to house prisoners here that has created such difficulty for our students and faculty, and, it seems, our servants. Perhaps, in future, the Council should reconsider the decision to stay at a school where the free movement of people must be allowed."

By the time she finishes, Jeweltongue has come to a stop to my right. She is no taller than I am, and is very well built, rounded arms filling out her sleeves. Despite the fact that she has just essentially revoked the Council's welcome at her school, she appears entirely unruffled—both by the Council and the ramifications of her words. I have a feeling there are few people indeed who would cross her willingly, and not because she is anything like Blackflame.

There are so many people here I wish I could have learned from, I tell Val.

I'm sure there are.

"This is, perhaps, a discussion for after the hearing," Nightblade says yet again. "Thank you, Headmistress Jeweltongue, for explaining your stance."

She inclines her head in deference and returns to her seat.

Nightblade gestures toward me, as if welcoming me to speak, as if there were no truth spell to force out my answers. "How did you manage to steal the key?"

I tell them, giving all of the ensuing details in complete honesty. Let Talon deal with the ramifications of leaving her book detailing the binding spells out. Let her explain why the key was only a cat's head key, and placed on her housekeeper's key ring. I feel a momentary regret having to name both Yilmaz and Esra, but there is no way around it, and they can hardly be blamed for failing to suspect me when I had duped Blackflame himself.

"So very honorable," Blackflame murmurs as I finish

describing how I'd stolen the key from Yilmaz as she rested. "For a girl who claims to value justice and honor, your ability to steal, deceive, and use people is quite exceptional. You would do anything, would you not, to achieve your ends?"

If I had my body, I would curl in on myself against his words. They're true, all true.

"No," Val says for me, voice strong and clear. "Not anything. I would not kill."

Blackflame hardly looks impressed. "But you would lie and poison. I see."

It wasn't poison. I gave Yilmaz a morning-long stomachache. But perhaps it was still unforgivable in its way. I drugged her, caused her pain, for my own ends.

Ignore him, Val says tersely. *We need to go on.*

Nightblade nods toward me. "What then? After you had the key?"

I touch on my run-in with Blackflame again, then describe leaving the Mekteb in company with the servants, and their introduction of me to the guards at the gate.

"And yet the Mekteb has no trouble with security," Bastion says, cutting his eyes to the place behind me where Jeweltongue must be sitting.

"They were your guards," Jeweltongue replies easily. "And as yet, no harm has been done to the Mekteb by the young woman in question, other than the loss of the two enchanted swords that were on display in Susulu Hall. That, Miss Hibachi, I do regret."

"I'm sorry for it," we say, half-turning in order to see her over my shoulder. "I was trying to avoid harming anyone."

"Indeed," she says. She must dislike Blackflame intensely, to have called into question the Council's future welcome to her Mekteb, and then gone so far as to suggest that all her concern regarding my actions amounts to is a couple of broken swords of purely magical curiosity.

"Enough," Blackflame says. "You left the Mekteb for the city, then. What allies did you meet there?"

I'll have to lie, I tell Val, so that he's ready.

That's fine. Go on.

"Only the phoenix. I paid an elderly woman to let me bake a bread roll at her fire. I baked in the key, my look-away charm, and a note telling Stormwind to wait in her cell for me. Then I burnt the feather the phoenix gave me and requested his help rescuing Stormwind."

"I was under the impression that he did not care for

politics," Arch Mage Nightblade says, his voice quiet.

"I can't speak to that," I say after a moment. "I doubt he would have done anything had I not asked for his help. But we spoke for some time, and he considered his actions. Had he not believed Stormwind innocent, he would never have helped me." He'd been swayed most by Jabir's involvement, but he had still carefully pondered his decision before agreeing.

"I see. And in return, you promised to travel back to the Burnt Lands?"

"Yes."

The mage with the scar shakes his head. "What exactly did he think you would accomplish there, by yourself?"

"He wished for me to try my hand at dismantling the spells there."

"And he still considered it worth the risk," Nightblade murmurs. He shakes his head. "Once you had his agreement, what did you do?"

"I returned to the Mekteb in time to distract the servant taking Stormwind's dinner in to her, and put the bun I had baked on her tray."

"Distract how?" Blackflame demands.

Last lie, I promise. At least, I will try to make it my last.

"A construct." The Council stares at me, and well they should. I am relatively certain I could not actually create a construct, a working of the highest order, difficult to maintain without complete and ongoing concentration. But the truth spell helps me convince them where I wouldn't be inclined to believe myself. "I created a construct of a teacher and used him to demand the help of the servant as he passed by. The servant put his tray down as ordered and went into the classroom, I placed the bun beneath a covered dish where it wouldn't be noticed, and the construct dismissed the servant."

Val shrugs my shoulders. "You know most of the rest of the story. I hid in the servants' washing room in the next building until the alarm was raised. Then I put on my mages' robes, 'discovered' the window I altered the protections on, and convinced the patrol I joined to take me to Stormwind's cell. I opened the door for her, gave her the space to come out, gave her a handful of smokers and stinkers, and a note telling her to use the roof if we got separated.

"I was caught on the stairs going up. She was directly behind me at the time. I cannot say precisely where she went after that."

The mages shift, glancing down at the papers before them, one or two murmuring something to the person beside them. My story is over, or at least I hope it is. I still can't be sure that Osman Bey didn't report my inhuman speed and fighting skill to the Council. It seems too much to hope that he did not.

"We have two reports here that we will ask you more about," Blackflame says, shifting a paper before him. "The first is from the head healer, Mistress Brightsong, who notes that your magical core has been touched by both fire and stone."

"The fire was from the sunbolt that nearly killed me. As far as I can tell, the stone was from the spell-creature in the Burnt Lands. There was no magic there to raise a shield as protection against the magical backlash from it."

A number of heads nod, accepting these explanations.

"The second is a report regarding your ability to fight the lycan guard. They believe your speed and ability to be beyond that of a human."

Val cants my head to the side. "Did the medical report find me at all inhuman?"

Blackflame regards me with disgust. "No."

"Then I expect it was merely the glamors and sleights of hand I used to confuse the guards, since I cannot be both human and not."

The spiky-haired woman says, "Then why shout 'No' and disarm yourself?"

"I was on the verge of killing someone. I had to remind myself that it was not something I could allow myself to do."

The mage with the scar looks at me strangely. "You wouldn't kill at all? Ever?"

"I could feel my fire calling to me. It would have been easier than breathing, to bathe them all in flame and escape. To kill them as I killed Kol. I would rather pay this price than do that. They were only upholding their honor, doing what they believed was right.

"I tried to stop them without magic because I did not trust myself. When I had no other choice, I tried to disarm them with a spell without fire at its heart. That's all."

The mage glances toward Blackflame, and I recall with sudden panic that I'd admitted to Osman Bey that I hadn't fought him—that it had been something else in me. Did he report that or hold it in confidence? And why hasn't he spoken up now? He must still be in the room....

"Are there any further questions for the prisoner?" Blackflame asks.

Why the panic? Val asks, his voice tired but steady. *You're almost done.*

The lycans. They know it wasn't me—I told one of them.

You what?

I didn't think I'd be able to escape the truth spell. I admitted I hadn't been the one to fight them.

Val makes no comment, which makes me feel even more the fool.

"Very well," Blackflame says into the quiet. "The prisoner will be escorted out and the Council will begin deliberation on the case."

As Nightblade approaches, Val returns my body to me. It feels as brittle as glass riddled with cracks, held together more by a memory of shape than by any true strength. Every breath comes as a jagged, painful gasp. I have to school myself to breathe slowly, as steadily as I can, let the pain ebb and flow until it begins to ease.

I remain seated until Nightblade lifts the truth spell from me. Even then, the pain does not dissipate, but lingers. How did Val bear this for a whole day?

Thankfully, Nightblade drops his fingers from my forehead and departs without a word. I open my eyes to see the blurry image of his robes moving away.

My escort materializes around me.

I will check in on you later, Val says. *Call if you need me.*

Thank you.

My body answers me in jerky movements as I rise, as if it doesn't quite remember the way of things. I push myself to my feet and teeter there uncertainly, as if half-drunk, until Ravenflight once more offers me her arm.

Halfway down the aisle, I remember to look for Osman Bey. He stands quietly, expression unreadable, golden eyes steady. I glance the other way to Stonefall, who appears equally inscrutable. As for Jabir, well, he looks like a harmless old man leaning on his staff, his gaze so bland it's hard to believe he's actually the sworn Guardian of the Mekteb, let alone a dragon-shifter. He certainly doesn't look like he just watched me pull off the biggest heist in the history of truth spells.

I keep my focus on my footing as we pass them. It is all I can do to make it out of the room and down the hall to the next room. There are new trays of food laid out, but my stomach balks at the thought of eating.

I ease myself down on a sofa, close my eyes, and let myself breathe. Whatever the Council chooses, I have done what I can.

MARKED

"Miss Hibachi."

It can't have been more than a few minutes since I sat down. I make myself open my eyes.

Ravenflight holds out a steaming bowl to me. "You would be wise to keep up your energy."

She's right, of course. I cannot afford my current weakness.

I take the bowl, nod as she sets a second plate on the sofa beside me. The food is wholesome and well seasoned, but my body wants none of it. I force down a few bites of the soup, try an equal number of bites from the food on the plate. When I have eaten what I can, I set the dishes to the side. Wordlessly, Ravenflight hands me a cup of water. I take it from her, wondering a little at her care. But she says no word, nor does anyone else speak as they finish their meals.

I stare at the floor with its covering of intricately designed carpets, following each twisting vine and uncurling flower on them, then trace my way back around to where I started in an attempt to focus on something other than my fate being decided in the room next door.

A knock comes at the door. I look up with a jerk, as do the other mages. The lycans were already watching the door, as if they'd heard who approached. The lycan stationed beside the door opens it and speaks to the mage in the hallway. I recognize him as the Council's scribe. He speaks softly, but from the way his eyes flick to me, the brisk nod of the lycan, I know it's a summons.

"The Council will see you, Miss Hibachi," the lycan tells the room, his eyes resting on me for a moment before moving away.

Interesting. It is the first time the lycans have referred to me as anything other than "the prisoner." And, other than Osman Bey, not once have they addressed me directly.

The remaining members of my escort stand up, waiting for me to rise. This time, my body answers me a little better, though my fingers have begun to shake. I hide them in my tunic as we make our way to the hearing room. Inside, I stand before the Council. The chair I'd used earlier has been removed, leaving me feeling exposed without its presence.

I risk a glance toward Nightblade. His expression is steady, the lines at the corners of his eyes slightly deeper. They tell me nothing for certain. I focus on Blackflame instead. He's talking to the mage to his right, but he seems tense. Blackflame unhappy with the verdict can only be a good thing, I try to tell myself. Unless of course he's happy with it, but still concerned about dealing with the stories I've told about him.

As the Council settles down and the scribe rings his bell again, I focus on the table before Blackflame's chair, so that I don't have to look at him or anyone else. *Breathe. Don't let him see what this verdict will cost you.*

I wish I had greater courage, strength enough to keep my hands from trembling, to keep my breath from shuddering. It's easier to be brave when you can still take some action of your own. It's much, much harder when you stand completely at someone else's mercy.

The scribe, still seated at his table to the side, clears his throat and begins to read from a parchment. "Kiki Hibachi has been found guilty on the charges of aiding and abetting the unlawful escape of a convicted prisoner, and unlawfully hiding a magical talent from the purview of the High Council. However, in light of her efforts to preserve the life of High Mage Harith Stonefall, the High Council requires further time to debate the final sentence. The High Council of Mages has thus decreed the following measure to be taken immediately. Kiki Hibachi is to be marked such that her magic is bound within her. The Council will reconvene tomorrow to finish discussing the case."

His words blur together in my mind, his voice echoing strangely in my ears. *Marked.* One step away from being bound as a source slave. I've said the words before, talked about it both seriously and flippantly, but this, the heart-clenching realization that it is happening, to me, here, now—that it has been read to me in a monotone, half-bored voice—this I cannot comprehend.

When I lost everything else, I always had my magic running through my veins, flowing in my blood. Now what I have will be sealed within me. And the Council has not yet decided whether to bind me to a mage as a source slave, or imprison me, or strip my magic from me completely. I swallow hard, tasting bile, and become aware that someone is grasping my good arm, just below the elbow. The grip steadies me, keeps me from swaying. I look slowly to my side to see Ravenflight gazing straight ahead, her features expressionless. I likely would have fallen without her.

It takes an agonizing moment or two for my legs to regain their strength. Blackflame is speaking now, but the words are garbled. I watch his face, the flat blue of his eyes, the way the skin around the corner of his mouth sags a little when he pauses. But the words— what is he saying? Something about tomorrow? It's all running together. And then he's done, and the bell chimes again, and Ravenflight gives my arm a slight squeeze.

I turn toward her automatically. She moves with me, guiding me out.

It seems a hundred leagues to the door. Beyond the door, an immeasurable distance rolls out before my feet. My escort forms around me, and I follow their lead, one impossible, unfelt step after the other. Instead of returning to the infirmary, we leave through a different side door and enter the nearest building. A few students catch sight of us; they are nothing but flickering shapes glimpsed from the corner of my eye, fading into the twilight.

Another hallway, stairs, and then a room. I pause just inside, surprised out of my stupor by the very normalcy of this room. It's a workshop of sorts, cluttered and comfortable. But for the tall windows, the walls are covered in shelves full of potions and powders. Two work tables crowd the center of the room, half-buried beneath books, stacks of parchment and paper, and more bottles and jars. The room is lit by a host of glowstones, some in holders along the wall, more in lamps anchored beneath the jumble on the tables. At the back of the room sits a wooden chair with leather straps attached to the armrests and the two front legs.

I halt, not caring that I'm blocking half my escort from entering.

"Keep going," Ravenflight says. Her words have the quiet ring of authority to them, and something else I cannot quite place.

I turn my head to look at her. I feel empty inside, hollowed out, but whatever she sees in me puts her on edge. She tenses. The lycans around me go still, focused completely on me. One false move, and they'll cut me down, strangle me with magic.

She's right, there's no running now. But hell if I'm going to get herded about like a goat to the slaughter. If I go quietly, then I'll do it my way. I offer her a brittle smile that is probably more snarl than softness, gather my strength, and stride into the room, sweeping past the first of my escort. Now that I've decided what I'm going to do, it's easy enough to pretend courage.

"You need to sit," Ravenflight says as I come to a stop beside the worktables.

"I'll sit," I agree, resolutely ignoring the chair. "When the mage who's supposed to do this is here."

She eyes me with faint amusement. Perhaps she can see through my bravado to the quaking girl beneath. The lycans make no comment, stationing themselves by the windows but for two by the door. The remaining mages enter warily, congregating around Ravenflight until, with a sharp word, she sends them to take up posts alongside the lycans.

I lean against the table, scanning its contents even though I know that, with a dozen guards watching, I won't be able to pocket anything that might aid me in an escape attempt. A parchment lying by my hand catches my attention: notes on improving a charm used to keep foxes away from chicken coops. *Really?* This is what the mage who's going to bind me spends time on? Curious despite myself, I shift my gaze to another paper near me. It details the shortcomings of a standard novice-level spell for lighting a candle.

"I'll need you to step away from the table," Ravenflight says.

There's no point in arguing, so I take a step away and ask, "Who *is* this mage?"

"Mistress Splinter," she replies.

"And? She works on basic charms and spells, but she's skilled enough to— do that?" I nod toward the chair.

Ravenflight considers her answer. When she speaks, it's with a certain weight. "She does not refuse a request for aid if she can help it."

Indeed. "Think she'll help me?" I quip, careful not to look toward the just-opened door.

"I do not aid criminals," a woman's voice says, the words hard as stone.

I force the corners of my mouth down. "Then we'll get along fine."

Facing her, I dip my chin in the semblance of a bow. "Kiki Hibachi." I want her to think of me as a person, not merely a job to get done.

"Splinter," she says. She is neither young nor old, her face unlined but tired, her eyes surprising me; they lack the warmth one might expect of brown eyes, yet they are not hard either, as her voice led me to expect. Her entire appearance seems a series of unintentional paradoxes. Her nightdark hair is braided back into a single long rope that falls over her shoulder, resting against her crossed arms. I would have thought she would pull her hair back tightly, in the almost severe way of Mistress Stormwind, but this braid is all softness, her hair lying gently against her skin, framing an otherwise austere face. Indeed, she stands bony and tall, her shoulders sharp angles beneath her robe. The robe itself flows in fold upon fold of cloth, darkening from a mossy green at her shoulders to a swath of forest green where it touches the floor. A golden dragon crawls down her sleeve, the embroidery glimmering in the light of the glowstones.

"Please take a seat," she says, and the dragon flicks its tongue at me between sharp teeth.

"Tell me about it first," I reply, wishing I were still leaning against the table. "I want to know exactly what you're going to do before they strap me in." I'm playing for time, a desperate, pointless strategy, and from the press of Splinter's lips she knows it. But she humors me.

"I will give you a potion to drink. The ink will enter your bloodstream and from there come up to your skin." She eyes me thoughtfully before continuing. "There are three things you should know. First, the ink is indelible and, once it marks you, you will not be able to rid yourself of it. Second, it will hurt more than anything you've ever felt." I doubt that, but I don't interrupt. "Third, if you do not fight it, the markings will create a pattern on your arms that one might call delicate. The more you fight it, the harsher the markings. Once they set, they do not change."

"You're telling me that if I want to look pretty I should sit still?" I say with disbelief. Around the room, my dozen guards exchange glances, then eye Splinter uncertainly.

"It doesn't matter how you sit," Splinter replies, moving toward a shelf of jars between the windows nearest me. The guards there take a few steps out of her way. "The struggle will be within."

I don't answer.

It takes her a quarter of an hour to mix what she needs. She measures the ingredients from the bottles with precision, using silver measuring spoons and a dropper. Then, her back to me, she pauses over the potion. I feel the focused flash of power, snapping bright and strong from Splinter to the cup, transforming the potion. She turns, the cup in her hands, and nods toward the chair.

Fighting to keep my expression still, I walk over and sit. Don't fight, I tell myself as a pair of lycans approach to strap down my arms. At least they are considerate of my wounded arm, careful not to jar it. They push up my sleeves, buckle the wide leather straps over my forearms, then kneel to secure my legs. My fingers curl around the ends of the armrests, my grip so hard it hurts. I can't fight my way free, nor does Splinter want me to fight this potion. But what do I care about looking pretty? Why would Splinter even tell me that?

As she steps before me, I meet her gaze. She is all hard angles and grim flatness. She is not beautiful, but she is exceptionally striking. Hers is a face one is unlikely to forget. She holds the cup out to me, ready for me to sip from, but I continue staring at her, as understanding dawns: pretty things are easier to pass off, more easily accepted, and more easily forgotten.

"Thank you," I say, and drink the potion.

It tastes like nothing in particular, mud and grass and metal and— apple? And then it slides into my stomach and I forget about the taste. *It burns.* For a heartbeat, I fight it, my stomach churning as the magic in the potion spreads its acid. Don't fight, I remind myself, my whole body clenched around it. Images flash before my closed eyes...Val telling me to choose this. Stonefall warning me I sought my own death. The phoenix speaking of ash, his path through the sky a line of flame.

Ash.

I have already burned, and this pain, this potion, is but an echo of what I chose with my sunbolt. *Welcome home,* I tell the inferno. *Come and be done with it.*

The pain expands from my center to my entire being in the space of a single breath. And then it focuses, my arms blazing until I feel the skin peel back, blackening and falling away, my bones charring. *Come and be done,* I repeat, and in my mind I think of Kol, monster though he may have been, burning as I burn now.

I have done this to others. Let it come back to me.

The burning ceases. It stops so completely that I can barely comprehend it. I feel myself sag in the chair, am suddenly aware of the faint whisper of breath in my lungs, the rush of my blood in my ears, the reawakening of the wound in my arm.

"Well done," Splinter says, somewhere above me. I nod my head once, without opening my eyes.

"Give her a few moments to rise," Splinter tells my guards.

Are you there? I ask, wondering if Val would have sensed what was happening to me and already come. He doesn't disappoint.

Yes. Are you well?

Well enough.

What just happened?

I've been marked, which means I might still have some hope of becoming a source slave. It's a temporary measure while they decide.

I see, Val says. Perhaps there really isn't anything more to say.

There's a rustle of footsteps, and I open my eyes as two lycans unstrap me. I expect Val will leave when he needs to. I doubt I'll notice when he goes.

"That's a marking?" Ravenflight stands behind the lycans, studying my arms. Her voice is soft with surprise. "It looks like lace!"

"Yes," Splinter agrees coolly. "She welcomed it. It did not have to fight its way across her arms."

I rest my head at a tilt, make myself look down. Starting on the back of my knuckles and spinning out across my arms to disappear beneath my sleeves, a dark tracery shows, as fine as lace but shaped like the work of a calligrapher's pen, swirls and flourishes and intricate interweavings. It is lovely in its way, as a spiderweb might be to the spider, though not its prey.

One of the mages behind me makes a sound of disgust. "What kind of coward *welcomes* it?"

Splinter spares me having to answer. "It takes greater courage to welcome fire into your bones than to push it away. Struggling is the natural instinct." Her expression, as she considers me, is one of mild curiosity.

"Fire and I are old friends," I tell her, my voice rasping. "Ice would have been different." Even the comparatively light touch of the truth spell was difficult to bear.

"Perhaps," she says. "But you also know what it is to burn."

I shrug, and find that my body does not hurt quite as badly as I thought it would. I heave myself out of the chair, take two wobbly steps, and realize I've used most of my strength welcoming my future.

Ravenflight, barely an arm's length away, steps quickly forward to steady me. The rest of my escort forms around me, some moving into the hallway to await me there, the others coming up behind me.

"Farewell," Splinter says as we reach the door. I glance at her quizzically, still somewhat disoriented, but she has already returned to her papers and potions.

My escort slows to a stop just inside the building's entrance. There are more guards here, guards I didn't notice on our way in—or perhaps they were only posted here once I entered. They've closed the doors and don't seem keen to open them. Ravenflight transfers my arm to one of the lycans and steps forward to speak with the guards.

I'm exhausted to the point of numbness, and my magic is irreversibly bound inside of me now. Whatever is on the other side of those doors doesn't seem to matter very much. Except that I won't be able to lay my head down and let go until I get back to my room in the infirmary.

"What's wrong?" I ask the lycan beside me.

A slight hesitation. "Students outside," he says, voice low. "The garden is filling."

"You know I can't hurt them now." I say the words loud enough to draw the attention of Ravenflight and the two lycans conversing ahead of us. They glance back.

"Yes," she replies.

"Then let them look. What does it matter?" I meet her gaze evenly. "After all, the more they see of me, the less likely I'll be able to escape." Unless I look like a weak, incapable girl, unable to stand on my own, with my head downturned so that all they'll see is my hair. It's the beginning of a plan, and not one of my better ones, but there it is. Make it clear that I don't expect to escape, give those around me an image of my weakness, and run like a hunted deer. Assuming, of course, that I can get through the doors that will be locked against me.

One thing at a time, I caution myself. They should reduce my guard now that I'm marked and can't use magic. That's a start. Right now, I need to rest. There is still some time between now and tomorrow, when the Council finally decides what to do with me.

Ravenflight murmurs something to the lycans, they respond, and she turns back to me. "We'll move as quickly as possible. Do not respond to the crowd, nor speak out loud."

I nod. My escort pulls in around me. The guards at the door step outside to clear a space for our passage. And then we're out, walking faster than I know how to place my feet. I stumble as we pass through the hastily cleared arcade. At the front, Ravenflight lights a bright blue ball of magefire to precede her, sending students scurrying out of the way. It won't burn them, but it makes it abundantly clear that she will not allow our way to be impeded.

As we step down from the arcade, I lose my footing again, and only the lycan's grip on my elbow keeps me from sprawling flat.

"Slow down," he snarls at the mages ahead of us, steadying me yet again. They do, but not much. We hustle across the gardens, cutting corners where the curving paths and low growing bushes allow. Night is falling, the glowstones lighting the paths so that the world seems bathed in shadows.

I can hear the voices of the students now, can see them following us, or hurrying through the gardens to line our path, faces seeking mine. I drop my chin another notch, wishing my hair was long enough to mask my face, and let my feet still falter when they will. I am weak. No one need worry about the threat I pose—there is none.

But as we turn right past the gardens and make for the infirmary, I hear a student call out, her voice carrying clearly over the shuffle and murmur. "You ought to be ashamed! She can barely walk and you're making her run—for what? She could have killed half the guard but she didn't, and you can't let her walk in peace? Shame!"

Another voice echoes, "Shame!"

Someone else responds with a rather eloquent curse word, and a few choice descriptions of what they think of the speakers for defending me, and the next thing I know, the lycan has scooped me into his arms and we're running. I bury my face against the stiff leather and velvet armor and consider how quickly these rumors escaped the confines of the hearing room. Who did the talking? And how much got out? Or perhaps the rumors were already out this morning, the comments I heard from the crowd their reaction to putting a face to the circulating stories. They had certainly sounded like they expected see a great towering warrior mage instead of me.

The lycan carries me all the way to my room. Once we enter the building, I expect him to put me down. When he doesn't, I tell him, "It's all right. I can walk now." He ignores me, as does the rest of my escort. A few minutes later, he deposits me wordlessly on my bed, turns, and walks out.

The mages mill about, checking the wards in my room one last time. They complete their work, casting me glances as they leave. I don't look up. Whatever they're thinking doesn't seem all that important right now. The remaining lycans file out with them.

Ravenflight pauses at the foot of my bed. "There'll be a guard posted outside your room. I'll tell Brightsong to check on you."

"Thank you." My voice is raspy and small in the room.

She hesitates a moment longer, then departs, closing the door behind her.

I sit alone on the edge of my bed, my fingers curled into the sheets beneath me. I should take off my boots and lie down. I know this, but it seems a far greater effort than I can manage now. Slowly, I turn my head to gaze at the dark sigil brushed onto the wall above my bed. In my mage's sight, it pulses with a muted light, nothing like the bright blue-white of the sigils on the other walls.

At least I have this: I can still see the magic in the world around me, still sense the spells enveloping me. Even if I will never again be able to cast one.

My hands tighten into fists around the sheets.

I am still a thief. One way or another, I will steal my freedom back.

But without my magic, I no longer quite believe myself.

A MOTHER'S LOVE

I look up from contemplating the near impossible feat of taking off my boots. From the hallway I can hear raised voices: the gruff tone of a male guard, and a cool steely voice that cuts right through his. I've barely been in my room three minutes. Who could they possibly be arguing with?

The door flies open. My mother sweeps into the room in a rustle of silk, the door slamming itself shut behind her before the lycans can reach it.

I stare at her, my thoughts stuttering. She is wrapped in a sea-green kimono, lavender embroidery spreading over the silk in a cascade of flowers and petals. Her hair has been done up in an elaborate styling of curls and waves, pinned with hair combs that glitter with amethysts and pearls.

Wordlessly, she drops a charm on the floor and steps on it. I hear the faint crackle as it breaks, and then a familiar pressure builds against my ears.

"You know who I am," she says. Behind her, a guard pounds on the door. She gives no indication of noticing.

"I—"

"I neither know nor care how you lied about your name to the High Council. I cannot believe you do not know me."

"My name," I stumble. *My mother is here*, my heart whispers. She came here for *me*. But I told a story of my past before the Council that wrote my mother out of my life—my mother, who cares nothing for Blackflame's source slave, and whom I am not sure I can trust. "I gave the only name I remember. If I had another one, I lost it with the spell I cast a year ago."

She considers me, the slight narrowing of her eyes the only sign she feels anything at all. "What is my name?" she demands.

Outside, the hallway falls silent.

"Hotaru Brokensword," I say, my voice cracking. *Okaa-san,* my heart cries. *Mother.* I don't want to lie to her. I want to know why she's here, if she'll help me, if she'll tell me truly whether or not she supports Blackflame. Now, after I've lost so much else, I want my mother back.

"You used my name-spell. Did you think I would not take notice?"

I shake my head. Perhaps, in those desperate moments before casting my spell, some part of me had hoped she would know me by it. Know me and help me. "I don't recall learning it from anyone. I'd heard of it, and I didn't want to kill the guards, so I tried it."

She must have first cast it for the same reason, all those years ago—not wanting to kill in order to defend herself. Surely that still lives in her as it lives in me now?

"Do you know my past?" I ask, unable to help myself. "My family?"

My mother does not speak.

"Please?" My voice is small and uncertain.

"No."

My heart stops, pain stabbing through my chest before it stutters back to life. The sound of this one word hurts in a way that the fire of Splinter's potion never touched me. I keep my eyes wide so Brokensword won't notice the tears pooling there. In all the possibilities I envisioned of meeting her, I never imagined this: that my mother would disown me with a single word.

"I did not know you that well," she continues. "However, I would not see you dead for your actions. I have managed to convince Arch Mage Blackflame that it would be wise to keep you alive for the time being."

I try to focus on her words, their meaning. "I'm...to be a source slave?"

"Yes." The word is not quite as firm and cool as the rest of her. But then she goes on, equilibrium restored, "There is a list of masters who have requested source slaves, should they become available. Arch Mage Blackflame did not consider any of them capable of holding you."

A list? Available? The very callousness of the system my mother describes leaves me appalled. I've always known how source slaves are used—but this, the idea that there are mages waiting for wild Promises to be found so that they might be enslaved, jockeying for a position on a list in order to get them first, this I had not fully considered.

"I requested another mage add herself to the list. Both Arch Mage Blackflame and Arch Mage Nightblade have separately agreed to grant you to her if she consents."

I cannot guess at Nightblade's motivations. I suspect that Blackflame wants me to suffer. I do not believe for a moment that he wishes me anything well by granting me this reprieve. If it would be impolitic for him to demand my death, then this would merely be a slower path to the same end. Whoever he would approve as a master for me can't be good.

"What mage?" I ask.

"She is a rogue hunter, and therefore makes the perfect match for keeping you in check. She also has very little to do with the High Council and its politics."

Which means what? That she'll keep me away from Blackflame? Or my mother? "Who is she?" I demand.

"The same woman who headed your escort of mages today: Ravenflight. I am hopeful she will agree."

My mouth opens in a small, silent O. It takes all my presence of mind to click my jaw shut again.

Brokensword says carefully, "She will not treat you unfairly."

"Unfairly?" I echo, incredulous.

"If you cared for your freedom or your magic, you should not have come here." Though the words are harsh, her voice is soft, tired.

"Some things are worth fighting for." I wonder if my words will touch her at all. This woman who did not fight for me five years ago, and won't acknowledge me as her own, and now thinks she has done me a service by choosing a rogue hunter as my master? When she *knows* how source slaves are treated—when she has stood by and watched what Blackflame does to his source slave? When she must know that, of all the mages I might escape, a rogue hunter will be the most difficult?

Brokensword dips her head, all cool detachment. "If they are worth fighting for, then they are also worth losing what you risk. You have lost. That will have to be enough for you."

"It is," I say, surprised by the truth of the words. "Stormwind—she was all the family I've had this last year. I couldn't let her be imprisoned unjustly."

"Indeed." Her expression remains neutral, but there is something in the slight tilt of her head, the hint of tension in her shoulders, that tells me she is displeased. She gestures toward me, an elegant opening of her hand. "Show me your markings."

I almost argue with her, but I can't see any harm in it. I push back my sleeves and straighten my arms. She takes a step closer. I see the slight widening of her eyes, the way her lips part, as she focuses on them.

"They are— delicate, indeed."

Delicate. That had been the word Splinter used.

"You expected them to be?" I ask.

Brokensword raises her gaze to me. "I hoped. You will recall that I saw you before your trial." I nod. "I sought out Mistress Splinter while you were in the hearing room. She agreed to explain to you how the potion worked, should you be sent to her. Though she doubted that someone as young as you could withstand the pain the markings incur without at least attempting to fight back."

"You," I begin and then stop. "Why?"

"We have met before," Brokensword says, as if this encapsulates all our history. "Where I can speak a few words to ease your way, I have. Your markings will not appear as such to most who see them. Your master will not treat you cruelly. This is what I may do for you."

Behind her, the door shudders. The wards on the wall flare up, magic pulsing around the room.

"Brokensword," a woman's voice calls. "Open this door at once!"

My mother sighs and raises her hand toward to the door. It bursts open. On the other side stands Mistress Brightsong, her hands raised—one shielding, the other ready to send forth a magical attack. Behind her stand the lycan guards, swords and daggers drawn.

"I was merely having a word with the prisoner," my mother says with cool amusement. "There's no call for worry, healer."

Brightsong's gaze flicks to me, checking to make sure I'm all right. "I understand you forced your way past the guards."

"They were being tiresome," my mother says, moving toward the door. Brightsong has to back up to let her by. "Really, they should be trained to understand the orders of their superiors."

"The prisoner is not allowed visitors," Brightsong says.

"I was not *visiting*." Brokensword's voice drips disdain. "Arch Mage Blackflame requested that I verify some information. I have done so, small thanks to you or your guards. Good evening."

Brightsong glares after my mother as she departs. I hold my breath, listening, hoping against all reason that she will come back, speak with me once more, promise that she is still my mother, will always be my mother. Or simply bid me farewell.

In the quiet, the faint tap of her shoes fade to an inaudible echo.

"Let's see your arm then," Brightsong says briskly, crossing the room to me. I stumble back a step.

"It's fine," I say, my voice rough with tears. I pull my hands to my chest, fingers curled. "I'm fine. Nothing to check."

A silence.

"Did she hurt you?"

I shake my head jerkily. I cannot give voice to this lie.

"Mistress Brightsong?" Arch Mage Nightblade stands at the door, head tilted, eyes sharp. "Is something amiss?"

I swallow my tears, drop my chin a notch to hide my unease. Nightblade. Could it not have been anyone else? I push the conversation I just had with my mother to the back of my mind. I will need my wits about me now.

"No," Brightsong says, her gaze lingering on me a moment longer. "Not anymore. Can I help you?"

"I understood Miss Hibachi had returned to her rooms and I wished a word with her."

"By order of the Council, she is not to have any visitors," Brightsong says coolly.

"I know." Nightblade smiles faintly. "I helped set that rule. It does not to extend to Council members."

He waits, his expression amiable.

"Miss…Hibachi," Brightsong says to me. "Do you wish me to remain here?"

Nightblade gives an almost imperceptible shake of his head. I don't trust him, don't want to know why he's here, but tomorrow he'll vote on my future…I am not sure I trust him to keep his word to my mother.

I swallow down the lump in my throat. "No," I tell Brightsong. "You can go."

She departs without a word, closing the door behind her.

"Miss Hibachi," Nightblade says.

I nod, cornered suddenly, my hip pressed against the bed and nowhere in the world I can go from here.

He lifts his hand and a spell spins out, radiating out to attach to the walls and dampen all sound. It is far beyond the charms both Talon and my mother used, and appears to cost him nothing at all.

He wastes no time on pleasantries.

"My people are long-lived, and our mages study widely," he says, watching me intently. Whatever he's looking for, I don't want to betray myself to him. I take stock of my face, my stance, and make myself slide into stillness as he goes on. "There are few breathers left in the world since the Great Burning, but we still know something of them."

I keep my expression blank, even as fear prickles the back of my neck. *He knows.*

"You are bonded to your breather, are you not?"

It takes all my presence of mind to answer with just a note of curiosity, "I don't know what you mean by bonded."

"Don't you? Tell me, how did you evade the Huq spell today?"

I shake my head, pretending confusion. "I didn't."

He doesn't believe me. I can see it in the slight narrowing of his eyes, the flare of his nostrils. He paces to the wall. With his back to me, he lifts a finger and touches the sigil anchored there. It flares to bright life, pulsing.

I stiffen at the sudden rush of magic tightening around me, as if I were a fly caught in its web.

He half-turns toward me, finger still touching the sigil. "Call him to you."

Sweat dampens my palms. I take a shaky breath, staring at him, and remember suddenly that Val had come to me when I was marked. And when Osman Bey recognized me on the stairwell. And when the tentacled beast chased me. He came when I was afraid or in pain.

I clamp down on my fear, breathing slowly. "There is no one to call."

His finger moves, barely more than a twitch, and the magic woven through the room yanks at me. I fall to my knees with a strangled gasp as it cuts into me, binding my arms to my side, a tide of pain flowing through my veins. It deadens my hearing, washes out my vision until the world turns a blinding white.

Breathe. He won't kill me. He's just trying to frighten me. *Breathe.* I will not give him this truth. I cannot trust what he will do with it. *Breathe.*

The pain subsides, ebbing away.

"Call him to you, Miss Hibachi. I do not wish to see you in pain."

It takes two tries to get the words out. "Then don't...hurt me."

He leaves the sigil, his robes sweeping the floor as he comes to kneel before me. If I raised my chin, I could look him straight in the eye. I don't. Instead, I ease back on my heels and wait. The pain is fading quickly, but I don't let myself relax. He could easily activate the sigil from here. There's no need for him to physically touch it. That was simply for show.

And then I feel Val's presence in my mind, slight but steady.

No. Go away.

What's happening? Val demands.

He's guessed about you. He wants me to call you. You need to leave before he realizes you're here.

Nightblade sighs. "You must understand. A breather bonded to a mage of your ability is no small thing."

"I have no ability," I say carefully, the words a little easier this time. "I've been marked. You need not...fear anything of me now."

"Markings by themselves only do so much." He drops his gaze to my hands, missing my look of disbelief. I don't know much about how the enchantment works, but the basics are pretty straightforward. Markings bind a person's magic within them so that it cannot be used in a casting. The usual second step binds the intended source slave to a mage, allowing that mage to access and channel the slave's magic whether or not they wish it.

Nightblade gestures, slim fingers indicating my hands. "Show me."

Val, if you're still here, you need to leave now.

Call me if I can help you.

I uncurl my fists and hold my hands out, palms down, as Val's presence fades in my mind. I don't push my sleeves up, and Nightblade has the grace not to ask. Instead, he studies what he can see, reaching out one finger to touch the dark flourishes above my knuckles. I try not to flinch at his touch, but I'm sure he notices.

"He helped you through it."

"*Nobody* helped me through it. I am well acquainted with fire. I've killed with it, and it seemed perfectly just to be consumed by it." His eyes widen slightly, as if he were seeing me for the first time. I go on while I have his attention, letting a little of the helpless anger building in me show. "You know nothing of me, or of Stormwind, if you think I am somehow bonded to a breather, and yet in the last year neither she nor I noticed anything amiss. Surely you don't think she would have failed to report such a thing? Or did you actually believe the idiocy of that trial and support her conviction?"

"I didn't support it," he says, his words soft. "But Stormwind may not have known of your bond. Such things can be hidden."

"Or not exist at all."

"Or..." he pauses, tilts his head, considering me, "not be found until a moment of need."

It takes all my willpower to reply steadily, "There is no bond."

He eases himself back, until he sits cross-legged before me. "Miss Hibachi, it was my responsibility to cast the truth spell upon you. I knew it had not taken properly."

"That's not possible. Arch Mage Bastion even checked it with you."

"He checked the casting of it. It was perfectly cast. It even took upon you as it should have at first. But the moment I turned my back on you and walked away, it shifted and lost its hold."

"That's—"

"Not possible," he says blandly. "Unless you are possessed. Since you gave no sign of a malign spirit possessing you, that leaves the breather."

"Why didn't you say something if you truly believed that? You take your duty to the Council very seriously."

Another faint smile. "I did not realize what had happened until some time after I checked the spell with Bastion. At that point, you were telling a story I wanted to hear, one that I didn't doubt the veracity of. So I let you go on."

"But you don't believe anything else I said, or anything I say now."

"I don't know what to believe."

"Why did you come here?" I demand. "You must have known that I wouldn't admit a 'bond' with a breather whether or not one existed."

He tips his head toward the wall. "I thought I might frighten the truth out of you. Failing that, I thought I should warn you, there is still a good chance you will be executed."

"Oh?" Execution hadn't actually crossed my mind, but it seems a far better future than a madwoman or a source slave.

Somehow, though, I doubt they'd let my magic go to waste. They'd harvest it first, and their ethics would get in the way of executing the madwoman produced as a result. Assuming, of course, that my mother's machinations fall through. Nightblade must have just missed her on his way in—or passed her without realizing she'd been to see me.

Still, this might be the only opening I'll get to be sure of the sigil above my bed. "You didn't think the blood magic would frighten me enough?"

"Blood magic?"

I don't answer. He's already lifted his head to scan the walls, and the next moment he rises to his feet, stepping around me to reach the wall above my bed.

"Who did this?"

I lean my head against the bed. I don't know how much more of this day I can get through. "It was there when I woke up. Surely you knew what you were doing just now."

He doesn't answer. He was too busy with his strategies to notice that the sigil he used to hurt me was tied to blood magic, that the pain would lance through my every vein and artery.

"Can't you tell who did it?" I ask, remembering Stonefall's words about magical signatures.

"Yes," Nightblade says absently. "But that's not always dependable." I sense a flicker of magic behind me. I twist in time to see the magic in the room shift, lines merging and reforming, the whole web remaking itself. Nightblade turns, the fingers of one hand brushing the top of my head. I swallow a gasp as a coil of magic encircles me, anchoring the web before it fades from sight.

"There," he says.

I wrap my arms over my chest, trying to still my trembling before he notices. Another flare of magic, this one short and sharp and focused on the wall before him, and the faint scent of burning drifts through the room. When he steps away, all that is left of the painted sigil is a dark, sooty smudge on the wall.

"You destroyed it?" I ask.

"It cannot be allowed." He pulls a cloth from his pocket and wipes his fingers. Then he looks down to where I crouch on the floor. "The wards are still in place, and keyed to you, but not through your blood anymore."

I nod. "Thank you."

He puts away his handkerchief without any indication that

my words require a reply. "Miss Hibachi, I can offer you only this much: Tell me your truths, and I will strive to assure you survive. A bond such as yours should be studied, understood. It is a rare chance to further our knowledge of such things."

Nightblade would have me betray Val and the trust he put in me, betray his people who have done no wrong but to be born as breathers, all for what? A slightly different future of pain and fear? I shake my head and offer Nightblade a rueful smile. "I think you had better kill me and be done with it. There is nothing to study."

He regards me for three long breaths. His eyes are dark and deep and hellish in their beauty. "As you wish."

He moves to the door, the faint *shhh* of his leather slippers on the floor loud in the quiet between us.

"Although," he says, pausing with his hand on the door, "it is interesting how fiercely you protect him."

I don't have the energy for his games, can't summon the necessary anger to glare at him. Instead, I wait until the door closes, and then lower myself to lie on the floor. I rest my head on my good arm, no longer fighting the trembling that racks my body.

I should get up, but the bed seems terribly far above me. It is far easier to lie here, staring across the floor at the far corner and pretending that the worst of my troubles is how I will climb back into bed.

I drift in and out of consciousness, dully aware that I need to make myself get in bed. It is only when I hear voices outside my door that I attempt to sit up. It's late night—the hours when the night stretches out and there is still no sign of dawn. The world outside my stained glass window lies dark and dormant, the shutters forgotten open.

There should not be any voices now. My guards rarely speak to each other. As the voices cease, I push myself upright, my wounded arm throbbing. I'm cold from lying on the tiles, my body stiff and my mind slow. I wipe the wet from the corner of my mouth, try to clear my thoughts.

The lock clicks, loud in the silent building, and Osman Bey opens the door. I blink at him, my brain finally waking up.

His face is drawn, grim. He scans the room once before letting his gaze settle on me. He holds the key in his fingers, the door still cracked open behind him. Something is very wrong.

"Get up."

I stumble to my feet, my hip thumping against the bed. He studies me silently, assessing me. I take a shaky breath, remind myself not to panic, not to bring Val into this unless I must. Except that, without Val, I am completely at Osman Bey's mercy.

I lift my hands, my left higher than my right, in mock surrender. "I still can't fight."

My sleeves slide down, baring the upper half of the markings. His gaze fastens on them. "No," he says quietly.

He pulls the door shut behind him, turning the key in the lock. I drop my hands, clench my jaw to keep my teeth from chattering. I'm desperately cold and weary, and I don't have any weapons. In a closed room I have no hope of escaping him. *Breathe.*

"Look," I say quickly. "I'm sorry—"

Osman Bey faces me, his back to the door. "You are?"

I nod jerkily. "Yes. Please— don't—" I cut myself off as bewilderment flickers over his features.

"Don't what?"

"Whatever it is you're doing," I finish uncertainly. He's already proven I can't fight him without Val's help. Without my magic, locked in this room with him, I have no protection whatsoever. But he wouldn't look confused if he was planning to attack me.

His eyes widen with understanding. "I won't hurt you."

He turns to the wall at his right, giving me the opportunity to recover my balance. "Tell me about this," he says, waving at the wall, the sigils it carries invisible to his eyes.

I take another breath to steady myself. "The worst of them means death. What else do you want to know?"

"Death if you do what?"

"If I use magic, which I can't anymore."

"What if you use something else?"

I sigh, what's left of my fear draining away. He's trying to figure out how to prevent any other escape attempts. Though why he's asking me and not the mages who cast these sigils I can't fathom. I cross the room to stand beside him. "The strongest ones ward against magical interference."

Laying my hand against the wall, I open my senses to the magic in the walls, watch as the layered wards present themselves to my eyes. With my hand so close to them, they pulse, strands of magic forking away from the wards closest to me to flash across the wall beneath my fingers, seeking my touch. Nightblade has done his work terrifyingly well. The blood magic might be gone, but the sigils are anchored directly to me.

"They're keyed to me," I tell Osman Bey. "I can't use magic here, of any sort. I can't open the door of my own accord. If I tried—say, if I had a lockpick set, the lock would freeze up, and these wards," I wave my hand toward the wall, "would incapacitate me."

"What if you used force on the door?"

I eye him askance. "Meaning?"

He shrugs. "Could you kick the door down?"

I almost laugh. "I'm not that strong, or well trained. But if I did, these wards—" I shudder, take a step away, the magic reaching after me— "they'd hold me here until your guards arrived."

"You would survive it?"

"Probably."

His eyes search my face. "Would you prefer to die than to become what they would make of you?"

"I'm not going to kill myself," I say, keeping my gaze on the sigil. "I had that chance and I let it go."

"Would you risk death to escape?"

"Of course." It isn't even a question. "But I don't have the capacity to make the attempt."

"I see." Osman Bey transfers his attention to the door. He runs a finger over the doorjamb. "I took your suggestion and spoke with Master Jabir. It seems we were holding prisoner a woman who had done no harm. And now we hold prisoner her rescuer."

He looks back at me, and this time I see the smoldering rage in his eyes, the wire-taut tension of his shoulders. "My brothers and sisters and I do not appreciate being misused," he continues, his voice almost a growl. "Our agreement with the mages was to provide protection from dark powers, using our iron and steel where their spells do not hold. Today we learned that they have violated our pact—that we have been made to hold an innocent as prisoner."

I have to bite my lip to keep from apologizing. I'm not sorry he spoke with Jabir, or that he and his pack are furious about what they've become a part of, but I am sorry that he is growling out his anger at me.

"So," Osman Bey says, "we will not hold you any longer."

He turns, his movements elegant and graceful and lethal. I hadn't realized he was standing in a ready stance until he slides into motion. His kick is pure poetry, from the perfect, ringing *thud* as his boot slams into the door, to the *snap* of hinges as the door rips free and crashes into the hallway beyond.

The wards around the room flare, a soft white rush of light that streaks around the walls before fading. It doesn't touch me. I'm still standing immobile by the bed. It wasn't me that kicked down the door. Nor did Osman Bey touch the magic of the protections themselves. I can see the faint flicker of the sigil traced on the door still glimmering on it as it lies on the floor.

Osman Bey gestures to the empty doorway with a flourish. "Are you coming?"

My mouth opens and closes once before I find my voice. "They'll be able to tell. I mean, that the door's sigil is no longer aligned with the other ones. At some point, it will strike them as odd that no one has closed the door."

"Then we had better close the door behind us, hadn't we?"

He really is breaking me out. I stare at him, my mind still not quite caught up with this new reality.

"Make sure you have everything you came with."

I nod, glance about.

"Quickly," he says. I scan the bed as fast as I can, pulling back the sheets and turning over the pillow. I'd only sat on the bed since my return to the room, though, and I don't appear to have shed any hair. That's all I have that hasn't already been taken from me.

"Ready?" Osman Bey asks as I finish. He stands in the hallway, the door propped up in his hands.

"Yes." I walk through the doorway, then watch as he shunts the door back into place. It's mostly aligned, leaning into the frame a bit. No one even glancing at it would miss that there was something wrong, but the sigils are all aligned now. The mages they are set to alert may not think anything of the door being kept open for the minute or so that has passed since Osman Bey first kicked it down.

"Upstairs," Osman Bey says softly, moving past me.

I follow him up. The stairway lies silent, and there is no sign of any guard anywhere. My blood thrums in my veins. My exhaustion has fled for the time being. I am alert and well aware that there are typically only two ways off a roof:

climbing down, or jumping to another roof. I'm not sure my wounded arm will hold me if I try to climb, and I'm quite certain the surrounding rooftops are too far for jumping.

We reach the door at the top of the stairs. Osman Bey pauses to pull out his key ring. The stairwell lies mostly in shadow, dimly lit by a glowstone that illuminates the hallway below, but he seems to have no trouble seeing.

"What now?" I ask him, leaning against the wall.

He selects a key and slides it into the lock. "Now we meet your other ally."

My stomach gives an unpleasant lurch. "Who?"

He chuckles, the sound deep and friendly. His eyes glint gold in the sudden fall of moonlight as he steps outside and glances back at me. "Did you have another you managed to omit mentioning to the Council?"

I keep my response measured as I follow him onto a rooftop garden of potted plants and benches and unlit glowstone lamps. "I was under a truth spell."

"I think the Council gravely underestimated your ability to tell them only a part of the truths they sought."

"You overestimate my cunning."

"I doubt that," he replies, coming to a stop before an ornately wrought bench. "You mentioned the Degaths to me before the trial. I went to see them."

"Did you?" What did I say about the Degaths during the hearing? Surely nothing beyond what had happened in Karolene? In which case, if they admitted seeing me….

He grins. "They were excessively courteous, their story as to their escape from Karolene matched your account, and they were grieved to hear that you had survived only to be caught aiding what they termed a 'political' prisoner. They assured me that they knew nothing further of you, and so I left."

I know very well this isn't the end of his story.

"I went to a public garden, as I'd told the Degaths I might," Osman Bey goes on. "Perhaps a half hour later, I was joined by a creature I never imagined I would have the honor of meeting."

"The phoenix," I breathe.

His lips quirk. He knows as well as I that it wasn't a coincidence, but it's not one I want to explain. Instead, I say, "You told him I've been marked."

Osman Bey nods, squatting beside the bench. He pulls out a cloth bag left beneath it. "He was not pleased."

No, the phoenix would not have been. I doubt I'll be much

good to him without the ability to use my magic. Osman Bey extracts a bundle of rope attached to a wooden slat from the cloth bag, as if he's said all he needs to. "But?" I say hopefully.

"But," he agrees and sets about arranging the rope. It isn't until he stands and slides a loop over my head that I realize what it is: a harness for me to ride in. The phoenix still wants me, perhaps because I haven't been bound yet. Or perhaps to make a point to the Council. Either way, I'm grateful.

Osman Bey helps me fit a loop of cloth-padded rope under my hips, creating a seat of sorts. Then he wraps another rope tightly around my waist, tying me in. I am thankful for this, for the care he is taking so that the phoenix does not have to lift me by my shoulders, jar my injured arm. I watch Osman Bey's bent head, the bright white of his turban, the faint shine of moonlight on his leather armor.

"Why are you doing this?"

He sits back on his heels. "Are the reasons I've given you not enough?"

"You're breaking their laws." He knows this as well as I. I simply can't quite grasp the *why* of it. Stormwind had been innocent, and I had helped her, but that is hardly convincing enough grounds for the lycan guard to not only break their oaths to the High Council but break me out as well.

He pushes himself upright, looks out over the rooftops and then back at me. "You've traveled the Burnt Lands," he says. "You should know precisely why we do not give our loyalty blindly, nor remain with those who have betrayed us."

Remembering the dark creatures that had chased me, I do.

"I also know perfectly well that I should be dead. You did not simply spare my life in that fight. You saved it."

I look away, pushing aside thoughts of killing, and Val, and breathers, and the breath my life is built on.

"By your own testimony, you could have destroyed half my guard that night with a single spell. You refrained, knowing you would pay the price for it."

A life debt—a whole host of life debts. I can hardly look at him anymore. I wanted his help. I told him what I did when he visited my room precisely to sway him to help me, impossible as it seemed. But I did not want this, to twist his actions because of a debt he owed me. Returning a life for a life is a good philosophy, but not when it forces you to give up your honor.

"I see." My voice is small in the space between us.

"No, I don't think you do." Osman Bey shifts, and I look

back at him without thinking. "You've already been punished for your crimes. When we discussed it, we agreed we could not send you into slavery as well, or something worse than that. And considering what the mages of the past have done, we are grateful to leave our post before causing more harm than we have already."

"Thank you," I manage.

He shakes his head. "Look there." He points toward the far side of the roof. Gliding down from the starry dark comes the phoenix. He flies without his fire tonight, only the soft gleam of moonlight on his feathers suggesting he is more than a mere bird.

As the phoenix circles around, Osman Bey holds up the looped top of the rope sling—it's wound through a short length of wood, making the perfect grip for the phoenix's talons. "Hold tight."

His body tenses. I grip the ropes at my side, careful not to raise my right hand too high.

"Run far, run fast, keep the wind in your hair," Osman Bey murmurs. The words have the sound of a traditional farewell. I open my mouth, unsure how to respond, and catch the amusement in his golden wolf's eyes.

"*Peace be upon you*," I say.

Then the phoenix's talons close on the wooden slat, and Osman Bey darts aside. The ropes snap tight, swinging me upward into the air. I grip the rope with all my strength, my arm flaring with pain. We hurtle across the rooftop, narrowly missing the potted plants on either side of the path. I curl my legs up beneath me, watching helplessly as we careen toward the low wall edging the rooftop.

A pillow of air wraps around me, buoying me upwards, and the phoenix's flight smooths out, wingbeats lengthening as he uses his magic to ease my weight. Together, we soar upwards, passing over the sleeping Mekteb to freedom.

REVELATIONS

The city slides by below us in a series of moonlit rooftops, glowstone-lit streets and darkened windows. The squares lie open and empty, the Festival now a thing of the past. Eventually, the crowded city buildings give way to houses with wide gardens, and then small farms, the land growing dark with crops.

We begin to descend, low boundary walls and bushes gliding by below us. The phoenix spreads his wings, slowing as we enter a date palm grove. We brush past the feathery tips of palm fronds, descending between long thick trunks. My feet touch down and I take a few running steps, stumbling over the uneven dirt underfoot. The phoenix releases the harness's slat and flaps past to land a few paces away.

I stand a moment, the sling still hanging off of me, and listen to the night, the soft rustle of the breeze through the palm fronds. It's a beautiful sound, gentle and free.

"Hitomi." Kenta walks toward me, a glowstone lantern in his hand. In its light, his face is hard, expression closed.

I look down at the knot binding the sling to me. "Hey."

My fingers, clumsy from the cold of my flight, struggle to undo the knot.

Kenta sets down the lantern. "Here." He pushes my hands away and with a few deft tugs loosens the remaining ropes so the sling slides down my legs.

"The ward," the phoenix reminds him.

Kenta slips a leather cord from his pocket and thrusts it at me. A pendant dangles from it: a circle of obsidian, hollowed out at the center.

Taking it, I run my fingers over the faint carving tracing its way around the center. "This is powerful," I murmur, the magic within it tingling at my fingertips. It's a warding stone strong enough to block perhaps even the most powerful traces the Council might put on me—assuming they can find something of mine to use. I can only hope Brightsong disposed of my bloody clothing.

Kenta clears his throat. "It seems the Degaths take their debt to you very seriously. That's been in their family for generations. Lady Saira sent one for you and its mate for Stormwind."

I slide it over my head awkwardly. I can't lift my right arm very high without considerable pain, but I manage it. I'm rewarded with a comfortable brush of magic over my skin that fades almost at once.

"How bad is it? Your wound?" Kenta asks.

"It's healing," I say, which is neither here nor there.

"Will you be able to travel?"

I nod, aware of how much he isn't saying, how hard he's trying to act like he isn't furious with me.

"We must move quickly," the phoenix says. "The search for you will start within moments. They will shut the city down looking for you." Which is why he flew me right out of it, no doubt. "Once they realize you have left the city, they will widen their search. We must use this time wisely."

I kneel so that I'm eye-to-eye with the phoenix, my legs steady again. "I don't know why you helped me now, after I've been marked, but I will do my best by the work you ask of me."

He cants his head to the side, eyeing me keenly as he resettles his wings. "You have not been bound yet?"

"No."

"I am glad the lycan had that right. You are still able to manipulate magic, which is something. Though it would be better, now, if you had a full mage to assist you."

Any full mage who came along to "assist" me would likely only be assisting my magic right out of me.

"You still have the feather?" he asks.

"No. They took it from me."

The phoenix eyes me with displeasure. "That was not well done."

"It wasn't my choice."

He ruffles his feathers, then bends to comb through them with his beak. Without a word, he offers me a new feather, small but burnished bright.

"Travel to the Burnt Lands as quickly as you can. When

you reach its borders, call me."

"I will."

The phoenix spares a glance for Kenta. "See that she reaches the desert safely."

Kenta nods gravely. "I will."

A moment later, the phoenix is gone, winging away between the palm trunks and up through their fronds, the rope sling swinging along beneath him. I expect he'll drop it somewhere far away as a decoy for those who hunt me.

Kenta stands quiet and tense beside me.

"I thought the Shadow League wasn't operating here," I quip.

"And I thought you understood you were to get out," Kenta snaps.

I flinch away from his anger. He ducks his head, abashed, takes a step back.

"I tried," I tell him. "I really did. But I would've had to kill someone to escape, and I couldn't." I study his face, the press of his lips, the tightness around his eyes, looking for some sign of comprehension. He gives a jerk of his chin. "I'm sorry," I tell him. "If I could have gotten away without blood on my hands, I would have."

He runs a hand through his hair. "And now?" he asks. "What will you do with what's on your hands?"

"I don't know," I admit. "I was just trying to help Stormwind. Now Blackflame has the High Council." I pull my sleeve up, baring the full markings to Kenta's gaze. "And I have this."

He studies the dark designs in the lantern light. "You should add some color."

"What?"

"Add color," he repeats, touching a swirl. My arm twitches at the brush of his fingers on my skin, as if I were expecting it to hurt. He withdraws his hand at once. "Markings are always black, and they're rarely beautiful. Add a bit of colored ink and only a mage who comes close enough to touch them will know what they are."

"That's...brilliant."

Kenta smirks. "Of course it is. It's my idea."

I shake my head at him, amused.

"Let's move."

I fall into step with him, the lantern lighting our way. "What are you planning next for yourself?"

He raises his brows. "I'm coming with you. Considering

your propensity for nearly getting killed, I think you'll need me."

"No." I'm surprised by how light this decision is, how much more I understand of Kenta now. Behind his words is the truth of his emotions: the guilt he still feels for letting me protect him in Karolene, for nearly dying for him.

"You need to return to the city," I say gently.

"The Ghost will kill me if he knows you survived and I sent you off to fend for yourself, rogue-hunting mages on your trail and your magic all bound up inside of you."

"Don't tell him. Or don't go back to Karolene."

"What do you expect me to do instead?"

"Start another Shadow League here. Now that Blackflame presides over the High Council, he'll give up his position as Arch Mage of Karolene—or rather, he'll appoint someone to take over for him there. If we want to stop him, and not merely stop what he's doing in Karolene, then the Shadow League needs to follow the High Council."

Kenta rubs his mouth. "I don't know how we're going to stop him."

"I was under a truth spell for my trial. I told the Council about the Degaths. They'll relaunch their investigation into Blackflame. Just because he's first mage doesn't mean he's protected from that."

We reach the edge of the palm orchard. Kenta turns to look at me, eyes dancing. "You didn't."

"I did. Someone needs to tell the Degaths to renew their petition to the Council." I grin at Kenta. "This is where it will happen. Not Karolene. And not the Burnt Lands. The Ghost needs you here. We all do."

"I'm sure the Ghost will send others."

How many others are there? Unless the Shadow League has grown by leaps and bounds, I suspect there are only a few who would be willing to devote their all to it. The rest have families, occupations, lives they cannot leave on a moment's notice.

"At least agree to come back once I've reached the desert," I say. "Blackflame's current position is the most precarious it's been in years. If there isn't someone from the League here to watch, to take advantage, we may miss an opportunity that won't come again."

He shrugs. "I gave my word to the phoenix. I'm not letting you out of my sight till I'm sure you're safe."

Safe is not a state I think I'll ever achieve. I try a different approach, "Blackflame has a source slave. A boy. I don't know his name, but I saw him after Blackflame used him. He was so weak he couldn't stand, could barely speak. Steal him, break the bond on him, and Blackflame will think you're me—because I mentioned the boy before the Council. He knows it made me furious. He'll put all his efforts into searching the city. And it will continue to undermine him in the eyes of the Council."

Kenta doesn't answer, uncertainty flickering in his eyes. Faintly, a long eerie wail begins, so far away it has the tinny unreality of a half-imagined sound. My eyes go to the horizon. Far off in the distance, a pale pinkish cloud rises above the faint outline of buildings. It's the smoke barrier above the Mekteb's walls, barely discernible from such a distance, but there nonetheless.

"We need to move," Kenta says abruptly, shuttering the lantern. "There's someone waiting for you by the wall."

It takes me a moment. "Stormwind's still here? She should have left by now!"

Kenta snorts, starting forward. "You expected her to leave while you were being held prisoner?"

I break into a shuffling run, heading toward the low boundary wall, the figure that has just stood up from its shadow. It didn't occur to me that Stormwind might endeavor to help me as much as I tried to help her. Especially considering the Council is hunting her.

"Hitomi?" Stormwind says as I pass over the ward stones spread around her sheltered spot. I ignore the faint twinge of magic, reaching out with my good arm to wrap her in a hug.

She chuckles softly, the sound breathy with relief as she hugs me back.

"You're not angry?" I ask finally, stepping back.

"I feared you were dead," she says. "I was so relieved to see you walk into my cell, it's been hard to get too angry."

"Why would you think I was dead?"

"The house wards were destroyed," she reminds me. "I asked that the Council look into it, but…."

"I left before that," I assure her. "Someone stole your mirror and tried to use a locator spell on it. We should probably thank them."

She shakes her head. Despite the faint smile on her lips she looks old, as if she's aged ten years in the last few weeks. But she still holds herself straight, her bun as severe as always, gaze as shrewd as I've come to expect. I'm glad of these things, that her trial and short imprisonment haven't robbed her of them.

"You're a fool," she says. Her voice sounds strangely rough. "You should never have come after me."

I open my mouth to argue, but Kenta cuts me off. "The alarm's already been raised. Tomi, you need to change and then we'll start moving. You can talk while we travel. Stormwind has clothes for you."

I nod.

"Be quick." He starts back to the grove.

Stormwind passes me a stack of clothes. I take them and squat down to change, beside the wall. "Where are we headed from here?"

"North. About four hours walking will get us to a town. By dawn, there should be horses waiting for us there. We would have met you closer to it, but we only had so much time to get here at all."

I nod, trading my creased white *selvar* for a faded and frayed one. I'm not sure I'll make it four hours, but there's no point worrying about it.

"Where will you go from there?" Not the desert—that much I've already deduced.

"To the Northland Council."

My hands still on the knot and loop closures of my tunic. "The *what*?"

She offers me a wry smile. "They do have their own council, even if we have a permanent delegate appointed to it. And…Blackflame will not expect me to go there. If I can gain their support, it may help in opposing his longer term plans. Although he likely has most of their arch mages in hand already. At any rate, if anyone is to do it, I should."

I start to ask her what she means, but she's not looking at me anymore. Her eyes have fastened on my hands, the dark swirls and scrolls that skim the edges of my knuckles. She steps forward, taking my good hand and sliding up the sleeve so that the moonlight falls bright on the markings there.

"Oh, Hitomi," she whispers, and in the speaking of my name I hear sorrow and anguish and a love I did not know she held for me. Here is what I wished for from my mother.

"It's all right," I say, my voice cracking. We both know it for a lie.

"I am sorry for it," she says. "And sorry that you already knew so much of pain that you could embrace it as you must have."

I smile so she won't see my sorrow. "It burned. I already taught myself all about that."

"So you did." She lets my arm go. "Were you bound as well?"

"No."

"That will make it easier."

"Easier?"

"If you were bound, your master would be able to trace you no matter how strong a charm you wore unless we could find a mage capable of breaking the bond. Nor would you be able to control their pull on your power. But if you were only marked, they have no hold on you."

She glances toward the palm grove. "Here, let me help you finish changing."

She helps me work my arm out of my tunic, taking a moment to inspect my wound in the moonlight. "It's healing well. Try to be as gentle as possible with it. Stretch it out thrice daily to make sure you retain full movement."

"I'll try," I say grimly, shimmying out of the gray tunic and pulling on the patched one they've given me in its place. "What about the markings?" I ask through gritted teeth.

She makes no answer.

I look over my shoulder at her. "They're spell made. There must be a counter-spell."

"None that I ever heard of."

I bite my lip, concentrating on fastening buttons. No apparent hope, but no time to dwell on it either. We need to run before the search widens past the city. If there's anything else I need to ask…. "What about the spell binding you?"

"It will fade in strength until I am able to break it myself. It should take no more than a week."

"Ready?" Kenta calls from the darkness.

"Yes," she replies, thrusting my clothes into a pack and holding it out to me. "Hitomi, this is yours."

A smile touches my lips as I take it from her. There is something inexplicably wonderful about getting back what I left behind.

"There's food and we've refilled your flask. There's a pouch of coins from the Degaths that ought to keep you well should you two get separated."

"Disguises ready?" Kenta asks as he reaches us.

"Here." Stormwind hands me a hammered silver band set with an oval of green malachite, a man's bracelet.

The moment I clamp the band over my wrist, I feel the faint

tingle of magic. Kenta's grin widens to an all-out smile. I look down at myself, the men's *selvar*, faded white tunic with billowing sleeves, and short, dark vest over a completely flat chest. I'm a boy. My hands appear larger, stronger, and somewhat hairier than I have ever wished them. And completely unmarked. I stare at them a moment longer, the skin pale in the moonlight, free of ink.

"It's a glamor I purchased from that theater troupe's costume master," Kenta says, clearly enjoying my bewilderment. "The same one who sold me the mage glamor."

"Unless you're directly confronted by a mage who's looking for you," Stormwind tells me, "the glamor should hide you quite well. Besides, it's better than mine." She wraps a natty red triangle scarf over her head, knotting it beneath her chin, and transforms into a stocky old peasant woman, wide face creased with age, callused hands still strong.

"How is being a boy better?"

Kenta turns a look of pure disbelief on me.

"No one will take notice if you need to run," Stormwind says pragmatically.

True enough. "I suspect running is something I have a lot of experience with."

Kenta snorts and starts forward at a brisk pace, following the wall to the road. The peasant woman who is Stormwind shakes her head as we fall into step behind him. "It doesn't make a good life, though," she says dryly.

"Neither does hiding," I point out.

"There's nowhere left to hide now," Stormwind says. "And only so much time left to run."

Kenta walks some distance ahead of us, keeping a watch for anyone traveling toward us. Stormwind and I are under strict orders to get off the road should he signal us.

As we walk, I run through our earlier conversation, coming back to her words about going north. "You said Blackflame might already have the Northland Council in hand," I say, glancing at her. "Does he have some plan beyond becoming first mage?"

She reaches out a hand to touch my shoulder. "Don't blame yourself for that."

Anger and regret twist in my gut at her words. "Why shouldn't I? When I broke you out, I *gave* him the High Council."

Stormwind lets out a harsh bark of laughter. "No, Hitomi. He would have had it eventually. You merely gave him an earlier opportunity than he expected."

"I always thought he wanted Karolene. He wanted the High Council as a whole."

"No, he wants it all. He wants the Eleven Kingdoms to serve the Northlands. He will force them to bow to the Northland king of his choosing."

"A king? Why would he choose a king?"

"Kings are easily controlled by a man such as him. With the king will come an army, a fleet of ships, and a certain legitimacy Blackflame will never have on his own."

I stare down the long silvered line of the road, the dark form of Kenta far ahead. "Well," I finally say, "I guess we're just going to have to do something about him."

Stormwind's gaze flicks to the backs of my hands. She makes no other answer.

"I told the Council about his assassination of old Lord and Lady Degath. Their investigation might not stop him, but it will slow him down for a while, don't you think?"

Stormwind nods, but there is no surety in it. "Perhaps. Perhaps not. I cannot say what he would do, but he's not the kind of man who lets power slip through his fingers. If the Council tries to remove him, he might attempt to destroy the Council itself."

"He— he can't do that."

"Blackflame will do whatever he deems necessary."

He will. I can feel the truth of her words deep in my bones. Outing Blackflame before the Council may have been the most dangerous thing I could do. The worst of what he will do is yet to come. He will hold on to the power he has gained with every weapon in his arsenal.

"How do you know so much about him?" I ask Stormwind. "And why did he go after you?"

Stormwind doesn't answer at once. The high wail of the Mekteb's siren drifts over the fields, faint and unrelenting. When she speaks, it is with regret. "You don't yet know my history, do you?"

"I know you're innocent of what he charged you with."

"Innocence isn't everything."

"What do you mean?" A cold dread settles in my stomach. This isn't right. Stormwind hasn't done anything. She's innocent. That's what's kept me going. But I know I'm wrong. I've always known I might be wrong, because Stormwind held her secrets so tightly, all I've ever known is the mage of the valley. Who or what she was before, I have no idea. And I have not dared to ask anyone else.

"Twenty years ago I fell in love with a young mage from the Northlands. I had been apprenticed in the Eleven Kingdoms, and he in the Northlands, but we shared our heritage and— he had a way about him." She stares down the road, her eyes trained on a past I cannot see. "He dreamt of helping our people, of raising them in power and making them again a force to be reckoned with. He believed that it could be done if only we Northland mages banded together."

"What are you saying?" I ask, my voice uneven.

"Blackflame is—or once was—my husband."

My mind goes blank. I stare at her. I cannot make sense of her words.

"I helped him gain recognition as a high mage by the Council, and make the connections he would need to be elected as an arch mage. It was then, when I saw what he was willing to do to achieve his vision, that I began to understand what I had done, what I was doing. I left him mere weeks before he poisoned your father for opposing his election as arch mage, and for assuring that he was placed over the smallest of the Eleven Kingdoms."

"You *married* him?"

"I am sorry, Hitomi. We all make mistakes. Mine was to love a man whose vision overrode his conscience."

She'd loved him? How could anyone look at him and not see the cruelty in his eyes? How could they not see his machinations for what they are? How could *Stormwind* have worked to put him in power?

"I thought you knew," she says. "You brought the pouch with you. It was in your pack. The one with my wedding brooch and the journal from the year before I married him."

"I didn't— I didn't know," I say, stumbling into silence.

"They were stored with my wedding dress."

I shake my head.

"Your breather knew."

He had. He'd made a very strategic gamble on the possibility that she would take me in as payment for the things she'd come to regret doing. Small wonder Kenta had been so startled when I'd revealed whom I intended to help.

Stormwind waits for me to speak, perhaps to absolve her of her guilt, or rail against her for hiding her secrets. But I can barely come to terms with who she is, what she's done, what everyone but I had known. Only I probably *had* known. There is no way I wouldn't have heard about Stormwind leaving Blackflame, not while living with my parents. I simply lost it in the ash, and was so focused on helping Stormwind, I didn't dig deep enough, didn't ask when I had the chance—not the Degaths, not Kenta, not even Stonefall.

Almost as overwhelming as my own stupidity is the taste of betrayal, acrid as smoke on my tongue. "Why didn't you tell me?" I ask, my voice cracking.

"At first, you were weak and I merely followed the lead your breather gave me. Later, there didn't seem to be any need. It was in the past for me and would only have caused tension between us."

I shake my head, though she's right. It would have changed our relationship. But I don't care anymore. She put him in power—the man who killed my father and changed my mother into someone else entirely.

"I considered telling you when Stonefall came with the summons," Stormwind goes on. "But we had so little time, and in the end I could not make myself. I did not want to part with you so."

I close my eyes. Perhaps it wasn't a betrayal, it wasn't meant as a betrayal; it was an old story, long dead. Easier to leave buried than to dig up and dissect. It was one of the many silences that filled that valley, silences I'd grown used to, barely audible over the lap of the lake water, hardly noticeable beneath the quiet patter of our lives together.

"I'm sorry," Stormwind says again.

"It's all right," I say, my voice rough. The past is gone now, our decisions made and no way to change them even if we wished. We walk on, the gravel crunching loud beneath our boots. It is still some time till dawn, the world a wash of whites and grays and deep black.

"I still would have come for you," I tell her. "Even if I'd known."

"I know," she says softly.

In the darkness, her smile holds a lifetime's worth of remorse.

FUGITIVE

"Hitomi."

I push myself upright, my hands press against dirt and weeds. Stormwind kneels beside me, already wearing her pack.

"Where's Kenta?" I ask, voice scratchy.

She nods to where a golden-haired tanuki waits beside the road. "There is a wagon headed our way. We're going to ask the driver for a ride."

I clamber to my feet. It's perhaps an hour past sunrise now. Stormwind called a halt near dawn, after I'd stumbled for the third time in as many minutes. Nearly two hours rest has helped, but I'm still achy and slow. Catching a ride sounds wonderful as long as we can do so without arousing suspicion.

"Do you know the language?" I ask as the wagon draws closer. "It will look suspicious that I'm dressed as a local and don't know three words of their tongue."

Stormwind hesitates. "Perhaps this isn't such a good idea. I can speak the language, but explaining you will be hard."

"No it won't." I stretch out the kinks in my back as my mind works through the story we'll need. "I'm a bit of simpleton. You're my grandmother. We're traveling to your other daughter's home to help with a birth. I'm along to help carry things and the dog is to keep us safe."

She glances at me wryly. "You are frighteningly good at this."

"Must be my previous life," I murmur, keeping my voice low lest the wagon driver see through our charade before we've begun to play it.

When Stormwind hails him a minute or two later, he pulls

the horses to a stop, inspecting us warily. A thick cloth tarp secures his load, covering it from sight. He must be a merchant of some sort.

He listens with a frown as Stormwind details our story of travel, her gestures indicating sore feet and a long road. He eyes me at one point, muttering a question. I keep a vague smile on my face and watch the birds hopping along the ditch on the opposite side of the road while Stormwind answers him.

Eventually, though, when Stormwind holds out a pair of coppers, he nods and takes them from her, gesturing to the back of the wagon. And it's as easy as that. We climb up, Kenta leaping up beside us, and make ourselves as comfortable as we can on whatever pots or parcels remain hidden beneath the covering. Once we are all safely settled, the wagon rolls forward once more.

I let myself doze, lying on the tarp and its lumpy bed of wares. Stormwind sits beside me, watching the road for trouble. Kenta lies curled up somewhere behind us.

After some time, houses begin to appear alongside the road, and then there are people passing around us, and the sound of other carts and animals. I make myself sit up and find we are nearing the center of a good-sized market town.

"That rider," Stormwind murmurs, gesturing with her chin back down the road.

A man rides toward us, a second horse on a long lead trotting along behind him. I tense, squinting to make out details. He's still too far away to recognize, but I have the distinct feeling he wears desert robes.

"Stonefall?" I ask, keeping my voice low. Kenta sits up, turning his gaze to the rider.

"It could be. Or another mage. Do they have any way to trace you despite that ward?"

I should have known better than to hope this wouldn't happen. "My room had wards that were keyed to me. Only to me, and one was stronger than the rest. Arch Mage Nightblade removed it when he visited my rooms because it should not have been used in the first place."

Even though her glamored eyes are another color, her face shaped differently, the lines upon it utterly unlike her own skin, I can see Stormwind working through the possibilities, coming to the right conclusion, and not wanting to accept it.

"They had my tunic," I say, "covered in blood from my wound. They used it. And they probably still have a piece of it set by for surety. I need to run far and fast, without either of you. There's no need for us to get caught together."

Kenta growls softly.

Stormwind shakes her head. "They wouldn't have...."

"They were desperate," I reply. "You disappeared and they didn't know how. They weren't going to allow for my escape. I don't know who sanctioned it, but it was done. Whoever this mage is, he's ahead of the rest, but they'll be coming."

Stormwind narrows her eyes. "It's Stonefall, I think. He wouldn't use blood magic. What's in his hand?"

I squint against the morning sunshine. He is still a good ways back, and has slowed his horses to a walk to move safely through the morning traffic. He wears his desert robes, as well as his sword, daggers, and crossbow. He scans the streets, each person he passes. He's searching for someone. The only question is whether it's me or Stormwind. In one hand, he holds his reins. The other he holds slightly forward, fisted, and suddenly I know.

"A glowstone," I say quietly, my voice cracking.

"Yours?" Stormwind asks. "You used it for something bigger than a basic charm?"

I nod. "I used it to...help him, and he ended up with it. But I can't quite believe he would hunt me with it." Not after I saved his life and then lied for him before the Council.

"He may not be," Stormwind allows. "But it's too great a risk to take. He is a hunter, he's following us, and we have to assume it is not to help us. We need to lose him."

Kenta rises to all fours, his gold-flecked eyes flashing a question.

"Do you think you can get it from him?" Stormwind asks, her voice barely audible.

He dips his muzzle.

"No," I say at the same time that Stormwind says, "It could work. Without the charm, he won't be able to follow. As it is, the ward should keep him from homing in on you any further."

"But he knows he's close. And he's a rogue hunter."

Kenta snorts and leaps down from the wagon.

"Be careful," I say, louder than I intended, but he's already gone, darting past the people on foot, his ringed tail disappearing in a matter of moments.

Stormwind touches the back of my hand. I look down to see my fingers curled tight into fists. "Kenta can afford to attract attention. You cannot."

I glance toward Stonefall. He's closer but he still hasn't spotted us. It's only a matter of time. And then Stormwind and I will both be caught, and Kenta as well, because he won't let us go without a fight.

I take a breath. Hold it. Exhale. Stonefall has the glowstone. And behind him could be mages with my old, bloodied tunic.

"I have to leave you," I tell Stormwind.

She looks out over the road to where Stonefall rides. "I know," she says. "But Kenta would not have let you walk away."

A shout goes up down the street. I tense, head whipping around in time to see Stonefall's horse rearing, the second horse backing up and yanking at its lead. Stonefall clings grimly to his mount, fighting to regain control of her. The people around him back away. A golden shape leaps out of the crowd, launching itself off the back of a terrified, bent over bystander to sail right into Stonefall. He shouts again, barely managing to keep his seat between the dog landing in his lap and his horse coming down. A flurry of movement, so quick I barely register it, and the dog leaps into the crowd and races away, ringed tail streaking out behind it.

Stonefall takes a few moments to calm his horses, sparing no more than a glance after the disappearing tanuki. I've no idea if he can still find Kenta among the milling crowd, but then he pivots slowly in his saddle, eyes gliding over everyone near him. Seeking.

He knows Kenta was a distraction, a ploy. He knows I have to be near.

I slip over the side of the wagon before his gaze reaches me, keeping my head down and walking alongside it, pack in hand. Stormwind says nothing. With my back to Stonefall, I can't tell what's happening, but Stormwind's stillness suggests that he hasn't seen through her glamor yet. Not that I know precisely how easy it is to see through a glamor from a distance. Stormwind made it sound like a mage would have to be quite close to discern its effect, but Stonefall is used to hunting rogues. After all I've gone through, there's no way

I'm leading him or any other mage straight to Stormwind.

"I'm leaving now," I say just loudly enough for her to hear.

She turns her head halfway toward me, as if she were speaking over her shoulder to the driver. "What shall I tell Kenta?"

"Tell him I'm sorry. He needs to stay here, for the League. I'll send word when I can. Tell him I have friends in the desert who can help me."

I expect her to argue, but she says only, "You're sure?"

"Yes. Kenta can't help me where I'm going. Make sure he doesn't follow, or he'll just leave another trail behind me for them to follow."

"I'll tell him," she agrees. "But I don't know how well he'll listen. Will you be able to reach your friends on your own?"

"Yes. And I still have the feather. I'll be fine." It's an exaggeration of epic proportions, but Stormwind doesn't gainsay me. Instead, she slips her fingers into a pocket that doesn't exist in her glamor, then holds her hand out to me. I reach over the high side of the wagon and take her offering. It is thin and round, wire and thread and bead. The look-away.

I glance up at her, but she's already turned away to watch the road. I can just make out her profile, past the edge of the old red scarf, steady and unsmiling.

"Go in peace," she says. That is all the farewell we can afford.

"And you," I murmur and step away from the wagon.

I walk briskly to the next cross-street, sandwiched between the boundary walls guarding the neighboring houses. It's hardly more than an alley, empty for now. Halfway down, I step into a recessed doorway, slide on the look-away and pull off the glamor charm. I wait a count of five breaths to ensure that anyone near the mouth of the alley has passed on and then walk back up to entrance to scan the street.

Stormwind bumps along in the back of the wagon, now another block away and very near what looks like an open market square. Kenta is still not in sight—I doubt he'll rejoin the wagon while Stonefall might see him. Stonefall himself is still there, walking his horse along the road and scanning the people as he goes. He knows I'm close. Knows it both from the glowstone and the fact that it was stolen from him. Within minutes he will catch up with Stormwind, and whatever her glamor may be good for, I don't doubt he'll see through it from ten paces away. It is precisely the sort of thing he is trained for.

My fault. My fault he has the glowstone—why didn't I demand it back from him in his bed chamber? It's too late for regrets, now, but that doesn't stop me from having them.

The horse behind him—the same little chestnut mare he brought to collect Stormwind with from our valley—means he intends to catch one of us. The glowstone makes it clear that he's looking for me. I may not be able to use magic to defend myself now, but he owes me a debt and I will shred his honor to pieces if he attempts to take me back to the High Council.

When he is still some thirty paces away, I loosen the look-away charm on my finger, sliding it halfway off for the briefest of moments. I feel its magic flicker around me. Stonefall's gaze snaps to me as I jam the ring back on. A pair of young boys, walking between the two of us, glance toward the alley, blinking uncertainly. Then they shrug off the shadow they'd seen and continue on.

Stonefall kicks his horse into a trot, swerving around the youths, the chestnut following after him. I turn and jog into the alley, keeping alongside the wall so I don't accidentally get trampled. Twenty paces in, I feel a wall of magic flow up from the ground ahead of me. The magic curves around to join with the walls on either side of me, rushing past me in the space of a breath. I pivot, heart hammering, and watch as the magic—bluish white to my mage senses—jumps across the alley's entryway, weaving itself together until it's as impenetrable as armor.

One should never underestimate a rogue hunter.

The only things that remain within this makeshift prison with me are Stonefall sitting easily on his horse, and the second horse behind him. The chestnut rolls her eyes uncertainly, lifting one front hoof and then the other. His own mount stands perfectly still.

Stonefall continues scanning the alley, trying to pin down my location. The moment I speak, he'll find me, of course. He'll find me regardless, because he knows what charm I'm wearing, what to look for. So I do the one thing I can think of before I lose my courage. I slide the look-away from my finger and wait.

He is every inch a rogue hunter now, from the ready stillness with which he sits, to his measuring gaze, to the magical walls he maintains around us effortlessly. I can't read his expression, can't guess at his thoughts from the inscrutable mask he wears. His horse shifts, takes a step forward. I raise my hand, palm out, as if I could stop him with all the magic I can no longer use.

"*Peace be upon you,*" he says.

Peace. It's a promise, in its way. An offer of safety.

"*And upon you, peace,*" I return, and find myself smiling crookedly at him. "Why the trap?" I ask. I can't afford to make a mistake, even with such a greeting.

"I can't spend all day chasing you." He dismounts and approaches, reins in hand. The walls of the spell contract, pulling in until we stand in an elongated bubble of magic, much harder to detect now. It must also be easier to maintain.

I hold my hand up again as he nears me. "You have other things planned for your day?"

His lips quirk as he comes to a stop five paces away. "Not exactly. Though the Council would like me to hunt down Stormwind."

"Because they don't trust you to not let me go?" On the other hand, if he wants to prove he's trustworthy, catching me and bringing me in will restore his reputation in the eyes of the Council.

"Perhaps," he says. "Perhaps they're afraid you'll turn me against them, the way you did the lycan guard."

"Bah," I scoff. "I didn't turn them. I explained the situation. I don't think they like being misused."

"It would seem not," Stonefall agrees wryly. "Though the Council hasn't yet realized you were at the root of the Guard's defection."

I eye him uncertainly. "But you said—"

"It was my guess, not theirs. I suspect I have a greater appreciation for your powers of persuasion than they do." He looks past me to the end of the alley, then back over his shoulder. "Where are your friends?"

"I already told the Council I don't have any."

"You also told them I gave you no help at all, other than a way out." He studies me as if I were a puzzle he can't quite put together. And he is a man who is accustomed to working things out. "You made no mention that I told you where Stormwind was being held, or who had the key to her shackles."

"I didn't, did I?" I feel a smile growing, and then I'm laughing for the first time in what feels like weeks, laughing even though the movement sends ripples of pain down my arm. "You just want to know how I did it."

Stonefall almost smiles. "I'm curious."

305

An understatement, if ever I heard one. "And if I tell you, then what? You give me your spare horse and directions to a safe haven?" It isn't a serious question. I'd no more dare tell Stonefall of Val's bond than I would announce it to the Council.

"The horse?" He glances toward the chestnut as if taken aback. "She's already yours."

"What?" I ask, certain I heard him wrong.

Stonefall shrugs. "I kept two horses as a rogue hunter, but I won't be needing her anymore. I resigned my post this morning as well—on the grounds of my own safety, given the nearly successful attack on my life. If you don't want her, I suppose I can sell her."

I stare at him. A rogue hunter resigning his post on the basis of personal safety sounds utterly absurd. A rogue hunter providing a mount to a fugitive seems equally outrageous. Laughter lurks in his eyes, the crinkle of his crow's feet. "You're serious."

"If you want to escape, you'll need to travel faster than a walk."

"You really think I can escape?"

He blinks, startled by the question.

"I know you found me because of the glowstone. But I think they—the other mages looking for me—might have my blood. I don't know how to escape that."

He smiles thinly, all amusement gone. "You don't have to. Brightsong wasn't pleased when the mages who warded your room used your blood—she was there, and even registered a complaint about it with the Council's scribe. At any rate, as soon as they were done, she evicted them from the room and had your clothes disposed of. Burned, actually. With the sigil itself destroyed, the Council doesn't have anything to trace you with."

"She— she did?"

"She was questioned quite thoroughly about it immediately after your escape." He shrugs. "She pointed out both the health issues and the ethical ones, and suggested that they should have taken greater precautions beforehand so they wouldn't be on the verge of violating their principles again. It seems half the Council was kept in the dark about the use of blood magic to hold you, and they are not pleased."

I think I want to be just like Brightsong one day.

Stonefall removes the second horse's halter and fits her with a proper bridle and reins. As he works, he says, "You'd better get moving. Zahra may be small, but she's fast and was born in the desert. There's a change of clothes in the saddlebags, plus some food and water, money, a couple of basic charms. Stormwind's pack."

"Stormwind's—" I begin, and understand. No one has thought to demand the pack from him yet. Without it, the other rogue hunters won't have anything to establish a trace with. "Why?" I ask. "Why are you doing this?"

He looks down for a moment, then meets my gaze. The anger in his eyes takes me by surprise. "I expected Talon to aid you. As far as I can tell, she did nothing. Then when you got out through your own means, I traced you, and you were moving far too slowly. Of course I'll help you. I don't know how you subverted the truth spell, but I do know you not only saved my life, but protected me from the Council. Because of that, I've had to answer for some of my actions—for letting you go before you caused any trouble—but I've retained both my honor and my freedom." His eyes drop to my hands. "The *least* I can do is bring you a horse."

"I see," I say. "And I thank you."

"I hope you can ride," he jokes as he offers me the reins.

I take them uncertainly. "I…don't think so." The horse, however "small" it might be considered, is still taller than me at its shoulder. I eye the saddle warily. "How am I supposed to get up there?"

Stonefall rubs a hand over his mouth. "I'll guide you through mounting. Once you're up, put on the look-away and we'll walk together for a bit, till you get a feel for it."

I smile my thanks at him.

He takes my pack to lash on behind the saddle and pauses. "How long have you been traveling on foot?"

"A few hours."

A line appears between his brows. "Do you have anything in here you can give me? Something with your scent?"

I grin and hold out my hand for my bag again. "You'd make a great criminal if you ever turned your mind to it."

Stonefall shakes his head, the corner of his lips quirked. I dig out the skirt I'd worn from Stormwind's valley on through the Burnt Lands and the desert. I'd changed out of it at the caravanserai, so that my spare clothes would be clean for my foray into the Mekteb. And it seems Kenta hadn't thought to do my laundry. Even if the Council manages to hire a pack of mercenary lycans, the skirt probably reeks of me more strongly than my own skin.

Stonefall tosses the fabric over the back of his horse, straps on my pack behind the saddle, and helps me through the awkward process of clambering up on my patient new mare, with only my left arm to aid me, bruised fingers and all.

"Use the charm," Stonefall says once he's mounted his own horse. "It won't hide the horse but at least you can use it for now."

"How about this one instead?" I ask, sliding on the silver wristband.

He nods, eyes crinkling. "That will do very well. Let's walk. Press your legs gently against her sides."

On the second attempt, Zahra starts forward at a relaxed walk. Stonefall lets his spell go and urges his horse into step beside me. I suspect the spell had built-in shieldings that kept others away, for no one even glances in our direction from the street beyond. Nor have I seen any sign of Kenta.

Stonefall rides beside me a quarter of an hour, murmuring instructions and twice correcting my grip on the reins. We bypass the town's central square, taking back streets. He explains not only how to sit a horse, but how to care for it. Then, in another empty alleyway, we come to a stop.

"You really don't have any other allies out here?" he asks. "Not even that sharp-toothed tanuki?"

I grin, hoping Kenta didn't nip Stonefall too hard when he snatched the glowstone right out of his hand. "No— that was him leaving. I'm on my own now."

"You need to find a guide to take you into the desert."

"How do you know I'm going there?"

"We all know. You owe the phoenix a debt, don't you? Ravenflight will follow you there whether or not she can trace you." He gestures to my newly acquired mare. "You need to move fast, disappear among the tribes."

"I have an idea about that."

He considers me. I wonder what he can tell of me through the glamor. "You may have family in the desert."

"I doubt they'd want me."

He tilts his head, shrugging slightly. "Want has less to do with it than honor and responsibility. Blood ties in the desert are a serious matter." When I don't immediately answer, he says, "Think on it. They would do their best to protect you from capture."

"I'll think about it," I agree finally.

He doesn't look appeased. "The desert is not a forgiving place. Whatever you do, don't travel alone."

He cares about this, too. Perhaps it shouldn't surprise me, after he tracked me down to give me his spare horse. But it does, and it makes me feel warm and hopeful despite the odds. "I won't," I promise.

He gestures to the wider road our street intersects with. "Follow that road east, and you'll come to a small town that lies on the caravan route to Fidanya. You'll be able to get better directions from there."

"Thank you," I say. "For all of this."

He nods.

I knee the horse gently, as he'd taught me. She ignores me. I haven't quite got this riding thing down yet.

"Hikaru," Stonefall says. I turn to him, eyebrows raised. He thinks less of the name I gave the Council than the one Stormwind gave him.

"You're…"

"Yes?"

"Very brave."

I sit still for a heartbeat. "Thanks," I manage as Stonefall departs, the word tinged with a faint inflection of awe.

I hadn't expected to earn such a man's respect.

DESERT BOUND

The small town Stonefall directed me to is in fact tiny—composed of a smattering of houses, a smithy, and a small inn. It seems most caravans don't stop here for even a meal, what with the city and the great caravanserai so near.

I leave my mare at a hitching post outside the inn and go in to ask directions. The owners, an elderly husband and wife with at least eight children to help them, are more than happy to serve me a meal of white bean soup and fresh baked bread, with a few olives and some information on the side.

"The desert, hmm?" the woman says, easing herself down on the cushions set opposite me at the low table. "Don't have any guides here. Your best bet is to catch up with the caravan that went through here last night."

I brighten. "How far would they have gotten?"

She snorts. "Not too far. They travel at night, and must have gotten a late start yesterday. They were through here near midnight. They'll have just made the next town."

Which means they likely won't have heard of my escape either. Not unless someone else catches up to them bearing the news. And there is the small, no doubt absurd, hope that this is the caravan Huda joined to return to her tribe's lands. It *has* only been a week or so since I bid farewell to Huda at the caravanserai, and she would have stayed there through the Festival anyhow. Even if she found a caravan that left before this one, she may be no more than a couple days ahead of me.

I thank the woman, leaving as soon as I've downed my meal. I stop only for a short break in the afternoon. This late in fall, the sun is still strong enough to make it clear why the caravan would choose to rest through the day. After a half hour's nap, I pull myself back up on Zahra and continue on.

The road lies empty for the most part. I pass a few farmers, an equal number of wagons creaking along the road, and that is all. No couriers race by on lathered steeds, no mages pound after me, nothing makes me clutch the reins in fear. Not even a tanuki bristling with fury. Stonefall must have dragged my skirt through half the town before leaving to have shaken Kenta from my trail.

A couple of hours before sunset, I reach the next town, dusty and sore. One glance at the number of camels and horses grazing in the fields around the town tell me the caravan is here. I'm tempted to go straight to the small caravanserai to seek out whoever I can find, Huda or the owners of the caravan. But I can't wear my glamor in her company, and my markings will stand out in the memory of anyone who sees me. There are still a few hours till sunset. I need to take Kenta's advice right away.

The main square offers me nothing of use, but a few of the alleys have tiny shops squeezed in shoulder to shoulder. I've nearly given up searching when I finally spot a sign decorated with painted images of tigers and dragons jutting out from between a corner bakery and a tailor's workshop: an ink shop.

I ride on until I find an empty back street, dismount, and remove my silver wristband. This is the dangerous part, walking about without a disguise. But I can't see any way around it that wouldn't arouse further suspicion. So I straighten out my patched tunic and lead my horse back to the ink shop as if I hadn't a care in the world.

The proprietor stands at the door. He's a wizened old man, his hair iron gray but his eyebrows still black. His eyes, like my mother's and my own, mark him as having come from one of the eastern Kingdoms. Through the single, polished window I spot the tools of his trade laid out on a lacquered tray. I've guessed his heritage perfectly. He practices an eastern method of inking known as tebori, which uses slim sticks of bamboo or carved metal, each with a group of needles attached at the bottom.

"Greetings, uncle," I say in Tradespeak, hoping language at least won't be an issue.

He answers easily enough. "Good day, miss. Water for your horse?" He gestures to a small barrel along the wall.

"I thank you." I remove the wooden cover. The mare dips her nose in, drinking thirstily. I'm not sure how well she'll do in a desert, certainly not as well as a camel. I'll worry about that when I must. If I can catch up with Huda—if she's even with the caravan—perhaps she'll know what to do.

I turn to the old man. "I had a design inked on my arms some time ago, and wanted to add some color. Can you help me?"

"Of course. Come in and we will take a look."

Once inside, I seat myself on the cushions on the floor. He pulls up a stuffed bolster, positioning it under my arm. I start with my wounded arm, because at this point, having it braced on a bolster seems a heavenly idea. I roll up my sleeve, consider my markings. A touch of color on the backs of my hands, a swirl or two on my arms, and it will look much less like a death sentence even to me.

The old man murmurs with surprise. With a glance at me for permission, he studies the markings, turning my arm over carefully, his eyes tracing the pattern of interlocking designs. Then he asks to see my other arm. I can only hope they don't look like something other than ink to his expert eye.

"Where was this done?"

"I went to a master back home." Well, not a master inker, but close. "I don't know when I'll go back. The design's a little too stark for me. I was hoping you could add some color here," I touch the back of my hand, "and maybe a little more at the top."

"Certainly," he says, his gaze still moving over my arms. "Why the firebird, though?"

"What?" I ask, taken aback.

He taps the inside of my arm, where the design wraps around to meet. There, at the center, a phoenix flies, its wings outspread. I stare at it. I haven't wanted to look at the markings. In truth, I've taken every opportunity to cover them, so I never noticed the phoenix. Now, having seen it, I wonder if I've been blind.

"I met one once," I finally say.

"Ah," he says. "That is special indeed. So, we will color it, and we will do your hands."

"How long will it take?"

He shrugs. "As long as it takes. An hour, perhaps two. These things should not be hurried."

Maybe not generally, but I have no idea how much time I have to spare, nor when the caravan will move on. He waits patiently for my response, so I make myself nod. If it takes too long, I'll pay him for his work and pretend that I'll return tomorrow.

After consulting me on colors, he sets to work. He stretches my skin taut with one hand, and uses the other to hold the tebori tool, resting it against his thumb as he slides the needles in and out of my skin. They make a faint, rhythmic sound as they pull out, *sha-sha-sha*. Compared to Splinter's potion, they hurt about as much as a mosquito bite would after a lion's.

The inker gives the phoenix its sunset flames, his tebori allowing him to create subtle gradations of color that transform the bird from a marking that imprisons me into a work of art. Well over an hour passes before he finishes both birds and moves on to my hands. The shadows outside have grown longer, the caravan that much closer to leaving.

I should have had him start with my hands—stupid to start with what few will see.

"I may have to leave soon," I say as he adds more ink to his tebori. "I can come back tomorrow."

"Only little while longer, miss," he says. "This hand is nearly done."

I nod. I need both hands done, at least a little. It has to look balanced, as if I had planned these markings, chosen them.

Did I miss something? a familiar voice asks in my mind, breaking me from my thoughts.

I have to bite my lip to keep from laughing. *What gives you that idea?*

You're decorating your markings. In a city shop?

Outside the city, I tell Val. *Remember the lycan that caught me?*

Yes.

He was the captain of the lycan guard. I hesitate, not sure how to go on.

You are a very dangerous woman, Val says. *I assume you somehow convinced him to break you out.*

Well, yes, but only because I told him the truth. He and his guard decided to leave their post to the Council. They didn't want to hold me prisoner, so they broke me out before they left.

Val's amusement is a warm thing, deep and sweet. But all he says is, *You did well not to let me kill him.*

I can't help the smile that spreads across my face. I keep my head bowed, my eyes on my arm, so that the old man doesn't notice.

There's something you should know, Val says. His voice in my mind is calm now, measured.

Is something wrong?

My prince knows.

I close my eyes, blocking out the sight of my markings.

About our bond?

My sudden retreat to my room caused some concern yesterday. At the end, just before I woke, he came to investigate himself. He is…much longer lived than I, and recognized what he saw.

Will you be okay?

A flash of frustration. *I'll be fine.*

Wrong question, then. *What will he do?*

I cannot say. For now, don't worry over it. Get as far from the Council as you can.

Sound advice. Whatever the breather prince decides to do, my first priority is evading the Council. I open my eyes as the inker tilts my hand, stretching another section of my skin tight. Not that the idea of a breather prince who might be curious about me is easy to brush past.

I'll leave you now. Call if you need me.

Thank you, I reply.

Val's presence fades quickly, but I turn his words over in my mind until the inker finally sets his tebori down for the last time and sits back.

"There," he says with evident satisfaction. "If you come back tomorrow, we'll continue the color up your arm. It will be beautiful."

"It already is," I say truthfully. The backs of my hands are decorated in amethyst and turquoise and cobalt. I never considered having my skin inked before, but the colors make the harsh reality of the markings easier to bear.

"Your *master* will hardly recognize them."

I start. He continues to clean his tools, the picture of equanimity. But he knows. He *knows* these are not regular tattoos. I glance outside, but nothing seems amiss: no mages, no guards closing in. Has he not alerted anyone?

"Uncle?" I say, my voice uncertain.

"Your mother is from the east, yes? Or perhaps your father?"

"Yes."

"Give them my greetings when next you meet."

I nod, even though he asks an impossible thing, one more promise I can't keep.

The small caravanserai at the far edge of town is filled to the brim with travelers. Men and women spill into the open yard. Many sit together in small groups, passing around food and tiny cups of coffee. A group of older children huddle together in a circle, their eyes intent on the game they play. More than a few animals are saddled and ready to be ridden out, their reins tied to hitching posts. No one takes any notice as I clumsily tether my mare to a post. She really is a good horse, with bright, intelligent eyes and a gentle disposition. I pat her shoulder and continue on to the building.

A servant girl greets me just within the door. Apparently, a tribeswoman traveling alone with a caravan is quite a remarkable fact, for the girl nods at once at my inquiry. "There is a desert woman here. I don't know her name, but she was out back a little while ago. If you would follow me?"

I do, barely able to believe my luck. *Please let it be her,* I pray silently. It will be so much easier if Huda is here. The girl leads me through the building and out the back to a second open yard. There, at the edge, sits a woman in desert robes, her hair covered and her face turned toward the not-so-distant hills.

The girl calls a greeting. I grin as Huda looks in our direction, then springs to her feet, beaming. "Ya Hikaru! You are here!"

"Ya Huda," I reply. "*You* are here!"

She laughs, stepping forward to wrap me in a hug.

I inhale sharply when she presses against my wounded arm, stiffening with pain. She steps back, her eyes on my face. I work to keep my smile easy. Her grin reappears in full force and she kisses me on each cheek in the desert tradition. "I did not think to see you again so soon!"

"Nor I. But I must return to the desert, and I thought we might travel together."

"We will," she assures me. To the servant girl hovering nearby, she says, "Can you tell me where Abu Jameel is?"

"Out front," the girl responds easily in the desert tongue. "He just finished up the accounting for the caravan's stay."

"Then we will meet him there. Thank you."

The girls nods and departs. Huda slips her hand into mine, and tugs me along after her. "If we travel together, we can leave the caravan. We are far enough north now that it will not be that much farther to reach the lands of our allies and cross through there."

"Did Laith ibn Hamza and his friends return to their lands already?"

Huda frowns slightly. "They departed once I left with the caravan. They should be entering their territory now, so you needn't worry for them."

Ah. So they did ensure she had a safe way back to her family before they left. I'm glad for the honor of the desert tribes.

"I will speak with the head caravan driver, and then we can make our own way," Huda continues as we round the corner of the building.

"Let me see to my horse," I say, having no interest in meeting anyone who might remember me. "She'll need to eat before we depart."

"Of course," Huda says, eyeing my little mare with interest. "I'll come find you when I am ready. Do you wish to rest a while, or ride out?"

"Ride," I say, even though I would like nothing better than to lie down and sleep for three days straight. "Though we may not get too far tonight," I add.

"We can set an easy pace to start with." She squeezes my hand. "And now you must come to my sister's wedding."

I laugh. I had completely forgotten her invitation when I'd last bid her farewell. "I would like that."

"Then it is decided," Huda says, as if I have nothing more pressing to consider. Eyes dancing, she hurries off to make her arrangements.

I return to my horse. Down the road rise the desert mountains, and beyond them, the Burnt Lands, with its dead city and its undying spells.

But for today I am alive and free. I have a horse who seems happy enough to put up with my fumblings, and a friend who might have been my sister and might also be my family's mortal enemy, and a disguise for the markings that have locked up the gift that defines me.

I smile as I stroke my mare's satin-smooth neck. What did Osman Bey say? *Run far, run fast, keep the wind in your hair.*

Good advice, that. I intend to take it.

ACKNOWLEDGEMENTS

It seems that with every book I write, my community grows a little larger and a great deal more wonderful. I am so very grateful for the veritable city of readers, writers, bloggers, friends, and family members who have helped me through the three years it has taken to bring this book to completion.

When I set out to write *The Sunbolt Chronicles*, I aimed for a novella serial, thinking that would allow me to publish with some regularity despite being a mom with two lovely young children. But beta readers of a novella-sized draft of *Memories of Ash* made it clear to me that I had better stop pretending I was the one in charge. I listened, and the story grew into itself, a full-sized novel.

For this, I have my Round 1 beta readers to thank: Mus'ifah Amran, Shy Eager, Ahmed Khanani, Hailey McCann, Tia Michaud, Theresa Shreffler, Bekah Trollinger, Elisabeth Wheatley, Janelle White and Kat Wise. Together, they recommended a series of "minor" changes that resulted in sweeping revisions, and pushed *Memories of Ash* to be the story it has become.

Round 2 beta readers have my sincere apologies for How Outrageously Long this beta reading round took, and receive a heartfelt (if virtual) medal of honor for sticking with me for as long as it took. I am most indebted to Anne Hillman and Elisabeth Wheatley for making it through this round. Early chapter feedback from Annie Bahringer, Claire Hermann, Leah Rothstein, and Janelle White was also deeply appreciated.

Amazingly, miserably, *Memories of Ash* went on to a Round 3. I am so very grateful to Shy Eager and my dear husband,

Anas Malik, for doing double duty as beta readers and working through this final round. Thoughtful feedback on pacing, tone, and the development of themes helped me to bring *Memories of Ash* past the point of cringe-worthy and into the realm of quite-possibly-okay.

I am deeply indebted to my copyeditor, Laurel Garver, for her fine grasp of language, her bald honesty (especially regarding characters dithering about when they should have been hurrying!), and her eye for detail. In addition, the wordsmithing magic Ann Forstie worked on the first seven chapters of *Memories of Ash* helped take the beginning sequence from good to great. I cannot thank either of you enough!

I am grateful to Melissa Sasina—and Elisabeth Wheatley whenever she could join us—for almost nightly online writing sessions for the last year (or more?), which made sitting down to write a fun, social time rather than a nightly misery. Without our regular check-ins, mutual cheerleading, and plot-hole problem solving over so many months, this book would probably still be in the works.

I want to give a shout out to all the bloggers and readers who have read and reviewed *Sunbolt*, and stepped forward to read advance review copies of *Memories of Ash*. Thank you for believing in my writing, and waiting for it, and for giving your time and energy to make this latest book a success. Whether you joined my launch team or wrote a review, or just tweeted your love of books, your support means the world to me.

I am as always thankful for the love of my family, for their understanding and kindness as I make my way through the wilds of writing. You have always been there for me, and only laughed sometimes when you happened to overhear me working through dialogue out loud, with voices. I appreciate that.

And, ultimately, I am grateful to God for all that He has given me, in my life and in my writing.

ABOUT THE AUTHOR

Intisar Khanani grew up a nomad and world traveler. Born in Wisconsin, she has lived in five different states as well as in Jeddah on the coast of the Red Sea. She first remembers seeing snow on a wintry street in Zurich, Switzerland, and vaguely recollects having breakfast with the orangutans at the Singapore Zoo when she was five.

Intisar currently resides in Cincinnati, Ohio, with her husband and two young daughters. In her last job`, she wrote grants and developed projects to address community health and infant mortality with the Cincinnati Health Department— which was as close as she could get to saving the world. Now she focuses her time on her two passions: raising her family and writing fantasy.

To find out what Intisar is working on next, and connect with her online, visit www.booksbyintisar.com.

CPSIA information can be obtained
at www.ICGtesting.com
Printed in the USA
LVHW091529050319
609565LV00005B/53/P